ABOUT THE AUTHOR

Born to a South African Dutch family in 1935, André Brink was one of a group of South African writers who, in the 1960s, helped to break down national taboos on the treatment of sex and religion in fiction. In a highly charged atmosphere he insisted on the need for confronting the social and political realities of his country. In 1967 he moved to Europe but later returned to South Africa to, in his words, "accept full responsibility for everything I write— not as a member of a small white enclave, but as a writer belonging more to Africa than to Europe." Although he has received the CNA Award, South Africa's most prestigious literary prize, three times, two of his novels, *Looking on Darkness* and *A Dry White Season*, were banned in South Africa. André Brink is currently a Professor of English at the University of Cape Town. In addition to his many other honors, he has received Great Britain's Martin Luther King Memorial Prize for the literary work best reflecting the ideas to which Dr. King dedicated his life, and in 1980 Mr. Brink was awarded France's Prix Médicis Etranger. In early 1983 the French Government made him a Chevalier of the Légion d'Honneur. His work has been published in twenty countries. His novels include *A Chain of Voices* and *Imaginings of Sand*.

A
DRY WHITE SEASON

ANDRÉ BRINK

HARPER ● PERENNIAL

NEW YORK ● LONDON ● TORONTO ● SYDNEY

HARPER ● PERENNIAL

Nothing in this novel has been invented, and the climate, history, and circumstances from which it arises are those of South Africa today. But separate events and people have been recast in the context of a novel, in which they exist as fiction only. It is not the surface reality that is important but the patterns and relationships underneath that surface. Therefore, all resemblance between the characters and incidents in this book and people and situations outside is strictly coincidental.

Mongane Wally Serote's poem "For Don M.—Banned" is reprinted with the kind permission of the publisher, Ad. Donker, Johannesburg.

First published in Great Britain in 1979 by W. H. Allen & Co. Ltd.

First U.S. edition published in 1980 by William Morrow and Company, Inc.

A DRY WHITE SEASON. Copyright © 1979 by André Brink. All rights reserved. Printed in the United States of America. No part of this book may be used or reproduced in any manner whatsoever without written permission except in the case of brief quotations embodied in critical articles and reviews. For information address HarperCollins Publishers, 10 East 53rd Street, New York, NY 10022.

HarperCollins books may be purchased for education, business, or sales promotional use. For information please write: Special Markets Department, HarperCollins Publishers, 10 East 53rd Street, New York, NY 10022.

First Harper Perennial edition published 2006.

Library of Congress Cataloging-in-Publication Data is available upon request.

ISBN-10: 0-06-113863-0 (pbk.)
ISBN-13: 978-0-06-113863-8 (pbk.)

12 13 14 15 RRD 10 9 8 7 6 5 4

For

ALTA

who sustained me in the dry season

it is a dry white season
dark leaves don't last, their brief lives dry out
and with a broken heart they dive down gently headed
  for the earth
not even bleeding.
it is a dry white season brother,
only the trees know the pain as they still stand erect
dry like steel, their branches dry like wire,
indeed, it is a dry white season
but seasons come to pass.

Mongane Wally Serote

FOREWORD

I used to think of him as an ordinary, good-natured, harmless, unremarkable man. The sort of person university friends, bumping into each other after many years, might try to recall, saying: "Ben Du Toit?" Followed by a quizzical pause and a half-hearted: "Oh, of course. Nice chap. What happened to him?" Never dreaming that *this* could happen to him.

Perhaps that is why I have to write about him after all. I used to be confident enough that, years ago at least, I'd known him reasonably well. So it was unsettling suddenly to discover he was a total stranger. Or does that sound melodramatic? It isn't easy to rid oneself of the habits of half a lifetime devoted to writing romantic fiction. "Tender loving tales of rape and murder." But I'm serious. His death challenged everything I'd always thought or felt about him.

It was reported in a humdrum enough fashion – page four, third column of the evening paper. Johannesburg teacher killed in accident, knocked down by hit-and-run driver. Mr Ben Du Toit (53), at about 11 o'clock last night, on his way to post a letter, etc. Survived by his wife Susan, two daughters and a young son.

Barely enough for a shrug or a shake of the head. But by that time his papers had already been dumped on me. Followed by this morning's letter, a week after the funeral. And here I'm stuck with the litter of another man's life spread over my desk. The diaries, the notes, the disconnected scribblings, the old accounts paid and unpaid, the photographs, everything indiscriminately lumped together and posted to me. In our student days he constantly provided me with material for my magazine stories in much the same way, picking up ten

9

per cent commission on every one I got published. He always had a nose for such things, even though he himself never bothered to try his hand at writing. Lack of interest? Or, as Susan suggested that evening, lack of ambition? Or had we all missed the point?

Looking at it from his position I find it even more inexplicable. Why should he have picked on me to write his story? Unless it really is an indication of the extent of his despair. Surely it is not.enough to say that we'd been room-mates at university: I had other friends much closer to me than he had ever been; and as for him, one often got the impression that he never felt any real need for intimate relationships. Very much his own man. Once we'd graduated it was several years before we met again. He took up teaching; I went into broadcasting before joining the magazine in Cape Town. From time to time we exchanged letters, but rarely. Once I spent a fortnight with him and Susan in Johannesburg. But after I'd moved up here myself to become fiction editor of the woman's journal, we began to see less and less of one another. There was no conscious estrangement: we simply didn't have anything to share or to discuss any longer. Until that day, that is, barely two weeks before his death, when he telephoned me at my office, quite out of the blue, and announced that he had to "talk" to me.

Now although I've come to accept this as an occupational hazard I still find it difficult to contain my resentment at being singled out by people who want to pour out their life stories on me simply because I happen to be a writer of popular novels. Young rugger buggers suddenly becoming tearful after a couple of beers and hugging you confidentially: "Jesus, man, it's time you wrote something about a bloke like me." Middle-aged matrons smudging you with their pale pink passions or sorrows, convinced that you will understand whatever their husbands don't. Girls cornering you at parties, disarming you with their peculiar mixture of shamelessness and vulnerability; followed, much later, as panties are hitched up or a zip drawn shut, by the casual inevitable question: "I suppose you're going to put me in a book now?" Am I using them – or are they using me? It isn't me they're interested in, only my "name", at which they clutch in the hope of a small claim on eternity. But one grows weary of it; in the end you can hardly face it any more. And that is what defines the bleakness of my middle-aged writing career. It is part of a vast apathy which has been paralysing me for months. I've known dry patches in the past, and I have always been able to write myself out of them again. But nothing comparable to this arid present landscape. There are more than enough stories at hand I could write; it is not from a lack of ideas that I had to disappoint the Ladies' Club of the Month. But after twenty novels in this vein something inside me has given up. I'm past fifty. I am no longer immortal. I have no wish to be mourned by a few thousand housewives and typists, rest my chauvinist soul. But what else? You cannot teach an old hack new tricks.

Was this one of the reasons why I succumbed to Ben and the disorderly documentation of his life? Because he caught me in a vulnerable moment?

The moment he telephoned I knew something was wrong. For it was a Friday morning and he was supposed to be at school.

"Can you meet me in town?" he asked impatiently, before I could recover from the surprise of his call. "It's rather urgent. I'm phoning from the station."

"You on your way somewhere?"

"No, not at all." As irritably as before. "Can you spare me the time?"

"Of course. But why don't you come to my office?"

"It's difficult. I can't explain right now. Will you meet me at Bakker's bookshop in an hour?"

"If you insist. But — "

"See you then."

"Good-bye, Ben." But he'd already put down the receiver.

For a while I remained confused. Annoyed, too, at the prospect of driving in to the city centre from the journal's premises in Auckland Park. Parking on Fridays. Still, I felt intrigued, after the long time we hadn't seen each other; and since the journal had gone to press two days before there wasn't all that much to do in the office.

He was waiting in front of the bookshop when I arrived. At first I hardly recognised him, he'd grown so old and thin. Not that he'd ever been anything but lean, but on that morning he looked like a proper scarecrow, especially in that flapping grey overcoat which appeared several sizes too big.

"Ben! My goodness — !"

"I'm glad you could come."

"Aren't you working today?"

"No."

"But the school vac is over, isn't it?"

"Yes. What does it matter? Let's go, shall we?"

"Where?"

"Anywhere." He glanced round. His face was pale and narrow. Leaning forward against the dry cold breeze he took my arm and started walking.

"You running away from the police?" I asked lightly.

His reaction amazed me: "For God's sake, man, this is no time for joking!" Adding, testily, "If you'd rather not talk to me, why don't you say so?"

I stopped. "What's come over you, Ben?"

"Don't stand there." Without waiting for me he strode on and only when he was stopped by the traffic lights on the corner I did catch up with him again.

"Why don't we go to a café for a cup of coffee?" I suggested.

"No. No, I'd rather not." Once again he glanced over his shoulder – impatient? scared? – and started crossing the street before the lights had returned to green.

"Where are we going?" I asked.

"Nowhere. Just round the block. I want you to listen. You've got to help me."

"But what's the matter, Ben?"

"No use burdening you with it. All I want to know is whether I may send you some stuff to keep for me."

"Stolen goods?" I said playfully.

"Don't be ridiculous! There's nothing illegal about it, you needn't be scared. It's just that I – " He hurried on in silence for a short distance, then glanced round again. "I don't want them to find the stuff on me."

"Who are 'they'?"

He stopped, as agitated as before. "Look, I'd like to tell you everything that's happened these last months. But I really have no time. Will you help me?"

"What is it you want me to store for you?"

"Papers and stuff. I've written it all down. Some bits rather hurriedly and I suppose confused. But it's all there. You may read it, of course. If you promise you'll keep it to yourself."

"But —"

"Come on." With another anxious glance over his shoulder he set off again. "I've got to be sure that someone will look after it. That someone knows about it. It's possible nothing will happen. Then I'll come round one day to collect it again. But if something does happen to me – " He jerked his shoulders as if to prevent his coat from slipping off. "I leave it to your discretion." For the first time he laughed, if one could call that harsh brief sound a laugh. "Remember, when we were at varsity, I always brought you plots for your stories. And you always spoke about the great novel you were going to write one day, right? Now I want to dump all my stuff on you. You may even turn it into a bloody novel if you choose. As long as it doesn't end here. You understand?"

"No, I'm afraid I don't understand you at all. You want me to write your biography?"

"I want you to keep my notes and journals. And to use them if necessary."

"How will I know if it's necessary or not?"

"You'll know, don't worry." A pale smile twitched his tense mouth. He stopped once more, an unnatural glare in his grey eyes. "They've taken everything from me. Nearly everything. Not much left. But they won't get that. You hear me? If they get that there would have been no sense in it at all."

We drifted along with the crowd.

"That's what they're aiming for," he proceeded after a while. "They want to wipe out every sign of me, as if I'd never been here. And I won't let them."

"What have you done, Ben?"

"Nothing. I assure you. Nothing at all. But I can't go on for very much longer and I think they know it too. All I'm asking of you is to keep my papers."

"But if the whole thing is really all that innocent —"

"Are you also turning against me now?"

There was something paranoic in his attitude, as if he'd lost his grasp on the world, as if we weren't really in that street in that city at that moment, as if he weren't really aware of my presence at all. As if, in fact, he himself were a stranger whose slight and superficial resemblance to the Ben du Toit I'd once known was pure coincidence.

"Of course I'll keep your stuff for you," I said, the way one would comfort or humour a child. "Why don't you bring it round to my house tonight, then we can have a quiet chat over a glass of wine?"

He looked even more perturbed than before. "No, no, I can't do that. I'll make sure it gets to you. I don't want to cause you any problems."

"All right then." I sighed with resignation. All the sob stories I'd seen in my time. "I'll look through it and let you know."

"I don't want you to let me know. Just keep the stuff like I told you. And if something happens —"

"Nothing will happen, Ben," I insisted, not without some irritation. "It's just hypertension. All you need is a good holiday."

Two weeks later he was dead.

By then I had already received the bulky parcel postmarked in Pretoria. And after our meeting that morning I was curious to find out more about the whole baffling affair. At the same time I couldn't repress a feeling of resentment, almost of nausea. Not only at the impossible mess of the papers I'd received, but at the embarrassment of having to work through them. It was bad enough to get mixed up with the life stories of total strangers, but at least one remained objective, uninvolved, a more or less indifferent spectator. With an acquaintance it was different. Too private, too bewildering. I was expecting to have to tell him, as to so many others: "Sorry, old chap, but I really can't find a worthwhile story in this." Only, with him it would be so much more difficult. And even more so in view of the state of his nerves. Still, he'd assured me he wasn't expecting anything beyond keeping them safely.

That night I stayed at home, trying to sort out the mess on my carpet. The black notebooks, the school exercise books, the bits and pieces of card or paper torn from magazines, the type-written pages, letters, newspaper cuttings. Aimlessly I started skimming and dipping into odd passages. Some names recurred regularly and a couple of them appeared vaguely familiar – Jonathan Ngubene, Gordon Ngubene – but it was only after I'd looked through the cuttings that my memories were clarified. Even then I couldn't make out what Ben's connection with them had been. Actually, it put me off. My novels deal with love and adventure, preferably in Old Cape settings or in distant romantic surroundings; politics isn't my "line". And if Ben had chosen to get involved in that way I didn't want to be drawn into it as well.

Glumly stowing away the piles of papers in the dilapidated box they had arrived in, I noticed a couple of photographs that had fallen from a large brown envelope I hadn't examined yet. One was quite small, passport size. A girl. Long black hair tied up with a ribbon, large dark eyes, small nose, rather generous mouth. Not beautiful in the sense of the heroines ambling through my books. But there was something about her which struck me. The way she looked right into the camera. A fierce, unsettling, uncompromising stare, challenging one to a duel of the eyes. It was an intensity belied by the gentleness, the femininity of the small oval face: *Look at me if you wish, you won't find any-thing I haven't discovered for myself and come to terms with. I've probed my depths: you're free to try too if you want to. Provided you do not expect it to give you any claim on me.* – It was something along these lines I found in the photograph, used as I was to constructing "characters". At the same time the face seemed disturbingly familiar. Had I come across it in a different context I might have recognised it more readily, but how was I to expect her among Ben's papers? It wasn't until the following day, working through the cuttings and notes again, that I recognised the same face on some of the newspaper photographs. Of course: Melanie Bruwer. The recent rumpus in the press.

The second photograph was an eight-by-ten on glossy paper. At first I took it for one of the pornographic pictures so readily available abroad; and it didn't interest me much. If that was Ben's way of getting a brief private kick it was none of my business and harmless enough. Not a very clear shot, as if the light had been bad. A background of fuzzy out-of-focus wallpaper, a bedside table, a crumpled bed; a man and a girl naked in a position of intimate caressing, apparently preparing for coitus. I was on the point of restoring it to the brown envelope when something prompted me to take a closer look.

The girl, the dark-haired girl, recognisable in spite of the heavy grain, was the same Melanie Bruwer. The man with her was middle-aged. The man was Ben.

The Ben I'd known at university was different. Reserved without being secretive; rather quiet, at peace with the world and himself; and, yes, innocent. Not that he was a prude or that he scorned student pranks, but never a ringleader. I never saw him drunk; at the same time he didn't try to avoid "the boys". A hard worker, above all, perhaps because he had to see his way through university on grants and loans and couldn't afford to disappoint his parents. Once, I remember, I saw him with a history book at an intervarsity rugby match. During the game he joined in the singing and merriment; but in the interval he quietly went on studying, oblivious of the noise around him. Even in a room filled with talking or carousing students he could carry on working steadily when there was something he'd set his mind on finishing. Not much of a sportsman, but in tennis he sometimes surprised one with his speed and agility. Whenever teams had to be chosen, he would lose convincingly. One got the impression that he did so deliberately to avoid official matches, because in friendly games he often beat the regular team players; and on the few occasions when, as a reserve member, he was forced to step in for someone else, he amazed the lot of us. On these occasions, with something really important at stake for his team, he returned the most incredible shots. But when the time came to pick new teams for the following year, Ben du Toit would cheerfully lose hands down.

His main diversion, a characteristically private one, was chess. It would be too much to call him a brilliant player, but he was stolid and meticulous and more often than not wore his opponents down by the sheer doggedness of his slowly unfolding strategies. In the more public area of student affairs he was seldom noticed, except for a certain unexpected flair which he sometimes revealed at mass meetings. Not that he liked these public appearances – and he consistently refused to stand for the Student Representative Council – but when he did get up to say something there was such an air of conviction and sincerity about him that everybody paid attention. And in his senior years many students, including girls, used to come to him with their personal problems. I still remember thinking enviously: Jesus, pal, you don't know your own strength with these chicks. The rest of us, experts at impressing the ladies with swaggering savoir-faire, don't stand a chance against that slow apologetic smile of yours – yet you don't seem to realise it yourself. Instead of making a grab you sit there like a clumsy young dog, allowing all the bright chances to slip past. In fact, you don't even acknowledge them as "chances"!

Only once, as far as I can remember, I caught a glimpse of something else in him, something normally obscured by his attitude of placid withdrawal. It happened in our third year, in History, when for one semester during the sabbatical of our regular Senior Lecturer a temporary bloke took over. We couldn't stand his schoolmasterly habits and discipline soon became a problem. On the day in question, catching me in the act of launching a paper missile, he promptly, in nearly apoplectic rage, ordered me out of the room. That would have been the end of it, had Ben not decided to emerge from his habitual lethargy and protest against my being singled out for punishment while the whole class had been equally guilty.

When the lecturer refused to budge Ben drew up a petition and spent a weekend collecting the signatures of all the class members, threatening a boycott of lectures unless an apology was offered. When the ultimatum was delivered, the lecturer read it, turned white, and summarily tore it up. Whereupon Ben led the threatened walk-out. In this era of demos and Student Power his action might appear ludicrously insignificant; but in those days, in the heart of the war years, it caused a sensation.

Before the end of the week Ben and the temporary lecturer were both called in by the Head of the department. What happened during the meeting leaked out to us much later, via some of the other academic staff, as Ben himself offered no more than a very brief summary.

The prof, a benevolent old bod loved and respected by everybody, expressed his regrets over the whole unfortunate affair and announced that he was prepared to treat it as a mere misunderstanding, provided Ben would apologise for his impetuous action. Ben politely expressed his appreciation of the prof's goodwill, but insisted on an apology from the lecturer who, he said, had offended the class with his unjust behaviour and ineffectual teaching methods.

This caused the lecturer to lose his temper once again and to start fulminating against students in general and Ben in particular. Ben quietly reacted by pointing out that this outburst was typical of the behaviour the students had been protesting against. Just when everything was becoming hopelessly complicated the lecturer offered his resignation and walked out. The prof punished the class by setting a test (in which Ben eventually obtained third or fourth highest marks); and the Administration solved their part of the problem by rusticating Ben for the rest of the semester.

It probably hit him harder than it would any of us, for his parents were poor and his grants were dependent on living in residence, so he had to find money for digs in town. I suppose we all felt a bit guilty about the outcome but the general attitude was that he had really brought it on himself. In any case no-one ever heard him complain. Neither did he embark, as far as I know, on any further rash ventures of that kind. Almost effortlessly he sank back below the unrippled surface of his sedate existence.

The evening paper carried a brief announcement on the funeral arrangements. I had planned to attend, but in the end it didn't work out. That morning I had to come in to the city centre for a lunch date with a visiting woman writer and I'd hoped to use the funeral as a pretext for getting rid of her in reasonable time: one of those ladies addicted to cream cakes and the wearing of lilac hats, who write about blood, tears and unmarried mothers, and who guarantee tens of thousands of readers for our journal. Which explains why I wasn't in the best of moods as I set out on foot from my parking spot towards the Carlton

Centre, more than fifteen minutes late to start with. Moodily withdrawn into my own thoughts, I wasn't paying much attention to my surroundings, but in the vicinity of the Supreme Court I became aware of something unusual and stopped to look about. What was happening? It took a while before it struck me: the silence. The customary lunchtime din of the city had subsided around me. Everywhere people were standing still. Traffic had stopped. The very heart of the city appeared to have been seized in a cramp, as if an enormous invisible hand had reached into its chest to grasp the heart in a suffocating grip. And what sound there was resembled nothing so much as the dull thud of a heartbeat, a low rumble, almost too low for the ear to catch, so it had to be insinuated into the body through blood and bone. Like a subterranean shudder, but different from the mine shocks which one experiences in Johannesburg every day.

After some time we became aware of movement too. Down from the station a slow wall of people were approaching in the street pushing the silence ahead of them: a dull, irresistible phalanx of blacks. There was no shouting, no noise at all. But the front lines were marching with raised clenched fists, like branches protruding from an indolent tide.

From the streets where we were standing innumerable other blacks started drifting towards the oncoming crowd, as silent as the rest, as if drawn by a vast magnet. We whites – suddenly very isolated in the expanse among the stern concrete of the buildings – began to edge towards the reassurance of walls and pillars. No-one spoke or made a sudden gesture. All action was delayed like a playback on TV.

It was only later I realised that judgement had been set for that day in one of the numerous terrorism trials of these recent months; and this crowd was on its way from Soweto in order to be present at the verdict.

They never arrived, though. While we were still standing there police sirens started wailing and from all directions vans and armoured vehicles converged. The sudden sound shocked us from our trance. In a moment noise came washing over the central city like a tidal wave. But by that time I had already moved away from the scene.

At least that gave me a valid explanation for arriving late at the Carlton Centre; and I still proffered the funeral as an excuse to make an early escape from my lilac lady. But by that time I no longer wanted to attend; I simply couldn't face it.

In the CNA Bookshop in Commissioner Street I bought a card of condolence which I signed in the shop and posted in Jeppe Street on my way back to the car. And then I went straight back home — I wasn't expected back at the office anyway — and began to work almost compulsively through Ben's papers again.

So far, there hasn't been a thank-you note from Susan. Of course, I didn't write my address on mine and she may not know where to reach me. Perhaps it's better that way, for all of us.

There were those who didn't regard Susan as the right sort of wife for Ben; but I cannot agree. He always needed someone to urge him on, to prevent him from getting stuck in a rut, to define goals for him and supply him with the energy and the drive to reach them. If it hadn't been for Susan he might have ended his life in some small, forgotten backveld village, quietly content to teach a bit of history and geography to one generation of school children after the other, or to spend his leisure time "uplifting" the children of the poor. As it turned out, he at least managed to end up in one of the top Afrikaans schools in the city. Whether he would have been happier in a different environment or in different circumstances is a moot point. How am I to judge the components of another man's happiness? But I really believe Susan knew how to handle him: how to let him have his way when he got one of his crazy notions; how to prod him when he had to do something constructive.

She probably inherited it from her father who made it from small-town attorney to M.P. Her mother, I believe, was something of a sentimental wash-out who meekly followed her lord and master whever his ambition led them. Of course, the fact that he'd never made it beyond M.P. would have added to Susan's determination. Caught between a father with great ambition but not enough talent to really reach the top, and a husband with enough talent but no ambition, she made up her mind very early as to who was going to make the important decisions. And in my efforts, at this stage, to sort out and clarify my meagre personal recollections of Ben I find it easier to explain Susan.

There was something – a magnetic field, a tension, an electricity – between us when I once spent a fortnight with them. It was just before I moved from Cape Town to the North, some twelve years after their marriage. I'd met her a few times before that, of course, but never for long enough really to get to know her. Not that I would like to convey anything improper in talking about a "magnetic field". We were both too well conditioned by our respectable backgrounds to indulge in anything rash; and both of us, albeit for different reasons I imagine, respected Ben's position in the middle. At the same time there's no denying that sometimes, in a sudden and unnerving way, one "recognises" a stranger as an equal, as an ally, as a companion, someone significant to oneself. It doesn't happen rationally or consciously. It is intuitive, a guts reaction. Call it a soundless cry for help. That was what happened when I saw Susan. Unless it's the fanciful writer in me taking over again. I really don't know: I'm not used to this sort of stock-taking and fiction still comes much more naturally to me than brute indecent truth.

From the beginning she proved to be the perfect hostess, protected by an impenetrable wall of courtesy, correctness, friendliness. Not being of a disposition to get along well with servants, she did everything in the house herself; and her thoroughness and good taste were evident in the smallest detail: the turned-up sheets at night, the small ice-container beside the water carafe, the exquisite little flower arrangement on the tray on which she brought me breakfast in bed in the mornings. Even at that early hour her make-up used to be immaculate, the merest suggestion of moisture on her lips, eye-shadow and mascara heightening discreetly the intense blue of her eyes, her curly blonde hair coiffed in a skilfully contrived look of naturalness. During the last few days of my stay she grew more at ease. Ben had the habit, late in the evening, just before going to bed, of withdrawing to the study he'd installed in what must have been intended as the servants' quarters in the back yard. Perhaps he left his preparation for the next day's lessons till then but I had the feeling that his real reason was to have a brief period of silence all to himself; wholeness, self-containment, reassured and surrounded by his books and the familiar objects he'd accumulated over the years. And after he'd withdrawn in this way Susan would bring me a last cup of coffee to my room and unceremoniously seat herself on the edge of my bed to chat.

On the Friday there was some school function or other which they'd been expected to attend, but at lunchtime Susan casually announced that she was in no mood for the "boring business" and would rather stay at home. "After all," she added, "we have an obligation to our guest."

"I'm sure he wouldn't mind being left alone for one evening." Ben looked at me. "He's not a stranger who must be amused at any cost."

"I'll gladly stay," I said.

"I wouldn't have gone, whether you were here or not," she insisted, suggesting a rock-hard will of her own below the slightly deliberate musicality of her voice.

So he went alone, but only after he'd performed his evening ritual of putting the children to bed: two pretty little blond girls, both of them variations of their mother's beauty – Suzette nine and Linda, if I remember correctly, five.

In spite of my repeated assurance that I'd be happy with a very simple supper, she prepared an impressive meal and laid the table as formally as was her wont, the full show of crystal and candles and silver. We remained at table for hours. I kept on refilling our glasses and fetched a new bottle from the cabinet after we'd emptied the first; followed by liqueur. Once or twice she covered her glass with her hand as I approached the bottle, but later she no longer bothered. She undoubtedly had too much to drink. One of the narrow straps of her dress slipped from a tanned shoulder but she made no effort to push it back. From time to time she pushed the fingers of one hand through her hair, and as the evening deepened her coiffure became less severe, more gentle, softer. One notices trifling things at a time like that. The sensuality of a lipstick smudge on a white damask napkin. Candlelight touching a ring as the hand makes a gesture. The curve of a neck and naked shoulder. Moisture on the

22

swelling of a lower lip. A conversation pursued in innumerable ways behind the casual movement of words.

I cannot pretend to remember what we said – it's seventeen years ago – but I can recall the feel and general drift of it. By that time it was very late. The wine had brought a flush to her cheeks.

"I envy you, you know," I said lightly, intimately. "Whenever I find myself in a family like yours I begin to doubt the sense of a bachelor existence like my own."

"All happy families are alike." A small, cynical line tensed her mouth. "But every unhappy family is unhappy in its own way."

"What do you mean?" I asked, puzzled.

"Isn't that what Tolstoy said?"

"Oh. Yes, of course."

"You don't sound very convinced."

"It's just that I – well, the sort of twaddle I write doesn't bring me in touch with Tolstoy very much any more."

She shrugged. The narrow white band remained slack across her arm.

"Does it matter?" she asked in a brief surge of passionate feeling. "You can write, whether it's twaddle or not. In one way or another you can give some sort of shape to whatever happens to you. But what about me?"

Here we go again, I thought. The story of my life.

"What are you complaining about?" I asked deliberately. "You have a good husband, you have two beautiful children, you've got lots of talent . . ."

She drew in her breath very slowly and very deeply.

"God!"

I kept my eyes intently on her face.

For a long time she sat motionless without looking away. Then, with passion just below the surface of her rich voice, she asked: "Is that all you can say to me? Is that all I can hope for?" And, after a pause: "In a year's time I'll be thirty-five. Do you realise that?"

"That's young. A woman's best decade."

"And if the Bible is anything to go by, I'm halfway now. What do I have to show for it? My God! For years on end one keeps thinking: *One day . . . One day . . . One day . . .* You hear people talking about 'life'. You start talking about it yourself. You wait for it to happen. And then? Then, suddenly, you realise: *This* is the 'one day' I've been waiting for. 'One day' is every bloody day. And it's never going to be any different." For a long time she was silent again, breathing deeply. She took a sip of liqueur, then said, as if deliberately trying to shock me: "You know, I can understand very well why some women become terrorists. Or whores. Just to have the experience of knowing you're alive, to feel it violently and furiously, and not to give a damn about whether it's decent or not."

"Is it really so bad, Susan?"

She stared past me as if she were not really talking to me – and perhaps she wasn't. "They always kept me on a tight leash when I was small. Said I was too wild, I had to control myself. 'Girls don't do this. Girls don't do that. What will people think of you?' I thought, once I'm grown up it will be different. Then I met Ben. We were both teaching in Lydenburg. I don't suppose there really was anything extraordinary about him. But you know, whenever he sat so quietly while everyone else was talking their heads off, I always tried to imagine what he was thinking. It made him seem different, and special. The way he handled the children, the way he just gently smiled when everybody else was arguing in the common-room . . . And he never tried to force his opinions on me like other men. I began to think he was the man I'd been waiting for. He seemed to understand people, to understand a woman. He would allow me to live the way I'd always wanted to. I suppose I was being unfair to him. I tried to imagine him the way I wanted him to be. And then — " She fell silent.

"Then what?"

"You mind if I smoke?" she asked suddenly. It surprised me, because on previous occasions she'd been very disparaging when Ben took out his pipe at table.

"Feel free," I said. "May I – ?"

"Don't bother." She rose and went to the mantlepiece, lit a cigarette, and came back to me. As she sat down she resumed unexpectedly: "It's not easy for a woman to admit that she's married to a loser."

"I don't think you're being fair to Ben now, Susan."

She looked at me wordlessly, took another sip of liqueur, then filled up her glass again.

At length she asked, "Who was it who said people who are afraid of loneliness should never marry?"

"Must have been someone who burnt his fingers." I consciously tried to be facetious, but she paid no attention.

"After twelve years I still don't know him," she went on. The small bitter line appeared at her lips again. "Neither does he know me." And after a moment: "The worst of all, I suppose, is that I don't even know myself yet. I've lost touch with myself."

Angrily she stubbed out the half-smoked cigarette and got up again as if in search of something; then she took another cigarette from the packet on the mantlepiece. This time I got up to light it for her. Her hands were trembling as I briefly touched them. She turned away to the piano and opened the lid, moving her fingers across the keys without depressing them; unexpectedly she looked up at me:

"If I'd been able to play really well it might have been different. But I'm a dabbler. A bit of music, playreading for the radio, all sorts of unimportant things. Do you think I should resign myself to the thought that one day my daughters may achieve something on my behalf?"

"Do you know how beautiful you are, Susan?"

She turned round, leaning back with her elbows resting on the piano, her breasts pointing at me, gently provocative. She still hadn't replaced her shoulder strap.

"Virtue is supposed to outlast beauty," she said with a vehemence which surprised me. Then, after a brief, tense inhalation of smoke: "All I have is the happy family you spoke about. Full time. Not a moment for myself."

"Ben does a lot to help you. I've noticed. Especially with the children."

"Yes. Of course." She returned to the table and we sat down again. "Why," she asked suddenly, "why does one allow oneself to be reduced to a domestic animal? Don't you think I also want to do something, make something, create something?"

"You have lovely children, Susan. Don't underestimate your creativity."

25

"Any bloody dairy cow can produce offspring." She leaned forward. Once again I was conscious of her breasts. "Did you know," she asked, "I had a miscarriage?"

"No," I said.

"Two years after Suzette. They thought I wouldn't be able to have another baby after that. I had to prove to myself that I was, well, normal. So I had Linda. It was hell. The full nine months. I resigned myself to being maimed for life."

"You look more beautiful than ever."

"How do you know? You didn't really know me then."

"I'm convinced of it."

"And in five years I'll be forty. Do you realise what that means? Why must one be condemned to a body?" This time she was silent for so long I thought it was the end of our conversation. We drank again, in silence. When she finally spoke it was much more restrained. "I've always had this feeling, ever since I started 'developing'." She looked straight at me. "There was one time, when I was fifteen or sixteen, when I believed in castigating my body like some mediaeval nun. To rid myself of evil desires. I would tie a knotted rope round my waist and wear rough underclothes. Even tried flagellation in a mild way. In the hope of setting myself free from my body."

"Did it do any good?"

She gave a short laugh. "At least I'm no longer wearing the rope."

"What about a chastity belt?"

Once more that unflinching gaze of her steady eyes, but she didn't reply. Was it defiance or invitation, confirmation or defence? Between us was the table with the burning candles, the treacherous light.

"And Ben?" I asked deliberately.

"What about Ben?"

"He loves you. He needs you."

"Ben is very self-sufficient."

"He wanted you to go with him tonight."

Another of her brief surges of passion. "I've brought him where he is today. I wonder what would have become of him if it hadn't been for me. Probably stuck in Krugersdorp giving alms to the poor. He should have become a missionary. It's up to me

26

to keep the family going."

"Aren't you trying too hard, perhaps?"

"What do you think will happen if I let go? I married him because I believed in him. So how can he – " She stopped; then spoke in a more subdued tone: "I don't think he really needs me. Or anyone. What do I know about my own husband? If only you knew—"

"What?"

Her blue eyes were dark behind the candlelight. Absently one of her hands was toying with the shoulder left bare by the dropped strap. Then, still looking straight at me, she replaced the strap and pushed back her chair: "I'm going to make us some more coffee."

"Not for me."

She stayed away for a very long time. And when she came back she was distant and formal. We moved to two easy chairs and drank our coffee in silence, and while we were still sitting like that Ben came home. She poured him a cup too, but didn't enquire about his evening out. Later he rose to go to the bathroom. She arranged the cups on a tray, then suddenly stopped to look at me:

"You must please forgive me for losing my self-control tonight."

"But Susan—"

"Forget what I said. I had too much wine. I'm not usually like this. I don't want you to think I've got anything against Ben. He is a good husband and a good father. Perhaps I don't deserve him."

She went out, to the kitchen. The next day she gave no hint at all of having the slightest recollection of our conversation. As if everything had been cancelled, obliterated, just like that.

Imperturbable and benign, Ben went his way. Getting up at dawn for a jog round the block, followed by a cold shower, off to school at half-past seven, back at lunch, then an hour or so of preparation or marking, and off again to school for tennis coaching or something; home at five, withdrawing into the garage to occupy himself with his hobby, carpentry, until it was time to bathe the children. On Sundays they all went to church:

Susan impeccable in a two-piece costume, the girls in frilly dresses and white hats, their blond hair plaited so tightly as to leave them sloe-eyed; Ben in his black tails — he was a deacon. An ordered and patterned life, with a place and time for everything. I don't mean that he meekly or slavishly followed his schedule, only that he seemed to derive an indispensable sense of security from his routine.

He was amused by what he regarded as my "unsettled" nature — I was in Johannesburg to explore the possibilities of a move to the North where one could count on more rapid progress and success — and he took my ambition with a pinch of salt.

"Surely you would also like to get ahead?" I asked him pointedly, one afternoon when I'd joined him in the garage where he was working on a doll's house for the children.

"Depends on what you mean by 'getting ahead'," he said gently, holding a piece of wood up to his eye to check its evenness. "I tend to be suspicious of mathematical minds with their straight lines from A to B to C."

"Don't you want to become a school principal one day, or an inspector?"

"No. I don't like administrative work."

"Don't tell me you just want to go on doing what you're doing at the moment?"

"Why not?"

"When we were at varsity you had such definite dreams about a 'happy society', a 'new age'. What's become of all that?"

With a grin he resumed his planing. "One soon finds out there's no point in trying to reform the world."

"So you're happy to stay out of it?"

He glanced up, his grey eyes more serious than before. "I'm not sure it's a matter of staying out of it. It's just, well, I suppose some people are more private than others. Rather than trying to take the world by storm I think one can achieve more by doing quietly what your hand finds to do in your own little corner. And working with kids is a thankful job."

"Are you happy then?"

"Happiness is a dangerous word." He started marking the

piece of wood for cutting dovetails. "Let's say I'm content." For a minute or so he went on working intently, then he added: "Perhaps that isn't true either. How shall I put it? – I have the feeling that deep inside every man there's something he is 'meant' to do. Something no one but he can achieve. And then it's a matter of discovering what your own personal something is. Some find it quite early in life. Others drive themselves to distraction trying to find it. And still others learn to be patient and prepare themselves for the day when, suddenly, they'll recognise it. Like an actor waiting for his cue. Or does that sound too far-fetched?"

"Are you one of those?"

He started tapping the chisel into the first joint. "I'm just marking time." Shaking the hair from his eyes. "The main thing is to be ready when your moment comes. Because if you let it pass – why, then it's gone, isn't it?"

"In the meantime you're making doll's houses."

He chuckled. "At least there's some satisfaction in making something with your hands, in seeing an ordinary piece of wood take shape. And seeing the children's faces when it's finished" – he sounded almost apologetic – "well, it makes you realise it's been worthwhile."

"You're really devoted to your children, aren't you?"

"'Devoted' sounds too easy, too mushy." He obviously regarded my question much more seriously than I'd intended it. "You see, when you're a child, you tend to live blindly. It's only afterwards, once you have your own children, that you look back on yourself through them. And for the first time you begin to understand what happened to you, and why it happened." And then he confessed what he'd hidden from me before: "That's why I'd love to have a son, you see, even though it may be selfish of me. I feel I cannot really come to grips with all my former selves unless I can relive it through a son. But of course that's out of the question."

"Susan?"

A brief sigh. "Well, she had a bad time with Linda and I cannot expect her to go through all that again."

There was something cruel about pursuing my questions, but I did. Why? Because his contentment, his serenity struck

29

me as a criticism of my own restlessness, a challenge to my way of life? Or because I refused to accept that one could really be so phlegmatic and at peace with oneself? Whatever it was, I asked him in a tone of deliberate provocation: "D'you think this is the 'happily ever after' I write about in my novels?"

"Probably not." He made no attempt to evade me. "But there's no point in sulking about what one hasn't got, is there?" Using a small wad of sandpaper he began to smooth the wood. Then, with his apologetic chuckle: "I know Susan used to have other plans for me. She's still dreaming her dreams."

"Have you given up?"

"Of course I still have dreams. But I have the advantage of having learned, from a very early age, to make allowances for damn hard facts."

"Meaning?"

"Don't you remember then? I'm sure I told you long ago."

It came back to me; and he filled in what I had forgotten. His father, who'd had to take over the farm of his wife's family in the Free State. Not without a humble measure of success. Then came the Great Drought of 'Thirty-three, when Ben was nine or ten years old. They had to trek with the sheep, all the way to Griqualand West where, according to reports, there was some grazing left. A fatal mistake. When the drought closed in on them in the godforsaken district of Danielskuil, there was no way out.

"By that time I had some ewes of my own," said Ben. "Not many. But every year my father had marked a few lambs for me. And that year the first lambs of my own were being born." He fell quiet for a long time. Then, abruptly, angrily, he asked: "Have you ever cut the throat of a new-born lamb? Such a small white creature wriggling in your arms. Such a thin little neck. One stroke of the knife. Every single new lamb that's born, because there's nothing for them to eat and the ewes have no milk. In the end even the shrubs disappear. The thorn-trees grow black. The ground turns to stone. And day after day there's the sun burning away whatever remains. Even the big sheep have to be slaughtered. When you look up you see the vultures above you. God knows where they come from, but they're there. Wherever you come or go, they follow you. At night you start dreaming about them. Once you've been in a drought like that you never forget it. Just as well Ma and my sister had stayed behind on the farm. I don't think they'd have been able to stand it. It was only Pa and me." His tone became aggressive. "We had two thousand sheep when we set out for Danielskuil. When we came back a year later we had fifty left."

"So you had to give up?"

"Yes, that was the end. Pa had to sell the farm. I'll never forget the day he told Ma the news. He'd left the house very early that morning, not saying a word to anyone. We saw him walking to and fro on the dry fields, it seemed like hours. Then he came back. Ma was waiting in the passage as he came in from outside with the sun behind him. And on the stoep – what makes one remember something so ridiculous? – on the stoep our old servant, Lizzie, was standing with a chamber pot in her hand, on her way to empty it outside. When she heard Pa telling Ma we had to go away she dropped the pot. Scared to death she was, because Ma had a hell of a temper those days, but that morning she didn't even scold Lizzie."

"And then?" I prompted Ben when he stopped.

He looked up as if, for a moment, he'd forgotten what we had been talking about. Then he said laconically: "Then we left the farm and Pa found work on the railways. Later became a station master. We children loved it, my sister Louisa and myself. Those long train journeys every Christmas. But Pa had lost his spark. And Ma didn't make it any easier for him. She carried on moaning and complaining, whining away year after year, until in the end she died. And Pa couldn't get on without her, so he also died."

He turned his back to me and went on with his work. There really was no more to be said.

The only other memory of my visit to them is of the last night. I stayed at home to baby-sit: Susan was rehearsing a radio play for the South African Broadcasting Corporation and Ben had gone to some meeting or other. When he came back we went to his study for a game of chess which went on for longer than I'd anticipated. So it was very late before I left him to enjoy his customary pause of solitude and silence. It was drizzling faintly as I walked across the yard to the kitchen door. Tiny insect sounds in the wet grass. A fresh earth-smell. When I came into my room the coffee tray was already waiting placidly on the bedside table, brightened by the inevitable little flower-pot. I was disappointed, having got used to the late last chat with Susan at night. I'd probably spent too much time with Ben.

I was already in bed when she came, after all. An almost inaudible knock. When I called, not quite sure that I'd really heard something, she came in. As always, she left the door open. A light summer gown. Her hair soft and curly on her shoulders. The scent of a woman who has relaxed in a warm bath. A scene from any of my best-sellers.

She sat on her usual place on the foot of my bed while I drank my coffee. I have no recollection of what we talked about. But I was intensely aware of her mere presence, sitting there, like that.

After I'd finished my coffee she got up to take the cup, leaning over me. Deliberately, or entirely by accident, the front of her gown fell open, revealing briefly, behind the sheer material, her breasts, vulnerable and white in the soft shadow, and the light-brown aureoles of her nipples.

I put out my hand and folded my fingers round her wrist.

For a moment she froze, looking straight at me as I still clutched her. What I saw in her eyes was fear. Of me, of herself? An expression I would have no trouble in describing in one of my love passages but which I can define only with difficulty now that I must try to be true to what really happened. "Naked anguish"?

I let go of her arm, and she kissed me briefly, nervously on my forehead before she went out and closed the door.

The real shock came much later. Nine months later, to be exact, when she gave birth to their son Johan.

Within the framework of our three lives, jointly and severally, that fortnight's visit is an insignificant episode. But there is so little I can rely on now that I have to write about Ben that I had no choice but to explore it at some length. I'm not sure I really found anything; but I had to try. For the rest, I am left with the jumbled papers he dumped on me. The press cuttings and letters and photocopies and journals and scribbled notes.

A passport photo of a girl with a sweet provocative face. The other photograph. Names. Gordon Ngubene. Jonathan Ngubene. Captain Stolz. Stanley Makhaya. Melanie Bruwer. And the possibilities suggested by my often misused imagination. I have to immerse myself in it, the way he entered into it on that first fatal day. Except that he did not know, and had no way of knowing, what was lying ahead; whereas I am held back by what I already know. What was unfinished to him is complete to me; what was life to him is a story to me; first-hand becomes second-hand. I must attempt to reconstruct intricate events looming behind cryptic notes; what is illegible or missing I must imagine. What he suggests I must expand: *He says — he thinks — he remembers — he supposes*. With my assortment of probabilities and memories and his disorganised evidence I must forge ahead against the dull obstacles of worry and confusion, trying to maintain at least a semblance of confidence or certainty. This is the burden I must take up, the risk I must run, the challenge I must accept. Trying to reconcile the calm and self-contained man I knew with the paranoic fugitive I met in town that day.

In a sense I owe it to him, or even to Susan. Report me and my cause aright! At the same time I have to grasp at him in an effort to write myself out of my own sterile patch. A complicating and aggravating factor.

Perhaps I would still have found it possible to accept that he deliberately walked into the passing car that night to lend suicide the more respectable appearance of an accident. But there was something amiss. I couldn't put my finger on it, yet I knew something didn't quite make sense. Now that final letter has arrived, a full week after his funeral, placing everything in the balance again. Now I have no choice. And it's no use trying to blame him, for he is dead.

ONE

I

It all really began, as far as Ben was concerned, with the death
of Gordon Ngubene. But from the notes he made subsequently, and from newspaper cuttings, it is obvious that the matter
went back much further. At least as far as the death of Gordon's
son Jonathan at the height of the youth riots in Soweto. And
even beyond that, to the day, two years earlier — represented in
Ben's papers by a receipt with a brief note scribbled on it —
when he'd started contributing to the schooling of the then fifteen year old Jonathan.

Gordon was the black cleaner in the school where Ben taught
History and Geography to the senior classes. In the older journals there are occasional references to "Gordon N." or just
"Gordon"; and from time to time one finds, in Ben's fastidious
financial statements, entries like "Gordon — R5.00"; or
"Received from Gordon (repayment) — R5.00", etc. Sometimes
Ben gave him special instructions about notes on his blackboard; on other occasions he approached him for small personal jobs. Once, when some money disappeared from the
classrooms and one or two of the teachers immediately blamed
Gordon for it, it was Ben who took the cleaner under his wing
and instituted inquiries which revealed a group of matric boys
to be the culprits. From that day Gordon took it upon himself to
wash Ben's car once a week. And when, after Linda's difficult
birth, Susan was out of action for some time, it was Gordon's
wife Emily who helped them out with housework.

As they came to know each other better Ben discovered more
about Gordon's background. As a young boy he had arrived
from the Transkei with his parents when his father had found

37

employment in the City Deep Mine. And since he showed interest in reading and writing from an early age he was sent to school – no cheap or easy undertaking for a man in his father's position. Gordon made steady progress until he'd passed Standard Two, but then his father died in a rockfall in the mine and Gordon had to leave school and start working to supplement his mother's meagre income as a domestic servant. For some time he was houseboy for a rich Jewish family in Houghton; later he found a better paid job as messenger for a firm of attorneys in the city, and then as an assistant in a bookshop. Somehow he managed to keep up his reading and the manager of the bookshop, pleased by his interest, helped him to continue his studies. In this way he eventually passed Standard Four.

At that stage Gordon went back to the Transkei. A traumatic experience, as it turned out, since there was no work for him back home, apart from lending a hand with the paltry farming activities of a great-uncle: planting maize, scouring the veld with a lean dog in search of hares for meat, sitting in the sun in front of the hut. He'd left the city because he couldn't stand life there any more; but it proved to be worse on the farm. There was something fretful and desultory in his blood after the years he'd been away. All the money he'd brought with him had gone into *lobola* – the dowry for a wife; and barely a year after his arrival in the Transkei he returned to the only place he really knew, Johannesburg, Gouthini. After a brief unsettled spell he landed at Ben's school.

One after another his children were born: in Alexandra, then Moroka, then Orlando. The eldest was Jonathan, his favourite. From the outset Gordon had resolved to rear his son in the traditions of his tribe. And when Jonathan turned fourteen he was sent back to the Transkei to be circumcised and initiated.

A year later Jonathan – or Sipho, which Gordon said was his "real" name – was back, no longer a *kwedini* but a man. Gordon had always spoken about this day. From now on he and his son would be allies, two men in the house. There was no lack of friction, since Jonathan obviously had a mind of his own; but on the main issue they agreed: Jonathan would go to school for as long as possible. And it was just after he'd passed Standard Six and secondary school was becoming an expensive business, that they turned to Ben for help.

Ben made enquiries at Jonathan's school and the family's church and, finding everybody in agreement on the boy's intelligence and perseverance and promise, offered to pay for Jonathan's school fees and books for as long as he continued to do well. He was quite impressed by the youngster: a thin, shy, polite boy, always neatly dressed, his shirt as starkly white as his teeth. In exchange for the financial support, Gordon saw to it that Jonathan agreed to help out in Ben's garden over weekends.

At the end of the first year there were smiles all round when Jonathan produced his school report, showing an average of over sixty per cent. As a reward for his achievement Ben gave him an old suit that belonged to his own son Johan – the two boys were roughly the same age – as well as an almost new pair of shoes and two rand in cash.

But in the course of the second year Jonathan began to change. Although he was still doing reasonably well he seemed to have lost interest and often played truant; he no longer turned up over weekends for his stint of gardening; his attitude became sullen and truculent and a couple of times he was openly cheeky with Ben. According to Gordon he was spending more time on the streets than at home. Surely no good could come of it.

His fears were soon realised. One day there was trouble at a beer-hall. A gang of *tsotsis* – hooligans – attacked a group of older men, and when the owner tried to throw them out they ran amok in the place, smashing everything in their way. The police arrived in two vans and carted off whatever youngsters they could lay hands on in the vicinity of the beer-hall, Jonathan among them.

The boy insisted that he'd had nothing to do with the commotion, that he'd been on the scene purely by accident when the fighting broke out; but the police witnesses testified that they'd seen him with the gang. The trial was very brief. Owing to a misunderstanding Gordon didn't attend: he had been told it would take place in the afternoon but when he arrived at the courtroom it was all over. He tried to protest against Jonathan's sentence of six cuts, but by that time the flogging had already been administered.

39

The following day he brought the boy to Ben's home; Jonathan had difficulty walking.

"Pull down your pants and show the Baas," ordered Gordon.

Jonathan tried to protest, but Gordon promptly undid the belt and slid the soiled and blood-stained shorts from his son's body, exposing the six cuts incised on his buttocks like six gashes with a knife.

"That's not what I'm complaining about, Baas," said Gordon. "If I know he did wrong I will give him a beating on top of this. But he says he is innocent and they didn't believe him."

"Didn't they give him time to state his case in court?"

"What does he understand of the court? Before he knew what was going on it was all over."

"I don't think there's anything we can do about it now, Gordon," said Ben unhappily. "I can get you a lawyer to appeal, but that won't heal Jonathan's buttocks."

"I know." While Jonathan was fumbling fiercely with his shorts, Gordon stood watching him. After a while he looked up and said almost apologetically: "Those buttocks will heal in time, Baas. I'm not worried about them. But those marks are right *here*." With barely repressed indignation he put a hand on his chest. "And I don't think they will ever heal."

He was proved right. Jonathan no longer showed much interest in school. According to Gordon he'd become resentful against the "Boere" and refused to learn Afrikaans. He started talking about things like Black Power and the African National Congress, which scared and depressed his father. At the end of the year Jonathan failed. He didn't seem to care in the least: for days on end, Gordon reported, he would simply disappear from home and refuse to answer any questions about his whereabouts. Ben was in no mood to continue what he now regarded as wasting money on his studies. But Gordon pleaded very strongly.

"Baas, if you stop now it'll be the end of Jonathan. And he will infect the other children in my house too. Because this is a bad sickness and it can only be cured by the school."

Ben reluctantly agreed. And, somewhat to his surprise, the

next year started in a more promising way than the previous one had ended. Jonathan continued to be secretive at home, given to moodiness and sudden outbursts; but he did go back to school. Until June, the sixteenth to be exact, that Wednesday, when Soweto erupted. The children massing in the school playgrounds like swarms of bees preparing to leave their hives. The marches. The police. The gunshots. The dead and wounded carted off. From that day Jonathan hardly showed his face at home any more. Dazed with fear and worry Emily kept the little ones indoors, listening to the explosions, the sirens, the rumbling of the armour-plated vehicles; at night there were bonfires of bottlestores, beerhalls, administration buildings, schools. And in the streets the charred skeletons of Putco buses.

It happened in July, in one of the demonstrations which by then had become an almost daily ritual: children and youths assembling for a march to Johannesburg, police converging in armoured trucks, long rattling bursts of automatic gunfire, a hail of stones and bricks and bottles. One police van was overturned and set alight. Shots, shouts, dogs. And from the clouds of dust and smoke some children ran to the Ngubenes' home to report, breathless with excitement, that they'd seen Jonathan in the crowd surrounded and stormed by the police. But what happened afterwards, they couldn't tell.

By late evening he hadn't come home yet.

Gordon went to see a friend, a black taxi-driver, Stanley Makhaya, a man who knew everything about everything in the townships, and begged him to sound out his contacts for news of Jonathan. For Stanley had contacts on both sides of the fence, among the blackjacks as well as in the deeper recesses of the underworld. Whatever you needed to find out in Soweto, said Gordon, Stanley Makhaya was the one man who could help you.

Except this once, it seemed, for even Stanley was stumped. The police had picked up so many people on that particular day that it might take a week or more to obtain a list of names.

Early the next morning Gordon and Emily set out in Stanley's great white Dodge, his *etembalami*, to Baragwanath

41

hospital. There was a crowd of other people on the same mission and they had to wait until three in the afternoon before a white-uniformed assistant was available to lead them to a cool green room where metal drawers were opened in the walls. The bodies of children, mostly. Some in torn and dusty clothes, others naked; some mutilated, others whole and seemingly unharmed, as if asleep, until one noticed the neat dark bullet-hole in the temple or chest and the small crust of dried blood clinging to it. Some wore tickets tied to a neck or a wrist, an elbow or a big toe, bearing a scrawled name; most were still nameless. But Jonathan was not among them.

Back to the police. There were no telephones working in Soweto in those days; the bus services had been suspended and for the time being there were no trains either. Once again they had to call on Stanley Makhaya's taxi to take them, however hazardous the journey, to John Vorster Square. A full day's waiting yielded nothing. The men on duty were working under pressure and it was understandable that they were crusty and brusque when approached for information on detainees.

After two more days had passed without any news of Jonathan, Gordon came to Ben for help. (No one had been surprised that he hadn't turned up at his work lately. There was such widespread intimidation of black workers in the townships that very few risked going into the city to their jobs.)

Ben tried his best to cheer him up: "He's probably gone into hiding with some friends. If anything serious had happened I'm quite sure you would have heard by now."

Gordon refused to be persuaded. "You must talk to them, Baas. If I ask, they just send me away. But if you ask they will give you an answer."

Ben thought it wise to approach a lawyer, one whose name had been prominent in the newspapers recently in connection with scores of youngsters brought to court in the wake of the riots.

A secretary answered the telephone. Mr Levinson, she regretted to say, was busy. Would Ben be prepared to make an appointment for three days later? He insisted that the matter was urgent. All he needed was five minutes to explain it to the lawyer on the telephone.

Levinson sounded irritable, but consented to take down a few particulars. A few hours later his secretary phoned to tell Ben that the police hadn't been able to give any information but the matter was being attended to. And it was still receiving their attention when Ben arrived at Levinson's office three days later.

"But it's ridiculous!" he protested. "Surely they should know the names of their own detainees."

Levinson shrugged. "You don't know them as well as I do, Mr Coetzee."

"Du Toit."

"Oh yes." He pushed a silver cigarette case across his enormous cluttered desk. "Smoke?"

"No thanks."

Ben waited impatiently while the lawyer lit his own cigarette and exhaled the smoke with a show of civilised relish. A tall, athletic, tanned man, his smooth black hair slick with oil, long sideburns, neatly trimmed moustache, Clark Gable redivivus. Large well-groomed hands, two solid, golden rings; tiger-eye cuff-links. He was working in his shirtsleeves, but the wide crimson tie and crisp striped shirt lent formality to the studied nonchalance of his bearing. It was a difficult interview, interrupted constantly: by the telephone, the well-modulated voice of a secretary on the intercom, or an array of assistants – all of them young, blond, lithe, competent, with the poise of entrants for a beauty competition – coming and going with files, rustling papers, or confidentially whispered messages. But in the end Ben managed to arrange for Levinson to follow up his telephone appeals to the police with a written demand for specific information.

"Now don't you worry" – with a hearty gesture reminiscent of a soccer team manager offering his confident prognosis for the coming Saturday – "we'll give them hell. By the way, do we have your address for the account? I presume you'll be responsible for the costs? Unless" – he checked his notes – "unless this Ngubene chap has money of his own?"

"No, I'll look after it."

"Right. I'll be in touch then, Mr Coetzee."

"Du Toit."

"Of course." He took Ben's hand in a firm conspiratorial

43

grip, pumping it like a mother bird feeding its young. "See you soon. 'Bye."

A week later, after another telephone call, there was a letter from John Vorster Square: their query, it stated, had been referred to the Commissioner of Police. After another week had passed without further reaction, Levinson addressed a letter directly to the Commissioner. This time they received a prompt reply, advising them to take up the matter with the officer in charge at John Vorster Square.

There was no reply to their next letter; but when Levinson made yet another sarcastic phone call to the Square, an unidentified officer at the other end curtly informed him that they had no knowledge whatsoever of any Jonathan Ngubene.

Even then Gordon didn't give up hope. So many youngsters had fled the country to find asylum in Swaziland or Botswana that Jonathan might well be among them. It would be in keeping with his behaviour of recent months. They just had to be patient, there would be a letter soon. In the meantime they had four other children to look after.

But the uncertainty, the anxiety, the suspicion persisted. And they were hardly surprised when, about a month after Jonathan's disappearance, the young black nurse arrived at their home.

She'd been trying for nearly a week to find them, she said. She was helping out in the black section at the General Hospital. Ten days ago a black boy of about seventeen or eighteen had been admitted to a private ward. His condition seemed to be serious. His head swathed in bandages. His belly bloated. Sometimes one could hear him moaning or screaming. But none of the ordinary staff had been allowed near him and they'd posted policemen at his door. Once she'd heard the name "Ngubene". And then she'd learned from Stanley – yes, she knew him, didn't everybody know him? – that Gordon and Emily were looking for their son. That was why she'd come.

They didn't sleep at all that night. The next morning they went to the hospital where an impatient matron denied that there had ever been anyone by the name of Ngubene in her wards; nor had there been any police on guard duty. Would they please go away now, her time was valuable.

44

Back to Ben; back to Dan Levinson.

The hospital superintendent: "It's preposterous. I would have known if there had been such a case in my hospital, wouldn't I? You people are always raking up trouble."

Two days later they received another visit from the young nurse. She'd just been sacked by the hospital, she told them. No one had given her any reason for it. Only a few days ago she'd been commended for her conscientiousness; now, all of a sudden, her services weren't required any more. However, she assured them that the black boy was no longer there. The previous evening she'd slipped round the building and climbed up the waterpipes to peep through a fanlight, but the bed had been empty.

Two more letters by Dan Levinson to the police failed to elicit even an acknowledgement of receipt.

Perhaps, Gordon grimly insisted, perhaps it really had been just a rumour; perhaps there would still be a letter from Mbabane in Swaziland or Gaberone in Botswana.

In the end it was Stanley Makhaya, after all, who found the first positive lead. He'd been in touch with a cleaner at John Vorster Square, he said, and the man had confirmed that Jonathan was being held in one of the basement cells. That was all the man had been prepared to say. No, he hadn't seen Jonathan with his own eyes. But he knew Jonathan was there. Or rather: had been, until the previous morning. Because later in the day he'd been ordered to clean out the cell and he'd washed blood from the concrete floor.

"It's useless just to write another letter or make another phone call," Ben told Levinson, white with anger. "This time you've got to *do* something. Even if it means a court interdict."

"Just leave it to me, Mr Coetzee."

"Du Toit."

"I've been waiting for a break like this," said the lawyer, looking pleased. "Now we'll give them the works. The whole titty. What about dropping a hint to the newspapers?"

"That will just complicate everything."

"All right, have it your way."

But before Levinson had framed his plan of action he was telephoned by the Special Branch with a message for his client

45

Gordon Ngubene. Would he kindly inform the man that his son Jonathan had died of natural causes the night before?

2

Once again Gordon and Emily put on their Sunday clothes for the trip to John Vorster Square – by that time the trains were running again – to enquire about the body: where it was; when they could get it for burial. One would have expected it to be a simple and straightforward matter, but the enquiry turned out to be yet another dead end. They were sent from one office to another, from Special Branch to CID, told to wait, told to come again.

This time Gordon, for all his old-worldly courtesy, was not to be moved. He refused to budge until his questions had been answered. In the late afternoon a sympathetic senior officer received them. He apologised for the delay but there were, he said, some formalities that still had to be attended to. And an autopsy. But everything should be finished by the Monday.

When on Monday they were once again sent away with empty hands they returned to Ben; and with him to the lawyer.

As on all previous occasions the tall man with the Gable looks dominated, with spectacular self-confidence, the enormous desk covered with files, telephones, documents, empty coffee cups and ornamental ash-trays. His teeth flashed against the deep tan of his face.

"Now this has gone too far," he exclaimed. In an impressive and elaborate show of efficiency he telephoned police headquarters immediately and demanded to speak to the officer-in-charge. The officer promised to make enquiries.

"You better start pulling out your fingers," said Dan Levinson aggressively, winking at his attentive audience. "I give you exactly one hour. I'm not taking any more nonsense, right?" He turned his wrist to look at his large golden chronometer. "If I haven't heard from you by half-past three I'll be phoning Pretoria and every newspaper in the country." He slammed down the instrument, flashing another grin at them. "You should have gone to the newspapers ages ago."

"We want Jonathan Ngubene, Mr Levinson," said Ben, annoyed. "Not publicity."

"You won't get far without publicity, Mr Coetzee. You ask me, I know all about it."

Much to Ben's surprise the Special Branch did ring back at five past three. Levinson didn't say much; he was listening, obviously flabbergasted by whatever the officer on the other side was telling him. After the conversation he remained sitting with the receiver in his hand, staring at it as if he were expecting it to do something.

"Well I never!"

"What did they say?"

Levinson looked up, rubbing his cheek with one hand. "Jonathan has never been in detention at all. According to them he was shot dead on the day of those riots and as nobody came to claim the corpse he was buried over a month ago."

"But why did they tell us last week—?"

Levinson shrugged, scowling as if to blame them for the latest turn in the affair.

"What about the nurse?" said Gordon. "And the cleaner at the Square? They both spoke about Jonathan."

"Listen." Levinson pressed the tips of his strong fingers together. "I'll write them an official letter demanding a copy of the medical report. That'll do the trick."

But in the simple reply from the police, a week later, the matter was closed with the brief statement that, unfortunately, the medical report was "not available".

It is easy to imagine the scene. Ben's backyard at dusk. Johan and his friends splashing and cavorting in the neighbours' pool. Susan preparing supper in the kitchen: they had to eat early,

47

she was going to a meeting. Ben at the back door. Gordon standing with his old hat pressed flat against his lean chest with both hands. The grey second-hand suit Ben had given him last Christmas; the white collarless shirt.

"That's all I say, Baas. If it was me, all right. And if it was Emily, all right. We are not young. But he's my child, Baas. Jonathan is my child. My time and your time, it's passing, Baas. But the time of our children is still coming. And if they start killing our children, then what was it that we lived for?"

Ben was depressed. He had a headache. And he could think of no ready answer.

"What can we do, Gordon? There's nothing you or I can change."

"Baas, that day when they whipped Jonathan you also said we can do nothing. We cannot heal his buttocks. But if we did something that day, if someone heard what we had to say, then perhaps Jonathan would not have got the sickness and the madness and the murder in his heart. I don't say it is so, Baas. I say *perhaps*. How can we know?"

"I know it's a terrible thing that's happened, Gordon. But now you have other children to live for. And I'll help you if you want to send them to school too."

"How did Jonathan die, Baas?"

"That's what we don't know."

"That's what I got to know, Baas. How can I have peace again if I do not know how he died and where they buried him?"

"What good can it do, Gordon?"

"It can do nothing, Baas. But a man must know about his children." He was silent for a long time. He wasn't crying, yet the tears were running down his thin cheeks, into the frayed collar of his grey jacket. "A man must know, for if he does not know he stays blind."

"Please be careful, Gordon. Don't do anything reckless. Think of your family."

Quietly, stubbornly, while the boys went on yodelling behind the neighbours' high white wall, he repeated, as if the words had got stuck inside him: "If it was me, all right. But he is my child and I must know. God is my witness today: I cannot

48

stop before I know what happened to him and where they buried him. His body belongs to me. It is my son's body."

Ben was still standing at the back door when the boys returned from the neighbours', bright towels draped over their smooth brown shoulders. Recognising Gordon, Johan gaily greeted him; but the black man didn't seem to notice him.

3

In order to devote all his time to the enquiries which had become an obsession with him, Gordon resigned from his work at the school. Ben, of course, only found out about this investigation much later; too late.

One of the first steps was to trace as many as possible of the crowd who had gathered on the day of the shooting. The problem was that so few people could remember anything specific about that chaotic day. Several, young and old, confirmed that they had seen Jonathan among the marching children; but they were much less sure about what had happened after the shooting.

Gordon was not discouraged. The first breakthrough came when a boy who had been wounded on the fatal day was released from hospital. He'd been blinded by buckshot in the eyes; but he recalled how, just before it happened, he'd seen Jonathan bundled into a police van with several others.

One by one they were tracked down by Gordon: some who'd seen Jonathan being arrested and taken away; others who had, in fact, been carted off to John Vorster Square with him. From that point, however, the accounts varied. Some of the arrested had been locked up for the night only; others had been transferred to Modder Bee, Pretoria and Krugersdorp; still others had been taken to court. And it wasn't easy to find Jonathan's tracks in that crowd. The only fact established beyond all possible doubt was that Jonathan had not been killed on the day of the riots.

Painstakingly, laboriously, like an ant, Gordon toiled on his antheap of evidence, in hate and love. He couldn't explain what he would do with it once he'd collected everything he needed. According to Emily, afterwards, she'd constantly prodded him about it, but he had been unable or unwilling to reply. Collecting evidence seemed to have become an end in itself.

Then, in December, a whole bunch of detainees still awaiting trial were released by the Special Branch. Among them was a young man, Wellington Phetla, who had been detained with Jonathan for a considerable period; and even after they had been separated they'd continued to be interrogated together. According to Wellington the SB had tried to force admissions from them that they'd been ringleaders in the riots, that they'd been in touch with ANC agents, and that they'd received money from abroad.

At first Wellington was reluctant to discuss anything with Gordon. According to Emily there was something wild in his manner. If one spoke to him he would be looking this way and that all the time as if scared of being attacked unawares. And he was famished, like an animal that had been kept in a cage for a long time. But slowly he grew more normal and less terrified, and at last he allowed Gordon to write down what he had to tell, notably the following:

a) that from the second day of their detention, when their clothes had been taken away, they'd been naked all the time;

b) that in this condition they had been taken to "a place outside the city" one afternoon, where they'd been forced to crawl through barbed wire fences, spurred on by black policemen wielding batons and sjamboks;

c) that on one occasion he and Jonathan had been interrogated by relay teams for more than twenty hours without a break; and that for much of this period they'd been forced to stand on blocks about a yard apart, with half-bricks tied to their sexual organs;

d) that on various occasions both he and Jonathan had been forced on their knees, whereupon bicycle tubes had been wrapped round their hands and inflated slowly, causing them to lose consciousness;

e) that one day, while interrogated on his own in an office, he'd heard people shouting continuously at Jonathan in the room next door, accompanied by the sound of blows and by Jonathan's screaming and sobbing; towards nightfall there had been a tremendous noise next door, like chairs or tables being knocked down. Jonathan's crying had subsided into a low moaning sound followed by silence, and then he'd heard a voice calling out many times: "Jonathan! Jonathan! Jonathan!"; the following day someone had told him that Jonathan had gone to hospital, but he'd never heard of him again.

With much pleading and coaxing Gordon persuaded Wellington Phetla to repeat his statement under oath before a black lawyer; at the same time an affidavit was taken of the young nurse Stanley Makhaya had sent to them. But the cleaner who had discovered the blood on Jonathan's cell floor was too scared to put anything in writing.

At least it was a beginning. And one day, Gordon believed, he would know the full story of what had happened to Jonathan from the day of his arrest until that Wednesday morning when the news of his alleged death of natural causes had been conveyed to them. Then he would trace the grave of his son. Why? Perhaps he was planning to steal the corpse and bring it back for proper burial in *Umzi wabalele*, the City of the Dead, Doornkop Cemetery in Soweto, near his house.

But it never went as far as that. The day after Gordon had obtained the two statements signed by Wellington Phetla and the nurse, he was taken away by the Special Branch. And with him, the affidavits disappeared without a trace.

4

The only person Emily could approach for help was Ben. Stanley Makhaya brought her in his large white Dodge. During the first four periods of the day, while Ben was teaching, she waited patiently on the stoep outside the secretary's small office. It was barely a fortnight after the schools had reopened for the new year. When the bell rang for the tea interval the secretary, flustered and mildly disapproving, came to tell Ben of the visitor and while the other teachers gathered in the common room for tea he went outside to see her.

"What's the matter, Emily? What brought you here?"

"It's Gordon, my Baas."

The moment she said it, he knew. But almost perversely, he wanted to hear it from her before he would believe it.

"What about him? Has something happened to him?"

"The Special Branch has come for him."

"When?"

"Last night. I don't know the time. I was too scared to look at the alarm clock." Fiddling with the black fringe of her shawl she looked up at him helplessly, a large shapeless woman with a face aged before its time; but very erect, and without tears.

Ben stood motionless. There was nothing he could do either to encourage or restrain her.

"We were asleep," she continued after a while, still preoccupied with the fringe. "They knocked so loud we were stiff with fright. Before Gordon could open for them they kicked down the door. And then the whole house was filled with police."

"What did they say?"

"They said: 'Kaffir, you Gordon Ngubene?' The children woke up from the noise and the little one began to cry. They mustn't do that in front of the children, Baas," she said in a smothered voice. "When they went away my son Richard was very bad. He's my eldest now that Jonathan is dead. I tell him to be quiet, but he won't listen to me. He's too angry. Baas, a child who saw the police take away his father, he don't forget it."

Ben was listening, numb, unable to respond.

"They turn over the whole house, Baas," Emily persisted. "The table, the chairs, the beds. They roll up the carpet, they tear open the mattress, they throw out the drawers of the cupboard. They look in the Bible. Everywhere, everywhere. And then they start to beat Gordon and to push him around and they ask him where he hide his things. But what can he hide, I ask you, my Baas? Then they push him outside and they say: 'You come with us, kaffir!'"

"Was that all they said?"

"That was all, Baas. I went outside with them, with the two smallest children in my arms. And when we get to the car one man he say to me: 'Ja, better say good-bye to him. You not going to see him again.' It was a long thin man, with white hair. I remember his face too much. With a cut here, on his cheek." She touched her own face. "So they took Gordon away. The neighbours they come to help me clean up in the house. I try to put the children to sleep again. But what will happen to him now?"

Ben shook his head in disbelief. "It must be a mistake, Emily," he said. "I know Gordon as well as you do. They'll release him. I'm quite sure they will, and soon too."

"But it's the papers."

"What papers?"

It was the first Ben learned about Gordon's investigation of the previous months, and of the affidavits about Jonathan's death. Even then he refused to regard it as particularly serious: an administrative error, an unfortunate mistake, surely no more than that. It wouldn't take them long to find out that Gordon was an honourable man. He tried to comfort Emily as best he could. She listened in silence and said nothing; but she didn't seem to be convinced.

The school bell rang; it was the end of the tea interval.

Ben walked with her round the building to where Stanley Makhaya's car was waiting. When he saw them coming Stanley got out. It was the first time Ben met him. A corpulent man, over six feet tall, with an enormous belly and the neck of a bull, and several double chins, resembling some of the traditional representations of the 19th century Zulu chief Dingane. Very black. With light palms. Ben noticed them as Stanley put out his hand, saying:

"How's it? Is this your Boer, Emily? This the *lanie*?"

"This is Stanley Makhaya," Emily said to Ben. "He is the man who help us all the time."

"Well, what do you say, man?" said Stanley, a smile on his

53

broad jovial face, expressing some secret, perpetual enjoyment. Whenever he laughed, Ben soon discovered, it was like a volcanic eruption.

Ben repeated what he'd already told Emily. They mustn't worry too much, it was a terrible mistake, but no more. Gordon would be back with his family in a day or two. Of that he was absolutely convinced.

Stanley paid no attention. "What do you say, man?" he repeated. "Gordon of all people. Never hurt a fly and look what they done to him now. He was a real family man, shame. And he always used to say—"

"Why do you keep on talking about him in that way?" said Ben, annoyed. "I tell you he'll be home in a few days."

The broad smile deepened: "*Lanie*, with us, when a man gets picked up by the Special Branch, you just start talking about him in the past tense, that's all."

With a final wave of his big hand he drove off.

When Ben came round the building he found the principal waiting for him.

"Mr Du Toit, aren't you supposed to be with the matrics this period?"

"Yes. I'm sorry, sir. I just had to attend to some people."

The principal was a bulky man too, but more fleshy than Stanley Makhaya, more marshmallowy, with a thin cobweb of red and blue veins covering his nose and jowls. Thinning hair. A small muscle flickering in his cheek whenever he felt constrained to look one in the eyes.

"Who was it?"

"Emily Ngubene. Gordon's wife. You remember Gordon who used to work here?" Ben came up the red steps to stand on a level with his principal. "Now he's been arrested by the Security Police."

Mr Cloete's face grew redder. "Just shows you, doesn't it? You can't trust one of them these days. Just as well we got rid of him in time."

"You know Gordon as well as I do, Mr Cloete. It must have been an error."

"The less we have to do with such people the better. We don't want to have the school's name dragged into it, do we?"

54

"But sir!" Ben stared at him in amazement. "I assure you they made a mistake."

"The Security Police won't make a mistake like that. If they arrest a man you can rest assured that they have reason to." He was breathing heavily. "I hope it won't be necessary for me to reprimand you on this sort of behaviour again. Your class is waiting."

Within the four walls of his cramped study, that night. He hadn't switched on the main light, contenting himself with the small stark circle of the reading lamp on his desk. Earlier in the evening there had been a summer storm over the city. Now the thunder had passed. A broken moon was shining through shredded clouds. From the gutters çame the irregular drip-drip-dripping of water. But inside the room a hint of the pre-storm oppressiveness still lingered, huddled in the gloom, an almost physical dark presence.

For a while Ben tried to concentrate on the marking of the Standard Nines' scripts, his jacket flung across a chair, his blue shirt unbuttoned, the right sleeve clasped by a shirt-garter. But now the red ballpoint pen lay discarded on the top paper as he sat staring at the bookshelves on the opposite wall. The placid books whose titles he could recall even though it was too dark to see. A slight movement in the gauze curtain covering the open steelframed window: caressing almost imperceptibly the conventional pattern of the burglar-proofing.

In this silence, in this defined small circle of white light, everything that had happened appeared unreal, if not wholly impossible. Stanley's broad face shining with perspiration, the subterranean rumbling of his voice and his laughter, the eyes unmoved by the wide grin on his lips. His familiarity, the tone of mocking deprecation: *Is this your Boer? This the lanie?* Emily on the high stoep of the redbrick building. The blue headscarf, the full-length old-fashioned chintz dress, the black fringed shawl. A lifetime in the city hadn't changed her. She still belonged among the hills of the Transkei. Would her eldest be sleeping more resignedly tonight? Or was he out with friends to smash windows, to set fire to schools, to blow up cars? All because of what had happened to his father. Gordon with his thin body, the deep furrows beside his mouth, the dark flickering of his eyes, the shy smile. *Yes, Baas.* The hat in both hands, pressed against his chest. *I cannot stop before I know what happened to him and where they buried him. His body belongs to me.* And then last night. *You just start talking about him in the past tense.*

Susan entered so quietly with the tray that he only became aware of her when she put it down on the desk. She'd had her bath and her body still suggested the luxury of nakedness and warm water. A loose floral housecoat. Her hair undone and brushed, a slightly unnatural blond hiding the first touches of grey.

"Haven't you finished marking?"

"I can't concentrate tonight."

"Are you coming to bed?"

"In a while."

"What's the matter, Ben?"

"It's this business of Gordon's."

"Why do you take it to heart so much? You said yourself it was only a mistake."

"I don't know. I'm just tired, I suppose. At this time of the night things don't look the same."

"You'll feel better once you've had a good night's sleep."

"I said I'd come in a while."

"It really has nothing to do with you, Ben. It will get sorted out, you know."

He wasn't looking at her. He was gazing at the red pen, motionless and menacing on the unmarked script.

"One always reads about this sort of thing," he said absently. "One hears so many things. But it remains part of a totally different world really. One never expects it to happen to someone you actually know."

"It's not as if you knew Gordon well. He was just a cleaner at your school."

"I know. But one can't help wondering, can one? Where is he tonight while we're talking here in this room? Where is he sleeping? Or isn't he sleeping at all? Perhaps he's standing in some office under a bare bulb, his feet on bricks and a weight tied to his balls."

"It's not necessary to be obscene."

"I'm sorry." He sighed.

"Your imagination is running wild. Why don't you rather come to bed with me?"

He looked up quickly, his attention caught by something in her voice; aware of her warmth of body and bath, her scent. Behind the loose folds of the housecoat the subtle promise of her breasts and belly. It wasn't often she conveyed it so openly.

"I'll be coming just now."

She was quiet for a while. Then, drawing the housecoat more tightly round her, she tied up her belt.

"Don't let your coffee get cold."

"No. Thank you, Susan."

After she'd gone out he could hear the gentle dripping of the gutters again. The small and intimate wet sounds of the departed rain.

Tomorrow he would go to John Vorster Square himself, he thought. He would talk to them personally. In a way he owed it to Gordon. It was little enough. A brief conversation to correct a misunderstanding. For what else could it be but a regrettable, reparable mistake?

5

At the wrong end of Commissioner Street, leaving the centre behind you, where the city grows toothless and down-at-heel, with peeling, barely legible ads for *Tiger Balm* and Chinese preparations on the blank walls beyond gaping vacant lots and holes and broken bottles, the building appears oddly out of place: tall and severely rectilinear, concrete and glass, blue, massive; yet hollow and transparent enough to offer an unreal view of the cars travelling on the high fly-over of the M1 beyond.

57

Constables loitering on the pavement with deliberate idleness. Cypresses and aloes. A hospital atmosphere inside. Stern corridors; open doors revealing men writing at desks in small offices; shut doors; blank walls. At the back, in the parking basement, the blank lift without buttons or controls, shooting upwards to a predetermined floor the moment you enter. Television cameras following your movements. On the high floor the bullet-proof glass cage, the thickset man in uniform watching you suspiciously while you write down the particulars required.

"Just a minute."

An unduly long minute. Then you are invited to follow him, through the clanging iron gate which is carefully locked behind you, effectively severing all links with the world outside.

"Colonel Viljoen. I've brought the gentleman."

Behind the table in the centre of the office, the middle-aged man pushing back his chair and getting up to greet you. "Come in, Mr Du Toit. How do you do?" Friendly ruddy face; grey crew-cut.

"Meet Lieutenant Venter." That's the young well-built bloke with the dark curly hair at the window, paging through a magazine and smiling a boyish welcome. Safari suit. Large tanned hair legs. A comb protruding from the top of a pale blue stocking.

Colonel Viljoen gestures towards the person beside the door: "Captain Stolz." The man nods, unsmiling. Tall, lean, checkered sports jacket, olive green shirt and matching tie, grey flannels. Unlike his colleague he does not need the pretence of a magazine as he leans against the wall, playing with an orange which he throws up and catches, and throws up and catches monotonously; and every time it lands in his white hand he pauses momentarily to squeeze it briefly, voluptuously, his gaze unflinching on your face. He remains uncomfortably out of sight behind your back when you sit down on the chair the colonel has offered you. On the table you notice a small framed photograph of a woman with a pleasant, shapeless face, and two small blond boys with missing front teeth.

"It seems you're having problems."

"Not really, Colonel. I just wanted to come and see you to find out – to discuss this Gordon you've arrested. Gordon

58

Ngubene."

The colonel looks at the piece of paper before him, carefully flattening it with his palm. "I see. Well, if there's anything we can do—"

"I thought I might be in a position to help you. I mean, in case there's been a misunderstanding."

"What makes you think there may have been a misunderstanding?"

"Because I know Gordon well enough to assure you . . . You see, he just isn't the sort of man to fall foul of the law. An honest, decent man. A churchgoing man."

"You'll be surprised to know how many honest, decent churchgoing men we come across, Mr Du Toit." The colonel leaned back comfortably, balancing on the back legs of his chair. "Still, I appreciate your willingness to help us. I can assure you that with the necessary co-operation on his part he'll be back with his family very soon."

"Thank you, Colonel." You would like to accept it implicitly, to acknowledge relief, yet you find it necessary to persist, in the urgent belief that you may be frank with this man in front of you. He is a family man like yourself, he has seen the good and bad of life, he may well be a few years older than yourself; it would come as no surprise to see him among the elders in church on a Sunday. "What is it you're really after, Colonel? I must admit that I was quite dumbfounded by his arrest."

"A routine enquiry, Mr Du Toit. I'm sure you'll appreciate that we can't leave a stone unturned in trying to clean up the townships."

"Of course. But if you could only tell me—"

"And it's not a pleasant task either, I assure you. We cannot raise a finger without the press screaming blue murder. Especially the English press. It's so easy for them to criticise from outside, isn't it? Whereas they'll be the first to squeal if the Communists took over. I wish I were in a position to tell you about some of the things we've been uncovering since the riots started. Have you any idea of what will happen to the country unless we investigated every possible lead we get? We've got a duty, an obligation to all our people, Mr Du Toit. You have your job, we have ours."

"I appreciate it, Colonel." There is the curious feeling, in such a situation, of being an accused yourself; uncomfortably, you become aware of sinister undertones to everything you say. "But from time to time one needs the assurance — and that's what I've come for — that in your search for criminals you do not also, unwittingly, cause innocent people to suffer."

It is very quiet in the office. There are steel bars in front of the window. It hits you in the solar plexus. Suddenly you realise that the friendly chap with the curly hair and the safari suit hasn't turned a page in his magazine since you arrived. And you start wondering, your neck itching, about the thin man in the checkered jacket behind your back. You cannot restrain yourself from turning to look. He is still standing in the doorway, leaning against the frame, the orange moving up and down in a slow mechanical rhythm, his eyes cool and frank, as if he hasn't looked away for a second. Strangely dark eyes for such a pale face. The thin white line of a scar on his cheek. And all of a sudden you know. You'd better memorize the name. Captain Stolz. His presence is not fortuitous. He has a role to play; and you will see him again. You *know*.

"Mr Du Toit," says Colonel Viljoen at the table. "While you're here, would you mind if I asked you a few questions about Gordon Ngubene?"

"I'd welcome it."

"For how long have you known him?"

"Oh, years and years. Fifteen or sixteen, I think. And in all that time—"

"What work did he do at your school?"

"He was appointed as cleaner. But because he could read and write he also helped out in the stockroom and so on. Totally reliable. I remember once or twice when the Department accidentally overpaid him, he immediately brought back the rest."

The colonel has opened a file and picked up a yellow ballpoint pen, but apart from doodling on a blank page he isn't writing down anything.

"Have you ever met the other members of his family?"

"His wife sometimes visited us. And his eldest son."

Why this sudden tension in your jaws when you utter the words? Why this feeling of divulging incriminating information

60

–and suppressing other facts? Behind you, you know, the lanky officer is watching you with his unflinching, feverish eyes while the orange is being thrown and caught and gently pressed and thrown again.

"You're referring to Jonathan?"

"Yes." You cannot help adding, with a touch of malice: "The one who died some time ago."

"What do you know about Gordon's activities since Jonathan's death?"

"Nothing. I never saw him again. He resigned his job at the school."

"Yet you feel you know him well enough to vouch for him?"

"Yes. After so many years."

"Did he ever discuss Jonathan's death with you?"

What should you reply? What is he expecting you to say? After a moment's hesitation you say, laconically: "No, never."

"Are you quite sure, Mr Du Toit? I mean, if you really knew him so well—?"

"I don't remember. I told you he was a religious man." – Why the past tense, following Stanley's example? – "I'm sure he would have learnt to resign himself to it in the end."

"You mean he wasn't resigned in the beginning? What *was* he, Mr Du Toit? Angry? Rebellious?"

"Colonel, if one of your children were to die so unexpectedly" – you indicate, with your head, the photograph on the table – "and if no one was prepared to tell you how it happened, wouldn't you be upset too?"

A sudden change of approach: "What attracted you to Gordon in the first place, Mr Du Toit?"

"Nothing in particular, I'm sure." Are you once again suppressing something of which you're not even conscious? "We exchanged a few remarks from time to time. When he was short of money I sometimes lent him a rand or two."

"And you paid for Jonathan's education?"

"Yes. He was a promising pupil. I thought it would be better for him to go to school than to loiter on the streets."

"Not that it made much difference in the end, did it?"

"No, I suppose not."

There is something very sincere and confidential in the

61

officer's attitude as he shakes his head and says: "That's what I fail to understand. Look at everything the Government's doing for them – and all they can think of in return is to burn down and destroy whatever they can lay their hands on. In the end they're the ones who suffer for it."

Half-heartedly, dejectedly, you shrug your shoulders.

"No white child would behave like that," he persists. "Don't you agree, Mr Du Toit?"

"I don't know. It all depends, I suppose." Another surge of resentment, stronger than before. "But if you were given the choice, Colonel: wouldn't you rather be a white child in this country than a black one?"

Is there the shadow of a movement behind your back? Once again you cannot resist the urge to turn your head to see Captain Stolz still watching you, immobile except for his slow and studied juggling act with the orange; as if he hasn't even blinked in the interval. And when you turn back, there is an engaging smile on the face of the brawny young man with the *Scope* on his lap.

"I think that more or less covers it," says Colonel Viljoen, putting his pen down on the ruled page covered with meticulous doodles. "Thank you very much for your co-operation, Mr Du Toit."

You get up, frustrated and foolish, but hopeful in spite of everything. "May I take it, then, that Gordon will be released soon?"

"As soon as we're satisfied he's innocent." He rises to his feet and offers his hand, smiling. "I assure you we know what we're doing, Mr Du Toit – and it's for your own good too. To make sure you and your family can sleep peacefully at night."

He accompanies you to the door. Lieutenant Venter raises his hand in a cordial greeting; Captain Stolz nods, unsmiling.

"May I ask you one last favour, Colonel?"

"By all means."

"Gordon's wife and children are very worried about him. It would make things easier for them if they could be allowed to bring him food and a change of clothing while he's still here."

"He's certainly fed well enough. But if they feel they'd like to bring him some clothes from time to time – " He draws up his broad shoulders. "We'll see what we can do."

"Thank you, Colonel. I'll rely on you then."

"Will you find your way out?"

"I think so. Thanks. Good bye."

6

Minor ripples of Ben's preoccupation with Gordon were beginning to affect the members of his family, almost imperceptibly in the beginning.

The two little blond girls of years ago had both grown up and left home by then. Suzette, always "her mother's child", an effortless and charming achiever in music and ballet and the hundred and one other activities Susan had chosen for them, must have been about twenty-five or twenty-six at the time, married to an up-and-coming young Pretoria architect who was beginning to win major contracts from the Transvaal Provincial Administration for some of their more spectacular projects. After completing her B.A. in Pretoria she'd obtained a diploma in commercial art, spent two years working for an exclusively female advertising company, and then accepted a top editorial post with a newly-launched glossy interior decoration magazine. The work involved regular business trips, most of them abroad, which didn't leave her much time for attending to the needs of the baby boy she'd produced in between her other activities. It annoyed and pained Ben, and it must have been roughly about that time, just after Suzette had returned from yet another trip to the U.S. and Brazil, that he spoke to her rather pointedly about the matter. As usual, she shrugged it off.

"Don't worry, Dad. Chris has got so many conferences and consultations and things of his own, he hardly notices whether

I'm home or not. And there's someone to look after the baby; he gets all the attention he needs."

"But you assumed certain responsibilities the day you got married, Suzette!"

Smiling, she pulled a mocking face and ruffled his thinning hair: "You're really an old stick-in-the-mud, Dad."

"Don't underestimate your father," Susan said, entering at that moment with their tea tray. "He's developed an extra-mural interest of his own lately."

"What's that?" Suzette asked, intrigued.

"Champion for political detainees." Susan's voice was cool and hard: not deliberately sneering, but with a smooth edge acquired through many years.

"Now you're exaggerating, Susan!" He reacted more sharply than one would have thought necessary. "I'm only concerned with Gordon. And you know very well why."

Suzette burst out laughing before he'd finished. "Are you trying to tell me you're turning into James Bond in your old age? Or is it The Saint?"

"I don't think it's very funny, Suzette."

"Oh but I do." Another calculated ruffling of his hair. "The role doesn't suit you, Dad. Drop it. Just be the sweet old square we've grown so fond of."

Linda was easier to manage. She'd always been "his" child, from the time when, as a baby, Susan had been too ill to attend to her. She'd grown into an attractive girl – about twenty-one at that stage – but less strikingly beautiful than her sister. More of an introvert; and, since puberty, when she'd survived a serious illness, deeply religious. A pleasant, well-adapted girl above all, an "uncomplicated" person. Holidays or weekends when she was home from university she often accompanied Ben when he went jogging in the morning, or on his late afternoon walks. In her second year at university she'd met Pieter Els, much older than she was and studying theology; soon afterwards she changed courses, abandoning the idea of teaching and turning to social work so that she would be better qualified to help Pieter one day. Ben never openly opposed the kind, somewhat colourless young man; yet Pieter's presence made him feel more inhibited towards Linda as if he resented, in anticipation, the idea of losing her. Pieter was determined to become a missionary. During the first year or two after he'd completed his university course he worked among the Ndebele near Pretoria; but his real ideal was to spread the Gospel further afield in Africa or the Far East, saving souls in a world rapidly approaching its doom. It was not that Ben despised his idealism, but he did regard it as somewhat exaggerated, cringing at the idea of the inevitable suffering and deprivation it would cause his daughter.

Unlike Suzette, she shared his concern over Gordon. Not that they had any really profound discussions about it – she was away in Pretoria most of the time and only came home for the occasional weekend, with or without the fiancé – but he felt encouraged by her sympathy. Above all, she was practical. What mattered to her was to make sure that Emily and her family did not suffer materially while Gordon was away; she made arrangements for food and clothing and rent. And, like Ben, but even more positively so, she was convinced that everything would be cleared up very soon.

"After all, we *know* he didn't do anything wrong," she said when, during that first weekend after the arrest, she and Ben went for a stroll to the Zoo Lake. "And the police are bound to discover it very soon."

"I know." In spite of himself he was feeling morose. "But sometimes unfortunate things do happen."

"They're human, just like us, Daddy. Anybody can make a mistake."

"Yes, I suppose so."

"You'll see: any day now they'll let Gordon go. Then we can find him a good new job."

Her Pieter had a slightly different approach: "The first thing we must do after he's released is to make him come over to the Dutch Reformed Church. Those sects are just a breeding ground for all sorts of evil, misleading the poor trusting members. With a more solid foundation they won't land in trouble so easily."

"I honestly don't think the church has anything to do with their problems," said Ben tartly. Followed by prolonged sucking on his burnt-out pipe.

And then there was Johan, the son Ben had always wanted and who'd been born so unexpectedly at a time when they had really given up thinking of having more children. But while Ben was prepared to spoil the boy, Susan had always been unreasonably strict with him. — *Now don't be a sissy, boys don't cry. You're just as hopeless as your father. Come on, you've got to be tough.* — A lively, healthy boy. A promising chess player. A good athlete. But tense. Like a young horse straining to go but not yet certain about which way to head for.

On that Friday Ben and Johan were driving back home from athletic practice, Johan drumming his fingers on the glove box, accompanying some inaudible tune in his mind.

"It's been your best thousand metres I've seen yet," said Ben warmly. "You were a good twenty metres ahead of that Kuhn boy. And only the other day he beat you."

"But I had a better time on Wednesday. One-point-seven better. Why didn't you come to watch me then?"

"I had business in town."

"What business?"

"I went to see the Security Police."

"Really?" He looked at Ben. "What for?"

"To find out about Gordon."

Johan looked intrigued. "Did they say anything about Jonathan?"

"No. It doesn't look good to me."

Johan was silent for a minute. "Hell," he exclaimed suddenly. "It's so strange to think about it, isn't it? I mean: he used to work in our garden and everything. I rather liked him. He made me that steelwire-cart, d'you remember?"

"And now they've got Gordon too."

"Did you manage to convince them?"

"I don't know. At least the Colonel was very understanding. He promised they'd let him go as soon as possible."

"Did you see Gordon?"

"No, of course not. No one is allowed to see a detainee. Once they've got you — " He stopped at an intersection, waiting in silence for the lights to change. Only after they had started up again he resumed: "Anyway, they're allowing his family to bring him a change of clothes when they want to." After a while

66

he added: "If you don't mind, I'd rather you didn't mention to Mother that I'd been to see them. She may not like it."

With a conspiratorial smile Johan turned to him. "You bet I won't."

7

It was, in fact, the arrangement about the clothes that led to a new development in Gordon's case.

About ten days after Ben had sent a message to the family about Colonel Viljoen's promise, a stranger brought news to Emily – and she promptly reported to Ben. The man, it turned out, had been detained at John Vorster Square for a few days on a suspected assault charge; when it proved to have been a case of mistaken identity he was released. But during his detention, he said, he'd seen Gordon briefly and had been shocked by his condition: he was unable to walk or speak properly, his face was discoloured and swollen, one ear was deaf, his right arm in a sling. Was there anything Ben could do about it?

Without delay he telephoned the Special Branch and demanded to speak to Colonel Viljoen personally. The officer sounded very cordial to begin with, but grew more severe as Ben repeated what he'd been told. In the end he regained his heartiness: "Good heavens, Mr Du Toit! You don't mean you're serious about such a wild story? Look, there's no way a man held on an ordinary criminal charge can communicate with one of our detainees. I can assure you Gordon Ngubene is in perfect health." A slight but significant change of tone: "I do appreciate your interest in the case, Mr Du Toit, but you're really not making things any easier for us. We have more than enough problems as it is and a bit of trust and goodwill will go a long way."

"I'm relieved by your assurances, Colonel. That's why I phoned you. Now I can tell the family not to worry."

"We know what we're doing." For a moment the officer sounded almost paternal: "In your own interest, Mr Du Toit, don't just believe any rumour you hear."

He would have been relieved to accept it at face value. But he kept on imagining Captain Stolz somewhere in the background while the Colonel was talking, his pale face expressionless, the thin scar on his cheek a deadly white on white; and although he tried his best to reassure Emily there was something restless and unhappy in his own mind.

Barely a week later it suddenly came to a head when Emily and two of her children left another change of clothing for Gordon at the Square. When they arrived home and prepared to wash the old clothes returned to them, there was blood on the trousers. Closer examination revealed three broken teeth in the back pocket.

With the trousers wrapped in a crumpled copy of *The World* Emily arrived at Ben's house in Stanley Makhaya's taxi. It was a difficult situation to handle, not only because of Emily's state of near-hysteria, but also because the Du Toits had guests for dinner: a couple of Susan's friends from the South African Broadcasting Corporation, the newly arrived young minister of their congregation, and a few of Ben's colleagues, including his principal. They had just sat down for the first course when the knock came.

"It's for you," Susan announced tersely, as she returned from the front door. Adding in a whisper: "For heaven's sake try to get rid of them soon. I can't wait with the main dish."

Stanley was less communicative than the previous time. In fact, he appeared almost aggressive, as if he were blaming Ben for what had happened; and there was a heavy smell of liquor on his breath.

What was to be done at this time of the evening and with a weekend ahead? All Ben could suggest was to telephone the lawyer at his home; but it took two vain attempts before the third Levinson in the directory turned out to be the right one. And all the time Ben was conscious of Susan glaring at him in smouldering silence, while all conversation around the table stopped as the guests tried to follow what was going on. Understandably, Friday was not the best night of the week to discuss business with Dan Levinson. Why the hell couldn't it wait until Monday, he shouted. But when Ben went outside to report to Emily she was adamant. By Monday, she insisted, Gordon might be dead.

What about the black lawyer then, Ben asked Stanley, the one who'd helped Gordon with the affidavits?

"No go," said Stanley with a harsh laugh. "Julius Nqakula got his banning orders three days ago, man. First round knockout."

Grimly Ben returned to the telephone trying to avoid the guests' eyes as he dialled again. This time Dan Levinson exploded: "My God, I'm not a fucking doctor who's on standby all the time! What do these people expect of me?"

"It's not their fault," said Ben miserably, embarrassed by the presence of his guests. "They've been forced into it. Don't you see, it's a matter of life or death, Mr Levinson."

"All right then. But Jesus Christ—!"

"Mr Levinson, I can quite understand if you don't want to be disturbed over the weekend. If you'd prefer to recommend another lawyer—"

"Why? Don't they have any bloody confidence in me? Show me another lawyer who's done what I have done these last months to help clear up the Soweto mess. And now they want to drop me? That's gratitude for you."

It took some time before Ben managed to edge in another word; in the end they did arrange to meet at his office the next morning. He wanted everybody who could be of assistance: Stanley, Emily, the man who'd told them about Gordon's condition, any possible witnesses.

Stanley had obviously not expected a positive response. With his great hands on his hips he stood waiting for Ben to report, while Emily sat crying quietly on the steps, her head pressed against the face-brick pillar; round the stoep light moths and gnats were swirling. "You mean he's going to help us?" said Stanley. "You actually pulled it off?" An explosion of appreciative laughter. "You may be a *lanie*" – his red tongue caressed

69

the syllables of the taunting *tsotsi* word – "but you've got it right here." Theatrically, he slammed one of his huge fists against his barrel chest. "Shake!" And he offered Ben his hand.

Ben hesitated, then took the hand. For a while Stanley stood pumping energetically: whether it was prompted by emotion or by too much drink was difficult to make out. He dropped Ben's hand as suddenly as he'd taken it, and turned round to help Emily to her feet.

"Come on, Auntie Emily. Tomorrow it'll all be first-class again."

Ben remained outside until the big car had disappeared down the street in a great roar. Dogs were barking after it. With a heavy heart he went back to the dining room.

Susan looked up, announcing with deadly restraint: "Your food is in the oven. I'm sure you didn't expect us to wait."

"Of course not. Sorry chaps." He sat down at the head of the table. "I'm not feeling hungry anyway." As casually as possible he drank some wine from his glass, conscious of them all watching him in expectant silence.

Susan: "So did you solve their problems? Or is it a secret?" Before he could reply she told the guests, with a small bitter smile, "Ben has developed a whole new set of priorities recently. I hope you'll forgive him for it."

With a touch of irritation he replied, "I apologised, didn't I?" He put down his glass and a few drops splashed over the edge staining the white tablecloth. He noticed Susan's disapproving stare but ignored it. "A young boy died the other day. The least one can do is to try and prevent another death."

"Your wife told us about it," said one of the teachers, Viviers (Afrikaans, Standards Six and Seven), an intense young man, fresh from university. "It's high time someone started doing something about it. One can't just sit back all the time. The whole system is crumbling around us and no one lifts a finger."

"What can one man do against a whole system?" asked one of Susan's SABC friends good-naturedly.

"Ben still likes to think of himself in the role of an old-world knight," said Susan, smiling. "More Don Quixote than Lancelot though."

"Don't be silly," he said angrily. "It's not a case of 'one man

70

against a whole system' anyway. The system doesn't concern me. I'm just making a few small practical arrangements."

"Like what?" asked the principal, Cloete, wearing his chronically dyspeptic, disapproving expression. Unceremoniously pushing back his chair he rose to refill his glass at the drinks cabinet: while everyone else was having wine, he stuck to his brandy and water. Slightly breathless, as usual, he came back.

"I've arranged for a meeting with the lawyer tomorrow," Ben said briefly. "We'll try to get an interdict from the Supreme Court."

"Isn't that dramatising things a bit too much?" asked the young minister, Dominee Bester, in a tone of good-natured reproach.

"Not if you knew what's happened." Briefly, reluctantly, Ben told them the news. The trousers, the blood, the broken teeth.

"We're still at table," said Susan, disapproving.

"Well, you asked me."

"How can a system survive if it allows such things to happen?" said Viviers, visibly upset. Without asking permission he lit a cigarette, something Susan normally frowned on. "For heaven's sake, can you imagine—"

"I'm not talking about the system," Ben repeated, more controlled than before. "I know we're living in an emergency and that one has to make allowances. I'm also prepared to accept that the Security Police often knows more than we do. I'm not questioning that. I'm only concerned with a couple of people I happen to know personally. I won't pretend that I knew Jonathan well. For all I know he may have been involved in illegal things. But even if that were so I still want to find out what happened and why it was allowed to happen. As far as Gordon is concerned, I can vouch for him. And quite a few of you also know him well enough." He looked straight at the principal. "And if they start acting against a man like Gordon then it's clear there must be something wrong. That is what I'm trying to prevent."

"Provided you keep the school out of it," said Cloete sullenly. "We teachers must stay out of politics."

Like an aggressive young dog Viviers turned on him: "What

71

about the Party meeting in the school hall three weeks ago? Wasn't that politics?"

"It was outside of school hours," said Cloete, swallowing deeply from his amber glass. "It had nothing to do with the school."

"You personally introduced the minister."

"Mr Viviers!" Cloete seemed to inflate himself as he leaned forward on his two large soft hands. "With all due respect, you're just a pipsqueak in politics. And what you know about school affairs—"

"I just wanted to get some clarification."

While they sat glaring at one another Susan deftly changed the subject: "What I'd like to know is who's going to pay for this? Not you, I hope?"

"That's beside the point," said Ben wearily. "Why can't I pay for it if I have to?"

"Perhaps Dominee can take a collection," one of the men from the SABC joked. They started laughing. And with that the danger was bypassed. In a few minutes the atmosphere was further improved by Susan's exquisite sweets; and by the time the conversation came round to Gordon again the tension was relieved, the mood relaxed.

"Perhaps it would be a good thing for the case to go to court, all things considered," said the young minister. "Too much secrecy doesn't do anyone any good. I'm sure the Security Police themselves would welcome it. I mean, it gives them a chance to state their side, doesn't it? And when all is said and done there *are* two sides to every case."

"Not that there appears to be much doubt about this case," retorted Viviers.

"Who are we to judge?" asked Cloete, leaning back with a show of pleasure, his white napkin still spread across his belly, bearing traces of every dish served in the course of the meal. "Remember what the Bible says about the first stone? Not so, Dominee?"

"True," agreed the Rev Bester. "But don't forget: Jesus didn't hesitate to castigate the moneylenders either."

"Because He knew there was no malice in Himself," Cloete reminded him, burping gently into his hand.

Staring absently ahead of him Ben refilled his glass.

"What about your guests?" Susan reminded him.

"I'm sorry. I got lost in my own thoughts."

"Dare we offer a penny?" said Cloete, grinning.

"Only God can fathom our hearts," said the young minister.

"And what will be," said the SABC producer who had spoken before, "will be."

"That's precisely what I'm protesting against," said Viviers angrily. "We're much too eager to leave everything to God. Unless we start doing something on our own we're in for an unholy explosion." He raised his glass. "Here's to you, Oom Ben," he said. "Give them hell."

And suddenly they were all raising their glasses, beaming with benevolence and amusement, in a show of unity unpredictable barely a minute ago. Satisfied, her confidence restored, Susan escorted them to more comfortable seats in the lounge, for coffee and Van der Hum. And only an hour later, alone in their bedroom after everybody had left and the lights in the rest of the house had been turned off, did she unmask her deeper discontent in the mirror as she meticulously removed the make-up from her face.

"You very nearly succeeded in wrecking the whole evening," she said. "I hope you realise it."

"I'm sorry, Susan," he said from the bed, taking off his shoes. "It turned out all right though."

She didn't bother to reply as she leaned forward to daub cream on her cheeks. The gown hung loosely from her shoulders and in the mirror he could see the soft, elongated pears of her breasts. Without wanting it, he felt dull, weary desire stirring inside him. But he knew she would be unapproachable tonight.

"What are you trying to do, Ben?" she asked unexpectedly, clearly determined not to leave it at that. She threw the bit of cottonwool into the basket beside her dresser, and reached for another. "What is it you really want? Tell me. I must know."

"Nothing." He began to button up his striped pyjama jacket. "I told you already: I just tried to help them. From here the law will follow its own course."

"Do you realise what you're letting yourself in for?"

73

"Oh stop nagging!" He undid his trousers and allowed them to drop to his feet. The buckle of the belt tinkled. He folded the trousers and hung them over the back of a chair, then stepped into his pyjama pants and tied the cord.

"Did you have to do it this way? Why didn't you discuss it with the Security Police first? I'm sure they would have cleared everything up just like that."

"I've already been to see them."

She lowered her hand, staring at him in the mirror. "You never told me."

Shrugging, he went to the bathroom.

"Why didn't you tell me?" she called after him.

"What difference would it have made?"

"I'm married to you."

"I didn't want to upset you." He started brushing his teeth.

She came to the door, leaning against it. With a more urgent tone in her voice than he was used to she said: "Ben, everything we've built up together over the years – for God's sake make sure you don't spoil it."

"What on earth do you mean?"

"We have a good life. We may not have everything we might have had if you'd been more ambitious, but at least we've got somewhere in the world."

"It sounds as if you're expecting me to go to jail or something."

"I don't want you to do anything reckless, Ben."

"I promise you I won't. But how can I allow people I've known for years to be—"

"I know." She sighed. "Just be careful. Please. We've been married for nearly thirty years now and sometimes it still seems to me I don't really know you. There's something in you I feel I'm unprepared for."

"Don't worry about me." Coming towards her he impulsively took her face in his hands and kissed her briefly on the forehead.

She returned to the dressing table and sat down. Stretching her neck she began to massage the loose skin of her throat.

"We're growing old," she said suddenly.

"I know." He got into his bed, pulling the blankets over his

74

legs. "I've been thinking about it more and more lately. How terrible it is to grow old without ever really having lived."

"Is it quite so bad?"

"Perhaps not." Lying with his arms under his head he looked at her back. "We're just tired tonight, I suppose. One of these days everything will be all right again."

But after the light had been turned out he couldn't sleep, however exhausted he felt. He was remembering too much. The dirty bundle in the newspaper they'd brought him. The stained trousers. The broken teeth. It made him nauseous. He moved into another position but every time he closed his eyes the images returned. From a distant part of the house he heard sounds and raised his head to listen. The refrigerator door. Johan fetching something to eat or to drink. There was something both terrifying and reassuring in the knowledge of the closeness of his son. He lay back again. Susan turned in her bed, sighing. He couldn't make out whether she was asleep or not. Dark and soundless the night lay around him, limitless, endless; the night with all its multitudes of rooms, some dark, some dusky, some blindingly light, with men standing astride on bricks, weights tied to their balls.

The application for a court order nearly failed when the man who had allegedly seen Gordon at John Vorster Square refused to sign an affidavit, scared of what might happen if he were identified. But on the strength of the evidence of the blood-stained trousers and the teeth Dan Levinson managed to provide his counsel with an impressive enough brief which was presented to the judge in chambers that Saturday afternoon. A provisional order was granted, restraining the Security Police from assaulting or mistreating Gordon. The following Thursday was set as a deadline for the Minister of Police to provide affidavits opposing the application. And Mr Justice Reynolds made it clear that he regarded the case in a very serious light.

But at the official hearing of the application the following week, the position changed radically. The Special Branch submitted their affidavits: one by Colonel Viljoen, denying categorically that the detainee had ever been assaulted; one by a magistrate who had visited Gordon shortly before and who testified that the detainee had appeared normal and healthy to him and had offered no complaints about his treatment; a third by a district surgeon who stated that the police had called him the previous week to examine Gordon after he had complained of toothache: he had pulled three teeth and as far as he could judge there was nothing wrong with the prisoner.

The advocate instructed by Dan Levinson to handle the family's application, protested as vehemently as he could against the secrecy surrounding the case and pointed out the destructive implications of the rumours caused by it. But the judge obviously had to reject allegations based on speculation and hearsay; and so he had no choice but to refuse a final injunction. However unsatisfactory many aspects of the case might have been, he said, it was impossible to find, on the basis of acceptable evidence submitted to him, that there had been any proof of assault. He had no further jurisdiction in the matter.

Ben did not hear from Emily again.

About a fortnight later he was alone at home one night – Susan had gone to the SABC for the recording of a play and Johan was at an athletics event in Pretoria – when it was announced on the radio that a detainee in terms of the Terrorism Act, one Gordon Ngubene, had been found dead in his cell that morning. According to a spokesman of the Security Police the man had apparently committed suicide by hanging himself with strips torn from his blanket.

TWO

1

For the first time in his life he was on his way to the black townships of Soweto. To Sofasonke City, as Stanley used to refer to it. Stanley was sitting beside him, his eyes obscured by sunglasses with large round lenses, a cigarette stub stuck to his lips, a checkered cap perched at an angle on his head, striped shirt and broad multi-coloured tie, dark pants, white shoes. They were driving in his big Dodge sporting a pink plastic butterfly on the bonnet; the wheel was adorned by red and yellow tape wound tightly round it; and a steering knob had been fitted to it, made of transparent plastic or glass, through which a voluptuous nude blonde could be seen. From the mirror dangled a pair of miniature boxing gloves. The sheepskin covers on the seats were a venomous green. The radio was turned on loud, snatches of wild music interspersed with incomprehensible comments by the announcer of Radio Bantu.

Uncle Charlie's Roadhouse marked the end of the city. Pale yellow and greyish brown, the bare veld of late summer lay flat and listless under the drab sky. A dull, dark cloud obscured the townships: there had been no wind all day to disperse the smoke from last night's fires in a hundred thousand coal stoves.

"For how long have you been driving this car, Stanley?" Ben asked mechanically, just to break the silence, aware of his companion's sullen disapproval of their excursion.

"This one?" Stanley shifted on his large buttocks with an air of proprietorial satisfaction. "Three years. I had a *bubezi* before this. A Ford. But the *etembalani* is better." In a sensual gesture, as if caressing a woman, he moved his hand along the curve of the wheel.

"You like driving?"

"It's a job."

It was difficult to draw anything from him today. His attitude suggested: *You talked me into taking you there, but that doesn't mean I approve.*

"Have you been in the taxi business for a long time?" Ben persisted patiently.

"Many years, *lanie*" – using again, but playfully, the contemptuous word of previous occasions. "Too much." He opened up momentarily. "My wife keeps on nagging me to stop before someone tries to *pasa* me with a *gonnie*" – making a stabbing gesture with his left hand to clarify the tsotsi expressions he seemed to relish; the Dodge swerved briefly.

"Why? Is it dangerous to drive a taxi?"

Stanley uttered his explosive laugh. "You name me something that isn't dangerous, *lanie.*" Light flickered on his black glasses. "No, the point is this isn't an ordinary taxi, man. I'm a pirate."

"Why don't you do it legally?"

"Much better this way, take it from me. Never a dull moment. You want to diet, you want to feel a bit of *kuzak* in your arse pocket, you don't mind a touch of adventure – then this is the life, man. Spot on." He turned his head, looking at Ben through his round dark glasses. "But what do *you* know about it, hey *lanie*?"

The derision, the aggressiveness in the big man unnerved Ben: Stanley seemed bent on putting him off. Or was it some sort of test? But why? And to what purpose? The unimaginative afternoon light kept them apart from each other, unlike their previous meeting, which had taken place in the dark: an evening which now, in retrospect, appeared almost unreal.

First, there had been the night of the news on the radio. The strange sensation of being totally alone in the house. Susan gone, Johan gone; no one but him. Earlier in the evening he'd been working in the study and it was almost nine o'clock before he went to the kitchen to find something to eat. He turned on the kettle for tea and buttered a slice of bread. In the food cupboard he found a tin of sardines. More for the sake of companionship than from curiosity he switched on the transistor radio for the news. Leaning against the cupboard he'd made for Susan years ago, he stood sipping his tea and started picking at the sardines with a small fork. Some music. Then the news. *A detainee in terms of the Terrorism Act, one Gordon Ngubene*. Long after the announcement had been made he was still standing there with the half-empty tin of sardines in his hand. Feeling foolish, as if he'd been caught doing something unseemly, he put it down and began to walk through the house, from one room to the other, quite aimlessly, switching lights on and off again as he went. He had no idea of what he was looking for. The succession of empty rooms had become an aim in itself, as if he were walking through himself, through the rooms of his mind and the passages and hollows of his own arteries and glands and viscera. In this room Suzette and Linda had slept when they'd still lived at home, the two pretty blond girls he'd bathed and put to bed at night. Playing tortoise, playing horsey, telling stories, laughing at jokes, feeling their breath warm and confiding in his neck, their wet kisses on his face. Then the slow estrangement, slipping loose, until they'd gone off, each on her own remote course. Johan's room, disordered and filled with strange smells: walls covered with posters of racing cars and pop singers and pinups; shelves and cupboards littered with model aeroplanes and dissembled machinery, radio carcasses, stones, bird skeletons, books and comics and *Scopes*, trophies, dirty handkerchiefs and socks, cricket bats and tennis racquets and diving goggles and God knows what else. A wilderness in which he felt an imposter. The master bedroom, his and Susan's. The twin beds separated by small identical chests, where years before had been a double bed; photographs of the children; their wardrobes on the wall facing the beds, his, hers; the rigorous arrangement of Susan's make-up on her dressing table, a patterned order disturbed only by a bra hanging limply over the back of a chair. Lounge, dining room, kitchen, bathroom. He felt like a visitor from a distant land arriving in a city where all the inhabitants had been overcome by the plague. All the symptoms of life had been preserved intact, but no living creature had survived the disaster. He was alone in an incomprehensible expanse. And it was only much later, when he returned to his study – and even that appeared foreign, not his own, but belonging to a stranger, a room where he was not the master but an intruder – his thoughts began to flow again.

Tomorrow, he thought, Emily would come round to ask for advice or help. He would have to do something. But he felt blunted and had no idea of where to start. So he really was relieved when she did not turn up the following day. At the same time it made him feel excluded, as if something significant had been denied him – though he knew it was illogical: for what was there he could do? What claim did he have? What did he really know of Gordon's private existence? All these years he'd been remote from it and it had never bothered him in the least. Why should it unsettle him now?

He telephoned Dan Levinson, but of course there was nothing the lawyer could do without instructions from the family. And when Ben rang off, he couldn't help feeling just a bit idiotic. Above all, redundant.

He even telephoned the Special Branch: but the moment the voice replied on the other side he quietly put down the receiver again. There was an argument with Susan when she reproached him for being ill-tempered. He quarrelled with Johan for neglecting his homework. The uneasiness persisted.

Then came the night Stanley Makhaya visited him. Scared of opening the front door when he knocked, Susan sent him round the house to the study at the back, then went to the kitchen to tap on the window as she used to do to call Ben to the telephone or to attract his attention. When he looked up, Stanley was already standing on the threshold – it was a warm night, the door stood open – surprisingly soundless for such a big man. Ben was startled, and it took him a moment before he recognised his visitor. Even in the dark Stanley was wearing his dark glasses. But when he came in, he pushed them up across his forehead like a pilot's goggles. Susan was still drumming on the kitchen window and calling: "Ben, are you all right?" Irritably he went to the door to reassure her; and for a minute he and Stanley stood looking at each other, uneasy and apprehensive.

"Didn't Emily come with you?" he asked at last.

"No, she sent me."

"How is she?"

Stanley shrugged his heavy bull-like shoulders.

"It's a terrible thing that happened," said Ben awkwardly.

"Well, we knew it was going to happen, didn't we?"

Ben was shocked by Stanley's nonchalance. "How can you say that? I was hoping all the time—"

"You're white." As if that summarised everything. "Hope comes easy to you. You're used to it."

"Surely that's got nothing to do with black or white!"

"Don't be so sure." For a moment his violent laugh filled the small room.

"When will he be buried?" asked Ben, deliberately changing the subject.

"Not before Sunday. We're still waiting for the body. They said tomorrow or the day after."

"Is there anything I can do? I'd like to help with the funeral arrangements. Anything."

"It's all done."

"What about the cost? Funerals are expensive these days."

"He had an insurance book. And he's got many brothers."

"I didn't know he had any."

"I'm his brother, man. We all are." Once again, unexpected and uninvited, his great booming voice exploded with laughter which caused the walls to tremble.

"When did they break the news to Emily?" he asked in a bid to stop the bellowing.

"They never came." Stanley turned to spit through the open door.

"What do you mean? Didn't they send a message?"

"She heard it on the wireless like the rest of us."

"What!"

"The lawyer phoned the next day to find out. The cops said they were sorry, they didn't know where to contact her."

In the heavy silence, suddenly realising that they were still standing, he made a half-hearted gesture towards one of the two easy chairs he'd taken over when Susan had bought a new suite for the lounge. "Do sit down."

Stanley promptly lowered his heavy body into one of the floral chairs.

For a time they were silent. Then Ben got up again to fetch

his pipe from the desk. "I'm sorry I don't have any cigarettes," he apologised.

"That's all right. I got some."

After a while Ben asked: "Why did Emily send you? Is there something she'd like me to do?"

"Nothing much." Stanley crossed his massive legs. One trouser leg was pulled up, revealing a red sock above the white shoe. "I had to come this way for a fare, so she asked me to drop in. Just to tell you not to worry."

"My God, why should she be thinking about *me*?"

"Search me." He grinned and blew out a series of smoke circles.

"Stanley, how did you meet Gordon and his family? For how long have you been friends? How come you're always there when they need help?"

A laugh. "I got a car, man. Don't you know?"

"What difference does a car make?"

"All the diff in the world, *lanie*." That name again, like a small fierce ball of clay from a clay-stick hitting one right between the eyes. Stanley changed into a more comfortable position. "If you got a taxi like me, you're right there, man. All the time. I mean, here you get a bloke *pasa*'d by the tsotsis, so you pick him up and take him home, or you take him to Baragwanath Hospital. There you get one passed out from *atshitshi*: same thing. Or a chap who drank too much divorce in a beer-hall. Others looking for *phata-phata*" – illustrated by pushing his thumb through two fingers in the immemorial sign – "so you find them a *skarapafet*. A whore. See what I mean? You're on the spot, man. You pick them up, you listen to their sob stories, you're their bank when they need some *magageba*" – rubbing his fingers together – "all the time, I tell you. You got a taxi, you're the first to know when the *gattes* are coming on a raid, so you can warn your pals. You know every blackjack, you know his price. You know where to find a place to sleep or a place to hide. You know the shebeens. Man needs a *stinka*, he comes straight to you."

"A *stinka*?"

Gleeful, perhaps not without disdain, Stanley stared at him, then laughed again. "A reference book, man. A *domboek*. A pass."

"And you met Gordon long ago?"

"Too much. When Jonathan was just so high." He held out his hand, a foot or two from the floor. Behind his resounding laugh, moving like shadows, were all the things he left unsaid.

"Are you a Xhosa too?"

"Jesus, what do you take me for?" Another bellow. "I'm a Zulu, *lanie*. Don't you know? My father brought me from Zululand when I was a child." Suddenly confidential, he leaned over and stubbed out his cigarette. "You listen to me, *lanie:* one of these days I'm taking my children back there. It's no place for kids here in the city."

"I wish I'd taken my own children away from here when they were small," said Ben passionately. "They would have had a different sort of life then."

"Why?" asked Stanley. "This is your place, isn't it? It's your city. You made it."

Ben shook his head. For a long time he sat staring at his pipe-smoke in silence. "No, it's not my place. Where I grew up"—he smiled briefly—"you know, I was fourteen years old before I put shoes on my feet. Except for church. You should have seen my soles, thick and hard from walking in the veld watching the sheep."

"I looked after the cattle when I was small." Stanley grinned, revealing his strong white teeth. "We used to have great fights with *kieries* down at the water."

"We fought with clay-sticks."

"And made clay oxen. And roasted tortoises."

"And robbed birds' nests and caught snakes."

They both burst out laughing, without really knowing why. Something had changed, in a manner inconceivable only a few minutes earlier.

"Well, at least we both managed to survive in the city," Stanley said at last.

"You probably succeeded better than I did."

"You kidding?"

"I mean it," said Ben. "You think I found it easy to adapt?"

Stanley's sardonic grin stopped him. Concealing the sudden pang of embarrassment Ben said: "Would you like some coffee?"

"I'll come with you."

"No, don't bother. You stay here." (Thinking: *Susan . . .*) "I won't be long." Without waiting he went out. The grass was soft and springy under his feet; it had been cut that afternoon and the green smell lay heavily on the night breeze. To his relief he heard Susan in the bathroom, safely out of the way.

When the kettle started boiling he had a moment of uncertainty. Should he offer Stanley one of the new cups Susan used for guests, or an old one? It was the first time in his life he had to entertain a black visitor. Annoyed by his own indecision he opened and shut the cupboard doors aimlessly. In the end, picking two old, unmatched cups and saucers no longer in use, he measured out the teaspoons of instant coffee and poured boiling water into the cups. He put milk and sugar on the tray and, almost guiltily, hurried out of the kitchen.

Stanley was standing in front of a bookshelf, his back turned to the door.

"So you're a history man?"

"In a way, yes." He put the tray on a corner of the desk. "Help yourself."

"Ta." Then, laughing, with what seemed to be deliberate provocation: "And what has all your history taught you?"

Ben shrugged.

"Fuck-all," Stanley replied on his behalf, returning to his chair. "You want to know why? Because you *lanies* keep thinking history is made right here where you are and noplace else. Why don't you come with me one day, I'll show you what history really looks like. Bare-arsed history, stinking with life. Over at my place, in Sofasonke City."

"I want to, Stanley," Ben said gravely. "I must see Gordon before he's buried."

"No ways."

"Don't back out now. You've just said I should go. And I've got to see Gordon."

"He won't be a pretty sight. What with the post mortem and everything."

"Please, Stanley!"

The big man stared at him intently for a moment, then leaned over to take one of the cups, adding four teaspoons of sugar. "Thanks," he said evasively, beginning to stir his coffee. Adding in a mocking voice: "You know, your wife didn't even want to open the door for me."

"Well, it was very late. She's never seen you before. You must realise—"

"Don't apologise, man." Stanley laughed, spilling some of his coffee into the saucer. "You think *my* wife would have opened this time of the night?" He made a slurping sound as he tested the heat of his cup on his lips. "Except for the *gattes*, of course. The cops."

"Surely you're not bothered by the police?"

"Why not?" He laughed again. "Never a dull moment, take it from me. I know how to handle them. But that doesn't mean they leave me in peace. All hours of the night, man. Sometimes for the pure hell of it. I'm not complaining, mind you. Actually" —a broad smile—"actually, every time I see them, I feel a great relief in my guts. Real gratitude, man. I mean, hell: it's only because they're so considerate that the lot of us, me, my wife, my kids, aren't in jail." He was silent for some time, gazing through the open door as if he saw something amusing outside in the dark. At last he looked back at Ben. "Years ago, when I was still a youngster, it was touch and go. You know what it's like when you got a widow for a mother, your father is dead, your sister lines with the *rawurawu*, the gangsters, and your brother—" He took a big gulp. "That *bra* of mine was a real tsotsi, man. He was my hero, I tell you. I wanted to do everything Shorty and his gang did. But then they caught him. Zap, one time."

"What for?"

"You name it. The works, left, right and centre. Robbery. Assault. Rape. Even murder. He was a *roerie guluva*, I tell you, *lanie*."

Ben avoided his eyes and stared into the night; but what he saw there, he felt, was different from what Stanley had imagined.

"And then?" he asked.

"Got the rope, what else?"

"You mean—?"

"Ja. Round his neck."

"I'm sorry."

87

Stanley guffawed. "What the hell for?" He removed the dark glasses from his forehead to wipe the tears of laughter from his eyes. "What's it to you?"

Ben leaned over to replace his cup on the tray.

"I went to see him, you know," Stanley resumed, unexpectedly. "A week before he got the rope. Just to say good-bye and happy landings and so on. We had a good chat. Funny thing, man. You see, Shorty never was a talkative sort. But that day it was a proper spring-cleaning. More than twenty years ago, but I still remember it. Snot and tears. About life in jail. And being scared of dying. That tough *bra* of mine who'd never feared hell or high water. Told me about the way the condemns would sing before they were hanged. Non-stop all through the last week, day and night. Even on the very last morning as they went out to the gallows. Shitting in their pants. But singing." Stanley suddenly appeared embarrassed by his own frankness. "*Ag*, fuck it," he said. "Let bygones be bygones, man. Anyway, I went home to my mother to tell her about my talk with Shorty. She was standing there in the *mbawula,* in the goddam little shack we were living in those days, the whole place filled with smoke, and she coughing as she stood there making porridge. I can still see it as I sit here. The paraffin box covered with newsprint, and the primus, and the bucket standing on the floor, and a photo of our kraal's chief on the wall. And the boxes and suitcases under the bed, high up on its bricks. She said: 'Is it all right with Shorty?' And I said: 'He's all right, Ma. He's just fine.' How could I tell her he was condemned for the next week?"

After that they didn't speak for several minutes.

"Some more coffee?" Ben finally asked.

"No, thanks. I got to go." Stanley got up.

"Will you let me know when Gordon's body is released?"

"If you want to."

"And then you'll take me to Soweto?"

"I told you it's no use, man. There were riots all over the place, you forgot? Don't look for trouble. You're out of it, so why don't you stay out?"

"Don't you understand I've got to go?"

"I warned you, *lanie*."

88

"I'll be all right. With you."

For a long time Stanley stared fiercely into his eyes. Then, brusquely, he said: "All right then."

That had been two nights ago. And now they were on their way. Soon after they'd passed the old Crown Mines, near the power station, Stanley turned off the main road and started picking his way through a maze of dusty tracks running through a wasteland of eroded mine-dumps. ("Keep your eyes open for the vans. They're patrolling all the time.")

A sensation of total strangeness as they reached the first rows of identical brick buildings. Not just another city, but another country, another dimension, a wholly different world. Children playing in the dirty streets. Cars and wrecks of cars in tatty backyards. Barbers plying their trade on street corners. Open spaces devoid of all signs of vegetation, smoking from large rubbish dumps and swarming with boys playing soccer. In many places there were the hideous burnt-out skeletons of buses and buildings. Smaller groups of children running ahead of the white Dodge, laughing and waving, as if the wrecks and ruins didn't exist and nothing had ever happened. Clusters of policemen in battledress patrolling shopping centres, beer halls, schools.

"Where are we going, Stanley?"

"Nearly there."

He followed a broken stretch of tarred road down a low bare hill, through an erosion ditch cluttered with rusty tins, cardboard containers, bottles, rags and other unnamable rubbish, and stopped beside a long low whitewashed building resembling a shed and bearing the legend:

From Here to Eternity
FUNERAL PARLOUR

On the stoep an old man was moving about on hands and knees with red polish and brushes and dirty cloths. In a long, narrow, filthy trough of mud and water beside the building a group of children froze like small dusty wooden sculptures when the big car pulled up and the two men got out. Below the steps lay the mangled remains of two bicycles, covered in rust, their wheels missing.

Stanley spoke in Zulu to the old man on the stoep, who pointed towards a gauze door without interrupting his work for a moment. But before they could reach it, the door was opened and a small black man emerged, his limbs thin and stick-like, like a praying mantis; dressed immaculately in white shirt, black tie, black trousers, and black shoes without laces or socks.

"My condolences, sir," he whispered mechanically, without even looking up.

After a brief discussion with Stanley they were invited inside. Among those cool, stern, white walls the sun outside became a mere memory. The floor was bare, except for two trestles in the centre, obviously intended for the coffin.

"I have not quite finished," said the undertaker in his hoarse whisper. "But if you will be so kind—"

He led them through to the backyard, a shocking return to the white and blinding sun. There was a lean-to filled with stacks of coffins – most of them in pine, and barely smoothed down, simply hammered together; others, shinier and more expensive, with gleaming handles, were covered by a much too small canvas.

"In here."

The little man opened a metal door in an unplastered brick wall. Icy air struck them as if an invisible cloth had been flapped in their faces. As the door was shut behind them, it was suddenly dark, a single bare, yellowish globe glowing dully and ineffectually against the ceiling, its delicate wires glaring white. There was a low hum from the refrigerator engine. Outside, there would still be sun and children, but distant and improbable.

On either side of the door were metal shelves on which bodies were piled up. Seven altogether, Ben counted, as if it were important to take stock. His stomach turned. But he wouldn't look away. One pile of three, and another of four. Mouths and nostrils stuffed with cottonwool, dark with blood. All of them naked, except for two wrapped in brown paper: those, said Stanley, had already been identified by relatives.

The rest were still anonymous. An old woman with a gaunt face, a mere skull covered in leather; the breasts reduced to flaps and folds of skin, the nipples large and scaly like the heads of tortoises. A young man bearing a gaping wound on the side of the head, one eye-socket empty, allowing one to look right into the red inside of the skull. On the top of the pile on the left lay a young girl with an incredibly sweet face, as if in peaceful sleep, one folded arm half-concealing her pubescent breasts; but from the waist down she was crushed, a mass of broken bone-splinters and black coagulated blood. A mountainously obese woman, an axe imbedded in her skull. A frail old man with ludicrous tufts of white wool on his head, copper rings in his ears, an expression of consternation on his face as if the weight of the bodies on top of him was becoming too much to bear.

The coffin stood on the floor. It was one of the more ostentatious coffins, with brass fittings, lined with white satin. In it lay Gordon, incongruous, ludicrous in a black Sunday suit, hands crossed on his chest like the claws of a bird, his face grey. A barely recognisable face, the left side distorted and discoloured, a blackish purple. The rough stitches of the post mortem across his skull, and under his chin, not quite concealed by the high stiff collar.

Now he had to believe it. Now he'd seen it with his own eyes. But it remained ungraspable. He had to force himself, even as he stood there looking down into the coffin, to accept that this was indeed Gordon: this minute round head, this wretched body in the smart suit. He groped for contact, for some memory which would make sense, but he was unable to find anything. And he felt uncomfortable, almost vexed, as he went down on his haunches beside the coffin to touch the body, disturbingly conscious of the old undertaker's presence, and of Stanley's.

The sun was blinding when they came outside again. They didn't talk. After Stanley had thanked the old mantis they went round the narrow whitewashed building to where the children had started cavorting in the mud again. And now it was the turn of the funeral parlour to become an irrational and far-fetched memory. At the same time it was inescapable, haunting him like a bad conscience in this explosive sunlight where life was going its bustling and obscenely fertile way. Death, he thought angrily, really had no place here. To be overcome by it on such a summer's day, when the world was bright and fruitful, was absurd.

Stanley glanced at him as they slammed the car doors shut, but said nothing. The car pulled off again, following once more an intricate route through patterns of identical houses, as if they were passing the same ones over and over again. Brickwalls covered in slogans. Peeling billboards. Boys playing ballgames. The barbers. The wrecks and the charred buildings. Chickens. Rubbish heaps.

Emily's home looked like all the others in her township, Orlando West, cement and corrugated iron, a small garden obstinately staked off against the dusty road. Inside, a spattering of old calendars and religious pictures on the bare walls; no ceiling to hide the iron roof above; dining table and chairs; a couple of gas lamps; sewing machine; transistor radio. There was a group of friends with her, mainly women, but they parted wordlessly to make way for Ben and Stanley when they arrived. A few small children were playing on the floor, one with a bare bottom.

She looked up. Perhaps she didn't recognise Ben against the glare of the sun outside; perhaps she simply hadn't expected him at all. Expressionless, she stared at him.

"Oh, my Baas," she said at last.

"I've been to the undertaker's to see him, Emily," he said, standing clumsily erect, not knowing what to do with his hands.

"It is good." She looked down at her lap, the black headscarf obscuring her face. When she looked up again, her features were as expressionless as before. "Why did they kill him?" she asked. "He didn't do them nothing. You knew Gordon, Baas."

Ben turned to Stanley as if to ask for help, but the big man was standing in the doorway whispering to one of the women.

"They said he hanged himself," Emily went on in her low droning voice drained of all emotion. "But when they brought his body this morning I went to wash him. I washed his whole body, Baas, for he was my husband. And I know a man who hanged himself he don't look like that." A pause. "He is broken, Baas. He is like a man knocked down by a lorry."

As he numbly stared at her some of the other women started talking too:

"Master mustn't take offence from Emily, she's still raw inside. What can we say, we who stand here with her today?

We're still lucky. They picked up my husband too, last year, but they only kept him thirty days. The police were kind to us."

And another woman, with the body and the breasts of an earth-mother: "I had seven sons, sir, but five of them are no longer with me. They were taken one after the other. One was killed by the tsotsis. One was knifed at a soccer match. One was a staffrider on a train and he fell down and the wheels went over him. One died in the mines. The police took one. But I have two sons left. And so I say to Emily she must be happy for the children she has with her today. Death is always with us."

There was a brief eruption when a young boy came bursting into the little house. He was already inside before he noticed the strangers and stopped in his tracks.

"Robert, say good day to the baas," Emily ordered, her voice unchanged. "He came for your father." Turning briefly to Ben: "He is Robert, he is my eldest. First it was Jonathan, but now it is he."

Robert drew back, his face blunt with resentment.

"Robert, say good day to the baas," she repeated.

"I won't say good day to a fucking *boer*!" he exploded, swinging round viciously to escape into the angry light outside.

"Robert, I'd like to help you," Ben stammered wretchedly.

"Go to hell! First you kill him, now you want to help." He stood swaying like a snake ready to strike, overcome by all the hopeless, melodramatic rage of his sixteen years.

"But I had nothing to do with his death."

"What's the difference?"

An old black priest, who had been keeping his peace in the background until Robert exploded, now pushed through the women and gently took the boy by one of his thin arms. But with surprising strength Robert tore himself loose and burst through the crowd of mourners, disappearing into the street. All that could be heard in the shocked silence inside was the high, monotonous buzzing of a wasp against a window-pane.

"*Morena,*" said the old priest, clicking his tongue, "don't be angry with the boy. Our children do not understand. They see what is happening in this place and they are like that wasp when you burn its nest. But we who are old are glad that you have come. We see you."

93

Ben's ears were ringing. It was a curious experience: his senses were taking in acutely what was happening, yet he didn't seem to be there. Disoriented, a total foreigner to the scene, an intruder in their grief which, nevertheless, he wanted so desperately to share, he looked at the woman in the middle of the room.

"Emily," he said, startled by his own voice in the silence – only the wasp was still buzzing, separated by the pane from its element outside – "you must let me know if you need anything. Please, you must promise me."

She stared at him as if she hadn't heard.

"*Morena,* you are kind to us," said the priest.

Automatically, without really meaning to, Ben put his hand in his trouser pocket and took out a ten rand note. He laid it on the table in front of her. They were all staring at him, all the mourning women, as if deliberately trying to ignore the green note on the checkered plastic cloth. And after he'd said goodbye, when he looked back at them from the door, almost in supplication, they were still standing like that, utterly immobile, like a family portrait.

The big Dodge was like an oven after standing in the glaring sun for so long, but Ben barely noticed it. Even the group of youngsters further down the street, shouting at him and raising clenched fists as he emerged from the house, hardly registered in his mind. He slammed the car door and remained staring fixedly ahead, through the windscreen, at the innumerable rows of houses trembling and rippling in the heat. Stanley moved in beside him.

"Well, *lanie?*" he said loudly.

Ben clenched his jaws.

"We going home now?" asked Stanley. The question sounded more like an accusation.

Unable to explain his reaction, with a hint of panic at the thought of everything ending so abruptly and pointlessly, Ben said: "Do you think we could go somewhere and just sit quietly for a while?"

"Sure, if you want to go. But we'd better get a move on from here, before that crowd starts stoning my car." He motioned towards the youngsters approaching down the street in a slow,

94

menacing phalanx. Without waiting, he started the car, reversed into the nearest side street and drove off, tyres skidding. Distant, isolated voices called out after them; in the rear-view-mirror one could see them dancing oddly in the dust, arms outstretched. A squealing, squawking chicken fluttered past the car, feathers flying, missed by inches. Stanley shook with laughter.

Outside, Stanley's house differed in no way from all the others in his street. Perhaps he deliberately didn't want to attract attention. Inside, it was better furnished than Emily's, with something of a flashy flair, but in no way remarkable. Bright linoleum on the floor, furniture from Lewis Stores, an ostentatious display cabinet filled with plates and shiny objects; on the sideboard a large tray covered with multicoloured birds; a record-rack with the empty sleeve of an Aretha Franklin record on top of it.

"Whisky?"

"I don't really like such strong stuff."

"You need it, man." Laughing, Stanley went through to the kitchen where one could hear him talking in a low voice to someone; he returned with two tumblers. "Sorry," he said, "no ice. The bloody paraffin fridge has packed up again. Cheers!"

The first gulp caused Ben to shudder lightly; the second went down more readily.

"How long have you been living here?" he asked, ill at ease.

Stanley laughed harshly. "You just making conversation now. What the hell does it matter?"

"I'd like to know."

"You mean: Show me yours and I'll show you mine?"

"When you came round to see me the other night we got along so well," Ben said, emboldened by the whisky. "So why are you holding back all the time today? Why are you playing cat and mouse with me?"

"I told you it would be better not to come."

"But I wanted to. I had to." He looked straight at Stanley. "And now I have."

"And you think it's made a difference?"

95

"Of course it has. I'm not sure what it is, but I know it was important. It was necessary."

"You didn't really like what you saw, did you?"

"I didn't come here to like it. I just had to see it. I had to see Gordon."

"And so?" Stanley sat watching him like a great angry eagle.

"I had to see with my own eyes. Now I know."

"What do you know? That he didn't commit suicide?"

"Yes. That too." Ben raised his glass again, with more confidence than before.

"What is it to you, *lanie*?" Behind the aggressiveness in his deep voice lurked something different and almost eager. "This sort of thing happens all the time, man. Why bother about Gordon?"

"Because I knew him. And because – " He didn't know how to put it; but he didn't want to avoid it either. Lowering his glass, he looked into Stanley's eyes. "I don't think I ever really *knew* before. Or if I did, it didn't seem to directly concern me. It was – well, like the dark side of the moon. Even if one acknowledged its existence it wasn't really necessary to live with it." A brief moment, the suggestion of a smile. "Now people have landed there."

"You sure you can't just go on like before?"

"That is exactly what I had to find out. Don't you understand?"

Stanley looked at him in silence for a long time as if pursuing, without words, a more urgent interrogation than before. Ben looked back. It was like a children's game, trying to outstare one another; only it was no game. In silence they raised their glasses together.

At last Ben asked: "Was the family represented at the post mortem?"

"Sure. I saw to it there was a private doctor. Suliman Hassiem. Known him for years, ever since he qualified at Wits." Adding wryly: "Not that that guarantees anything. Those *boere* know the ropes."

"They won't get away with it in court, Stanley," he insisted. "Our courts have always had a reputation for impartiality."

Stanley grinned.

"You'll see!" said Ben.

"I'll see what I'll see." Stanley got up with his empty glass.
"What does that mean?"

"Nothing." Stanley went out. From the kitchen he called:
"Just remember what I told you!" He returned, carrying his
glass in one hand and a bottle in the other. "Can I top you up?"

"Not for me, thanks."

"Be a sport, man!" Without waiting, he filled Ben's glass
liberally.

"Emily needs help," said Ben.

"Don't worry, I'll look after her." Stanley gulped down half
his whisky, then added nonchalantly: "She'll have to give up
the house, of course."

"Why?"

"That's the way it is, man. She's a widow now."

"But where will she go?"

"I'll wangle something." An impish grin. "We're trained for
the job, man."

Ben looked at him intently, then shook his head slowly. "I
wish I knew what was going on inside you, Stanley."

"Don't look too deep." Convulsing with laughter in his disarming way.

"How do you survive?" asked Ben. "How do you manage to
stay out of trouble?"

"You just got to know how." He wiped his mouth with the
back of his hand, watching Ben as if he were trying to make up
his mind about something. From the kitchen came dull,
untranslatable sounds; outside, children were squealing and a
dog barked; once a car drove past at high speed.

"That time they picked up my brother," Stanley suddenly
said, "I decided I'd go straight. Didn't want to end up like him.
So I became a garden boy in Booysens. Not bad people, and I
had my own room in the yard. For a long time it went just fine.
Then I picked up a girl friend; she was a nanny a block or so
away. Her name was Noni, they called her Annie. Nice girl. I
started spending the nights with her. But one night there was a
knock on the door. Her master. Burst in on us, sjambok in his
hand. Beat the shit out of us even before we could put our
clothes on. I got out on all fours, as bloody naked as the day I
was born." He seemed to find the memory very funny as he

doubled up with laughter. "Anyway, I cleared out from my room the same night, before he could trace me." Stanley refilled his glass; Ben's was still full. "*Lanie,* that night I saw something I hadn't seen before, and that was that I wasn't my own boss. My life belonged to my white baas. It was he who organised my job for me, and who told me where I could stay, and what I must do and what I mustn't, the lot. That man nearly broke every bone in my body that night. But that wasn't what troubled me. It was this other thing. Knowing I would never be a man in my own right. I got to be free first. So what did I do? Started right at the bottom. Got me a job at the market. Then I bought job lots to hawk in the townships over the weekend, until I could open my own shop in Diepkloof. But it was juiceless, man. To get enough capital I had to borrow from the *lanies*, the big boys in iGoli. Back to square one. Every month they came to check my books and take their share of the profit. You call that freedom? So in the end a few of us clubbed together to buy a car. One year, then I bought my own. Never looked back."

"Now you're your own boss?"

Stanley looked down at his shoes, absently wiping the dust from their noses with his hand. "Right." He looked up. "But don't let that fool you, baby. I'm only as free as the white bosses allow me to be. Got that? Simple as shit. All right, I've learned to take it for what it's worth. One learns not to expect the fucking impossible any more, you learn to live with it. But what about my children? I'm asking you straight. What about Gordon's children? What about that mob that shook their fists at us out there in the street? They can't take it any more, man. They don't know what we older blokes have learned long ago. Or perhaps they do. Perhaps they're better than us, who can tell? All I know is something big and bloody has started and nobody knows what the hell is still going to happen."

"That is what I had to come to see for myself," said Ben quietly.

"Got to go now," said Stanley, emptying his glass and putting it down. "Before the people start coming home from work and the townships fill up. Then I can't guarantee anything." In spite of his brusque words his attitude was less forbidding than before; and as they went out he even put his hand on Ben's shoulder in a brief gesture of comradeship, restoring the confidence of the other night.

Silently they drove back through the labyrinth of building-blocks resembling houses; and in that silence, behind the events of the afternoon and the uncommitted light of the sun, lay the memory of Gordon, small and maimed in his coffin in the cool bare room, his grey claws folded on his narrow chest. The rest seemed interchangeable, transferable, unessential: but that remained. And, with it, the aching awareness of something stirred into sluggish but ineluctable motion.

As they drew up in front of the hawthorn hedge with its bright orange berries, Stanley said:

"I can't keep on coming here like this. They'll put their mark on you."

"Who? What mark?"

"Never mind." Taking an empty cigarette packet from his pocket, Stanley found a ball-point pen in the glove-box, and scrawled a number on the back of the packet. "In case you ever need me. Leave a message if I'm not there. Don't give your name, just say the *lanie* phoned, right? Or else write me a note." He added an address, then smiled. "So long, man. Don't worry. You're okay."

Ben got out. The car drove off. He turned round to the house and opened the wrought-iron gate with the post-box perched on top. And all at once *this* was what seemed foreign to him: not what he'd seen in the course of the long bewildering afternoon, but this. His garden, with the sprinkler on the lawn. His house, with white walls, and orange tiled roof, and windows, and rounded stoep. His wife appearing in the front door. As if he'd never seen it before in his life.

99

The funeral. Ben had wanted to attend, but Stanley had refused point-blank. There might be trouble, he'd said. And there was. Few people had known Gordon, but his death had evoked a violent, if short-lived, response which had been inconceivable during his life. Especially since it followed so soon after that of Jonathan. An entire society seemed suddenly to have grasped at his funeral as an occasion to give expression to all the tensions and confusion and passions provoked by the previous months: a great and necessary catharsis. Letters and telegrams arrived from people who, only a few weeks before, had never even heard the name of Gordon Ngubene. Emily, who would have chosen to bury her dead in private, was forced into the midst of a public spectacle. A photograph of her sitting at her kitchen table and staring past a candle eventually won some international award.

The World continued to give prominence to the case; soon the name of Dr Suliman Hassiem, who had attended the autopsy on behalf of the family, became almost as familiar as that of Gordon Ngubene himself. Although, on the instructions of the Special Branch, Dr Hassiem refused all press interviews, alarming particulars continued to find their way to *The World* and *The Daily Mail,* soon to be repeated as hard facts in spite of categoric and sarcastic denials by the Minister. Urgent appeals were made to all concerned to ensure that the funeral take place peacefully; but at the same time much prominence was given to reports of police reinforcements sent to Soweto from all over the Reef. And on the Sunday the townships looked like a military camp, overrun by armoured trucks and tanks and squadrons of riot police with automatic rifles, while helicopters surveyed the scene from the air.

From early morning the busloads of people began to arrive. Still, everything appeared calm. The people were tense, but there were no "incidents" – except for the bus from Mamelodi which was stopped by riot police outside Pretoria. All the passengers were ordered to get out, to run the gauntlet of two files of police who laid into them with batons, sjamboks and rifle-butts. There was something very calm and ordered about the whole operation: pure, unadulterated violence which needed no pretext or excuse and simply went its way systematically, thoroughly, neatly. Afterwards the bus was allowed to proceed to Soweto.

The funeral service lasted for hours. Prayers, hymns, speeches. In spite of the obvious tension everything remained remarkably subdued, but after the service, in the late afternoon, as the people came streaming from the graveyard for the ritual washing of hands in the house of the bereaved, a police cordon tried to cut off the majority of the guests. Some youths in the crowd started throwing stones and a police van was hit. Suddenly it was madness. Sirens. Tear gas. Volleys of gunshots. Squadrons of police moving in with batons. Dogs. It went on and on. As soon as one township fell silent under a cloud of tear gas, violence would erupt elsewhere. It continued after nightfall, illuminated in spectacular fashion by burning buildings – Bantu Affairs administrative quarters, a liquor store, a school in Mofolo – and exploding vehicles. Throughout the night there were sporadic new outbursts, but by daybreak everything was once again, according to the media, "under control". An undisclosed number of wounded were taken to hospitals and nursing homes all over Johannesburg; others simply disappeared into the maze of houses. The official death toll was four, surprisingly low in view of the extent of the riots.

Emily's eldest son, Robert, had disappeared during the night. It was more than a week, in fact, before she heard from him again in a letter from Botswana. With her remaining children gathered round her, she finally withdrew, weary and dazed, to their small kitchen which bore Gordon's photograph on the wall, surrounded by wilted flowers. And in Doornkop Cemetery a mountain of wreaths covered the mound under which lay the unknown little man on whose behalf it had all happened so inexplicably.

The next day it was reported that Dr Suliman Hassiem had been detained in terms of the Internal Security Act.

The image that presents itself is one of water. A drop held back by its own inertia for one last moment, though swollen of its own weight, before it irrevocably falls; or the surface tension which prevents water from spilling over the edge of a glass even though it may already bulge past the rim – as if the water, already sensing its own imminent fall, continues to cling, against the pull of gravity, to its precarious stability, trying to prolong it as much as possible. The change of state does not come easily or naturally; there are internal obstacles to overcome.

Ben's ability to resist was sorely tested by Dr Hassiem's arrest. But even then he tried to remain reasonable. His first reaction was to telephone Stanley.

The taxi driver was not available, but the woman who answered promised to convey the message. What was the name? Just tell him the *lanie* phoned, he said, obeying Stanley's instructions.

The call came on the Tuesday afternoon while Ben was working in the garage where, of late, he'd been finding refuge for longer hours than before among his chisels and saws and hammers and drills.

"*Lanie?*" Stanley didn't identify himself, but Ben immediately recognised the deep voice. "You in trouble?"

"No, of course not. But I'd like to talk to you. Can you spare the time?"

"I got to be in your suburb tonight. Let's make it eight o'clock, all right? I'll pick you up at the garage where we turned off to your place last time. So long."

Fortunately it was easy to get away without an explanation as Susan had to go to a meeting and Johan to some school function. When Ben arrived at the garage at eight o'clock the white car was already waiting for him, parked unobtrusively behind a row of dark pumps. The pungent smell of oil still lay heavily on the day's heat trapped under the low awning. A tiny spot glowing in the driver's window betrayed Stanley, smoking placidly.

"How's it, *lanie*? What's your trouble, man?"

Ben got in beside him, leaving the door open. "Have you heard about Dr Hassiem?"

Stanley started the engine, laughing. "Of course. Close your door." When they'd gone a block or two, he said gaily: "Those *boere* know their job, I told you."

"What now?"

"If they can play dirty, we do the same."

"That's why I wanted to see you," said Ben urgently. "I don't want you to mess everything up at this stage."

"*Me* mess everything up?! What you talking about, man? Is Gordon dead or isn't he?"

"I know, Stanley. But it's gone far enough."

A brutal laugh. "Don't kid yourself. It's just started."

"Stanley." It felt like pleading for his own life, putting his hand on the big man's wrist on the steering wheel as if to restrain him physically. "It's out of our hands now. We must let the law run its course. And whoever is guilty will pay for it."

Stanley snorted. "They all playing the same ball game, *lanie.*"

Ben preferred to ignore him. "There's one thing we can do," he said "One thing we must do. And that is to make sure we get the best advocate in Johannesburg to represent the family."

"What's the use?"

"I want you to go with me to Dan Levinson tomorrow. He must brief an advocate as soon as possible. One who won't allow them to get away with anything, no matter what the cost."

"Money is no problem."

"Where does it come from?"

"That's not your worries."

"Will you go with me tomorrow?"

Stanley sighed, irritable. "Oh hell man, all right. But I tell you it's no use."

They drove back to the filling station, stopping in the same dark nook behind the pumps where the smell of oil hit their nostrils with fresh violence.

"All I'm asking you is to give the court a chance, Stanley."

A harsh, bitter laugh. "All right. Meet you in our smart liberal pal's office tomorrow. See if we can get an advocate who'll bring Gordon and Jonathan back to us."

"That's not what I said."

"I know, *lanie*." His voice sounded almost soothing. "But you still believe in miracles. I don't."

4

The court inquest into the death of Gordon Ngubene coincided with the school holidays (21 April – 9 May), which made it possible for Ben to attend all the sessions. Most of the public interest stirred up by the funeral two months before seemed dissipated by then. There was a fair number of black spectators in the public galleries – some of them quite noisy and causing disturbances with shouts of "Amandla! – Freedom!" and a bristle of clenched fists – but, apart from the inevitable cluster of journalists, there were very few whites: some students and lecturers from Wits, representatives of the Black Sash and the Progressive Reform Party, a Dutch delegate from the International Commission of Jurists who happened to be in South Africa for consultations, and a small sprinkling of others.

A useful and dispassionate account of the proceedings was published subsequently by the Institute of Race Relations. It was banned soon afterwards, but there was a copy among Ben's papers.

GORDON NGUBENE (54) an unskilled labourer from Orlando West, Soweto, unemployed at the time of his arrest, was detained on 18 January this year in terms of Article 6 of the Terrorism Act and held at John Vorster Square. On the basis of certain information received by his family an urgent application was made to the Supreme Court on 5 February to restrain the Security Police from assaulting Mr Ngubene or from interrogating him in an unlawful manner, but on 10 February the application was rejected for lack of evidence. On 25 February Mr Ngubene's death in detention was announced by the SABC and confirmed by the police the following day, although his relatives had never been informed officially. On 26 February a post mortem examination was conducted on Mr Ngubene's body by the State Pathologist, Dr P. J. Jansen, assisted by Dr Suliman Hassiem on behalf of the family. Mr Ngubene was buried on Sunday 6 March and on the following day Dr Hassiem was detained in terms of the Internal Security Act, which prevented the legal representatives of the family from consulting with him. In anticipation of Dr Hassiem's release the inquest of Mr Ngubene's death, originally scheduled for 13 April, was postponed *sine die*. Soon afterwards the magistrate was informed that there was no likelihood of Dr Hassiem's release in the near future, and in view of the fact that he had also signed the post mortem report drawn up by Dr Jansen, a new date was set for the inquest and the proceedings opened in the Johannesburg Magistrate's Court on 2 May.

According to the medical report submitted on the first day Dr Jansen had executed a post mortem on the naked body of a middle-aged Bantu male, identified as Gordon Vuyisile Ngubene, on 26 February.

Mass: 51,75 kilogram. Height: 1,77 metres. Post-mortem lividity dependent on the lower limbs, scrotum, face and back. Some blood-stained fluid from the right nostril. Tongue protruding between teeth.

The report listed the following injuries on the body:

1. Ligature around the neck between the thyroid cartilage and the chin, and a broad ligature mark 4 cm wide below, more prominent laterally. No bruising or haemorrhage of the deep tissues of the neck. Tracheae compressed. Hyoid bone not damaged.

2. Swelling over right cheek bone with bruising of the underlaying tissues and fracture of the bone itself.

3. Three small round abrasions of 3 mm inside left ear and a larger abrasion of the same kind in the right ear.

4. A haematoma over the lumbosacral area.

5. The seventh right rib broken at the costochondral junction.

6. Abrasions and laceration marks on both wrists.

7. Marked swelling of the lower scrotum. A specimen taken from it had a dried-out parchment-like appearance and revealed traces of copper on the skin.

8. Horizontal lacerations and abrasions on both shoulder blades, the chest and abdomen.

9. The right ulna broken about 6 cm below the elbow.

10. Extreme congestion of the brain with small haemorrhages, brain fluid bloodstained. Also moderate congestion and waterlogging of the lungs.

11. A variety of other bruises and abrasions, concentrated on the knees, ankles, abdomen, back and arms.

Dr Jansen found that death had been caused by the application of force to the neck, consistent with hanging. Under cross-examination he conceded that such pressure could also have been exerted in other ways, but insisted it was beyond his jurisdiction to speculate on such possibilities. However, he admitted that some of the injuries had been older than others – several of them as old as fourteen to twenty days, others three to four days, still others of even more recent date. He confirmed that Dr Hassiem had been present at the autopsy and that, as far as he knew, Dr Hassiem's report had been identical to his in most respects. On a question by Adv Jan de Villiers, S. A., on behalf of the family, Dr Jansen said he did not know why Dr Hassiem would have taken the trouble of drawing up a separate report if he had co-signed the main one.

After that, several Special Branch witnesses were called to give evidence. Capt F. Stolz testified that on Tuesday 18 January, at about 4 a.m., acting on certain information, he had gone to the house of the deceased, accompanied by Lieut B. Venter, Lieut M. Botha and several black Security Policemen. Mr Ngubene had resisted arrest and a certain amount of force had

had to be applied to restrain him. Subsequently Mr Ngubene had been interrogated on several occasions. The police had reason to believe that the deceased had been involved in subversive activities and several incriminating documents had, in fact, been found in his house. In view of the fact that state security was involved, these documents could unfortunately not be submitted to the court.

According to Capt Stolz the deceased had declined to cooperate, although he had always been treated with courtesy and correctness. In reply to a question by Adv Louw, for the police, Capt Stolz emphasised that Mr Ngubene had never been assaulted in his presence and that he had always enjoyed good health while in detention, except for sporadic complaints of headaches. On 3 February he had also complained of toothache and the following morning he had been examined by a district surgeon, Dr Bernard Herzog. As far as he knew Dr Herzog had extracted three teeth and prescribed some tablets, but he had emphasised that he could find nothing seriously wrong with the deceased. Consequently the police continued their interrogation as usual. Asked what he meant by "as usual" Capt Stolz said it had been customary for the deceased to be taken from his cell at 8 a.m. and brought to the captain's office, where he would remain until 4 or 5 p.m., sometimes earlier. During the period of his detention members of the investigating team had bought food for Mr Ngubene "from their own pockets". He added that the deceased had been allowed at all times "to sit or stand as he wished".

On the morning of 24 February the deceased unexpectedly showed signs of aggression and tried to jump through an open window in Capt Stolz's office. He was acting "like a madman" and had to be restrained by six members of the Special Branch. As a precautionary measure he was then manacled and put in foot-irons attached to his chair. At that stage he appeared quite calmed down and by noon he announced that he was prepared to make a full statement of his subversive activities. On Capt Stolz's request Lieut Venter took down three pages of the statement in longhand, whereupon Mr Ngubene complained of feeling tired. He was then taken back to his cell. The next morning, 25 February, one Sergeant Krog reported to Capt Stolz that Mr

Ngubene had been found dead in his cell. A note found with the body was submitted to the court. It read: *John Vorster Square, 25 February. Dear captain, You can carry on interrogating my dead body, perhaps you will get what you want from it. I prefer to die rather than to betray my friends. Amandla! Your friend, Gordon Ngubene.*

Cross-examined by Adv De Villiers, for the family, Capt Stolz repeated that the deceased had always been treated well. Asked how he could account for the injuries found on the body he said he had no idea, detainees sometimes deliberately injured themselves in various ways. Some injuries might have been caused by the scuffle on 24 February. Adv De Villiers wanted to know whether he did not regard it as excessive to require six strong policemen to subdue a frail man who had weighed barely 50 kilograms at his death, whereupon Capt Stolz repeated that the deceased had acted "like a madman". Asked why there had been no bars in front of the window to prevent detainees from trying to jump out, the captain said that the bars had been removed temporarily the previous day for repairs to the window frame.

Turning to the note allegedly found on the body, Adv De Villiers said he found it strange that it should bear the date of 25 February since the body, discovered at 6 a.m. that morning, had already shown signs of advanced rigor mortis.

Capt Stolz: "Perhaps he was confused in his head."

Adv De Villiers: "As a result of torture?"

Capt Stolz: "He wasn't tortured."

Adv De Villiers: "Not even on February third or fourth when he complained of headache and toothache?"

Capt Stolz complained to the magistrate that the advocate was trying to cast unwarranted suspicion on the Special Branch. The magistrate, Mr P. Klopper, asked counsel to refrain from insinuations, but allowed him to proceed with his cross-examination. The witness stuck firmly to his earlier evidence, except for offering some elaboration on the alleged involvement of the deceased with the ANC and "activities endangering the security of the State". Asked about the portion of the written statement taken on the afternoon of 24 February, Capt Stolz said the document contained material which could not be disclosed in court as it would hamper the Security Police in an important investigation.

Adv De Villiers: "I put it to you that the only 'subversive activities' the deceased had ever been involved in were his efforts to establish what had happened to his son Jonathan Ngubene, allegedly shot in a riot in July last year, although several witnesses have been traced who are prepared to testify that in fact Jonathan died in detention in September, three months later."

The advocate for the police, Mr Louw, objected against the allegation on the grounds that it could not be proved and that it was irrelevant to the present inquest.

Adv De Villiers: "Your Worship, the present witness has gone out of his way to implicate the deceased through wild accusations of 'subversive activities'. It is my good right to put the other side of the case, especially if it can support my argument that we are dealing with an innocent man who died in the hands of the Security Police under what can only be termed highly questionable circumstances. If the Security Police are interested in clearing their reputation then surely they will not object to the real facts being presented to the court?"

At this stage magistrate Klopper adjourned the court to the next day. Upon resumption he announced that this was an ordinary inquest into the death of a specific person, not a full-scale judicial enquiry; consequently he could not allow Adv De Villiers to present evidence or to make allegations about the death of Jonathan Ngubene.

Adv De Villiers: "Your Worship, in that case I have no further questions to put to Capt Stolz."

In the course of the second day of the hearing several other witnesses for the Security Police were called to corroborate the evidence given by Capt Stolz. However, under cross-examination there was some difference of opinion on the removal of the bars in front of the window and the reasons for it, as well as on the exact nature of the scuffle on 24 February. In addition, Lieut Venter also conceded under cross-examination that there had been a previous scuffle in the same office on 3 February, the day before the district surgeon had been called in to attend to Mr Ngubene. Asked whether anyone else had visited the deceased before his death, Lieut Venter said a magistrate had paid him a routine visit on 12

February, accompanied by Capt Stolz and himself, but that the deceased had not complained of anything.

Adv De Villiers: "Does it surprise you that he had no complaint?"

Lieut Venter: "Your Worship, I don't understand that question."

Mr Klopper: "Mr De Villiers, I have asked you before to refrain from insinuations of this kind."

Adv De Villiers: "As it pleases your Worship. Lieutenant, can you tell me whether Capt Stolz was also present while the district surgeon examined the deceased on fourth February?"

Lieut Venter: "I wasn't there, but I presume the Captain was present."

Next, Sergeant Krog and two constables who had discovered the body on the morning of 25 February, were called to testify. One of the blankets in the cell of the deceased had allegedly been cut into strips with a razor blade (before the court) to form a rope, one end of which had been tied round the bars of the cell window and the other round Mr Ngubene's neck. The witnesses differed on the way in which the blanket had been tied round the bar and also about the position of the hanging body when they found it. (Sergeant Krog: "I'd say his feet were about six inches from the floor"; Const Welman: "He was hanging quite high, his head almost touching the bars, so his feet must have been a foot or more from the ground"; Const Lamprecht: "As I remember his toes just touched the floor".) They agreed that no one had seen the deceased alive after he had been locked inside the cell at about half-past five the previous afternoon. According to Sergeant Krog all cells were supposed to be visited at hourly intervals through the night to make sure everything was in order, but unfortunately this had been omitted on the night in question. "We were very busy and I suppose there was some misunderstanding about whose duty it was to do the rounds."

Adv De Villiers: "Suppose I put it to you that Capt Stolz or some other officer from the Special Branch had instructed you to stay away from the cell that night?"

Sergeant Krog: "I strongly deny that, your Worship."

When the enquiry resumed on 4 May, Adv Louw, for the

police, submitted four affidavits by detainees, testifying that they had all seen Gordon Ngubene between 18 January and 24 February, that he had been in good health on every occasion, and that they themselves had been treated very well by the same officers responsible for interrogating Mr Ngubene. However, under cross-examination the first of these detainees, Archibald Tsabalala, denied that he had ever met Mr Ngubene in detention, and stated that he had been forced to sign the affidavit before the court. "Capt Stolz hit me many times with a length of rubber hosepipe and said they would kill me unless I signed." Thereupon he pulled up his shirt and showed his bruised back to the court. When Capt Stolz was recalled to the witness box he testified that Tsabalala had slipped and fallen down a staircase a few days before. He insisted that Mr Tsabalala's original statement had been made voluntarily. After some further cross-examination Capt Stolz was allowed to take Mr Tsabalala back to John Vorster Square.

Following this testimony, Adv Louw, for the police, announced that the other three detainees whose affidavits had been submitted, could not be called for cross-examination as it would prejudice the security of the state. In the face of strong opposition from Adv De Villiers the magistrate ruled that the court would nevertheless consider their affidavits as evidence.

Dr Bernard Herzog, a Johannesburg district surgeon, testified that on the morning of 4 February he had been called by Capt Stolz to examine a detainee, identified to him as Gordon Ngubene. He could find nothing wrong with the man. Mr Ngubene had complained of toothache and as three molars had showed signs of advanced decay he had extracted them and given Mr Ngubene some aspirin for the pain.

The next time he'd seen the deceased was early on the morning of 25 February when he had been summoned to John Vorster Square where he'd found Mr Ngubene dead, lying on the floor of his cell, dressed in grey trousers, a white shirt and a maroon jersey. Sergeant Krog had informed him that he had personally discovered the body about half an hour earlier, hanging from the bars of his window, and that he had taken it down. According to the sergeant the blanket had been tied so tightly round the neck that they'd had to cut it loose with a razor blade discovered in the cell. Rigor mortis had already reached an advanced stage and he'd concluded that death must have occurred as long as twelve hours before.

Adv De Villiers embarked on his cross-examination in a decidedly aggressive manner, commenting extensively on the fact that Dr Herzog had not found it necessary to examine the deceased more thoroughly on 4 February (Dr Herzog: "Why should I? He only complained about his teeth"); and that he couldn't remember whether Capt Stolz or anyone else had been present during the examination in question. Accused by Adv De Villiers of having been "intimidated" by the Security Police or even of deliberately co-operating with them "in playing their disgusting little games of hide and seek" Dr Herzog objected strongly and appealed to the court for protection. As far as the preliminary examination of the corpse was concerned he declined to offer a definite opinion about the estimated time of death, pointing out that rigor mortis could be influenced by any number of extraneous circumstances. He could offer no explanation for the fact that, when the state pathologist Dr Jansen had performed the post mortem on 26 February, the corpse had been naked. Following a request by Adv De Villiers, Capt Stolz was again recalled to the witness box, but he was unable to say what had become of the clothes the deceased had worn at the time of his death, or why they had not been forwarded to the State laboratories for examination. He did, however, offer on behalf of the Security.Police to compensate the family for the loss of the clothes.

The court was adjourned briefly so that the attendant at the police morgue could be called, but he was unable to recollect whether the body had been clothed or naked when delivered to him.

The last witness called by Adv Louw was a police graphologist who identified the handwriting on the note found with the corpse as Gordon Ngubene's. This was strongly contested by a specialist called by Adv De Villiers, who listed a long series of discrepancies between the handwriting on the note and that found in several of Mr Ngubene's other papers. Mrs Emily Ngubene, wife of the deceased, also denied that it was her husband's handwriting. Continuing her evidence, she said that Mr

Ngubene had been "beaten and pushed around" on the occasion of his arrest on 18 January; that about ten days later a detainee released from John Vorster Square had brought her news of a serious assault on her husband; and that when she had delivered a change of clothing for her husband on 4 February she had discovered blood on the trousers returned to her, in addition to three broken teeth in the back pocket (before the court). She testified that in a conversation with the family doctor, Dr Suliman Hassiem, who had attended the autopsy, he had expressed serious doubt as to whether death had been caused by the strips of blanket as alleged earlier. Before she could pursue the matter, however, a strong objection against hearsay evidence was lodged by Adv Louw and sustained by the magistrate. Adv Louw also successfully opposed specialist evidence that the second signature on the State pathologist's post mortem report could not have been that of Dr Hassiem. Evidence led by Adv De Villiers on allegations of torture or assault against Capt Stolz in several other cases, was rejected as unfounded and irrelevant.

After further evidence of a more technical nature Adv De Villiers caused a commotion in court by calling as a witness a young girl, Grace Nkosi (18), to testify about her own detention at John Vorster Square. She had originally been arrested on 14 September last year, she said, and after being subjected to interrogation by several members of the Security Police (including Capt Stolz and Lieut Venter) over a considerable period, she had been taken back to Capt Stolz's office on the morning of 3 March. Several accusations had been brought in against her and every time she'd denied them she had been beaten with a sjambok. After some time she had fallen on the floor, whereupon she had been kicked in the face and the stomach. When she spat blood she was ordered to lick it up from the floor. Then Capt Stolz threw a large white towel over her head and started twisting the ends round her neck in a manner she illustrated to the court. She tried to struggle, but lost consciousness. According to Miss Nkosi this was repeated several times. The last time she heard Capt Stolz saying: "Come on, *meid*, speak up. Or do you want to die like Gordon Ngubene?" Then she lost consciousness again. She came round in her cell and on 20 March she was released without a charge.

In spite of lengthy attempts by Adv Louw to persuade her that she had either made it all up or had misheard the name "Gordon Ngubene" in a state of dizziness, Miss Nkosi insisted that she had told the truth.

After the two counsel had concluded their arguments the court was adjourned until the afternoon for the verdict. Mr Klopper gave his finding in less than five minutes. Although it was impossible to account for all the injuries on the body, he said, no conclusive evidence had been offered to prove beyond doubt that members of the Security Police had been guilty of assault or of any other irregularity. There were indications that the deceased had become aggressive on more than one occasion and had to be restrained with a measure of force. There was sufficient evidence to conclude that death had been caused by a trauma following pressure applied to the neck, consistent with hanging. Consequently he found that Gordon Ngubene had committed suicide by hanging himself on the morning of 25 February and that on the available evidence his death could not be attributed to any act or omission amounting to a criminal offence on the part of any person.

For the sake of formality the documents of the inquest were forwarded to the Attorney-General, but on 6 June he announced that no further steps would be instituted, for lack of a *prima facie* case against any person or persons.

5

She stood waiting for him on the steps outside the court building on the second or third afternoon of the inquest, after they had adjourned for the day: the petite dark-haired girl with the large black eyes he had absently noticed among the journalists before. It had occurred to him, when he'd seen her in court, that she looked startlingly young for such responsible work; surrounded by so many older, tougher, more cynical reporters her youth had struck him as almost vulnerable, an openness, a frankness, a freshness. But now, suddenly finding her directly in front of him and looking down into her small oval face, he was surprised to discover how much older she was than he'd thought. Certainly much closer to thirty than to eighteen or twenty. Delicate lines beside the eyes; deep and more definite lines of determination or pain on either side of her mouth. Still young enough to be his daughter, but mature and without illusions or callowness; an affirmation, unnerving in its force, of unflinching womanness.

Ben was disgruntled, irritable, lost in thought when he came out. Not only because of what had happened in court but by something specific: he had become accustomed to the presence of a whole contingent of Security Police in the courtroom at every session, taking turns to stare at the spectators, singling them out one by one for scrutiny and forcing one to feel guilty even when there was no reason at all for it; but that afternoon, for the first time, Colonel Viljoen had also been there. And when the eyes of the greyish, benign, paternal officer had suddenly discovered Ben in the crowd, his expression had revealed something — surprise? disapproval? not even that: a mere suggestion of taking cognizance – that had disturbed Ben. So he hardly noticed the girl when he came outside and only became conscious of her when, standing right in his way, she said, in a deeper voice than one might have expected of her:

"Mr Du Toit?"

He looked at her in surprise as if expecting to find that she'd confused him with someone else.

"Yes?"

"I'm Melanie Bruwer."

He stood waiting, defensive.

"I understand you knew him?" she said.

"Who?"

"Gordon Ngubene."

"You're from the newspaper," he said.

"Yes, I'm from the *Mail*. But I'm not asking on behalf of the paper."

"I'd rather not talk about it," Ben said in the tone of quiet finality he might have employed talking to Linda or Suzette.

He was surprised by her reaction. "I understand," she said. "Pity, though. I would have liked to know more about him. He must have been a very special kind of man."

"What makes you think so?"

"The way he persisted in trying to dig up the truth about his son's death."

"Any parent would have done the same."

"Why are you hedging?"

"I'm not. He was a very ordinary person. Just like myself or anyone else. Don't you see? That's the whole point."

She smiled suddenly, affirming the fullness and generosity of her mouth. "That's exactly what intrigues me," she said. "There aren't many ordinary people around nowadays."

"What do you mean?" He looked at her with a suggestion of suspicion, yet disarmed by her smile.

"Just that very few people seem prepared to be simply human – and to take responsibility for it. Don't you agree?"

"I'm really no judge." In a curious way she made him feel guilty. What, in the final analysis, had he done? Waited, procrastinated, made a few simple arrangements, that was all. Or was she mocking him?

"How do you know about it anyway?" he asked cautiously. "I mean that I knew Gordon?"

"Stanley told me."

"So you also know Stanley?"

"Who doesn't?"

"He couldn't have given you a very glowing report on me," he said awkwardly.

"Oh Stanley has quite a soft spot for you, Mr Du Toit." She looked him in the eyes. "But you said you'd rather not discuss it, so I won't keep you. Good-bye."

He looked after her as she went down the broad steps. Below, she turned and waved briefly, a small green figure. He raised his hand, more to call her back than to say good-bye, but she had already gone. And as he went down the steps to the busy

116

street, the image of her large frank eyes still in his mind, he was conscious of a sense of loss: as if he'd missed something which had been fleetingly and exquisitely possible, even though he couldn't explain it to himself.

She gave him no peace for the rest of the day, nor that night. What she'd said about Stanley; what she'd said about Gordon; about himself. Her narrow face with the dark eyes and vulnerable mouth.

At lunchtime two days later, as he was having his tea and toast in a small crowded Greek café near the court, she suddenly turned up next to his small square table with the stained plastic cloth, and said:

"Mind if I sit with you? There's no other place."

Ben jumped up, knocking against the edge of the table and spilling some tea into the saucer.

"Of course." He pulled out a chair opposite his.

"I won't bother you if you're not in a mood for conversation," she said, her eyes mocking. "I can occupy myself."

"I don't mind talking," he said eagerly. "It went so well in court this morning."

"Do you think so?"

"You were there, weren't you?" He couldn't supress his excitement. "What with Tsabalala turning against them and all that. Their whole case is beginning to collapse. De Villiers is making mincemeat of them."

She smiled slightly. "Do you really think it's going to make any difference to the outcome?"

"Of course. It's as clear as anything De Villiers is strangling them in their own lies."

"I wish I could be so sure."

The waiter brought her a dirty menu covered in torn plastic, and she gave him her order.

"Why are you so sceptical?" asked Ben after the waiter had gone.

Her elbows propped up on the table, she put her chin on her cupped hands. "What are you going to do if it doesn't work out?"

"I haven't even given it a thought."

"You scared?"

117

"Of what?"

"Not of anything in particular. Just scared."

"I'm afraid I don't understand you at all."

Her insistent eyes refused to let him off. "I think you understand only too well, Mr Du Toit. You desperately want it to work out."

"Don't we all?"

"Yes, we do. But you want it for a different reason. Because you're involved."

"So you're just looking for a story for your paper after all?" he said slowly, in bitter disappointment.

"No." She was still looking at him, unmoved, unmoving. "I assured you of that the day before yesterday. I want to know for myself. I *must*."

"Must?"

"Because I also manage to get involved all the time. I know I'm a journalist, I'm supposed to be objective and not to get drawn into things. But I wouldn't have been able to live with myself if it had been no more than that. It's – well, sometimes one starts wondering about one's own reasons. That's why I thought you might help me."

"You don't even know me, Melanie."

"No. But I'm prepared to take the risk."

"Is it really a risk?"

"Don't you think so?" There was something disarmingly playful in her grave tone of voice: "When one person unexpectedly finds himself on the edge of another – don't you think that's the most dangerous thing that can happen to anyone?"

"It depends, I suppose," he said quietly.

"You don't like straight answers, do you?" she said. "Whenever I ask you a question you say: 'It depends', or: 'Perhaps', or: 'I don't know what you mean'. I want to know *why*. Because I know you're different."

"What makes you think I'm different?"

"Stanley."

"Suppose he made a mistake?"

"He's seen too much of life to make that sort of mistake."

"Tell me more about him," said Ben, relieved to find an escape.

Melanie laughed. "He's helped me an awful lot," she said. "I'm not referring to newspaper stories only – that too, from time to time – but I mean finding my feet, especially in the beginning, when I first became a journalist. Don't be fooled by his happy-go-lucky attitude. There's much more to him."

"I presume his taxi is just a camouflage for other things?"

"Of course. It makes it easier for him to come and go as he chooses. He probably smuggles grass, if not diamonds." She smiled. "He's something of a diamond himself, don't you think? A big black rough uncut diamond. One thing I've discovered long ago: if you ever really need someone, a man you can trust with your life, it's Stanley."

The waiter arrived with her sandwiches and tea.

After he'd left, she deftly returned the conversation to Ben: "That's why I decided I'd take the chance and talk to you."

He poured himself a second cup, without sugar, looking at her keenly. "You know," he admitted, "I still can't make up my mind about you. Whether I can really believe you or whether you're just a much more astute journalist than I'd thought."

"Test me," she said, unperturbed.

"In spite of what you may think," he blurted out, "there really is very little I can tell you about Gordon."

She shrugged lightly, munching her sandwich, a few small crumbs clinging to her lips. She flicked them off with her tongue, a swift, casual motion that moved him sensually.

"That's not the reason why I came to sit here."

"No, I know." He smiled, some of his restraint gone, feeling like a schoolboy.

"It shook me when I saw Archibald Tsabalala in the box this morning," she said. "Standing there and saying right to their faces what they'd done to him. Knowing that in a few minutes he would be led out by the very same men who'd tortured him." Her dark eyes turned to him in urgent confidence. "Still, in a sense I can understand it. All those Tsabalalas: perhaps they're the only ones who can really afford to do it. They have nothing left to lose. Only their lives. And what remains of life when it's been stripped bare like that? It can't get worse. Perhaps it can only get better. Provided there are enough of them. How can a government win a war against an army of corpses?"

119

He said nothing, sensing that she hadn't finished.

"But *you*," she said after a while. "You have everything to lose. What about you?"

"Don't talk like that. Please. I haven't done anything really."

Her eyes on his face, she slowly shook her head. The long dark hair stirred gently, heavily round her narrow face.

"What are you really thinking, Melanie?"

"It's time to go back for the afternoon session," she said. "Otherwise you may not get a seat."

For another moment he stared at her, then raised his hand to call the waiter. In spite of her protest, he paid for both. And then they went back through the crowded streets without speaking.

On the last day of the inquest, immediately after the verdict, he came from the building dazed and weary, and stopped on the pavement. There was a large crowd outside, mainly black, shouting and raising their fists and singing freedom songs, while from behind him people emerged from the courtroom, flowing past him, some bumping into him. He was hardly conscious of it. It had all ended too abruptly. The verdict had been too blunt, he was still groping in his mind to grasp it. *Consequently I find that Gordon Ngubene committed suicide by hanging himself on the morning of 25 February and that on the available evidence his death cannot be attributed to any act or omission amounting to a criminal offence on the part of any person.*

From the crowd two people broke away towards him, but he only noticed it when they touched him. Stanley, wearing his dark glasses and his irrepressible smile, although for once it looked more like a grimace. And leaning on his arm, a shapeless bundle, Emily.

As they reached him her mouth was distorted. She tried to shape a word but failed; then she simply threw her arms round his neck and started sobbing on his chest. Her great weight caused him to stagger back and in order to keep his balance he put his arms round her. While a few press cameras flashed on the stairs she went on weeping, swaying against him, until Stanley took her back gently but resolutely.

Like her, Ben was too overcome to speak.

But Stanley was firmly in command. Placing a heavy hand on Ben's shoulder, he said in his deep booming voice: "Don't worry, *lanie*. We're still alive, man."

Then they disappeared into the throng again.

A moment later a small figure with long hair came to him, and took his arm.

"Come," she said.

At the same time police were moving in with dogs to break up the crowd before it could turn into a demonstration; and in the confusion they escaped to the miserable little café of the previous time. At this hour it was nearly empty; one of the neon tubes on the ceiling had fused, and the other was flickering on and off at irregular intervals. They went to a table behind a large green plastic pot-plant and ordered coffee.

Ben was in no mood to talk, brooding over his own thoughts. Accepting it without comment, Melanie finished her cup in silence. At last she asked:

"Ben, did you really expect a different verdict?"

He looked up, stung by the question, and nodded in silence.

"What now?"

"Why do you ask me?" he said angrily.

Without answering she beckoned the waiter and ordered more coffee.

"Can *you* understand it?" he asked, challenging her.

Calmly she said: "Yes, of course I can understand it. What else could they have decided? They can't admit that they are wrong, can they? It's the only way they can keep going."

"I don't believe it," he said obstinately. "It wasn't just anything: it was a court of law."

"You've got to face it, Ben: it's not really the function of the court to decide on right or wrong in absolute terms. Its first duty is to apply the laws."

"What made you so cynical?" he asked, stunned.

She shook her head. "I'm not cynical. I'm only trying to be realistic." Her eyes softened. "You know, I can still remember how my father used to play Father Christmas when I was small. He always spoiled me, in every conceivable way, but his favourite diversion was that Christmas game. By the time I was five or six I'd found out that all this Father Christmas stuff was nonsense. But I couldn't bear to tell him, because *he* enjoyed it so much."

"What on earth has that got to do with Gordon?" he asked dully.

"We're all constantly playing Father Christmas to one another," she said. "We're all scared of facing the truth. But it's no use. Sooner or later we've got to face it."

"And 'truth' means that you must reject the notion of justice?" he said in a rage.

"Not at all." She seemed bent on mollifying him as if she were the older person. "I'll never stop believing in justice. It's just that I've learned it's pointless to look for it in certain situations."

"What's the use of a system if it no longer has any place for justice?"

She was looking at him with silent, ironic eyes. "Exactly."

He shook his head slowly. "You're still very young, Melanie," he said. "You still think in terms of all or nothing."

"Certainly not," she objected. "I rejected absolutes the day I rejected Father Christmas. But you cannot hope to fight for justice unless you know injustice very well. You've got to know your enemy first."

"Are you quite sure you know the enemy?"

"At least I'm not afraid of looking for him."

Irritable, cornered, he pushed his chair back and got up before he'd touched his second cup. "I'm going," he said. "This is no place to talk."

Unprotesting, she followed him outside, to where the home-going traffic had subsided and the streets looked empty and plundered; hot, smelly air was moving in listless, hopeless waves among the buildings.

"Don't brood on it too much," said Melanie when they came out on the pavement. "Try to sleep it off first. I know it's been an ordeal for you."

"Where are you going?" he asked in sudden near-panic at the thought of her leaving him.

"I'm catching my bus down in Market Street." She prepared to go.

"Melanie," he said, not knowing what had got into him.

She looked round, her long hair swinging.

"Can't I take you home?"

"If it isn't out of your way."

"Where do you live?"

"Westdene."

"That's easy."

For a moment they stood opposite one another, their vulnerability exposed in the grimy light of the afternoon. In such insignificant moments, he wrote afterwards, in such trivial ways, a life can be decided.

"Thank you," she said.

They spoke no more as they walked on to the parking garage; nor in the car, later, over the bridge and down the curve of Jan Smuts Avenue and left in Empire Road. Perhaps he was regretting it now. He would have preferred to be alone on his way home; her presence affected him like light beating on unsheltered eyes.

The house was in the older part of the suburb, on an incline, a large double plot with a white picket fence in which there were several gaps. An ugly old house from the Twenties or Thirties, with a low curved verandah sheltering the red stoep, rounded pillars covered in bougainvillea, green shutters, no longer rectangular, and hanging from half-broken hinges. But the garden was appealing: no landscaped lawns or streams or exotic corners, but honest well-kept flowerbeds, shrubs and trees, a luxuriant vegetable patch.

Ben got out to open the door for her, but when he came round the car she had already stepped out. Uncertain, crestfallen, he hesitated.

"Do you live here on your own?" he asked at last, unable to reconcile the house with her.

"My father and I."

"Well," he said, "I'd better go." He wondered whether he should offer her his hand.

"Wouldn't you like to come in?"

"No, thank you. I'm not in a mood for people now."

"Dad isn't home." She narrowed her eyes to look at him against the late glare. "He's gone climbing in the Magaliesberg."

"All alone?"

"Yes. I'm a bit worried, because he's almost eighty and his health isn't very good. But no one can keep him away from the mountains. Usually I go with him, but this time I had to stay for the inquest."

"Isn't this a very lonely place to live?"

"No, why? I can come and go as I wish." After a moment: "And one needs a place like this, where you can withdraw when you feel like it."

"I know. I tend to do the same." He was, perhaps, giving away more than he'd intended. "But then I'm a lot older than you."

"Does it make any difference? One's needs depend on one-self."

"Yes, but you're young. Don't you prefer being with other people and enjoying yourself?"

"What do you call 'enjoying yourself'?" she asked with light irony.

"What young people normally mean by it."

"Oh I enjoyed myself in my own way when I was younger," she said. "I still do." Then, not without a touch of wryness: "You know, I was even married at one stage."

It intrigued him; he found it hard to believe: she looked so young, so unscathed. But looking at her eyes again he felt less sure of himself.

"You said you were in a hurry to get home, Mr Du Toit," Melanie reminded him.

She had called him by his first name before; and it was this unexpected, slightly provocative formality which prompted him to say: "I'll come in if you offer me a cup of coffee. I didn't drink my second cup in the café."

"Don't feel obliged." But with a quietly satisfied air she went through the broken iron gate and followed the unevenly paved path to the stoep. It took her some time to find her key in her handbag; then she unlocked the door.

"Follow me."

She led the way to a large study comprising two ordinary rooms with the major portion of the wall between them knocked out to leave a wide archway supported by an enormous elephant tusk on either side. Most of the walls were covered with bookshelves, some built-in, a few lovely antique cases with glass doors; for the rest, ordinary pine boards balanced rather precariously on bricks. There were a few worn-out Persian rugs on the floor, and springbuck and oryx hides; the curtains before the large bay windows were of faded velvet, once probably old-gold, now a dirty yellowish brown. Prints in the open spaces between the book cases: Munch's three girls on the bridge, a Rembrandt *Titus,* a Braque still-life, an early Picasso, Van Gogh's cypresses. Several enormous easy chairs with cats sleeping on them; an exquisite inlaid chess-table with yellowed ivory and ebony chessmen, oriental in design; an old baby-grand piano, and a veritable ark of a military dropside desk. The desk, as well as two smaller tables and all other available spaces large and small, including the floor, were covered with piles of papers and books, some lying open, others with torn paper bookmarks protruding from the pages. On the floor lay tangled lengths of flex leading from a record-player to two voluminous speakers. The whole room was redolent of old tobacco and cats and dust and mould.

"Make yourself comfortable," said Melanie, sweeping an armful of books, newspapers and handwritten sheets from a chair and persuading one of the innumerable indolent fat cats to give up its place. Going across to a record cabinet standing with doors wide open because the shelves inside were too crammed for them to be closed, she turned on a reading lamp perched on top. It cast a dull, dusty, yellow glow across the splendid chaos of the room. In a strange way she seemed to belong to the room, even though at the same time she appeared wholly out of place. Belonged, because she was so obviously at home there and could find her way so surely in the confusion; out of place, because everything there was so old and musty and used and lived-in while she appeared so young and untouched.

"Sure you'd like coffee?" she asked, still standing beside the lamp, its light touching her shoulders and one cheek, one half of her dark shiny hair. "Or would you prefer something stronger?"

"Are you having something?"

"I think we need it after today." She passed under the arch flanked by the improbable tusks. "Brandy?"

"Please."

"With water?"

"Thanks."

She went out. He began to explore the double room, stumbling over the wires of one of the loudspeakers, mechanically running his hand along the spines of books in a shelf. There seemed to be the same lack of any discernible system in the books as in the room itself. Arranged haphazardly next to one another, he discovered books on law, a Greek Homer, the Vulgate and an assortment of Bible commentaries, philosophical works, anthropology, old leather-bound travel journals, art history, music, *Birds of South Africa,* botany, photography, dictionaries in English, Spanish, German, Italian, Portuguese, Swedish, Latin; a collection of plays; Penguin novels. Nothing appeared new, everything used and read and thumbed; in the few books he pulled out to scan, there were dog-eared pages, underlined passages, margins filled with comments in a minuscule almost illegible handwriting.

He lingered beside the chess-table, lovingly touching a few of the delicately carved pieces, executing a few moves in the classical, satisfying harmony conceived by Ruy Lopez – white, black; white, black – and feeling, for the first time, the pang of envy: to play with a set like this after handling the soiled, worn wooden pieces of his own; to live in daily contact with it, like this girl Melanie.

She entered so softly behind him that he never heard her; and he was startled when she said:

"I'll put it down here."

Ben looked round quickly. She had kicked off her shoes and was settling into the chair she'd cleared earlier, her legs folded under her, a cat on her lap. He removed the debris from a chair opposite her and took the glass she'd left on a pile of books. Two large grey cats approached him, rubbing against his legs, tails in the air, purring luxuriously.

In the heavy, sombre snugness of the disordered room they sat drinking in silence for a long time. He could feel the dull fatigue slipping from him like a heavy overcoat gliding from a hanger and landing on the floor. Outside the dusk was deepening. And in the dusk of the room inside, caressed

126

by the brooding yellow light of the single lamp, the cats were moving silently, invisible in the darker gloom where the light could not reach.

Temporarily, only temporarily, the harsher realities of the long day were softened: the courtroom, death, lies, torturers, Soweto and the city, everything which had been so unbearably vivid in the seedy little café. Not that it ever disappeared entirely: it was like a charcoal drawing over which a hand had lightly brushed, blurring and smudging the starkness of the lines.

"When will your father be back?" he asked.

She shrugged. "Don't know. He never sticks to a schedule. A few more days, I think. He left a week ago."

"This looks like the study of Dr Faustus."

She grinned. "That's him, all right. If only he'd believed in the Devil he might have decided to sell his soul to him."

"What does he do?" It was a relief to be talking about her father, bypassing himself and her and whatever had happened.

"He was a professor, Philosophy. Retired years ago. Now he does whatever he feels like. And every now and then he goes off into the mountains, collecting plants and things. He's been all over the place, up to Botswana and the Okavango."

"Don't you mind staying behind here all on your own?"

"Why should I?"

"I was just asking."

"We get along perfectly." In the obscure golden gloom of the lamp, surrounded by everything familiar to her, she seemed to shed her reticence more easily. "You see, he was nearly fifty when he came back from the War and married my mother in London. She was – oh, years younger than he, the daughter of old friends. And after a romance of only three weeks – when he'd known her before the War, she'd still been a child, he'd never paid any attention to her – they got married. But she couldn't adapt to South Africa and just a year after I was born they were divorced. She went back to London and we've never seen her since. He brought me up on his own." She sipped her brandy, smiling with all the generosity of her mouth. "God knows how he managed, he's the most unpractical man I've ever seen." For a while it was quiet, except for the cats purring, and the rustling sound of her chair as she moved her legs. "He studied law to start with," she said. "Became an advocate. But then he grew fed up with it and dropped everything and went to Germany to study philosophy. It was in the early Thirties. He spent some time in Tübingen and in Berlin, and a year in Jena. But he got so depressed by what was happening in the Third Reich that he came back here in 'Thirty-eight. When war broke out, he joined the army to fight Hitler and ended up spending three years in a German camp."

"What about yourself?"

She looked up quickly, studying him for a minute. "There isn't much to say about me."

"What made you become a journalist?"

"Sometimes I ask myself the same question." She fell silent again, her eyes large and mysterious in the dusky room. Then, as if she'd suddenly made up her mind, she said: "All right, I'll tell you. I don't know why, I don't like talking about myself."

He waited quietly, aware of a growing relaxation, an openness made possible by the increasing darkness outside and the gentleness of the old house.

"I was brought up in a very sheltered way," she said. "Not that he was possessive – not openly, anyway. I think he'd just seen enough of the mess the world was in to want to protect me as much as he could. Not against suffering as such, but against unnecessary suffering. And later, at university, I took a nice, safe course. Literature mainly. Hoping to become a teacher. Then I got married to a man I'd met at school, he'd been one of my teachers. He adored me, carried me on his hands, just like Dad had done." She moved her head; her dark hair stirred. "I suppose that was where the trouble started."

"But why?" He felt a sudden pang of longing for Linda.

"I don't know. Perhaps there's always been something contrary inside me. Or is it the opposite? I'm a Gemini, you see." A provocative smile. "Deep down, I suppose, I'm just lazy. Nothing would be easier than to indulge myself, to allow myself to sink back into it, like in one of these old easy-chairs. But it's dangerous. Do you understand what I'm trying to say? I mean, one can lead such a delightfully cushioned existence that you actually stop living, stop feeling, stop caring. As if you're in a trance, living in a constant high." She was toying with her glass. "Then, one day, you discover that life itself is slipping past and you're just a bloody parasite, something white and maggot-like, not really a human being, just a thing, a sweet and ineffectual thing. And even if you try to call for help, they don't understand you. They don't even hear you. Or they think it's just a new craze and start doing their best to humour you."

"So what happened? What made you break out of it?"

"I'm not sure that anything really dramatic or spectacular is necessary. It just happens. One morning you open your eyes and discover something prickly and restless inside, and you don't know what's the matter. You take a bath and go back to your room and suddenly, as you pass the wardrobe, you see yourself. And you stop. You look at yourself. You look at yourself naked. A face, a body you've seen in the mirror every day of your life. Except you've never *really* seen it. You've never really *looked*. And now, all of a sudden, it comes as a shock, because you're looking at a total stranger. You look at your eyes and your nose and your mouth. You press your face against the smooth, cold surface of the mirror, until it's fogged up, trying to get right into it, to look right into your eyes. You stand back and look at your body. You touch yourself with your hands, but it remains strange, you cannot come to grips with it. Some mad urge gets into you. An urge to run out into the street just as you are, naked, and to shout the filthiest obscenities you can think of at people. But you repress it, of course. And it makes you feel even more caged in than before. And then you realise that all your life you've been hanging around waiting for something to happen, something special, something really worthwhile. But all that happens is that time passes."

"I know," Ben said quietly, more to himself than to her. "Don't you think I know what it feels like? Waiting and waiting: as if life is an investment in a bank somewhere, a safe deposit which will be paid out to you one day, a fortune. And then you open your eyes and you discover that life is no more than the small change you've got in your back pocket today."

She got up out of the chair and went over to the window

behind the overloaded desk, a narrow figure against the darkening evening outside, a childlike defencelessness about her shoulders and the trim roundness of her bottom.

"If there really was a specific incident which made me open my eyes," she said, turning back to him, "it was something utterly trivial in itself. One day our housemaid fell ill at work and in the afternoon I took her home to Alexandra. She'd been with us for years, first with Dad and me; then, after my marriage, with Brian and me. We got along very well; we paid her decent wages and everything. But that was the first day I'd ever set foot in her house, you know. And it shook me. A tiny brick house with two rooms. No ceiling, no electricity, concrete floor. In the dining-room there was a table covered with a piece of linoleum, and two rickety chairs, I think, and a small cupboard for crockery; and in the other room a single bed and some paraffin boxes. That was all. That was where she lived, with her husband and their three youngest children and two of her husband's sisters. They took turns with the bed; the rest slept on the floor. There were no mattresses. It was winter, and the children were coughing." Her voice suddenly choked. "Do you understand? It wasn't the poverty as such: one knows about poverty, one reads the newspapers, one isn't blind, one even has a 'social conscience'. But Dorothy was someone I thought I *knew;* she'd helped Dad to bring me up; she lived with me in the same house every day of my life. You know, it felt like the first time I'd ever really looked right into someone else's life. As if, for the first time, I made the discovery that other lives *existed*. And worst of all was the feeling that I knew just as little about my own life as about theirs." With a brusque movement she came from behind the desk and picked up his empty glass. "I'll get you some more."

"I've had enough," he said. But she had already disappeared, followed by a couple of soundless cats.

"Surely you didn't get divorced because of that?" he asked when she came back.

Her back turned to him, she put a record on the player, one of the late Beethoven sonatas, turning the volume down very low; almost imperceptibly the music flowed into the cluttered room.

"How can one pinpoint such a decision?" she said, curling

up in her chair again. "That wasn't the only thing that happened. Of course not. I just felt more and more claustrophobic. I became irritable and unreasonable and uptight. Poor Brian had no idea of what was happening. Neither did Dad. As a matter of fact, for about a year I stayed away from him altogether, I couldn't face him, I didn't know what to say to him. And after the divorce I moved into my own flat."

"Now you're back with your father," he reminded her.

"Yes. But I didn't come back to get pampered and spoilt again. Only because, this time, he needed *me*."

"And then you became a journalist?"

"I thought it would force me, or help me, to expose myself. To prevent myself from slipping back into that old euphoria again. To force me to see and to take notice of what was happening around me."

"Wasn't that rather drastic?"

"I had to do something drastic. I knew myself too well. It wouldn't take much to sink back slowly into self-indulgence and the wonderful luxury of being cared for by others. But I dare not let it happen again. Don't you understand?"

"Did it work?" Ben asked. The second brandy was reinforcing the effect of the first, causing him to relax in heavy mellowness.

"I wish I could give you a straight answer." Her eyes were searching him keenly as if hoping for a clue or a cue from him. After a few moments she went on: "I went on a long journey first. Just wandering about. Mainly in Africa."

"How did you manage that on a South African passport?"

"My mother was English, remember. So I got a British passport. It still comes in handy when the paper wants to send out a reporter."

"And you came through it all unscathed?"

A brief and almost bitter laugh. "Not always. But then, I couldn't really expect to, could I? After all, that was one of the reasons I'd broken away."

"What happened?"

She shrugged, noncommittal. "I really don't see why I should pour out all my sob-stories on you."

"Now you're the one who is evasive."

131

She looked straight at him, weighing, reflecting. Then, as if she were depressed or threatened by something unless she could move around, she got up again and started wandering about the room, pushing the odd book into line with the others.

"I was in Mozambique in '74," she said at last. "Just when Frelimo was getting out of hand after the takeover." For a moment she seemed to have thought better of it; then, her back turned to him, she said: "One night on my way back to the hotel I was stopped by a group of drunken soldiers. I showed them my press-card but they threw it back at me."

"And then?"

"What do you think?" she asked. "They dragged me off to an empty lot and raped me, the whole lot of them, and left me there." An unexpected chuckle. "You know what was the worst of it all? Arriving back at my hotel long past midnight and finding that there was no hot water."

He made a hopeless, angry gesture. "But couldn't you report it or something?"

"To whom?"

"And the next day you flew straight back?"

"Of course not," she said. "I had to finish my assignment."

"It's madness!"

She shrugged, almost amused by his frustrated anger. "Two years later I was in Angola," she said calmly.

"Don't tell me you were raped again?"

"Oh no. But they arrested me with a group of other foreign journalists. Locked us up in a schoolroom until they could check our credentials. Kept us there for five days, about fifty or sixty people in that one room. It was so crowded, there was no space to lie down and sleep. One simply had to prop oneself up against one's neighbours." Another chuckle. "The main problem was not so much the heat or the lack of air or the vermin, but a stomach complaint. The worst squitters I've had in my life. And there was absolutely nothing I could do about it. I left in the same pair of jeans I'd been wearing when they caught me."

From the bottle of brandy she'd brought with her, she touched up his glass, uninvited, and her own as well.

"Soon after that the paper sent me up to Zaire," she went on.

"When the rebellion started. But that wasn't quite so bad. Except one evening, when we were on the river in a small motor boat and suddenly got caught in crossfire. We had to drift downstream, clinging to any old piece of wreckage, hoping they wouldn't shoot us all to bits. The man with me got a bullet in the chest but he pulled through. Fortunately it was getting dark, so they couldn't see us any more."

After a long silence he asked, aghast: "Didn't it muck you up completely? That time in Mozambique – didn't it make you feel you'd never be the same again?"

"Perhaps I didn't want to be the same."

"But for someone like you – the way you grew up – a girl, a woman?"

"Does that really make a difference? Perhaps it even made things easier for me."

"In what possible way?"

"To get out of myself. To free myself from my hangups. To learn to ask less for myself."

In one gulp he emptied his glass, shaking his head.

"Why does it surprise you?" she asked. "When you first got involved with Gordon – the things that came naturally to you I had to learn from scratch. I had to force myself every inch of the way to get there. And sometimes it still frightens me to think I haven't got there yet. Perhaps 'getting there' is just part of the great illusion."

"How can you talk about anything coming 'naturally' to me?" he protested.

"Didn't it then?"

And now it was inside *him* it was happening, the sudden loosening, like a great flock of pigeons freed from a cage. Without trying to stop or check it, encouraged by her own confessions and by the lived-in ease of the room in that comforting dusk which made confidence possible, he allowed it to flow from him spontaneously, all the years he'd cooped up inside him. His childhood on the Free State farm, and the terrible drought in which they'd lost everything; the constant wandering when his father had the job on the railways, and the annual train journey to the sea; his university years, and the ridiculous rebellion he'd led against the lecturer who had sent his friend from the classroom; and Lydenburg, where he'd met Susan; the brief fulfilment of working among the poor in Krugersdorp, until Susan had insisted on a change, embarrassed by living in such a place surrounded by people so far below them; and his children, Suzette headstrong and successful, Linda gentle and loving, Johan frustrated and aggressive and chomping at the bit. He told her about Gordon: about Jonathan working in his garden over weekends and growing moody and recalcitrant, and mixing with questionable friends and disappearing in the riots; and his father's efforts to find out what had happened, and his death; about Dan Levinson, and Stanley, and his visit to John Vorster Square; and Captain Stolz, with the thin scar on his white cheekbone, and the way he'd stood there leaning against the door throwing and catching the orange, squeezing it with casual, sensual satisfaction every time it came down in his hand; every single thing he could think of, important or irrelevant, up to that day.

After that it was quiet. Outside, night had fallen. From time to time there was sound – a car driving past, the distant siren of an ambulance or a police van, a dog barking, voices in the street – but muffled by the old velvet curtains and the many books padding the walls. The Beethoven had ended long ago. The only movement in the room, now and then, almost unnoticed, like shadows, was that of cats sidling or rippling past, looking for a new spot to sleep, yawning, smoothing their fur with small pink tongues.

Much later, Melanie got up and took his glass from him.

"Like some more?"

He shook his head.

For an instant she remained close to him, so close he could smell the slight scent of her perfume. Then she turned and left the room with the glasses, her dress swinging round her legs, her bare feet soundless on the floor. And in her soundlessness and the quiet grace of her movement he found something so intensely sensual that he could feel his face grow hot, his throat tautening. An awareness of him and her alone in this half-dark house, and the silent lustre of the light, the wealth of books, the stealthy shadows of the cats; and beyond the walls of the double room with its grotesque elephant tusks, there was the suggestion, a mere subconscious stirring, of other rooms and other dusks and darknesses, available emptiness, beds, softness, silence. A consciousness, above all, of her, this young woman Melanie, moving, invisible, somewhere through those darknesses, familiar and relaxed on her bare feet, attainable, touchable, overwhelming in her frank and unevasive womanness.

Almost terrified, he rose. And when she came back, he said: "I didn't realise it was so late. I'd better go."

Without saying a word she turned to lead him back to the front door, and opened it. On the stoep it was quite dark, the day's warmth still slumbering in the stone; she didn't turn on the light.

"Why did you invite me in?" he asked suddenly. "Why did you take me away from the courtroom?"

"You were much too alone," she said, with no hint of sentimentality in her voice, a simple statement.

"Good-bye, Melanie."

"You must let me know if you decide to do anything," she said.

"Like what?"

"Think it over first. Don't rush it. But if you do decide to follow up Gordon's case, and if you need me for anything"—she looked at him in the dark—"I'll be glad to help."

"I'm still too confused."

"I know. But I'll be here if you need me."

He did not answer. His face was burning in the half-hearted brush of the evening breeze. She stayed behind as he went to the car. There was an unreasonable, ridiculous urge in him to turn back and go into the house with her and close the door behind them, shutting out the world; but he knew it was impossible. She herself would send him back into the very world she'd delivered herself to. And without daring even to wave, he hurried through the rusty gate and got into his car. He switched on the ignition, drove a few yards uphill, turned into a driveway, and came back down the incline, past her house. He couldn't see whether she was still standing there. But he knew she had to be somewhere in the dark.

"Where have you been? Why are you so late?" Susan asked, vexed and reproachful, as he came from the garage. "I was beginning to think something had happened to you. I was on the point of phoning the police."

"Why would something happen to me?" he asked, peeved.

"Do you know what time it is?"

"I just couldn't come straight home, Susan." He wanted to evade her, but she remained standing in the kitchen door, the light behind her. "The court gave its verdict this afternoon."

"I know. I heard on the news."

"Then you must understand."

She looked at him in sudden suspicion and revulsion: "You smell of liquor."

"I'm sorry." He made no effort to explain.

Indignant, she stood aside to let him pass. But as he came into the kitchen she relented: "I knew you would be tired. I made you some *bobotie*."

Grateful and guilty, he looked at her. "You shouldn't have taken the trouble."

"Johan had to eat early, he went to the chess club. But I've kept ours."

"Thanks, Susan."

She was waiting in the dining room when he came from the bathroom, his hair damp, his mouth prickling with toothpaste. She had taken the silver out, and opened *Château Libertas*, and lit some candles.

"What's all this for?" he asked.

"I knew the case would upset you, Ben. And I thought the two of us deserved a quiet evening together."

He sat down. Mechanically she offered him her hand for the evening prayer; then she dished up the minced meat, rice and vegetables in her brisk, efficient way. He felt like saying: *Really, Susan, I'm not hungry at all.* But he didn't dare to; and for her sake he pretended to enjoy it, in spite of weariness lying like a heavy lump in his stomach, weighing him down.

She was talking brightly, eagerly, deliberately trying to humour him and make him relax; but with the opposite effect. Linda had telephoned and sent him her love; unfortunately she and Pieter wouldn't be able to come over the next weekend, he was working on a Bible-study course. Susan's mother had also phoned, from the Cape. Father had to open some administrative building in Vanderbijlpark in a few weeks' time and they would try to stay over. Ben resigned himself to the flow of her conversation, too tired to resist.

But she became aware of it, and stopped in the middle of a sentence to look at him sharply. "Ben, you're not listening."

He looked up, startled. "Pardon?" Then he sighed. "I'm sorry, Susan. I'm really flaked tonight."

"I'm so glad it's over now," she said with sudden emotion, putting her hand on his. "You've had me worried lately. You mustn't take these things to heart so much. Anyway, it'll be better now."

"Better?" he asked, surprised. "I thought you said you'd heard the news of the verdict? After everything that had come out in the inquest."

"The magistrate had all the facts, Ben," she said soothingly.

"I heard them too!" he said angrily. "And let me tell you—"

"You're a layman like the rest of us," she said patiently. "What do we know about the law?"

"What does the magistrate know about it?" he asked. "He's not a jurist either. He's just a civil servant."

"He must know what he's doing, he's had years of experience." With a steady smile: "Now come on, Ben, the case has run its course and now it's over. Nobody can do anything about it."

"They killed Gordon," he said. "First they killed Jonathan, then him. How can they get away with it?"

"If they'd been guilty the court would have said so. I was just as shocked as you were when we heard about Gordon's death, Ben. But it's no use dwelling on it." She pressed his hand more urgently. "It's all over and done with now. You're home again. Now you can settle down like before." With a smile – trying to encourage him or herself? – she insisted: "Now finish your food and let's go to bed. Once you've had a good sleep you'll be your old self again."

He didn't answer. Absently he sat listening, as if he couldn't understand what she was talking about; as if it were a different language.

On Sunday morning the photograph of Emily embracing Ben was splashed on the front page of an English newspaper with a banner headline, *The face of grief,* and a caption which briefly summarised the facts of the inquest (report on page two), referring to "Mrs Emily Ngubene, wife of the man who died in detention, comforted by a friend of the family, Mr Ben Du Toit".

It annoyed him, but he couldn't care much. It was something of an embarrassment, such a public display in a newspaper; but the woman had been beside herself, she'd obviously acted without knowing what she was doing.

But Susan was upset. So much, in fact, that she didn't want to go to church that morning.

"How can I sit there feeling everybody staring at us? What will people think of you?"

"Come on, Susan. I agree it was quite uncalled for to splash it like that, but what does it really matter? What else could I do?"

"If you'd kept out of it from the beginning you wouldn't have brought this shame over us now. Do you realise what problems it may cause my father?"

"You're making a mountain out of a molehill, Susan."

But later in the day the telephone started ringing. A couple of amused, teasing friends who asked Susan whether Ben had "acquired a new fancy"; one or two – including young Viviers – who wanted to assure them of their sympathy and support. But the others, almost without exception, were negative, some openly hostile. The school principal was particularly abrasive in his comment: Did Ben appreciate that he was an employee of the Department of Education and that political action by teachers was severely frowned on?

"But Mr Cloete, what on earth has it got to do with politics? The woman lost her husband. She was shattered with grief."

"A *black* woman, Du Toit," Cloete said coolly.

He lost his temper: "I can't see that it makes any difference."

"Have you grown colour blind then?" Cloete was gasping for breath in his characteristic asthmatic way. "And then you say it's not politics? What about the Immorality laws of the country?"

One of Ben's colleagues among the church elders, Hartzenberg, telephoned shortly after the morning service: "I'm not surprised you weren't in church this morning," he said, apparently in a clumsy effort to jest. "Too ashamed to show your face, I suppose?"

What hurt more deeply, was Suzette's call over lunch: "Good heavens, Dad, I always knew you were naïve, but this is going too far. Embracing black women in public!"

"Suzette," he retorted angrily, "if you had any sense of perspective—"

"Who's talking about a sense of perspective?" she interrupted scathingly. "Did you spare one single thought for the repercussions this may have for your children?"

"I've always shown rather more consideration for my children than you have for yours, Suzette." It sounded more vicious than he'd meant it to be; but he was getting sick and tired of the whole business.

"It wasn't Suzette you were talking to like that, was it?" asked Susan, as he sat down at the table again.

"Yes, it was. I was expecting more commonsense from her."

"Don't you think there's something wrong if the whole world seems to be out of step with you?" she asked sharply.

"Can't you leave Dad alone?" Johan burst out unexpectedly. "For Heaven's sake, what's he done wrong? Suppose something had happened to him – wouldn't you have been upset too?"

"I certainly wouldn't have thrown myself into the garden boy's arms!" she said icily.

"Now you're exaggerating," Ben reprimanded her.

"Who started it, I wonder?"

The telephone rang again. This time it was his sister Helena, married to an industrialist. More amused than anything else, even she couldn't suppress a touch of venom: "Well I never! All these years you've been accusing me of seeking publicity whenever a photographer happened to recognise me at a reception or something—now look at you!"

"I don't think it's funny, Helena."

"I think it's priceless. Except there must be easier ways of getting your picture in the papers."

Even Linda offered a gentle reproach when she phoned in the early evening: "Daddy, I know you meant well, but surely it's better to stay out of the newspapers if you're really sincere about wanting to help people?"

"Sounds like one of Pieter's arguments," he said, unable to hide his chagrin. All day he'd been waiting for her to call, convinced that she, of all people, would understand.

Linda was silent for a moment. Then she admitted: "Actually, it *was* Pieter who pointed it out. But I agree with him."

"Do you really think I specially arranged for the photographers to be present, Linda?"

"No, of course not!" In his mind he could see her blushing with indignation. "I'm sorry, Daddy, I didn't mean to make it more difficult for you. But it has been a rather depressing day for me."

"In what way?" Immediately all his concern was directed to her.

"Oh well, you know. All the other students . . . They didn't exactly make it easier for me. And it's useless to try and argue with them."

One telephone call never came. Not that he'd expected it; it was unthinkable. And yet throughout that oppressive day she had been the one closest to him, as acutely present in his thoughts as she had been in the shadows and dull light of the old house in Westdene two nights before.

After Linda's call he unplugged the telephone and went out for a walk. The streets were deserted and the peaceful evening brought more rest to his turbulent thoughts.

Susan was already in the bedroom when he came back; seated in front of her mirror in her night-dress, her face drawn and pale without make-up.

"You going to bed already?" he asked, unable to repress a feeling of guilt.

"Don't you think I've had enough for one day?"

"Please try to understand," he said, half-heartedly raising

his hands towards her, but allowing them to drop back.

"I'm tired of trying."

"Why are you so unhappy?"

She turned her head quickly, almost frightened, but regaining her composure in an instant. "You've never been able to make me happy, Ben," she said, expressionless. "So please don't flatter yourself by thinking you can make me unhappy either."

Amazed, he stared at her. Suddenly she turned her face away from him, pressing it against her hands, her shoulders shaking.

He came to her and touched her awkwardly.

She tensed. "Please leave me alone," she said, her voice smothered. "I'm all right."

"Can't we talk about it?"

She shook her head and got up to go to the bathroom without looking at him, closing the door behind her. After a few aimless minutes he went out to his study where he tried to find relief, as so often in the past, by opening one of his books on chess and repeating on his faded, well-worn board the moves of one of the classical games from the past. But tonight it gave him no joy. He felt an intruder and an amateur in a game played by two dead masters, long ago. Disgruntled, he abandoned it and put the set away in a drawer. Then, in a conscious effort to regain control and to sort out the confusion in his mind, he started making notes: a brief, cryptic catalogue of all that had happened from the very beginning. It helped to see it set out so objectively on paper, as neat and inevitable as the pattern of veins on a leaf. This way it was easier to handle, to judge, to evaluate. But in the end everything was reduced to Melanie's brief question:

What now?

For it was not over and done with as Susan had suggested. Now, after the newspaper, even less than before. Perhaps it had barely begun. If only he could be sure.

At eleven o'clock, on an impulse, he got up and went to the garage, raised the tip-door and got into his car. Outside the house of the minister he nearly changed his mind as he noticed that all the windows, with the exception of only one, were dark.

141

But he grimly overcame his own reluctance and knocked on the front door.

It was quite a while before the Rev Bester opened, in a red dressing gown and slippers.

"Oom Ben? My goodness, what brings you here at this time of the night?"

He looked at the eager, narrow face before him. "Dominee, tonight I'm coming to you like Nicodemus. I've got to talk to you."

For a moment the Rev Bester seemed to hesitate before he stood aside. "Of course. Do come in." There was the sound of a sigh in his voice.

They went through to the study with its bare walls and parquet floor.

"Can I offer you some coffee?"

"No, thank you." He took out his pipe. "I hope you don't mind my smoking?"

"Go ahead, by all means."

Now that he'd come he felt uncertain about how to broach the subject, where to start. And in the end it was the minister who suggested, in a "professional" tone of voice: "I take it you've come to talk about this business in the paper?"

"Yes. You were in my house the night Emily came to ask for help, remember?"

"Indeed, yes."

"So you'll know this thing has been going on for some time."

"What's the trouble, Oom Ben?"

Ben pulled on his pipe. "It's been a terrible thing right from the beginning, Dominee," he said. "What gave me confidence was knowing it would go to court, it would come into the open. I felt sure the right verdict would be given. That was what I kept telling other people too: people less prepared than I to have faith in the outcome of an inquest."

"Well?"

"Why do you ask, Dominee? You know what happened."

"Everything was examined in depth by the court."

"But didn't you read the papers, Dominee?" he asked. "Were you happy with what came to light there?"

"Indeed not," said the Reverend. "Only a few nights ago I

told my wife this is a terrible shame the Lord has brought over us. But now the case is closed and justice has run its course."

"You call it justice?"

"What else?"

"I was *there*!" he said in a rage. "I heard every word that was spoken. It was like Advocate De Villiers said—"

"But Oom Ben, you know the way advocates have of exaggerating their arguments, it's part of their work."

"Is it part of a magistrate's work to pretend that the facts which have come to light don't exist?"

"Was it really facts, Oom Ben? How can we be sure? There is so much bad faith in the world, on all sides."

"I knew Gordon. And what they said about him – that he was plotting against the Government – is a downright lie."

"No one but God can really see what's in our hearts, Oom Ben. Isn't it presumptuous to pretend we can speak for someone else?"

"Have you no faith in your fellow men, Dominee? Don't you love your neighbour?"

"Wait a minute," said Mr Bester with great patience, used to dealing with recalcitrants. "Instead of criticising blindly, don't you think we have reason to be proud of the judiciary we have? Suppose this had been Russia: what do you think would have happened then? Or one of the African states? I can assure you it would never have reached the courts at all."

"What's the use of reaching a court when a handful of people have all the power to decide what is going to be said in that court and by whom? The one man they allowed to speak for himself, that young Archibald Tsabalala, didn't he immediately deny everything they'd forced him to say in his statement? And the girl who spoke about her own torture—"

"Don't you realise it's the oldest and easiest manoeuvre in the world to blame the police if you want to save your own skin?"

"Did Archibald Tsabalala save his skin? It would have been much easier for him to stick to the statement they'd dictated to him. He might have left the court a free man instead of being

143

taken back to his cell by the same man he'd accused of torturing him."

"Now look here, Oom Ben," the young man said, this time with some irritation, "no one can deny that wrong and even evil deeds are committed in our society, as in all others. But if you start questioning your authorities you act against the Christian spirit. They are invested with the authority of God and far be it from us to doubt their decisions. Render unto Caesar what belongs to him."

"And if Caesar starts usurping what belongs to God? If he starts deciding on life and death, must I strengthen his hands for him?"

"There is no evil that cannot be cured by prayer, Oom Ben. Don't you think you and I should rather go down on our knees tonight and pray for our Government and for every man in a position of authority?"

"I find it too easy, Dominee, to shrug off our own responsibilities by referring them to God."

"I'm not so sure that this isn't sacrilege, Oom Ben. Don't you trust Him with this business any more?"

"It's not a question of whether I trust Him or not, Dominee. He can manage without me. The question is whether there may be something He expects *me* to do. With my own two hands."

"Like what?"

"That's what I've come to you for, Dominee. What can I do? What must I do?"

"I doubt whether there is anything you or I can do."

"Even if one sees injustice with one's own eyes? Do you expect me to turn my head the other way?"

"No. Everyone must make sure his own corner of the world is in order. That he is pure in his own heart. For the rest we must rely on His own assurance that the effectual fervent prayer of a righteous man availeth much." He was getting into his stride. "There will be no end of trouble if every man tries to take the law into his own hands. God created order in the world, not chaos. He expects us to obey. Remember what Samuel said to Saul: To obey is better than sacrifice."

"I have a problem that cannot be solved by a text, Dominee,"

Ben said, his voice strangled. "Help me!"

"Let us pray," said the young man, rising from his chair.

For a moment Ben stared at him, uncomprehending, resentful; then he yielded. They knelt down. But he couldn't close his eyes. While the minister was praying he kept staring straight at the wall; although he made an effort to listen, he couldn't grasp the words in his thoughts, they were too smoothly predictable. He was in need of something else, something different.

When they rose at last, the Rev Bester said, almost jovially: "Now what about that cup of coffee?"

"No, I'd rather go home, Dominee."

"I hope you've found more light on the matter, Oom Ben."

"No," he said. "No, I haven't."

Startled, the young man stared at him. Ben almost felt sorry for him.

"What do you want then?" asked the minister.

"I want justice. Is that too much to ask?"

"What do we know about justice if we move outside the will of God?"

"What do we know about the will of God?" he threw back the question.

"Oom Ben, Oom Ben." The young man looked at him, pleading. "For Heaven's sake don't do anything rash. It's bad enough as it is."

"Rash?" he asked. "I don't know whether it's rash. I simply don't know anything any more."

"Please think it over, Oom Ben. Think of everything that is at stake."

"What I think, Dominee, is that once in one's life, just once, one should have enough faith in something to risk everything for it."

"One can gain the world and still lose one's soul."

Through the smoke his pipe had introduced into the small stuffy room he glared at the minister with burning eyes. "All I know," he said, "is that it won't be worthwhile having a soul left if I allow this injustice to stand."

They went down the bare passage to the front door.

"What are you planning to do, Oom Ben?" asked the Rev Bester when they reached the cool air of the stoep.

"I wish I could give you an answer. I wish I knew myself. All I know is that I must do something. Perhaps God will help me." He went down the steps, slowly, his shoulders hunched. Turning back to the young man in the high rectangle of the doorway he said: "Pray for me, Dominee. I have a feeling that whatever happens from now on, there will be only a very narrow ridge between heaven and hell."

Then he went into the night.

7

For three hours he was kept waiting in the District Surgeon's room by the thin girl with the peroxide hair. She'd been annoyed with him from the first minute, when she'd discovered that he had neglected to make an appointment; to make it worse, he'd refused to tell her what his business with Dr Herzog was, and he hadn't shown the slightest interest in seeing any of the other surgeons available.

"Dr Herzog has gone out for consultations. He may not be back for hours."

"I'll wait."

"He may not come in at all today."

"I'll wait anyway."

"Even if he does come in he's got so much to do on a Monday that he won't have time to see you."

"I'll take the chance."

He didn't even seem conscious of her vexation. Passively he sat paging through the uninspiring secondhand copies of *Time* and *Punch* and *Scope*, pamphlets for expectant mothers, brochures on family planning and first aid and immunisation: from time to time he got up to stare through the window at the blank wall of the building opposite; but he never seemed to grow impatient. There was in his manner something of a cat prepared to keep watch beside a mousehole for half a day without getting bored.

Just before half-past twelve Dr Herzog appeared and, ignoring the waiting patients, exchanged a few whispered words with the thin receptionist; then he went through the door bearing his name in white on black. The girl followed him hurriedly; through the open door one could hear them conferring in low voices. For a moment Dr Herzog poked his head round the door to look at Ben. Then the door was closed and the girl returned to her desk in bitchy triumph.

"Dr Herzog says he's sorry but he won't be able to see you today. If you'd care to make an appointment for Wednesday—"

"It's only for a few minutes."

Ignoring her indignant protests, he walked past her to the closed door, knocked, and went in without waiting for an invitation.

Scowling, the District Surgeon looked up from his small desk littered with cards and papers. "Didn't Miss Goosen tell you I was busy?" he asked in obvious ill-humour.

"It's urgent," Ben said, offering his hand. "I'm Ben Du Toit."

Without getting up, Dr Herzog grudgingly took his hand. "What can I do for you? I really am snowed under today."

A bulky man with the physique of a butcher. Unkempt grey hair surrounding a bald pate. Fierce grey-black eyebrows; a pockmarked face covered with purple veins; tufts of hair in his ears and nostrils. The backs of his hands, resting on the papers before him, were hirsute, as were the forearms protruding from the short white sleeves of his safari jacket.

"It's in connection with Gordon Ngubene," said Ben, sitting down, uninvited, on the straight chair in front of the desk.

The burly man opposite him remained motionless. Even his face remained essentially unchanged: what happened was that his expression appeared to freeze, the way one's face is supposed to grow rigid when, as the old superstition has it, the clock strikes six. Behind his eyes invisible shutters seemed to close.

"What about Gordon Ngubene?" he asked.

"I'd like to find out everything you know about him," Ben said calmly.

"Why don't you ask the Attorney-General for a copy of the court proceedings?" Herzog suggested, with an expansive and almost generous gesture. "It's all in there."

"I attended the inquest from beginning to end," Ben said. "I know exactly what was said in court."

"Then you know as much as I do."

"You must forgive my saying so," said Ben, "but that wasn't exactly my impression."

"May I ask what interest you have in the case?" The question was simple enough; but the voice sounded a darker warning.

"I knew Gordon. And I've taken it on me not to rest before the truth has come out."

"That was what the inquest was for, Mr Du Toit."

"I'm sure you know as well as I do that the inquest didn't answer one single question of real importance."

"Mr Du Toit, aren't you treading on rather dangerous ground now?" Herzog put out his hand and took a cigar from an open box on the desk, pointedly declining to offer one to Ben. Without removing his eyes from his visitor he meticulously removed the band and lit the cigar with a small kitsch lighter in the shape of a naked girl emitting a flame from her vagina.

"Dangerous for whom?" asked Ben.

The doctor shrugged, blowing out smoke.

"Wouldn't you welcome it if the full truth were told?" Ben insisted.

"As far as I'm concerned the case is closed." Herzog started sorting his papers. "And I've already told you I'm extremely busy. So if you don't mind——"

"Why did the Special Branch summon you that Friday morning, fourth February? If he'd really complained of toothache, surely they would have called a dentist?"

"I'm used to attending to all the medical needs of the detainees."

148

"Because Stolz has a good working relationship with you?"

"Because I'm a District Surgeon."

"Did you take an assistant with you?"

"Mr Du Toit." The big man placed his hands on the arm-rests of his chair, as if preparing to push himself up. "I'm not prepared to discuss the matter with a total stranger."

"I was just asking," said Ben. "I should think an assistant would be indispensable if there were teeth to be drawn. To hand on the instruments and so on."

"Captain Stolz gave me all the assistance I required."

"So he was present when you examined Gordon. In court you said you couldn't remember."

"Now this is enough!" Herzog said, in a fury, pushing himself up on his hairy arms. "I've already asked you to go. If you don't leave this minute I'll have no choice but to throw you out."

"I'm not going before I know what I've come to find out."

Moving with surprising speed for such a corpulent man Herzog came round the desk, planting himself squarely in front of Ben.

"Get out!"

"I'm sorry, Dr Herzog," he said, restraining his voice, "but you can't force me to shut up the way the Special Branch did with Gordon."

For a moment he expected Herzog to hit him. But the doctor remained motionless in front of him, breathing heavily, his eyes blazing under the heavy eyebrows. Then, still blown up with rage, he returned to his chair and picked up his cigar again, inhaling deeply.

"Listen, Mr Du Toit," he said at last, in an obvious effort to sound light-hearted. "Why go to all this trouble for the sake of a bloody coon?"

"Because I happened to know Gordon. And because it's become just a bit too easy for too many people to shrug it off."

The doctor smiled with almost jovial cynicism, revealing the gold fillings in his many teeth. " You Liberals with your lofty ideals: you know, if you'd been working with those people the way I've got to, day after day, you'd soon sing a different tune altogether."

149

"I'm not a Liberal, Dr Herzog. I'm a very ordinary man who's had it up to here."

Another benevolent grin. "I see what you mean. Don't think I blame you. I mean, I can appreciate your sentiments, having known the chap and all that. But listen to me, it's not worth your while to get involved in this sort of business. No end of trouble. When I was younger, I often got all het-up about things too. But one soon learns."

"Because it's safer to co-operate?"

"What do you expect of a man in my position, Mr Du Toit? I mean, Jesus Christ, think for yourself."

"So you really are afraid of them?"

"I'm not afraid of anyone!" All his earlier aggressiveness welled up again. "But I'm not a damn fool, I tell you."

"Why did you prescribe tablets for Gordon if you found nothing further wrong with him?"

"He said he had a headache."

"Tell me, Dr Herzog, man to man: were you worried about his condition when you saw him that day?"

"Of course not."

"And yet he died a fortnight later."

Dr Herzog blew out smoke, not deigning to reply.

"Are you quite sure you never saw him again during that fortnight?"

"I was asked the same question in court. And I said no."

"But we're not in court now."

The doctor inhaled, and exhaled again. The heavy smell of his cigar smoke was pervading the room.

"You did see him again, didn't you? They sent for you again."

"What difference would it make?"

"So it's true?"

"I didn't say anything."

"Suppose I can produce witnesses who followed you wherever you went during that fortnight? And suppose they're prepared to testify that you did go back to John Vorster Square before Gordon died?"

"Where would you find such evidence?"

"I'm asking you."

Leaning forward, Dr Herzog peered intently at Ben's face through the smoke. Then he uttered a brief laugh. "Come off it," he said. "Bluff will get you nowhere."

"What clothes was Gordon wearing when you saw him that morning?"

"How do you expect me to remember every little detail? Do you know how many patients I see every day?"

"You remembered the clothes he was wearing when you examined his body in the cell."

"I had to draw up a report immediately afterwards, that's why."

"But surely you can remember whether he was wearing the same clothes the first time? I mean, this sort of memory tends to link itself to similar ones."

A sudden derisive laugh. "You're an amateur, Mr Du Toit. Now please, I've got work to do."

"You realise it's in your power to expose or to suppress the truth?"

Dr Herzog rose and walked towards the door. "Mr Du Toit," he said, looking back, "what would you have done in my place?"

"I'm asking you what *you* did, Doctor."

"You're on a wild goose chase," Dr Herzog said affably, opening the door. He caught the receptionist's eye. "Miss Goosen, please tell Dr Hughes I'm ready to see him now."

Grudgingly, unhappily, Ben rose and went to the door.

"Are you quite sure that's all you can tell me, Doctor?"

"There's nothing more, I assure you." His gold fillings gleamed. "Don't think I take your interest amiss, Mr Du Toit. It's good to know that there are still people like you, and I wish you the best of luck." Now he was talking easily, smoothly, filled with benevolence and understanding, as glib as any after-dinner speaker. "Only" – he smiled, but his eyes remained unchanged –"it's such a hell of a waste of time."

8

The moment he opened the door and saw the seven men crowding together on the stoep, even before he could recognise some of the faces, he knew what was happening. It was the first day of the new term and he had just arrived home from school.

Stolz produced a sheet of paper. "A warrant," he announced quite unnecessarily. On his cheek the thin white scar. "We've come to search your house. I hope you will co-operate?" A statement, not a question.

"Come inside. I have nothing to hide." There was no shock, no fear – seeing them in front of him on his own doorstep, it suddenly seemed totally unavoidable and logical – only a sense of not really being involved in what was happening, as if he were watching a bad play; as if the messages sent from his brain were obstructed on their way to his limbs.

Stolz turned towards the group behind him, and proceeded to introduce them. But most of the names escaped Ben, except for the one or two he already knew. Lieutenant Venter, the smiling young man with the curly hair he knew from John Vorster Square. And from the inquest he remembered Vosloo, squat and swarthy; and Koch, athletic, broad-shouldered, heavy-browed. They looked like a group of rugby players waiting for a bus to depart, all washed and shaven, in sports jackets or safari suits; all of them beaming with good health, exemplary young men, probably the fathers of small children; one could imagine them accompanying their wives to shop in supermarkets on Saturday mornings.

"Are you going to let us in?" Stolz asked, a keener edge becoming perceptible in his voice.

"Of course." Ben stood to one side and they came trooping into the passage.

"Were you expecting us?" asked Stolz.

Suddenly, with that question, Ben's lethargy was suspended. He even managed a smile.

"I can't say I've been sitting here waiting for you, Captain," he said. "But it's not entirely unexpected either."

"Oh really?"

In spite of himself he said: "Well, you turned up at Gordon's house as soon as you heard that he was making enquiries about the death of his son."

"Does that mean that you have also started making enquiries?"

For a moment it was deadly quiet in the passage, in spite of the cluster of people.

"I suppose that is what your visit implies," he said tartly. "Was it Dr Herzog who told you?"

"You went to see Dr Herzog?" Stolz's dark eyes remained expressionless.

Ben shrugged.

Susan's arrival from the dining-room ended their brief tug-of-war. "Ben? What's going on here?"

"Security Police," he said neutrally. And, to Stolz: "My wife."

"How do you do, Mrs Du Toit?" Once again the officer went through the formalities of introducing his men one by one. "Sorry about the inconvenience," he said after he'd finished. "But we have to search the house." He turned back to Ben: "Where is your study, Mr Du Toit?"

"In the backyard. I'll show you the way." The men stood with their backs pressed against the wall to let him pass.

Pale and rigid, Susan was still staring at them in disbelief. "I'm afraid I don't understand," she said.

"I'll appreciate it if you could come with us, Madam," said Stolz, adding with a stiff smile: "Just in case you try to slip out and warn someone."

"We're not criminals, Captain!" she retorted, stung.

"I'm sorry, but one can't be too careful," he said. "So if you'll be so kind?" In the kitchen he asked: "Is there anyone else in the family?"

"My son," said Ben. "But he stayed behind at school for cadets."

"Servants?"

"I do my own work," Susan said coldly.

"Shall we go then?"

The study was rather cramped for so many people and they all seemed to be in each other's way. After Susan had curtly refused to sit down, Ben seated himself on the easy chair beside the door to be out of their way while she remained tense and silent in the doorway. One of the men kept watch outside, cigarette in hand, his back to the door; the six others started working systematically through the room, as busy and thorough as a swarm of locusts. The drawers of the desk were pulled out and stacked in a pile on the floor to be emptied and examined, one after the other, by Stolz and one of his lieutenants. Venter squatted in front of the low cupboard Ben had built to house his papers: examination questions, circulars, progress reports, notes, memorandums, timetables, inspectors' reports. Koch and one of his colleagues ransacked the filing cabinet in the corner, working their way through all his personal documents: accounts, receipts, income tax forms, insurance, bank statements, certificates, correspondence, family albums, the journals he'd kept sporadically over the years. In his student years it had started as a regular diary; as a young teacher first in Lydenburg and later in Krugersdorp he'd made a habit of jotting down anything that had interested or amused him – examination howlers, phrases from essays by his best pupils, expressions of his children, bits of conversation which might prove useful one day; also comments and reflections on his subjects or on current affairs, on books he'd read – much of it totally irrelevant and incomprehensible to outsiders. In recent years he'd occasionally written more intimate notes, on Susan and himself, on Linda or Suzette or Johan, on friends. And through all that Koch and his colleague were paging steadily, meticulously, while the remaining policeman was examining the furniture, apparently in search of secret hiding places – under the chair cushions (Ben had to get up for it), behind the shelves, inside his chessbox and even inside a small bowl of polished semiprecious stones from South-West Africa; at last he rolled up the carpet to look under it.

"If only you would tell me what you were looking for," Ben remarked after some time, "I could save you a lot of time and trouble. I'm not hiding anything."

Stolz looked up – he was working on the third drawer from

the desk – and said laconically: "Don't worry, Mr Du Toit. If there's anything of interest to us, we'll find it."

"I was just trying to make it easier for you."

"It's our job."

"You're very thorough."

Across the pile of drawers the dark eyes looked at him. "Mr Du Toit, if you knew what we're working with every day of our lives, you would understand why we've got to be thorough."

"Oh I appreciate it." He was almost amused.

But Stolz replied sternly, even sharply: "I'm not so sure you really appreciate it. That's the problem with people who start criticising. They don't realise they're just paving the way for the enemy. You won't catch those Communists napping, mark my word. They're at it, every hour of the day and night."

"I wasn't accusing you of anything, Captain."

A brief pause, before Stolz replied: "I just wanted to make sure you understand. It isn't as if we always enjoy what we've got to do."

"But there may be more than one way of doing it, Captain," he said calmly.

"I can understand that you're upset about having your place searched," said Stolz, "but believe me——"

"I wasn't talking about this little visit," Ben said.

All over the room the men suddenly stopped working: the rustling sound, like the feeding of a multitude of silkworms in a big box, fell silent. Outside, in the distance, a bicycle bell shrilled.

"Well, what are you talking about then?" asked Stolz.

They were all waiting for him to say it. And he decided to accept the challenge.

"I'm referring to Gordon Ngubene," he said. "And to Jonathan. And to many others like them."

"Do I understand you correctly?" asked Stolz very calmly. The scar on his face seemed to turn even whiter than before. "Are you accusing us——"

"All I said was there may be more than one way of doing your job."

"You're suggesting——"

155

"I leave that to your own conscience, Captain."

In silence the officer sat gazing at him across the piled-up stuff in the small room. All the others were there too, a room filled with eyes: but they were irrelevant. He and Stolz were isolated from them. For that was the one moment in which he suddenly knew, very quietly and very surely: it was no longer a case of "them", a vague assortment of people, or something as abstract as a "system": it was *this man*. This thin pale man standing opposite him at this moment, behind his own desk, with all the relics and spoils of his entire life displayed around them. *It's you. Now I know you. And don't think you can silence me just like that. I'm not Gordon Ngubene.*

It was the end of their conversation. They didn't even continue searching much longer, as if they had lost interest. Perhaps they hadn't intended it very seriously anyway, a mere flexing of muscles, no more.

After they had replaced the drawers and closed the cupboard and the filing cabinet, Venter found a foolscap page on the desk, bearing Herzog's name and a series of brief notes on the interview. That was confiscated, together with all the other papers and correspondence on the desk, and Ben's journals; he was given a handwritten receipt of which they retained a duplicate.

Returning to the house they asked to be shown the bedroom. Susan tried to intervene: this, she felt, was too private, the humiliation too blatant. Stolz offered his apologies, but insisted on going through with the search. A concession was made, though, by allowing Susan to stay behind in the lounge in young Venter's company, while Ben showed the others the way to the bedroom. They wanted to know which bed was his, and which wardrobe, and briefly examined his clothes and looked under his pillow; one of the men got on a chair to check the top of the wardrobe; another flipped through the pages of the Bible and the two books on his bedside table. Then they returned to the lounge.

"Can I offer you some coffee?" Susan asked stiffly.

"No thank you, Mrs Du Toit. We still have work to do."

At the front door Ben said: "I suppose I should thank you for behaving in such a civilised way."

Unsmiling, Stolz replied: "I think we understand one

156

another, Mr Du Toit. If we have reason to suspect that you're keeping anything from us, we'll be back. I want you to know that we have all the time in the world. We can turn this whole house upside down if we want to."

Behind the formality of his tone and attitude Ben caught a glimpse, or imagined that he did, of a man in a locked office under a burning electric bulb, methodically going about his business, for days and nights if necessary: to the absolute end if necessary.

After they had gone he remained inside the closed front door for a minute, still conscious of the distance he felt between himself and the world. Almost tranquillity; perhaps even satisfaction.

Behind him he heard the sound of their bedroom door being closed. A key was turned. As if it were necessary! He was in no frame of mind to face Susan anyway.

Thought and feeling were still suspended. He couldn't – he wouldn't – start probing what had happened. All reactions were mechanical.

He went through the house to the garage and started planing a piece of wood – aimlessly, simply to keep himself occupied. Gradually his activity became more planned, more definite, even though there was no deliberate decision involved. He started making a false bottom for his tools cupboard, fitting it so neatly that no one would ever suspect its presence. In future, if ever he had anything he wanted to keep from their prying eyes, this was where he would hide it. For the moment the sheer physical action was sufficient in itself. Not an act of self-protection, but a counter move, something positive and decisive, a new beginning.

157

Wednesday 11 May. Strange day. Yesterday's visit by the Special Branch. Difficult to explore on paper, but I must. Writing it out in full sentences is salutary, like breathing deeply. Will try. A frontier crossed. So definite that from now on I'll be able to divide my life in Before and After. The way one talks about the Flood. Or the apple, the fruit of the Fall, that perilous knowledge. One can speculate about it beforehand, but you're unprepared when it happens. A finality, like I suppose death, which one can only get to know by experiencing it. Even while it was happening I didn't realise it as keenly as I do now. Too dazed, I imagine. But now: today.

Everything wholly strange. Children who say "good morning" and whose faces you see without recognising them or knowing why they are addressing you. A bell that sends you from classroom to classroom and which you obey without knowing the reason. When you open your mouth it is without any foreknowledge of what will follow. It happens by itself. Your own words seem unfamiliar to you, your voice comes from far away. Every building, every room, the tables and benches, the blackboard, pieces of chalk, everything is strange. Nothing wholly dependable. You have to assume that, previously, you managed to pick your way through it all, that in some mysterious way you "belonged", but it is inexplicable now. Inside you is a manner of knowing which you cannot share with anyone else. Nothing as commonplace as a "secret" ("Guess what: they searched my house yesterday"). Something essentially different. As if you now exist in another time and another dimension. You can still see the other people, you exchange sounds, but it is all coincidence, and deceptive. You're *on the other side*. And how can I explain it in the words of "this side"?

Third period free. Wandered about outside among the rockeries. Was it the autumn air? The leaves falling, the clear anatomy of the trees. No disguise, no ambiguity. But more strange than ever. From time to time a voice from a classroom, a phrase called out, unconnected with anything else. From the far end of the building someone practising scales, the same ones over and over. As basic as the trees, equally terrifying and meaningless.

In the hall the choir singing. The anthem. For the Administrator's visit in a week or so. The music broken up in parts. First, second; boys, girls; then all together. *At thy will to live or perish, O South Africa, dear land.* Once more please. *At thy will to live or perish.* No, that's not good enough. Come on. *At thy will to live or perish.* That's better. Now right from the beginning. *Ringing out from our blue heavens.* Open your mouths. At thy will to live at thy will to live at thy will to live or perish or perish or perish. The whole lot of us will perish. All you sweet young children, innocent voices singing, girls blushing and peeping at the boys, hoping this morning's acne ointment is covering up the blemishes; boys poking each other in the ribs with rulers or passing on cryptic notes in sweaty hands. At thy will to live or perish, O South Africa, dear land!

And in a few minutes we'll all be back in the classroom resuming our work as if nothing had happened. I'll teach you about this land and its prevailing winds and its rainfall areas, ocean currents, mountain ranges and rivers and national products, of efforts to produce rain and to control the ravages of dry seasons. I'll teach you where you come from: the three small ships that brought the first white men, and the first bartering with Harry's Hottentots, and the first wine, and the first Free Burghers settling on the banks of the Liesbeek in 1657. The arrival of the Huguenots. The dynasty of the Van der Stel governors, and the options open to them: Simon aiming at a concentration of whites at the Cape, allowing natural class differences to develop; his son Willem Adriaan opting for expansion, encouraging the stock farmers to explore the interior and settle among the natives; racial friction, disputes, frontier wars. 1836: Boer emigrants in a mass exodus in search of liberty and independence elsewhere. Massacres, annexations of the newly conquered land; temporary victory for the Boer Republics. Followed by the discovery of diamonds at Kimberley and gold at the Witwatersrand; the influx of foreigners and the triumph of British imperialist interests. Anglo-Boer War, concentration camps, Lord Milner, anglicisation in the schools. 1910: Unification and a new beginning, "South Africa first". Boers rebelling against the decision of their own government to support Britain in 1914. Impoverished farmers flocking to the cities. The mine revolts of '22, Boers and Bolshevists against the Imperialists. Official recognition of the Afrikaans language. Translation of the Bible, 1933. Coalition government. War. Afrikaners moving underground in the Ossewa-Brandwag. The indestructible dream of a Republic. And at last, a Nationalist Government in power. So you can see for yourselves, boys and girls, we've come a long way. Remember the words of the young Bibault in the revolt against Van der Stel in 1706: "I shall not go I am an Afrikaner and even if the landdrost kills me or puts me in jail I refuse to hold my tongue." Our entire history, children, can be interpreted as a persistent search for freedom, against the dictates of successive conquerors from Europe. Freedom expressed in terms of this new land, this continent. We Afrikaners were the first freedom fighters of Africa, showing the way to others. And now that we have finally come to power in our own land, we wish to grant the same right of selfdetermination to all the other nations around us. They must have their own separate territories. Peaceful coexistence. Plural development. It is an expression of our own sense of honour and dignity and altruism. After all, we have no choice. Outside this vast land we have nowhere to go. This is our fate. *At thy will to live or perish, O South Africa, our land!* No, I'm afraid it's not good enough. Try again.

This vast land. The train journeys of my boyhood. The last stage on the sideline to our station: seven hours for those thirty-five miles. Stopping at every siding, loading or unloading milk cans, taking in coals or water: stopping in the middle of nowhere, in the open veld, heat-waves rippling on the horison. A name painted on a white board, so many feet above sea-level, so many miles from Kimberley, so many from Cape Town. The pure senselessness of it all heightened by the fact that everything is recorded so fastidiously. What the hell does it matter that this is the name of the station, or that it is so many miles away from the next?

From a very early age one accepts, or believes, or is told, that certain things exist in a certain manner. For example: that society is based on order, on reason, on justice. And that, whenever anything goes wrong, one can appeal to an innate decency, or commonsense, or a notion of legality in people to rectify the error and offer redress. Then, without warning, there occurs what Melanie said and what I refused to believe: you discover that what you accepted as premises and basic conditions – what you had no choice but to accept if you wanted to survive at all – simply does not exist. Where you expected something solid there turns out to be just nothing. Behind the board stating a name and heights and distances there is a vacuum disguised, at most, by a little corrugated iron building, milk cans, a row of empty red fire-buckets. Nothing.

Everything one used to take for granted, with so much certainty that one never even bothered to enquire about it, now turns out to be illusion. Your certainties are proven lies. And what happens if you start probing? Must you learn a wholly new language first?

"Humanity". Normally one uses it as a synonym for compassion; charity; decency; integrity. "He is such a human person." Must one now go in search of an entirely different set of synonyms: cruelty; exploitation; unscrupulousness; or whatever?

Darkness descending.

Still, there is Melanie. Light in the gloom. (But why? Dare I even think about it?)

The problem is: once you've caught a glimpse of it, once you've merely started suspecting it, it is useless to pretend it's different. She was right. Melanie. Melanie. The only question that matters is the one she asked: *What now?*

It has begun. A pure, elemental motion: something happened – I reacted – something opposed me. A vast, clumsy, shapeless thing has stirred. Is that the reason of my dazed state? Let's try to be reasonable, objective: am I not totally helpless, in fact irrelevant, in a movement so vast and intricate? Isn't the mere thought of an individual trying to intervene preposterous?

Or am I putting the wrong questions now? Is there any sense in trying to be "reasonable", in finding "practical" arguments? Surely, if I were to consider what I might "achieve" in a practical sense I couldn't even hope to begin. So it must be something else. But what? Perhaps simply to do what one has to do, because you're *you*, because you're *there*.

I am Ben Du Toit. I'm here. There's no one else but myself

right here, today. So there must be something no one but me can do: not because it is "important" or "effective", but because only I can do it. I have to do it *because* I happen to be Ben Du Toit; because no one else in the world is Ben Du Toit.

And so it is beside the point to ask: what will become of me? Or: how can I act against my own people?

Perhaps that is part of the very choice involved: the fact that I've always taken "my own people" so much for granted that I now have to start thinking from scratch. It has never been a problem to me before. "My own people" have always been around me and with me. On the hard farm where I grew up, in church on Sundays, at auctions, in school; on stations and in trains or in towns; in the slums of Krugersdorp; in my suburb. People speaking my language, taking the name of my God on their lips, sharing my history. That history which Gie calls "the History of European Civilisation in South Africa". My people who have survived for three centuries and who have now taken control – and who are now threatened with extinction.

"My people". And then there were the "others". The Jewish shopkeeper, the English chemist; those who found a natural habitat in the city. And the blacks. The boys who tended the sheep with me, and stole apricots with me, and scared the people at the huts with pumpkin ghosts, and who were punished with me, and yet were different. We lived in a house, they in mud huts with rocks on the roof. They took over our discarded clothes. They had to knock on the kitchen door. They laid our table, brought up our children, emptied our chamber pots, called us *Baas* and *Miesies*. We looked after them and valued their services, and taught them the Gospel, and helped them, knowing theirs was a hard life. But it remained a matter of "us" and "them". It was a good and comfortable division; it was right that people shouldn't mix, that everyone should be allotted his own portion of land where he could act and live among his own. If it hadn't been ordained explicitly in the Scriptures, then certainly it was implied by the variegated creation of an omniscient Father, and it didn't behove us to interfere with His handiwork or to try and improve on His ways by bringing forth impossible hybrids. That was the way it had always been.

But suddenly it is no longer adequate, it no longer works. Something has changed irrevocably. I stood on my knees beside the coffin of a friend. I spoke to a woman mourning in a kitchen the way my own mother might have mourned. I saw a father in search of his son the way I might have tried to find my own. And that mourning and that search had been caused by "my people".

But who are "my people" today? To whom do I owe my loyalty? There must be someone, something. Or is one totally alone on that bare veld beside the name of a non-existent station?

The single memory that has been with me all day, infinitely more real than the solid school buildings, is that distant summer when Pa and I were left with the sheep. The drought that took everything from us, leaving us alone and scorched among the white skeletons.

What had happened before that drought has never been particularly vivid or significant to me: that was where I first discovered myself and the world. And it seems to me I'm finding myself on the edge of yet another dry white season, perhaps worse than the one I knew as a child.

What now?

THREE

In the dark it was a different city. The sun was down when they reached Uncle Charlie's Roadhouse; by the time they left the main road near the bulky chimneys of the power station, the red glow was already darkening through smoke and dust, smudged like paint. A premonition of winter in the air. The network of narrow eroded paths and roads across the bare veld; then the railway-crossing and a sharp right turn into the streets running between the countless rows of low, squat houses. At last it was there, all around them, as overwhelming as the previous time, but in a different way. The dark seemed to soften the violence of the confrontation, hiding the details that had assaulted and insulted the eyes, denying the squalor. Everything was still there, stunning in its mere presence, alien, even threatening; and yet the night was reassuring too. There were no eyes conspicuously staring. And the light coming from the small square windows of the innumerable houses – the deadly pallor of gas, the warmer yellow of candles or paraffin lamps – had all the nostalgic intimacy of a train passing in the night. The place was still abundantly alive, but with a life reduced to sound: not the sort of sound one heard with one's ears, but something subterranean and dark, appealing directly to bones and blood. The hundreds of thousands of separate lives one had been conscious of the first time – the children playing soccer, the barbers, the women on street corners, the young ones with clenched fists – had now blurred into a single omnipresent organism, murmuring and moving, devouring one like an enormous gullet that forced one further down, with peristaltic motions, to be digested and absorbed or excreted in the dark.

"What you looking at?" asked Stanley.

"I'm trying to memorise the way."

"Forget it, you're a foreigner." But he didn't say it unkindly, more in sympathy. "Anyway, I'm here to show you the way, aren't I?"

"I know. But suppose I have to come on my own one day?"

Stanley laughed, swerving to avoid a scavenging dog. "Don't try it," he said.

"I can't be a millstone round your neck, Stanley."

"The hell with it. We're in it together, man."

It moved him, more than anything Stanley had said before. So Melanie had been right, after all: in some indefinable way he had been 'accepted'.

He'd telephoned Stanley the previous evening, after his day of disconnected reflections, walking three blocks from his home to a public booth to make sure Susan wouldn't know. They arranged to meet between four and half-past, but Stanley had been late. In fact it had been nearly half-past five before the big white Dodge had pulled up at the garage where they'd met before. No word of apology; actually, he'd seemed surprised at Ben's annoyance.

He wasn't wearing his dark glasses today: they protruded from the top pocket of his brown jacket. Striped shirt, wild floral tie, chunky cuff-links.

They drove off, wheels spinning, engine roaring, watched by a startled and grinning gardener in blue overalls on a lawn in a garden opposite the garage.

"I thought I should discuss things with Emily," Ben explained once they were safely on their way. "And with you, of course."

Stanley waited, whistling contentedly.

"The Special Branch came to search my house two days ago."

The big man turned his head quickly. "You joking?"

"They did."

He wasn't sure about the reaction he'd expected: but it certainly wasn't the reverberating guffaw from the depths of Stanley's stomach, causing him to double up and nearly drive up a kerb.

"What's so funny about it?"

"They actually raided your place?" Stanley started laughing again. He slammed one hand on Ben's shoulder: "Well, shake, man." It took some time for the laughter to subside. Wiping tears from his eyes, Stanley asked: "Why did they do it, you think?"

"I wish I knew. I think they were tipped off by Dr Herzog. The one who was in court. I went to see him, to find out what he really knew about Gordon."

"Did he say anything?"

"We won't get anything out of him. But I'm convinced he knows more than he's prepared to say. He's either scared of the police or working with them."

"What else did you expect?" Stanley chuckled again: "So he put the cops on you? Did they grab anything?"

"Some old journals. A bit of correspondence. Nothing much. There wasn't anything anyway. They probably just wanted to scare me."

"Don't be too sure."

"What do you mean?"

"For all you know they may really think you're into something serious."

"They can't be as stupid as that."

"Lanie" – a smug grin – "don't ever underestimate the sheer stupidity of the SB. Sure, they can be as quick as hell and they got a finger in every pie: but, man, you just let them believe they're on to some sort of a conspiracy in the dark and I tell you nothing will get them off it again. Worse than leeches. For sheer stubbornness nothing can beat the *gattes*. I known them for years, man. If they decide it's a bomb they looking for, you can shove their noses right into a turd and they'll still swear to God it's a bomb."

In spite of himself Ben could feel his jaws tauten. But he refused to be convinced. "I tell you it was just to scare me, Stanley."

"So why didn't you get scared?"

"Precisely because they tried so hard. If they want to intimidate me, I want to find out why. There must be something there, and we're going to find it. I can't do a thing without you.

But if you're willing to help me, we can dig up whatever they're trying to cover up. I know it won't be easy and we can't expect too much too soon. But you and I can work together, Stanley. It's the least we owe to Gordon."

"You quite sure about this, Ianie? I mean, this is no time for show."

"Do you remember the day I said we must be careful before it went too far? Then you were the one who laughed at me. You said it had only started. And you were right. I know it now. And now I'm going all the way. If you'll help me."

"What's 'all the way', Ianie?" Stanley was deadly serious now.

"I can only find out by going on."

"You think they going to allow you to go on?"

Inhaling deeply, Ben said: "It's no use looking too far ahead, Stanley. We'll have to handle every bit as it comes up."

The only reaction from the big man behind the wheel was a relaxed chuckle. Through smoke and dust they drove on in silence for a long time until Stanley stopped in what might have been either a side street or a vacant lot, a black hole in the dark. As Ben touched the handle to open the door, Stanley restrained him:

"You wait here. It's further on. I'll check first."

"Didn't you warn Emily then?"

"I did. But I don't want people to find out." Noticing Ben's questioning look, he said: "The joint is full of informers, Ianie. And you got enough problems as it is. See you." Slamming his door he disappeared in the dark.

Ben turned his window down a few inches. An oppressive smell of smoke drifted into the car. The awareness of disembodied sound grew overpowering. And once again, but more intensely than before, he had the feeling of being inside an enormous animal body with intestines rumbling, a dark heart beating, muscles contracting and relaxing, glands secreting their fluid. Only, in Stanley's absence, it acquired a more ominous, malevolent aspect, an amorphous menacing presence. What forced him to remain there, every muscle tensed and in his mouth a bitter taste, wasn't fear of a gang of tsotsis or a police patrol or the thought that he might suddenly be attacked

170

in the dark, but something vague and vast, like the night itself. He didn't even know where he was; and if for some reason Stanley did not come back, he would never be able to escape from there. He had no map or compass, no sense of direction in the dark, no memory to rely on, no intuition to help him, no facts or certainties. Exposed to pure anguish, he sat motionless, feeling the tiny cold pricks of perspiration on his face where the air touched him.

In that total invisibility Soweto was more real to him than the first time he'd been there in broad daylight. Simply because Stanley was not with him. Never before had he experienced so acutely the total isolation of their respective worlds, and the fact that only through the two of them those worlds were allowed to touch briefly and provisionally, and that only through Gordon it had been made possible at all. Gordon: invariably it returned to him.

Trapped in the violence of his own thoughts, Ben remained in the car for what might have been hours until, suddenly, Stanley reappeared beside him.

"You seen a ghost?" asked Stanley, his face laughing in the dim interior light of the car.

"Perhaps I have." The sudden relief made him feel light-headed. "Now I know what this Black Peril is people are so scared of," he said mockingly.

Somewhere, in a street close by, a woman started screaming, long piercing sounds stabbing the night.

"What's happening?" asked Ben as he got out in a hurry.

"How should I know? Murder. Rape. It can be anything."

"Can't we do anything?"

"You got a death wish, lanie?"

The screams ended in a final low animal moan merging with the night's more general hum.

"But Stanley—"

"Come on. Auntie Emily's waiting for you."

Responding to the matter-of-fact tone in his voice, Ben followed him; but as they walked on he discovered that he was still listening tensely for the woman to make another sound. They proceeded from one tall lamp-post to the next, planted far apart and supporting white floodlights, creating the impression of a concentration camp. From time to time Ben would stumble over things in his way – a tin, a discarded fender, unrecognisable rubbish littering the dark street – but Stanley found his way surely and easily, like a big black cat in the night.

They went through the small rickety gate and up the two front steps to the door. Stanley knocked. It sounded like a code, part of his boyish love of cloak-and-dagger. Emily opened immediately, as if she'd been waiting with her hand on the key. Large and shapeless in her old-fashioned full-length dress, she stood aside to let them enter. There was only one gas lamp burning inside, and the corners of the small front room were in semi-darkness. Against the far wall a few children were sleeping under a grey blanket, small bundles close together, like loaves of bread set out to raise. On the sideboard the transistor was playing, turned down very low. Everything appeared unchanged, from the calendar pictures and the printed texts on the walls to the sewing machine on the scrubbed table and the old Dover stove in the corner. A vase filled with plastic flowers. The floral curtains drawn. There was a smoky stuffiness inside, aggravated by a stale smell of bodies. Beside the table sat a small grey man in a worn black suit, resembling a wizened lizard with two very bright, very black eyes twinkling among the many folds and wrinkles of his face.

"This is Father Masonwane of our church," said Emily, as if apologising for his presence.

The little man smiled, exposing toothless gums. "We met before," he said. "When the *morena* was here last time."

"The Baas must please sit down," said Emily. "Take this chair here, the other one is too broken."

Ben sat down rigidly, a little distance away from the table.

"Well," Stanley announced from the door. "I'm going. You can have your chat in peace. So long."

With a touch of panic Ben half-rose again. "Why don't you stay?"

"Got a customer waiting," Stanley said. "Don't worry, I'll be back." Before Ben could protest again he was out, once again surprisingly soundlessly for such a big man. The three of them were left behind; the gas-lamp stood hissing on the table.

"I put on water for tea," said Emily, "but it will take some time." She hovered near the stove, too uneasy to sit down in Ben's presence.

"I didn't mean to disturb you," he said, looking at the priest.

"Father Masonwane is a big help to me," she replied.

The small man merely smiled mysteriously.

"I've come to talk to you, Emily."

"Yes, it's good, Baas."

"Now that the court has let us down, we'll have to gather all the evidence we can ourselves. Stanley is going to help me. We must find out everything about Jonathan and Gordon, so that we can clear up the shame that has been brought over them."

After every sentence he paused, waiting for her to react, but she said nothing. The priest, too, remained silent. Once one of the children sleeping on the floor coughed; another mumbled briefly.

"We cannot bring them back to life," said Ben. "But we can make sure that this sort of thing won't ever happen again."

"You mean well, *morena*," said the old priest at last. He spoke slowly and very correctly, as if considering each word separately. "But it is better to forgive. If we keep the pain alive then hate and bitterness will remain with us."

"The air must be cleared so we can breathe again."

"The air can only be cleared if we forget about yesterday's thunder."

"No," Emily said suddenly. "No, the Baas is right. It's not that I want to go on with this thing, because it is a bad thing. That Jonathan died, that Gordon died" – she fell silent for a moment and had to control her voice first – "that is hard enough to bear, but I can forgive it. Father Masonwane has taught me a lot." She looked up, the light falling directly on her round face. "But they covered Gordon's name with dirt. They said things which he would never do. And we must clean it up, else he will never have peace in his grave."

"Sis Emily," the old priest said, shaking his head, "that is not the way to set about it." His dry voice became more urgent. "Those people who did it to him, they are poor sinful people who do not know what they are doing. We must have patience with them. We must learn to love them, otherwise everything will break down."

173

"They killed Gordon," Ben said vehemently. "He was a man who wouldn't even hurt a fly. And they killed Jonathan, who was only a child. How can you say they didn't know what they were doing?"

The priest shook his grey head. "I tell you they don't know," he repeated. "You don't believe me? I know it is a terrible thing to say, but it is true. They don't know. Even when they shoot our children they don't know what they're doing. They think it doesn't matter, they think it's not people, they think it doesn't count. We must help them. That is the only way. They need our help. Not hate, but love, *morena*."

"It's easy for you to talk," Ben said. "You're a priest."

The old man grinned, exposing his bare pink gums. "I also had to stand by when they took my sons to jail, *morena*," he said. "And every time I go into the city I must show the police my pass. Some of them treat me with respect. But there are others, young ones, younger than my sons, who throw it down on the ground after they have looked at it. There was a time when I also hated them, when my heart was bitter, like an almond. But I conquered it, *morena*, and now I know better. Now I pity them and I pray for them and I ask the Lord to help me so that I can learn to love them."

"They covered Gordon's name with dirt," Emily persisted calmly, staring straight ahead, as if she hadn't heard what he'd said.

"Aren't you afraid, Sis Emily?" the old priest reproached her.

She shook her head. "No. In the end one grows tired of being afraid," she said.

"This very afternoon you were crying about your husband. And now you are prepared to dry your tears just like that."

"I've cried too much, Father Masonwane," she said. "Now the Lord has sent the Baas to me."

"You must think about it."

Emily stared past him, into the semi-darkness where her children were sleeping. "Father, you always told me to trust in the Lord. You said He could still perform miracles. Tonight He sent my Baas in here, a white man. Don't you think that is a miracle?" And after a moment she repeated, in the same calm, resolute way: "They covered Gordon's name with dirt. We must clean it up."

"In that case I must go," said the old man, sighing as he got up. "There are ants in your heart tonight, Sis Emily." With an apologetic smile he opened the door and slipped out.

Now they were alone in the house, he and Emily, and the sleeping children. For a while they remained staring at each other uneasily, he rigid and lean on his straight-backed chair, she large and bloated beside the stove. And they were both relieved to discover that the kettle had started boiling, which gave her something to do. She poured his tea into a white cup with a faded gilt edge, shaking her head when he made a questioning gesture in her direction. Standing formally at attention she remained behind the priest's chair while Ben stirred his cup. One of the children was snoring lightly.

"What must I do now, Baas?" she asked.

"We must gather all the information we possibly can. You and Stanley must work together. Try to find every person who can tell us something about Jonathan or Gordon. Even if it doesn't sound important at all, bring it to me. Or send Stanley to me. You're right here, you have ears and eyes in this place. And I'll set to work with whatever you bring to me."

"I have something for you, Baas."

"What?"

She waited for him to finish his tea before she said: "I don't know if I can give it to you."

"Let me see."

"It is all I have left of Gordon."

"I'll look after it, whatever it is. I promise."

All of a sudden she seemed nervous, and first went to lock the door, standing with her back to him for some time before she put one hand into the front of her dress to extract something. Hesitantly she came back to him and put it on the table in front of him, still warm from her body. A small crumpled bit of paper.

Two separate ones, in fact, he discovered when he unfolded it. The first was ruled, like an exercise book, the other a square of toilet paper. Both were inscribed in soft pencil, almost illegible through handling and crumpling. The handwriting was shaky, the style oddly formal.

The first note was the easier to read:

My dear wife you must not have worries for me but I am longing for you and the children you must look after them in the fear of the Lord. I am hungry and I cannot understand what they require from me there is too much shouting going on but I think I shall be home some day I think about you all the time. With kind regards,

From your husband.

The piece of toilet paper proved more difficult to decipher:

My dear wife I am still in these conditions (followed by a few illegible words) *worse and too much pain you must try to help me for they do not want to* (illegible) *me. You must care for the children and if you need money you must ask the church or my* (illegible) *master who is kind to us. I do not know if I will come home alive they are very* (illegible) *but God will provide and I miss you very much. Try to help me because*

It ended abruptly, not torn off, but in the middle of a line, with ample space below.

"There's no name on it, Emily," Ben said.

"I know Gordon's writing, Baas."

"How did you get these letters?"

She took out a handkerchief, unfolded it very carefully and blew her nose. Then she put it away.

"Who brought them to you, Emily?"

"I cannot tell you." She avoided his eyes.

"I have to know if we want to take this matter further."

"It is a man I know, Baas. I cannot make trouble for him in his work."

He became suspicious: "Does he work for the police?"

She turned away and, quite unnecessarily, rearranged the blanket covering the children.

"Emily, you must discuss it with him. Tell him I'll keep it secret. But I've got to know."

"He cannot come out."

"Just tell me his name then."

She hesitated before she said, almost resentfully, "Johnson Seroke." Immediately she became very agitated again and insisted: "It is no use, Baas. He cannot talk."

"Won't you send him to me?"

She shook her head. Putting out her hand, she demanded: "It is better to give it back to me."

176

Ben covered the two bits of paper on the table with his hand. "It is to clear up his name, Emily. It's the only way."

After a long hesitation she withdrew her hand.

"When did you get the letters?" he asked.

"The first one came early. Two days, three days after they took him away. The other one" – she frowned with concentration, one hand fiddling with a loose thread from her dress – "the other one came later. Just before we got the trousers, Baas, with the blood and the teeth."

"And afterwards?"

She shook her head. "No, that was the last one."

"But Emily, why didn't you tell me long ago?"

"If they hear about the letters they make it more bad for him."

"But you could have told me after his death, when we went to court."

"Then they take my letters away from me. I was afraid, Baas."

"It might have made a difference."

"No," she said bluntly. "If I show it at the court they call that other man again and he say it is not Gordon's writing." She was breathing deeply. "I think you must give it back to me, Baas."

"I promise you I'll look after it, Emily. Nothing will happen to it. And it may still be very valuable to us, if we can find more evidence to go with it." Urgently he leaned forward, pressing both hands on the table: "Emily, you *must* talk to Johnson Seroke. He helped you once, he brought you these letters. Perhaps he'll be prepared to help us again. It's for Gordon and Jonathan, Emily."

"He didn't want to talk to me. He just give me the letters."

"Promise me you'll at least speak to him."

"I will speak to him, but he won't listen. The people are too much afraid, Baas."

"If they keep quiet because they are afraid, everything just gets worse. And then we'll never be able to clear Gordon's name."

Almost shamelessly he repeated it, knowing it was the only way to get through to her. And gradually their conversation became less urgent, as they began to talk about Gordon; and about Jonathan too, but more about Gordon. What they could recall of him, little things he'd said or done. Obviously beginning to feel more at ease, she refilled his cup and they went on reminiscing about Gordon and Jonathan; and about the second son, Robert, who'd run away to Botswana.

"You shouldn't worry about him too much," Ben said. "At his age all boys tend to be difficult. My wife also has constant trouble with our son."

It became very homely: two parents discussing their children. And the strangeness ebbed away. He was beginning to find it easier to communicate with Emily. At the same time Gordon reappeared in a different perspective, as if the focus of some inner lens had been adjusted. He felt involved in a different way, more immediate than before, more personal.

He was startled when the knock on the door came. But Emily said, without hesitation: "It's Stanley," and she went to open for him.

Immediately the whole room was filled with his boisterous presence as if the interior had become electrically charged; as if, all over the place, hidden forces were preparing themselves so that amazing things could start happening. Only the children slept through it all.

"So how's it, Auntie Emily? You had a nice talk?" Without waiting for an answer he offered Ben his packet of *Lucky Strike*: "Like a *fuse*?"

"No thanks," Ben said, automatically reaching for his pipe but without taking it from his pocket.

"Tea?" asked Emily.

"Thanks, Auntie, that's too strong for me. How about whisky?"

"You know I don't keep drink in the house," she said.

"Well, let's line," he said to Ben. "We can fill up at a she-been."

"I must be in my classroom early tomorrow morning, Stanley."

Pulling up his sleeve, Stanley revealed his large gold watch: "Judge the *jampas*, man, it's early times yet."

"Not in the week," Ben said politely.

"I see. The old puritan blood still running strong, hey?" His laughter caused the crockery on the sideboard to rattle. "All right, come along then. Someone at my place wants to see you." He waved from the door: "Notch you, Auntie Emily."

And suddenly they were outside, back in the night that had been going its way all the time he'd been inside, as if the hour spent in the small house had been a mere interlude between darker acts. They drove along the potholed streets, and across a railway line and an expanse of black open veld. In the distance Ben once saw red flames from the power station flickering through clouds of smoke. A few minutes later Stanley pulled up behind a house and led the way to the kitchen door.

This interior, too, was familiar to Ben: the gay linoleum and the display cabinet, the decorated plates, the birds of paradise on the tray, the settee and armchairs with multicoloured cushions.

The front door stood half-open. "What's happened to him?" muttered Stanley, going out. A minute later he came back supporting a man who was trying, not very successfully, to zip up his pants. He looked fortyish, wearing a checkered shirt and green trousers, with a large ornamental buckle on his belt; his two-tone shoes were spattered with drops.

"Godalmighty!" said Stanley, not really angry. "I wish you'd stop it. On my bloody doorstep!"

"My bladder was bursting."

"You're boozing too much."

"What else do you expect me to do?" the stranger said reproachfully, a dazed stare in his eyes, as he tried to wipe his face with a large coloured handkerchief. "It's killing me, man, sitting around on my arse like this. Gimme another drink."

"Forget about the drink. Meet Mr Du Toit. Ben, this is Julius Nqakula. The lawyer who took the first affidavits on Jonathan for Gordon."

The stranger glared at him aggressively.

"Don't bother about the state he's in," Stanley said, chuckling. "He only functions when he's pissed. Nothing wrong with his head." He deposited Julius on a chair, where he remained sprawled, his legs stretched out across the linoleum. Through half-closed lids he sat staring glumly at Ben while Stanley poured whisky for all three.

179

"What's he doing here?" asked Julius Nqakula after he'd gulped down half his glass in one go, not taking his eyes off Ben.

"I brought him here on Gordon's business," Stanley said nonchalantly, settling his great body on a settee with ridiculously thin legs.

"Gordon is dead. He belongs to us. What's this *mugu* got to do with him?"

Ben was vexed. He felt like walking out, but was restrained by a gesture from Stanley who looked smugly amused.

"You may not think it, looking at him like this," said Stanley, "but this rotter used to be one of the top lawyers in the townships, lanie. Last year, when they took all those kids to court after the riots, he was working day and night to save them. Hundreds of cases, I tell you. But then they gave him his banning orders, that was just after he got Gordon's affidavits for him. So he had to give up his practice and all he's doing nowadays is to get pissed on other people's booze."

Julius Nqakula did not look very impressed.

Stanley turned abruptly to him: "Listen," he said, "Ben wants us to keep working on Gordon's case."

"He's white," Julius snapped, still glaring at Ben, and moving one of his shoes in rhythmic jerks.

"The SB raided his house because of Gordon."

"He's still white."

"He can reach places we can't."

"So what?"

"And we can get into joints he can't. So what do you say: we join forces?"

"I say he's white and I don't trust him."

Ben had repressed his anger until now; but he refused to do so any longer. "I suppose you now expect me to say: 'You're black, I don't trust you'?" he burst out, slamming his glass down on the low coffee table. "Don't you think it's time we got past this stupid stalemate?" He turned to Stanley: "I really don't know how you can expect any help from him. Can't you see they've broken his spirit?"

To his amazement a slow smile moved across Julius Nqakula's bony face. He emptied the rest of his glass into his mouth, made a gurgling sound in his throat, and wiped his lips with his sleeve. "Come again," he said, almost appreciatively. "See if anyone can break *me*!"

"Why don't you help us then?" said Ben. "For Gordon's sake."

"Oh you White Liberals!" Julius said. "Fill up, Stanley."

An unreasonable, atavistic anger sprang to life inside Ben, as it had during his visit to the District Surgeon. "I'm not a bloody Liberal," he said fiercely. "I'm an Afrikaner."

Stanley refilled Julius's glass and his own, neat; they sat in silence, looking at Ben.

At last Stanley asked: "Well, how's it, Julius?"

Julius grunted, smiling slowly, appreciatively. "Oh he's all right," he said. Then he moved into a more comfortable position in his chair, propped up on his elbows, his backside hanging over the edge of the seat. "What you aiming to do?" he asked.

"The main thing is to dig up everything they're trying to hide. Until we've got enough to reopen the case. We mustn't stop before we're sure we've got everything. So the guilty can be punished and the world can know what happened."

"You got a hope!" said Julius.

"Are you going to help us or not?"

Julius smiled lazily: "Where do we start?" he asked.

"With your affidavits on Jonathan."

"No go. Those were confiscated when they caught Gordon."

"Didn't you keep copies?"

"I was raided too, man."

"Then we must find those people again and get them to make new statements."

"That nurse got such a fright she won't ever put pen to paper again. And the Phetla chap ran away to Botswana."

"Well," said Stanley jovially, "you got your job cut out. You just trace them and persuade them to make new statements."

"I'm under banning orders."

"You weren't banned so you could sit on your backside." Stanley got up. "Think it over while I take the lanie home. Before his missus gets the hell in."

"By the way," said Julius, still reclining casually, "Johnny Fulani came to me yesterday."

181

"Who's Johnny Fulani?" asked Ben.

"One of the detainees whose statements were read at the inquest. Remember? When Archibald Tsabalala turned against them, they decided not to call the other three. State security. Now they've released Johnny Fulani."

"What did he say?"

"What d'you expect? They *moered* him until he signed."

"Right. So you get another statement from him."

"I already have one."

Ben smiled. "Good. Do you mind sending me a copy with Stanley? I'll keep it safely."

"Suppose they raid you again?"

"Don't worry, I've thought of that," Ben said. "I made a hiding-place they won't ever find."

Unfolding in segments, Julius rose from his chair and offered Ben his hand.

"Now keep off my moonshine, Julius!" Stanley said, trying his best to look menacing.

On their way back in the shaky old Dodge, Ben asked: "Why did you want me to meet Julius?"

"Because we need him."

"Any other lawyer would have done as well."

Stanley laughed. "I know. But Julius got hit right under the belt by that banning. Going to pieces. Now we've given him something to do it will get him back on his two feet." A carefree and contented laugh. "Lanie, you wait. I got a feeling you and I are going a long way together. And all along the way we'll pick up people, until we get right to the other side. Then there'll be such a lot of us they won't be able to count us no more. An amountable majority." For the rest of the way home he sat singing, drumming with his fingers on the roof to keep the beat.

Sunday 15 May. Back to Melanie. Inevitably, I suppose. I do need her for the investigation and she said she would help. At the same time I felt some trepidation. Impossible to think of her as no more than a helper. What then?

An injustice to her to suggest that she threatens me. My middle-aged existence, my middle-class values. Teacher. Elder. 'Respected member of society'. What is happening to me?

On the other hand – or am I rationalising now? – she offers comfort. Restores my confidence. Encourages me. What exactly? The first time it happened by coincidence, utterly unpremeditated, in innocence. Would it have been better to leave it at that? Not to jeopardise the uniqueness of the experience. There are moments which, for one's own sake, one shouldn't ever try to repeat. Suddenly there is a pattern; there are expectations, possibilities, hopes. Needless to speculate. It is too late. I did go back.

Why should I feel uneasy about it? Perhaps the circumstances. This weekend. Even now they think I've withdrawn into my study to prepare for tomorrow. "On a Sunday!" Susan protested.

She'd been impossible ever since my return from Stanley on Thursday night. "You smell like a hut." "You've been drinking again." "Into what holes have you been crawling again?" Like in Krugersdorp years ago when I visited the parents of my pupils. She couldn't stand it. Even worse this time. Soweto. In all fairness to her, though, it must have come as a shock. She'd honestly thought it was all over. Worried and concerned, and not necessarily about herself only. The visit by the SB nearly broke her spirit. Been to the doctor twice already. Nerves, migraine, sedatives. I must be more considerate. If only she'd make an effort to understand.

To make things worse, Suzette and family also came over for the weekend.

Still, things were reasonably under control till Saturday morning. Took Suzette's little Hennie for a walk. Stepped into every puddle, played in mud like a little pig, talked non-stop. "You know, Grandpa, the wind's got a cold too. I heard it sniffing in the night."

Then Suzette threw a tantrum because I'd allowed him to get so filthy. I'm an "undesirable influence", teaching the child bad manners etc. Lost my temper too. Told her *she* was the undesirable influence, going off on her trips, gallivanting and neglecting the poor boy. That made her furious. "Who are you to talk about going off all the time? Mum told me she hardly sees you at home any more."

"You don't know what you're talking about, Suzette."

"Are you trying to deny it? What about all this hobnobbing with blacks in townships? You should be ashamed of yourself."

"I refuse to discuss my affairs with you if you use that tone of voice."

She was furious. A beautiful woman, the spitting image of her mother, especially when she's angry. "Well, I'd like you to know that that's what we've come for this weekend," she said. "To have a proper heart-to-heart with you. Things just can't go on like this. Chris is negotiating with the Provincial Council this very minute about a new project. Would you like to see them cancel it? These things are contagious, you know."

"You make it sound like an illness."

"Exactly. I've been wondering whether there's something wrong with you. There's never been such pally-pallying with blacks in our house before."

Chris was, as usual, much more reasonable. He was at least prepared to listen. I think he accepts that Gordon's case can't just be left like that, even though he may not approve of what I'm doing: "I respect your reasons, Dad. But the Party is in the process of preparing people for major changes. And if this business causes a new furore, as it's bound to, it will put a new brake on things. The whole world is ready to jump at our throats, we can't play into their hands. We Afrikaners are going through tough times right now and we should all stand together."

"You mean we should close our ranks round any sign of evil, the way a rugby team protects a man who's lost his pants on the field?"

Chris laughed. He hasn't lost his sense of humour yet. But

then he said: "We must put it right from the inside, Dad. We can't throw it open to the eyes of the world."

"For how long have these things been going on now, Chris? And nothing has been put right yet."

"You mustn't expect to see results too soon."

"I'm sorry, Chris. But these mills are grinding too slowly for me nowadays."

"You yourself will be crushed in the mill if you don't watch out."

If Suzette hadn't turned up at that moment and started interfering we might have come to some sort of understanding. I know he means well. But what with all the tension in the house since Thursday night, I couldn't take it any more. And after lunch I drove off in the car.

Even then I didn't deliberately head for Westdene. I was just driving to allow my feelings to settle. The quiet Saturday afternoon streets. For the first time it shook me. The men and women in white on tennis courts. The bowls greens. The black nannies in uniform, pushing prams across lawns. The men with bare torsos washing their cars. The women in curlers watering flowerbeds. The groups of blacks lying or sitting on streetcorners, chatting and laughing. The lazy stillness of the sun just before the cold sets in.

And then I was back in the street running uphill; in front of the old house with the curved verandah over the red stoep. I drove past, turning at the top of the incline, and then down again. But a mile or so away I stopped to think it over. Why not? There was nothing wrong with it. Actually it was most desirable, if not imperative, to discuss the possibility of future action with her.

At first sight I took him for a Coloured gardener, squatting on his haunches beside a flower bed, pulling out weeds. Soiled corduroy trousers, black beret sporting a guinea-fowl feather, khaki shirt, pipe in his mouth, and the filthiest pair of mudcaked shoes – worn without socks or laces – I'd ever seen. It was her father, old Professor Phil Bruwer.

"No, sorry," he grumbled when I spoke to him, "Melanie isn't at home."

His wild white mane couldn't have been combed in months.

185

Small goatee stained with tobacco juice. The skin of his face dark and tanned like old leather, like an old discarded shoe; and two twinkling dark brown eyes half-disappearing below the unkempt eyebrows.

"Then I suppose there's no point in staying," I said.

"What's your name?" he asked, still hunched over the bed.

"Du Toit. Ben Du Toit. I met Melanie the other day."

"Yes, she spoke about you. Well, why don't you wait a while? She may not be long, she went to the newspaper office to finish off something. Of course, one never knows with her, does one? Why don't you give me a hand with the weeding? I was off to the Magaliesberg for a while, now my whole garden is in a mess. Melanie doesn't know the difference between a plant and a weed."

"What plants are these?" I asked him, to keep the conversation going.

He looked up in mock reproach. "What's the world coming to? It's herbs, can't you see?" He started pointing them out to me: "Thyme, oregano, fennel, sage. Rosemary's over there." He got up to stretch his back. "But somehow they don't taste right."

"They seem to be flourishing."

"Flourishing isn't enough." He started cleaning his pipe. "Something to do with the soil. For thyme you should go into the mountains of Southern France. Or Greece. Mycenae. It's like vines, you see. Depends on whether it's a southern or a northern slope, how steep it is, how scaly, all sorts of things. Next time I want to bring me a small bag of soil from the mountain of Zeus. Perhaps the Old Man's holiness will do the trick." He grinned, exposing his uneven, yellow-stained teeth, many of them mere stumps. "One thing I seem to discover as I grow older is that the more one gets involved in philosophy and stuff, in transcendental things, the more surely you're forced back to the earth. We'll all go back to the old chtonic gods yet. That's the problem of people running after Abstractions. Started with Plato. Mind you, he's misunderstood in a shocking way. Still, give me Socrates any time. We're all living in the spell of the Abstract. Hitler, Apartheid, the Great American Dream, the lot."

"What about Jesus?" I asked, somewhat deliberately.

186

"Misunderstood," he said. "*Et verbum caro facta est*. We're running after the *verbum*, forgetting about the flesh. 'Our bodies which us to us at first convey'd'. Those Metaphysicals really had it by the short hairs. One's got to keep one's feet or hands on the ground, preferably all four of them."

I'm writing down haphazardly what I can recall of the running monologue he kept up as he pottered about in the garden, weeding and watering, raking leaves, digging for worms, straightening some plants and pruning dried-up leaves from others. An irrepressible warmth inspiring everything he said. "You know, those days when our people had to work like hell to gain a toehold on this land, it was a good life. But then this notion got into us that once we'd taken control we should start working out blueprints and systems for the future. Now look at the mess. It's all System and no God. Sooner or later people start believing in their way of life as an absolute: immutable, fundamental, a precondition. Saw it with my own eyes in Germany in the Thirties. A whole nation running after the Idea, like Gadarene swine. *Sieg heil, sieg heil.* Keeps me awake at night. I mean, I left there in 'thirty-eight because I couldn't take it any longer. And now I see it happening in my own country, step by step. Terrifyingly predictable. This sickness of the Great Abstraction. We've got to come back to the physical, to flesh and bone and earth. Truth didn't fall from Heaven in the shape of a word: it goes about bare-arsed. Or if we've got to talk in terms of words, then it's the word of a bloody stammerer like Moses. Each one of us stuttering and stammering his bit of truth."

An odd detail: not very seemly, I'm afraid, but it was as much part of Phil Bruwer as his stained teeth or his filthy shoes or his dry chuckle. I'm referring to his farting. He seemed to function in such a way that every change of thought, every new direction, every particular emphasis had to be punctuated by a fart. Improper as it may be, he is as much a virtuoso as any player of the trombone. It went something like this:

"The Government is handling the electorate as if it were a bloody donkey. Carrot in front and kick in the backside. The carrot is Apartheid, Dogma, the Great Abstraction. The kick is, quite simply, fear. Black Peril, Red Peril, whatever name you want to give it." A resounding fart. "Fear can be a wonderful ally. I remember once, years ago, on a trip to the Okavango, collecting plants; whole train of bearers following me. After the first week or so they became lazy, falling farther and farther behind. One thing I can't stand is dawdling when you're in the bush. Then a lion started following us. It was a dry year and most game had gone off, but this old male remained behind. Got our smell. Not that it could have been very difficult, for after a few weeks in the bush one stinks to high heaven. Anyway, the couple of days that lion followed us I had no trouble with people falling behind or dropping out. Those bearers were actually jogging to keep up. Jolly useful lion that." Fart.

When there was nothing more left to do in the garden we went inside, to the kitchen. Just as disordered as the study. There were two stoves, one electric, the other an ancient, lugubrious black coal stove. He saw me looking at it.

"It's Melanie who talked me into buying the white monster," he said. "Says it's more efficient. But I kept the old one for my own cooking. Not every day, but when the spirit moves me." Fart. "Like some tea?" Without waiting for an answer he took a blue enamel kettle from the coal stove and poured us some bush-tea in old-fashioned, chipped Delft cups without saucers, then added a teaspoonful of honey to each cup. "Honey is God's own sweetener. The only true elixir of life. Only one man died young after eating honey and that was Samson. But it was his own damned fault. Cherchez la femme." Fart. "Poor soul might have become a good, saintly man if it hadn't been for that little Philistine tart." We sat at the kitchen table with its red checkered oilcloth, sipping the sweet, fragrant tea. "Not that I have any aspirations towards sanctity," he went on, chuckling. "Too old for that I'm afraid. I'm preparing myself for a long peaceful sleep in the earth. One of the most satisfying things I can think of, you know. To turn slowly into compost, to become humus, to fatten worms and nourish plants, keeping the whole cycle of life going. It's the only form of eternity I can hope for." Fart. "Back to Pluto and his pomegranates."

"You must be a very happy man."

"And why shouldn't I? I've had a bit of everything in my life, from heaven to hell. And now I still have Melanie, which is more than an old sinner like me should hope for." Fart. "I've lived long enough to make peace with myself. Not with the world, mind you." His dry chuckle, like before. "Never too down and out to give the world a run for its money. But with myself I've made peace all right. To thine own self bla bla, even though it was an old turd like Polonius who said it. Even in turds God plants his humble truths." And then, with only the barest punctuation of a change in direction, he started talking about Melanie. "Pure accident that she ever saw the light of day," he said. "I suppose I was so mad with Hitler after the war, what with spending three years in one of his camps, that I deliberately fell in love with the first Jewish girl I saw. Lovely girl, mind you. But it was chewing off a bit much, trying to save the whole world by marrying her. Bad mistake. Never aspire to save the world. Your own soul and one or two others are more than enough. So there I was left with Melanie after my wife had gone off. You see, the poor woman was so out of her depth among the Afrikaners, what could she do but run away? And to think I actually blamed her for leaving me with a year-old baby. One tends to underestimate the strange ways in which God shows us his mercy." Once again he couldn't resist emphasising his point with a neat, dry fart.

His story explained the quaintly Semitic, Shulamithic nature of her looks; her black hair and eyes.

"She told me she met you at the court inquest on this Ngubene's death?" he said as if, having covered the whole field, he was now directing his assault in a more specific way. Except, of course, it wasn't an assault.

"Yes. If it hadn't been for her—"

He chuckled appreciatively, pushing one muddy hand through his wild white mane. "Look at me. Every single grey hair on this head of mine has been caused by her. And I wouldn't have missed one of them. You also have a daughter?"

"Two."

"Hm." His penetrating, amused eyes were searching me. "You don't show too much wear and tear."

"It doesn't always show on the outside," I said playfully.

"So what's the next move?" he asked, so suddenly it took me

189

a moment to realise that he had returned to the inquest.

I told him about what had happened so far. Dr Herzog. Emily's notes. The mysterious Johnson Seroke who'd delivered them to her. Stanley's lawyer friend. It was such a relief, after the bickering at home, to talk freely and frankly.

"Not an easy road you've chosen," he commented.

"I have no choice."

"Of course you have a choice, damn it. One always has a choice. Don't fool yourself. Only be thankful you made the choice you did. Not an original thought, I admit. Camus. But one can do worse than listening to him. All I want to say is: keep your eyes open. I remember—" Another fart coming, I thought; and he didn't disappoint me either. Fortunately he was lighting a match at the same time to coax new life into his dead pipe. "I remember a walking trip in the Tsitsikama forest a few years ago. Hit the coast at the mouth of the Storms River and crossed over the rickety suspension bridge. It was a wild day, awful wind, quite terrifying if you're not used to it. There was a middle-aged couple ahead of me, nice respectable people from the holiday camp. The husband was walking in front, his wife on his heels. And I literally mean right on his heels. In mortal terror. Holding her two hands on either side of her eyes, like the blinkers of a horse, to shut out the swaying bridge and the stormy water. There they were walking through one of the most incredibly beautiful landscapes in the whole damn world and all she saw of it was a few square inches of her husband's back. That's why I'm saying: Keep your eyes open. Make sure you stay on the bridge, right. But for God's sake don't miss the view."

Suddenly, somewhere in the unpredictable course of his verbal diarrhoea, while we were drinking our second or third cup of bush-tea, she was there with us. I'd never heard her coming, not a sound. When I looked up she was simply standing there. Small, delicate, like a halfgrown girl with the merest swelling of breasts under her T-shirt, her black hair tied back with a ribbon. No make-up, except perhaps a touch of something at the eyes. A hint of tenseness, tiredness in her face. On her forehead, beside her eyes, round her mouth. Like the first time there was the unnerving discovery of a person who'd seen more of life than might have been good for her. Still, it hadn't dulled her eyes. Or are my norms really very old-fashioned?

"Hello, Dad." She kissed him, and tried in vain to straighten his unruly hair. "Hello, Ben. You been here long?"

"We've had more than enough to talk about," Prof Bruwer said. "Like some bush-tea?"

"I'll make me something more civilised." While she was boiling water for coffee she looked at me over her shoulder: "I didn't mean to keep you waiting."

"How could you have known that I'd be here?"

"It's not all that unexpected." She took a mug from the cupboard. "You've had a very busy week, it seems."

Was it really only a week since I'd been with her the first time, that late afternoon and evening among the cats in the front room, she curled up, barefoot, in the big chair?

"How do you know about my 'busy' week?" I asked, surprised.

"Saw Stanley yesterday." She brought her cup to the table and sat down with us. "Ben, why didn't you phone me after they'd searched your house? It must have been a terrible experience for you."

"One learns to survive." I had meant to say it lightly, but as I spoke it sounded different; I was conscious of a sense of liberation.

"I'm glad. I really am."

The small slurping sound as she tested the hot coffee. A delicate fringe of foam on her lips.

The old man stayed with us for some time, joining in our conversation but without dominating it as before, as if the need for it had been suspended. Then he put on his black beret and went out without ceremony. Much later – he must have gone round the house, for we didn't see him again – we heard the piano playing in the front room. It sounded slightly flat; it had probably not been tuned in years; but the playing was effortless, compelling, flowing. Bach, I think. One of those pieces that go on and on, like the old man's conversation, with intricate variations, yet clear and precise in its complexity. She and I remained at the kitchen table.

"Stanley told me you'd decided to keep working on Gordon's case."

191

"I must."

"I'm glad. I thought you would."

"Will you help me?"

She smiled. "I told you I would, didn't I?" For a moment she scrutinised me as if to make sure I was serious. "I've already started working on some of my contacts. In fact, I was hoping to have something for you when you came. But they're terribly tight-lipped. One will have to be very circumspect." She shook back her hair. "But I think I'm on to something. That's why I was so late today. Dad thought I'd gone to the office, but I was in Soweto."

"But it's dangerous, Melanie!"

"Oh I know my way. And I'm sure they know my little Mini by sight." A brief, wry smile: "Although I must admit there was a rather tense moment today."

Her very nonchalance made my heart contract. "What happened?"

"Well, on my way back, in the open veld between Jabulani and Jabavu, I had a flat tyre."

"And then?"

"I changed the wheel, what else? But there was a crowd of youngsters playing soccer. And all of a sudden, when I looked up again, they were surrounding the car. Some were laughing, but others were raising clenched fists and shouting freedom slogans and insults. I must admit that for once I thought I'd had my chips."

Unable to make a sound I stared at her.

She gave a carefree smile. "Don't worry. I just followed their example and raised my clenched fist and shouted: '*Amandla!*' And then it was like the Israelites crossing the Red Sea: they made way for me and I went through without getting my feet wet."

"It might easily have turned out differently!"

"What else could I do? You know, I sat there behind the wheel thinking: *Thank God I'm a woman, not a man. They would kill a man. Now I suppose rape is about the worst that can happen to me.*"

"It's terrible enough!"

"I think I know what I'm talking about, Ben," she said

quietly, looking at me with those large black eyes. "You know, after that encounter with the Frelimo soldiers in Maputo, I started getting nightmares. It went on for months." For a moment she crossed her arms over her small breasts as if to shield herself against the memory. "Then I realised it was getting out of hand and I forced myself to think it through. All right, it is a terrible thing to happen to anyone. Not so much the pain—not even the forced entry into your body as such—but the breaking into your privacy, into what belongs exclusively to yourself. And yet, even that can be endured. Come to think of it: did it really happen to *me*, or only to my body? One needn't always place one's whole self at stake, you know. It's like prisoners in jail; I've spoken to so many of them. Some never get over it. Others manage to shrug it off, because they've never really been prisoners, only their bodies were locked up. No one has touched their thoughts, their minds. Not even torture could reach so far."

"But what about *you*, Melanie?"

"It's only when you fully appreciate your body that you can also accept its insignificance."

"You're your father's child all right!" I had to admit.

She looked round, and went to the kitchen dresser where she'd left her keys and her small handbag, and lit a cigarette. Coming back to me she moved the used cups aside and sat down on a corner of the table, so close I could have touched her.

More, I think, to protect me against her unsettling closeness than anything else, I said: "Shall I help you wash up the cups?"

"That can wait."

"I suppose I'm still conditioned by my mother," I said awkwardly. "She never gave us a moment's peace until everything in the house had been cleaned and put back where it belonged. Before going to bed at night she would go through the house to make sure everything was tidy, just in case she died in her sleep and left anything undone. It drove my father up the wall."

"Is that why you have this urge to clear up Gordon's case too?" she teased.

"Maybe." For a moment I felt lighthearted: "Not that I

have any intention of dying in my sleep."

"I hope not. I've hardly got to know you." It was a pleasantry, no more, I know. Or wasn't it?

In any case her reference to Gordon brought me back to the question I'd wanted to ask her earlier:

"What did you go to Soweto for, Melanie? What is it you're working on?"

With the characteristic gesture she swept back her long hair over her shoulders. "It may be a dead-end, of course. Still, I think it may lead to something. It's one of the black warders at John Vorster Square. He helped me a couple of times in the past and they don't suspect him. He knows something about Gordon. Only, it'll demand a lot of patience, he's very nervous. He wants to be sure that the dust has settled first."

"How do you know he has something on Gordon?"

"He gave me one bit of information. He said there definitely had been bars in front of Stolz's windows on the day of the so-called scuffle."

For a moment I was at sea. "What about it?"

"Don't you remember? They claimed Gordon had tried to jump out, that was why they'd had to restrain him. But if the window had been barred he couldn't possibly have tried to escape."

"It doesn't add much to the facts."

"I know. But it's a beginning. Do you remember how Advocate De Villiers managed to confuse them when he asked them about the bars? They concocted a silly story of how the bars had had to be removed temporarily and so on. This new bit of evidence is another small wedge in the log. It casts suspicion on the whole scuffle."

"You think your black warder will really be prepared to help us?"

"I'm sure he knows enough."

A sudden feeling of excitement, an almost boyish elation that persists as I'm writing. I know we're making progress. There was the bit Julius Nqakula told us. The new affidavits he's trying to find. Emily's notes and the Johnson Seroke she's been in touch with. And now the news from the warder. It's precious little. It comes to us in small bits, very very slowly. But we are making progress. And one day it will all be exposed to us and to the world. Everything about Gordon and Jonathan. Then we'll know it has been worthwhile all along. I'm as confident of this now as I was when I spoke to her, even in spite of her calm and reasonable attempts to keep everything into perspective:

"Don't get excited too soon, Ben," she said. "Remember, this is a game played by two sides."

"What do you mean?"

"They're not going to sit back and allow us to just gather whatever information we choose."

"What can they do about it?"

"Ben, there's nothing they cannot do."

In spite of myself, a numbness in my stomach.

She went on: "Remember, you're an Afrikaner, you're one of them. In their eyes that's just about the worst kind of treason imaginable."

"What about you?"

"My mother was a foreigner, don't forget. I'm working for an English newspaper. They've written me off long ago. They simply don't expect the same sort of loyalty from me that they demand from you."

Inside, the piano had stopped playing. The silence was almost eerie.

Ruefully, grudgingly, I said: "Are you really trying to put me off? You of all people?"

"No, Ben. I only want to make quite sure you have no illusions about anything."

"Are *you* so sure of what lies ahead, of the consequences of every single thing you do?"

"Of course not." Her lovely laugh. "It's like the river I landed in when I was in Zaire. You've got to believe you'll reach the other side. I'm not even sure it matters who or what you have faith in. It's the experience in itself that's important." The frank revelation of her eyes: "I'll help you, Ben."

That restored my confidence. Not elation like before, that had been too superficial, too easy. But something more profound and solid. Call it faith, as she had.

Later we went down the long passage to the junk-shop of the front room where we'd been the first time. Her father wasn't

195

there. Probably gone for a walk, she said, adding in a tone of reproach: "He refuses to take it easy. He just won't believe he's getting old."

"I must go now."

"Why don't you stay?"

"I'm sure you have other things to do."

"I'm going out tonight, but it's still early. No need to go before eight or so."

Why should that have disturbed me so deeply? Of course a woman like her would go out on a Saturday night; of course she wouldn't spend all her free time in that old house with her father. I doubt that it was something as straightforward and uncomplicated as jealousy: why should I be jealous? – I had no claim on her. Rather a painful acceptance of the obvious discovery that there were whole landscapes of her life inaccessible to me. However freely she'd confided in me about her life, however readily she'd answered all my questions, it had been no more than a narrow footpath on which I'd wandered through her wilderness. Was there any reason to be upset about that? Was there any hope of it ever being different?

I, too, have my own life to lead without her, independent of her. Wife, house, children, work, responsibilities.

Yes, I would have loved to stay. Like the previous time, I would have loved to sit with her until it became dark, until one could unburden more freely, until her presence would no longer be quite so unsettling: everything reduced to dusk and the purring of many cats. But I had to go away.

I must be sensible. What binds us is the mutual devotion to a task we have undertaken: to bring the truth to light, to ensure that justice be done. Beyond that nothing is allowed us, nothing is even thinkable. And apart from what we are allowed to share for Gordon's sake, neither has any claim on the other. Whatever part of my life falls outside that narrow scope, is exclusively mine; what is hers is hers. Why should I *wish* to know more?

"I'm glad you came, Ben."

"I'll come again."

"Of course."

I hesitated, hoping she might lean over and perhaps kiss me lightly as she'd kissed her father. That fullness of her mouth.

But she probably was as unprepared as I was to risk it.

"Good-bye."

"Good-bye, Melanie." The music of her name, the blood in my ears. My God, I'm *not* a child any more.

3

Maintaining the daily routine was becoming more and more of an irritation; at the same time it offered a sense of reassurance and security, linking one day to the next, tidily, predictably. Getting up at half-past six to go jogging, usually with Johan. Making breakfast and taking Susan's to her in bed. Off to school, and back at two. Lunch, a brief nap, then to school again for sport or other extramural work. Late in the afternoon a couple of hours spent on woodwork in the garage, a solitary walk, supper, withdrawing into the study afterwards. The daily timetable at school; the rotation of standards and subjects. Eight, nine, ten; eight, nine, ten. History, geography. The neat and solid facts, unassailable in black and white; nothing outside the prescribed syllabus was relevant. For years he'd been rebelling against the system, insisting that his pupils, especially the matrics, read more than had been set for them. Teaching them to ask questions, to challenge assertions. But now it had become much easier to resign himself to the given, as it liberated his thoughts for other things. He no longer felt the need to be so deeply involved in the work. It really happened by itself, carried onwards by its own momentum; all that was required of one was simply to be there, to execute the steps.

In between classes there were the few free periods for marking or catching up with reading; intervals in the common room; conversations with colleagues. The eager support of the young language teacher Viviers. Ben never gave away much beyond confirming that he was still 'working on it', preferring to shrug off direct questions, pleased by the young man's interest but embarrassed by his enthusiasm. He found Viviers too much of a young dog wagging his tail at every new idea.

Some of the younger staff members were just the opposite and started avoiding him after the newspaper photograph. Most of his colleagues were content with a comment or two, a snide remark, a witticism. Only one – Carelse, Physical Education – found it such a roaring joke that he returned to it day after day, laughing loudly at his own crude comments. "They should put you on the jury of the Miss South Africa Competition." "I say, Oom Ben, haven't you had a visit from the Vice Squad yet?" There was no end to it. But he was without malice or deceit, and when he laughed it was as frank and open as an unzipped fly.

Neither mockery nor resentment nor serious interest could really touch him. What happened at school was of so little concern to his life: his centre of gravity had moved elsewhere. Except, perhaps, as far as the pupils were concerned – the ones who came to him for advice and who, over many years, had used him as father confessor. Little ones bullied by prefects. Others struggling with certain subjects. Still others with very personal problems: How do you ask a girl to go steady? – Can't you talk to my dad? He doesn't want me to go camping this weekend. – How far can one go with a girl before it's sinful? – What does one do to become an architect?

Were there fewer of them lately, or was he imagining things? Once, coming into his classroom after interval, there was a copy of the notorious photograph pinned to the blackboard. But when he took it down, casually inquiring whether anyone would like it as a memento, the laughter was spontaneous and generous. If there were any undercurrent it certainly wasn't serious yet.

Outside school hours there was his other life, in which his home had become a coincidence and Susan merely an obstacle in the course of the current which churned and pursued its inevitable way.

One morning a young black man turned up at the school.

Ben was excited when the secretary told him about it during the interval. A messenger from Stanley? A new breakthrough? But it turned out the youth, Henry Maphuna, had come on entirely different business. Something very personal. He'd heard, he said, that Ben was helping people in trouble. And something had happened to his sister.

As it was the near the end of the interval, Ben asked him to come round to his house in the afternoon. Arriving home at two o'clock, he found Henry already waiting.

Susan: "One of your fans wanting to see you."

A pleasant young fellow, thin, intelligent, polite, and quite sure of what he wanted. Not very well dressed for such a cool day. Shirt and shorts, bare feet.

"Tell me about your sister," said Ben.

For the last three years the girl, Patience, had been working for a rich English couple in Lower Houghton. On the whole they'd been kind and considerate, but she'd soon discovered that whenever the lady was out the husband would find a pretext to be near her. Nothing serious: a smile, a few suggestive remarks perhaps, no more. But two months ago the wife had to go to hospital. While Patience was tidying up in the bedroom her employer made his appearance and started chatting her up; when she resisted his efforts to caress her, he knocked her down, locked the door and raped her. Afterwards he was suddenly overcome by remorse and offered her twenty rand to keep quiet. She was in such a state that all she could think of was to run home. Only the next day did she allow Henry to take her to the police station where she produced the twenty rand and laid a charge. From there she went to a doctor.

Her employer was arrested and summonsed. A fortnight before the trial the man had driven to the Maphuna's home in Alexandra and offered them a substantial amount to withdraw the charge. But Patience had refused to listen to his slobbering pleas. She'd been engaged to be married but after what had happened her fiancé had broken it off; the only satisfaction she could still hope for was for justice to be done.

It had seemed a mere formality. But in court the employer told a wholly different story, about how he and his wife had had trouble with Patience from the beginning; about a constant

199

string of black boyfriends pestering her during working hours; on one occasion, he said, they'd even trapped her with a lover in their own bedroom. And while his wife had been in hospital things had gone from bad to worse, with Patience following him about the house and soliciting him, with the result that he'd been forced to sack her, paying her a fortnight's notice money – the twenty rand produced in court. In an hysterical outburst she'd started tearing her own clothes, swearing she'd be revenged by accusing him of rape etc. Under oath his wife corroborated his evidence on Patience's general behaviour. There were no other witnesses. The man was found not guilty and the regional magistrate severely reprimanded Patience.

Now the family had heard that Ben was prepared to help the injured, and so Henry had come for help and redress.

Ben was upset. Not only by the case as such but by the fact that Henry had chosen to come to him for help. He already had his hands full with Gordon and Jonathan – and suddenly everything he'd done so far appeared so inadequate anyway. Now there was this too.

He could think of only one remedy. While Henry was waiting in the backyard Ben telephoned Dan Levinson and asked him to take over. Yes, of course he was prepared to pay for it.

After Henry had left he tried to telephone Melanie at her office but the lines remained busy. That was reason enough to drive to town. It was a new Melanie he met this time, in the small cluttered office she shared with two others; telephones, telexes, piles of newspapers, people running in and out. A cool and crisp and very capable Melanie; direct and to the point in the hubbub surrounding her. Only for a few moments, isolated beside the coffee machine in the passage, did he recognise the warmth of the smile he'd known before.

"I think you've done by far the best thing to refer it to Levinson," she reassured him. "But I think it's time we made an arrangement about money. You can't go on paying for everything out of your own pocket."

"One more case won't make so much difference."

Swinging back her hair in the gesture he remembered so well, she asked: "What makes you think Henry Maphuna will be the last to come to you for help? Now they know about you, Ben."

"How do they know?"

She merely smiled, and said: "I'll talk to the editor about funds. And don't worry. We'll keep it secret."

24 May. Stanley, earlier tonight. Hardly bothered to knock. When I looked up from my desk, he was standing there, blocking the doorway.

"How's it, lanie?"

"Stanley! Any news?"

"Well, depends. Tell you next week."

I looked at him quizzically.

"I'm off on a trip, lanie. Botswana. Got some business there. Thought I'd just drop in and tell you, so you won't get worried."

"What sort of business?"

His boisterous laugh. "Leave it to me. You got your own troubles. So long."

"But where are you off to now? You haven't even sat down yet."

"No time. I told you I just came to pay my respects."

He didn't want me to go out with him. As suddenly as he'd appeared he was gone. For a brief minute my little study had been scintillating with extraordinary life: now, immediately afterwards, one could hardly believe it had happened.

And even more than on the day I went to Melanie I was left with the burden of the unanswerable. In exactly the same way in which he'd entered into this room tonight and disappeared again, he'd come into my life; and one day, who knows, he'll be gone just as suddenly. Where does he really come from? Where is he off to tonight? All I know about him is what he allows me to know. Nothing more, nothing less. A whole secret world surrounding him, of which I know next to nothing.

Faith, she said. The jump in the dark.

I must accept him on his own terms: that is all I have to go by.

It was such a small report that Ben nearly missed it in the evening paper:

Dr Suliman Hassiem, detained three months ago in terms of the Internal

201

Security Act, was released by the Special Branch this morning, but immediately served with a banning order restricting him to the Johannesburg magisterial district.

Dr Hassiem had been appointed to represent the Ngubene family at the autopsy on Mr Gordon Ngubene who died in custody in February, but as a result of his own detention he was unable to testify in the subsequent inquest.

Ben had to restrain his impatience until the next day after school, when he had an appointment to discuss Henry Maphuna's case with Dan Levinson. The lawyer gave him Dr Hassiem's address. From the office he had to go home first, for his delayed lunch; and then back to school to give a hand with the coaching of the Under Fifteen rugby team. But just as he was preparing to leave the house the telephone rang. Linda. She had the habit of telephoning at odd times throughout the week, just for a chat.

"How's Father Christmas today?"

"Busy as usual."

"What's it this time? That fat new book on the Great Trek I saw on your desk last week?"

"No, the poor thing is still lying untouched by human hand. I've got so many other things."

"Like what?"

"Oh, well – I'm just on my way to rugby practice now. And then I'm going to see someone." Linda was the only one he could unburden his heart to. "Remember that doctor who was to testify in Gordon's inquest? The one who was detained. Well, they've let him out and I want to find out whether there's anything new he can tell me."

"Do be careful, Daddy."

"I will. We're making headway, you know. One of these days we'll have all Gordon's murderers lined up against a wall."

"Have you done anything about a new house for Emily? You said last time she would have to leave hers now that she's a widow."

"Yes. But I'm holding that over to discuss with Grandpa when he's here next week."

Some more small-talk, and then she rang off. But now that he'd talked to her he was in no mood for the rugby practice:

there was so much of greater urgency to attend to. The strict timetable he'd obeyed for so many years was beginning to chafe him. And impulsively, almost impatiently, he drove to young Viviers's flat near by and asked him to take his place in the practice. Too bad if Cloete was annoyed by the swop. Without wasting any more time he drove directly to the address Levinson had given him, heading south, out of the city, to the Asian township of Lenasia.

How odd to think that for more than twenty years he'd been living in Johannesburg, yet it was only in recent months that he'd set foot in these other townships. Never before had it been necessary; it hadn't even occurred to him. And now, all of a sudden, it was becoming part of a new routine.

A little girl in a frilly white dress opened the door. Two thin plaits, red bows; large dark eyes in a small, prim face. Yes, she said, her father was at home, would he like to come in? She darted out, returning in a minute later with her father, hovering on the doorstep to watch them anxiously.

Dr Hassiem was a tall, lean man in beige trousers and poloneck sweater; expressive hands. His face was very light-skinned, with delicate Oriental features and straight black hair falling across his forehead.

"I hope I'm not disturbing you, Doctor," Ben said, ill at ease after he'd introduced himself. "But I saw in the paper that you'd been released."

One eyebrow flickered briefly; that was Hassiem's only reaction.

"I'm a friend of Gordon Ngubene's."

Almost precipitate, but very polite, Dr Hassiem raised his hands: "The inquest is over, Mr Du Toit."

"Officially, yes. But I'm not so sure everything came to light that had to come out."

Unyielding, the doctor remained standing, pointedly neglecting to offer Ben a seat.

"I know it may be painful to you, Doctor, but I must know what happened to Gordon."

"I'm sorry, I really can't help you."

"You were present at the autopsy."

The doctor shrugged noncommittally.

203

"Emily told me you felt Gordon may not have been strangled by the blanket he was hanging from."

"Really, Mr Du Toit—" Hurriedly, he walked over to the window, pulled the curtain aside and glanced out, a hunted look in his eyes. "I only came home yesterday. I've been detained for three months. I'm not allowed to come and go as I like." With something cornered and helpless in his attitude he looked at the child standing on one leg in the doorway. "Go and play, Fatima."

Instead, she hurried to her father and grabbed one of his legs in both thin arms, peering round it, grimacing at Ben.

"But don't you realise, Doctor, if everybody can be silenced like this we'll never find out what happened."

"I'm really very sorry." Hassiem seemed to have made up his mind firmly. "But it would be better if you didn't stay. Please forget that you ever came here."

"I'll see to it that you are protected."

For the first time Hassiem smiled, but without losing his stern composure. "How can you protect me? How can anyone protect me?" Absently he pressed the child's face against his knee. "How can I be sure you weren't actually sent by them?"

Ben looked round in dismay. "Why don't you ask Emily?" he suggested feebly.

The young physician made a move in the direction of the door, the girl still clinging to his leg like a leech. "I have nothing to say to you, Mr Du Toit."

Dejected, Ben turned round. In the doorway to the passage he stopped: "Tell me just one thing, Doctor," he said. "Why did you sign the State Pathologist's report on the autopsy if you drew up a report of your own as well?"

Dr Hassiem was clearly caught unprepared. A sharp intake of breath. "What makes you think I signed Dr Jansen's report? I never did."

"I thought as much. But the report produced in court had both your signatures on it."

"Impossible."

Ben looked at him.

Dr Hassiem picked up the little girl, holding her on his hip. He came towards Ben. "Are you trying to bluff me?"

"No, it's true." Adding with sudden passion: "Dr Hassiem, I've got to know what happened to Gordon. And I know you can help me."

"Sit down," the doctor said abruptly. He briefly hugged the child, then persuaded her to go and play. For a while the two of them sat in silence in the quiet lounge. The clock on the wall went on ticking, unperturbed.

"What did you write in your report?" asked Ben.

"We didn't differ much on the facts," said Dr Hassiem. "After all, we were examining the same body at the same time. But there were differences in interpretation."

"For example?"

"Well, I thought that if Gordon had really been hanged the marks on his throat would have been concentrated on the front." He touched his larynx with the long slender fingers of one hand. "But in this case the bruises were more obvious on the sides." Another gesture. He got up to fetch cigarettes from the mantelpiece; after a brief hesitation he glanced through the window again before returning to his chair and offering Ben the packet.

"No thanks. I prefer my pipe, if I may."

"By all means."

For a while it seemed as if Dr Hassiem wasn't going to say anything more; perhaps he was regretting what he'd divulged already. But then he resumed:

"It was something else that really upset me. Perhaps it isn't important."

"What was it?" Ben demanded.

Perched on the very edge of his chair, Hassiem leaned forward. "You see, through a misunderstanding I arrived at the morgue too early for the autopsy. There wasn't a soul around, except for a young attendant. When I told him I'd come for the autopsy he let me in. The body was lying on the table. Clothed in grey trousers and a red jersey."

Ben made a gesture of surprise, but the doctor stopped him.

"There was something else," he said. "The jersey was covered in tiny white threads. You know, the sort one finds on a towel. That set me thinking."

"And then?" Ben asked, excited.

205

"I didn't have time to examine anything properly. As a matter of fact, I'd hardly bent over the body when a police officer came to call me. Said I wasn't allowed in the morgue under any circumstances before Dr Jansen arrived. He took me to an office where we had tea. About half an hour later Dr Jansen was brought in and the two of us went back to the morgue. This time the body was naked. I enquired about it, but no one knew anything about it. Afterwards I found the attendant in the passage and asked him what had happened. He said he'd been given instructions 'to prepare the corpse', but he knew nothing about the clothes."

"Did you put that in your report?"

"Of course. I found it most odd." His nervousness returned; he got up. That's all I can tell you, Mr Du Toit. I know absolutely nothing more."

This time Ben meekly allowed the man to lead him to the front door.

"I may come back to you," he said, "if I manage to find out more about this."

Dr Hassiem smiled without saying yes or no.

Ben drove home in the dusty afternoon.

The next day's evening paper reported briefly that Dr Suliman Hassiem and his family had been transported by the Security Police to a destination in the Northern Transvaal. His banning order had been amended by the minister to ensure that for the next five years he would not be allowed to leave the Pietersburg district. No reasons for the removal had been given.

27 *May.* Couldn't help being shocked when I opened the door to find him standing there. Stolz. Accompanied by another officer, middle-aged. Didn't catch the name. Very friendly. But I find the man in friendly mood more terrifying than otherwise.

"Mr Du Toit, we've just brought back your stuff." The journals and correspondence they'd confiscated a fortnight ago. "Will you sign for it, please?"

Must have been from pure relief that I said yes when he asked whether they could come in for a second. Susan, thank God, away at some meeting. Johan in his room, but the music turned up so loud he couldn't possibly hear us.

206

They'd barely sat down in the study when he said, jokingly, that his throat was dry. So obviously I offered them coffee. And only when I came back into the study with the tray and noticed the book on the Great Trek lying in a different position it hit me: of course! they'd had a quick search of the room while I'd been out.

Strange, but that was what finally put me at ease. Thinking: Right, here I am, and there you are. Now we're on our way. Feel free to search my house. You don't know about the false bottom in my tools cupboard. No living soul knows. Nothing will ever be left lying around again.

Not an easy conversation. Asked me about the school, about Johan's achievements, rugby, etc. Told me about his own son. Younger than Johan. Twelve or so. Would his son be proud of his dad? (Is mine proud of me?)

Then: "I hope you're not mad at us about the other day, Mr Du Toit?"

What could I say?

Found another house crammed with ammunition and explosives in Soweto this morning, he said. Enough to blow up a whole block in the city centre. "People don't seem to realise we're right in the middle of a war already. They're waiting for armies on the march, planes flying overhead, tanks, that sort of thing. They don't realise how clever these Communists are. Take it from me, Mr Du Toit: if we were to lay off for one week this country would be right down the drain."

"All right, I take it from you, Captain. I'm not arguing either. But what did Gordon have to do with it all? Would you still have had to fight this war of yours if your wheels hadn't rolled over people like him to start with?"

Not a very pleasant expression in his dark eyes. I suppose I should learn to restrain myself. Something defiant in me these days. But I've smothered it for so many years!

They were already on their way out when he said, in that casual, lazy way of his: "Look, if you want to help people like Henry Maphuna it's fine with us. A bit over-enthusiastic, if I may say so, but that's for you to decide." He looked at me in silence for a moment. "But in all sincerity, we don't take kindly to remarks like the one you made recently about lining up all

Gordon's murderers against a wall. You're playing with fire, Mr Du Toit."

Then, as easy-going as before, he offered me his hand. The thin line on his cheek. Who gave it to him? (And what happened to the man afterwards?)

Stood there half-paralysed after they'd gone. How did he know about Henry? How did he know about that line-up business?

Some leak from Levinson's office? I'll have to watch out. But that remark about Gordon – that was something I said to Linda.

Only one common denominator. The phone.

Thank God I didn't get through to Melanie that day. They mustn't find out about her.

4

30 May. Have always "got on" with Susan's parents, without much cordiality from either side. The feeling that they resent her marrying "below" her. The vast block of farms her grandparents acquired in the Eastern Transvaal. Her father the leading lawyer in Lydenburg. Loyal supporter of the Party. Opposed the Smuts government in the war. Even went underground for some time. Failed in the 1948 election but became M.P. in 1953 to live more or less happily ever after.

Has been threatening for a long time to retire (75 next November) but only, I suspect, in the hope of being begged to stay on and be rewarded with the position of Chief Whip or something similar. His only grudge in life this lack of "recognition" after having given his all for God and country. The proverbial man with a great future behind him.

More sympathy for her mother. Beautiful woman in her time. But her spirit broken at an early age, wilting in her husband's glamour; a meek shadow dragged along to Party rallies, the opening of Parliament, the inauguration of institutions for the aged, the blind, the maimed, or the mentally retarded, the opening of tunnels or boreholes. Wearing her perennial hat. Like the Queen Mother.

Admittedly, he has an imposing presence. Age has lent him dignity. Golden watch-chain across the bulge of his belly. White moustache and trimmed goatee. Silver hair. Black suit, even when he inspects his game farm. Somewhat too ruddy complexion owing to an increasing predilection for scotch. The bonhomie covering a will as hard as flint. The ruthless, unrelenting sense of Right and Wrong. Easy to see where Susan got her hangups. The almost sadistic righteousness with which he used to mete out corporal punishment to his daughters, even when they were eighteen or nineteen, and that for minor infringements like staying out after ten at night. The inexorable regularity of their household, determining even the Saturday night activities in the parental bedroom. Enough to scare her off for life. Like a young tree budding, then blighted by an untimely frost. Never quite candidly fruitful again.

They've been here since Saturday morning. Left today. Inauguration of a new industrial complex in Vanderbijlpark.

Yesterday afternoon the ladies withdrew in a very obvious manner, leaving me and Father-in-law rather ill-at-ease in the lounge. He refilled his glass. I sat fiddling with my pipe.

"Something I'd like to discuss with you, Ben." He drew courage from a large gulp of scotch. "I first thought it would be better left alone, but Susan seems to think you'll welcome a frank discussion."

"What's it about?" I asked, suspicious of her role in the matter.

"Well, you know, it's that photograph in the paper the other day."

I looked at him in silence.

"You see, well, how shall I put it?" Another gulp. "I suppose

209

every man has a right to his own opinion. But you know, a thing like that could become an embarrassment to someone in my position."

"Seems you'll always have the poor with you," I said.

"It's no joke, Ben. It is a grievous day when a man's family comes between him and his duty to his fatherland."

"Are you blaming me for trying to help those people?"

"No, no, of course not. I appreciate your concern for them. I've been doing the same thing all my life, sacrificing myself for my neighbours, be they black or white. But no member of our family has ever been seen in public with a kaffir woman before, Ben."

He went to refill his glass. Recognising the symptoms I tried to cut him short before he could warm up for a full-fledged speech.

"I'm glad you mentioned it, Father. Because I'd like to discuss it with you."

"Yes, that's what Susan told me."

"First, there's the matter of Emily Ngubene's house. Now that her husband has died she's no longer entitled to a home of her own."

He seemed relieved that the matter turned out to be so simple.

"Ben"—he made an expansive gesture, managing not to spill any whisky—"I promise you I'll take it up." Producing his little black notebook. "Just give me all the particulars. Soon as I'm back in the Cape next week—"

Short and sweet. I decided to press on, profiting from his magnanimous mood.

"Then there's the matter of Gordon Ngubene himself."

He stiffened. "What about him? I thought the case was closed?"

"I wish it was, Father. But the inquest didn't clear up half of what happened."

"Oh really?" He shifted uncomfortably.

I briefly brought him up to date, not only with the questions raised by the inquest but by the few facts I'd been able to uncover, insignificant as they were in themselves.

"There's nothing there that would stand up in a court of

law," he said almost smugly. He pulled out his pocket watch, studying it as if to calculate for how much longer I would be keeping him from his nap.

"I know that only too well," I said. "That's why I wanted to discuss it with you. We have no final, irrefutable evidence. But we have enough to indicate that something serious is being covered up."

"You're jumping to conclusions, Ben."

"I know what I'm talking about!" It came out more sharply than I'd intended. He started, and took another gulp of scotch.

"All right, I'm listening," he said, sighing. "Perhaps I can use my influence. But you'll have to convince me first."

"If they really have nothing to hide," I said, "why is the Special Branch going out of its way to intimidate me?"

The very word seemed to sober him up instantly, startling him from his complacency. "What's this about the Special Branch?"

I told him about the raid on my house, the tapping of my telephone, Stolz's straight warning.

"Ben," he said, suddenly sounding very formal. "I'm sorry, but I'd rather not have anything to do with this sort of thing." He rose from the settee and aimed for the door.

"So you're also frightened of them?"

"Don't be stupid! Why should I be frightened of anyone?" He glared at me. "But one thing I can tell you: if the Special Branch is mixed up with it they must have good reason. And then I prefer to stay out of it."

I managed to intercept him at the door. "Does that mean you're prepared to sit back and allow an injustice to be done?"

"Injustice?" His face grew purple. "Where's the injustice? I don't see it."

"What happened to Jonathan Ngubene? And how did Gordon die? Why are they doing their best to hush it up?"

"Ben, Ben, how can you side with the enemies of your people? Those who find in everything that happens ammunition to attack a freely elected government? Good heavens, man, at your age I expected something better from you. You've never been a hothead in your life."

"Isn't that enough reason for you to listen to me now?"

"Now come on." He had regained his composure. "Don't you know your own people then? We've always kept the commandments of the Lord. We're Christians, aren't we? Look, I'm not saying there aren't some exceptions among us. But it's ridiculous to start generalising about 'injustice' and so on."

"You're not prepared to help me then?"

"Ben, I told you." He was shuffling his feet uneasily. "If you'd come to me with something clear-cut and beyond all doubt, I would have been the first to take it up. But a bunch of vague suspicions and insinuations and bad feelings won't get you anywhere." He sniffed, annoyed. "Injustice! If you want to talk about injustice, then look at what our people have suffered. How many of us were thrown in jail in the Forties just because this land was more important to us than to be drawn into England's war – the same English who used to oppress us?"

"We had a freely elected government then, too, didn't we? Led by an Afrikaner."

"You call Smuts an Afrikaner?!"

"Now you're avoiding the issue," I reminded him.

"It's you who started talking about injustice. You, a man who teaches history at school. You ought to be ashamed of yourself, man. Now that we have at long last come to power in our own land."

"Now we're free to do to others what they used to do to us?"

"What are you talking about, Ben?"

"What would you do if you were a black man in this country today, Father?"

"You amaze me," he said contemptuously. "Don't you realise what the government is doing for the blacks? One of these days the whole bloody lot of them will be free and independent in their own countries. And then you have the nerve to talk about injustice!" He put a trembling, paternal hand on my shoulder, skilfully manoeuvring me out of the way so he could slip past into the passage on his way to the bedroom. "You give it another good think, Ben," he called back. "We've got nothing to be ashamed of before the eyes of the world, my boy."

Now I know it's hopeless to expect any help from him. Not because he is malicious or obtuse; not even because he is afraid. Simply because he is unable to consider, even for a moment, the merest possibility that I may be right. His benevolence, his dour Christianity, his firm belief in the rectitude of his people: these, tonight, are a much greater obstacle to me than any enemy who squarely opposes me.

5

It was a winter of fits and starts.

Nothing came of Henry Maphuna's complaint about the rape of his sister by her employer. Since the man had already been found innocent and discharged by the court there was no way of reopening the case. Dan Levinson suggested two alternatives: if the girl was prepared to testify that she had consented to intercourse a new charge could be laid under the Immorality Act; otherwise a civil action for damages could be brought. The family promptly dismissed the Immorality suggestion as it would bring disgrace upon Henry's sister. And damages were irrelevant. What they required was to have her name cleared and the culprit brought to justice. The outcome was, perhaps, predictable; still, it came as a shock to Ben when the aged mother arrived at his home to ask for help. Two nights before, taking the law into his own hands, Henry had gone to the house of his sister's ex-employer in Lower Houghton and bashed in the man's skull. Now he was in custody on a murder charge.

Back to Dan Levinson, smoothly groomed behind his imposing desk, radiating the virility one might associate with an ad for a sportsman's deodorant. Once again the parade of lissome blondes with files or messages or cups of coffee.

That was only one of the cases and causes Ben had to find time for. Melanie's prediction had come true: during those

213

winter months more and more strangers turned up on his doorstep to ask for help. People looking for jobs in the city and having trouble with reference books and official stamps. (Those magic words: *Permitted to be in the prescribed area of Johannesburg in terms of section 10 (1) (b) of Act No 25 of 1945 . . .*) It was easy enough to refer them to Stanley; and those he couldn't deal with personally were passed on to some fixer in the townships. There were others who had been evicted from their homes either because they'd fallen in arrears with the rent or because they had no permit to live in the area. Men prosecuted because they had brought their families from some distant homeland. An old widow whose sixteen year old son had been charged with "terrorism" when, sent to buy milk, he'd been arrested by police in search of youngsters who had set fire to a school elsewhere in Soweto an hour before. Countless others who reported that their fathers or brothers or sons had been "picked up" days or weeks or months before and were still being held incommunicado. Some, released without charge, returning with tales of assault and torture. A young couple, white man and coloured girl, who came to enquire whether Ben could arrange for them to get married. A venerable old father who complained that after he'd given his daughter away in marriage the man had refused to pay the *lobola* imposed by tribal custom. Some of the cases were shocking; others quite ludicrous. And in between the genuine supplicants there was a steady stream of chancers and common beggars.

In the beginning they came one by one, at intervals of a week or more. Later hardly a day went by without some appeal for help. They came in twos, in threes, in droves. More than once Ben felt reluctant to return home after school, dreading the new demands inevitably awaiting him. And Susan was threatening to acquire a dog to put an end to the throng in her backyard.

The very extent of the responsibilities imposed on him – and the impossibility of withdrawing once he'd offered to help the first few – was threatening to wear him down. There were symptoms of an ulcer developing. He was beginning to neglect his school duties. His manner with the pupils became more abrupt and there were fewer of them visiting him during the interval to chat or ask for his advice. If he had had enough time, if there hadn't been so many other worries, he might have coped. But all the while, ever since the day Stolz had come back to him, there was the awareness of being watched, of acting against invisible obstacles opposing him every inch of the way.

Often it happened so imperceptibly that he found it impossible to determine a starting point or a turning point. But at some moment, however subtly it was introduced, there must have been such a series of "firsts": the first time his phone was tapped; the first time his mail was tampered with; the first time an unknown car followed him to town; the first time a stranger was posted opposite his house to check on whoever arrived or left; the first time the phone rang in the middle of the night, with nothing on the other side but heavy breathing and a mirthless chuckle; the first time a friend informed Ben: "You know, I had a visitor last night who kept on asking questions about you——"

In between were brighter days. Stanley returned from Botswana with a new affidavit signed by Wellington Phetla: having left the country the boy was prepared to tell the full story of his arrest with Jonathan and the time they'd spent in detention together. Stanley had also traced a couple of Wellington's comrades who'd been willing to corroborate his evidence in writing. The news he brought of Gordon's second son, Robert, was less encouraging. When Stanley had found him he'd been on the point of leaving for a military camp in Mozambique; he'd been adamant that he wouldn't return unless he could do so with a gun in his hand.

But the despondency about Robert was offset by something else Stanley reported soon after his return. For the first time, he announced, they seemed to be on the verge of a real breakthrough: he'd traced an old cleaner working in the police mortuary and this man had told him that on the morning of the autopsy Captain Stolz had handed him a bundle of clothes with instructions to burn it.

And in Soweto the black lawyer Julius Nqakula was quietly and persistently going his way, rounding up his old clients to take down statements on Jonathan and Gordon. Even the nurse who had lost her nerve after telling them about Jonathan's spell in hospital was persuaded to sign a new affidavit. And all these bits and pieces Stanley brought to Ben for safekeeping in the hidden compartment of his tools cupboard.

There were setbacks too. Only two days after signing her new statement the nurse was detained by the Special Branch. Julius Nqakula himself was arrested late in August when, contravening the terms of his banning order, he visited his sister in Mamelodi. It meant a year's imprisonment, which Stanley accepted with surprising resignation:

"Old Julius won't give away a thing, don't worry. And anyway he's been hitting the bottle too hard lately. This year in the chooky will sober him up nicely."

"A year in jail just for visiting his sister?"

"That's the chance he took, lanie. Julius will be the last to complain."

"Don't you think the real reason for his arrest was that they found out he was helping us?"

"So what?" — If there was one expression which summarised the full reality of Stanley Makhaya it was the way in which he used to say *So what?* — "Lanie, you're not getting guilt complexes now, are you? That's a luxury only Liberals can afford. Forget it." A blow between the shoulder-blades sent Ben stumbling. "Julius will be back, man. All refreshed by his little spell in the deep-freeze."

"How can we just shrug off a man we've been working with?"

"Who said we shrugging him off? Best way of remembering a man, lanie, is to carry on fighting. We doing it for Emily, right?"

Emily also came to Ben's house late one afternoon. He was exhausted after dealing with the day's quota of visitors. It was Sunday to boot. Susan had gone to Pretoria to spend the day with Suzette and Chris, something she had been doing more and more frequently lately. Johan was out with some friends. For once, Ben tried to ignore the knocking. But when it persisted, leaving him no choice but to trudge wearily down the passage, he found Emily on the stoep. Behind her in the shadow of a pillar, stood a strange black man in a brown striped suit. Thirtyish, pleasant face, but very tense, looking round nervously all the time as if expecting invisible enemies suddenly to materialise.

"This is Johnson Seroke, Baas," Emily said meekly. "The man I told you about, the man of the letters."

In his study, the curtains drawn, Ben asked: "Do you really work for the Security Police, Johnson?"

"I had no choice," the man said with smouldering hostility.

"Yet you smuggled out letters to Emily?"

"What can you do if a man asks you and he's in trouble?" Johnson Seroke was sitting on the edge of his chair, pulling the fingers of his left hand one by one, cracking the joints, over and over.

"There is big trouble for Johnson if they find out, Baas," said Emily.

"Johnson, what do you know about Gordon?" Ben asked.

"I saw very little of him." Johnson spoke in a clipped, studied way.

"But you did talk to him from time to time?"

"He gave me the letters."

"When was the last time you saw him?"

"Just before he died."

"Were you there when they interrogated him?"

"No." He went through all five fingers of his left hand again. "I was three offices away. But I saw him when they carried him down the passage."

"When was that?"

"The Thursday. The twenty-fourth February."

"Do you remember what time it was?"

"It was late in the afternoon."

"What did he look like?"

"I could not see. He was limp."

With an effort Ben asked: "Was he dead?"

"No. He made a sound."

"Did he say anything you could make out?"

"Nothing."

"What did you do?"

"What could I do? I was there in the office. I pretended to be busy. They took him down to the cells."

"Did they say anything about it afterwards?"

Johnson Seroke jumped up and came to the desk, leaning forward on outstretched arms. The whites of his eyes were yellowish, with small red veins showing. "If you tell anybody I was here today I shall deny it. See?"

"I understand. I promise." He gazed up at the man leaning on his desk, upset by the look of panic in the bloodstained eyes. "No one will know you've been to see me."

"It was just because Emily asked me."

"I tell him the Baas is good to us," said the big woman uneasily.

"You never saw Gordon again?" Ben insisted.

"I was there when they took the body away to the morgue."

"When?"

"Next day."

"You sure you don't know anything about the night in between, Johnson?"

"How should I know? I keep away from such things when they happen."

"Why do you stay with the police?" Ben asked point-blank. "You don't really belong there."

"How can I go away? I love my family."

After they had left, the nervous young man and the large lumbering woman, Ben made brief notes of their conversation for his file.

The next morning, in plain daylight, his study was burgled while he was away at school and Susan in town. As far as they could make out nothing was stolen, but his books had been plucked from the shelves and the contents of his drawers emptied on the floor, the chair cushions ripped open with a sharp object.

"It's this lot of good-for-nothings swarming round the house all day," Susan said indignantly. "If you don't put an end to it soon something drastic will happen. And it'll be your own fault. You can't be that blind, Ben! Don't you see the writing on the wall?"

He didn't reply. He waited until she'd taken a sedative and gone to lie down before he hurried to the garage. But the tools cupboard was untouched.

6 September. Melanie off to Rhodesia last night, via Malawi. At least, that is the official version. Really going to Lusaka. For which she'll have to use her British passport. I warned her it was asking for trouble. She shrugged it off: "It's the only favour my mother has ever done me. So I use it when it suits me."

When her South African passport expired a month ago she was worried that it might not be renewed. In the end there was no hitch. Got it last Friday. Laughingly showed me the new photograph inside. She thinks it's hideous; I rather like it. She gave me one to cherish like a schoolboy in her absence. Only ten days, she tried to reassure me. But a strange emptiness surrounds me, as if she's left me wholly unprotected.

Over the weekend a new bit of information from her contact at the Square. It appears that he's responsible for serving supper to the detainees. On third February he was instructed that in future only white warders were to be admitted to Gordon's cell. That was the day of his "headache" and "toothache". Next morning Dr Herzog came.

Even more important: when the warders went down to the cells on the evening of twenty-fourth February he saw people at Gordon's door. Was told by one of his black colleagues: "The man is sick, the doctor is with him."

So my suspicion is confirmed. Herzog knows much more than he's prepared to tell. But who's going to get it from him?

In today's sudden desolation I drove round to see Phil Bruwer. Playing the piano when I arrived. Still that air of having slept in his clothes. Smelling of wine and tobacco and farting. Overjoyed to see me. Cold day, we played chess in front of the fire. He lit his pipe with long twigs kept in an iron pot specially for that purpose.

"How's the Sleuth?" he asked, his eyes twinkling under the brushwood of his brows.

"Making some headway, Prof. I suppose Melanie told you what she heard from the warder?"

"Mm. Like to have a game with me?"

Amazing for how long we went on playing without saying a word, yet without feeling isolated. Surrounded by those thousands of books. Cats sleeping on the rug in front of the fire. A wholeness about it all. That's the only word I can really think of to describe it. It seemed so *whole*, so unlike all the bits and pieces of my jigsaw.

I'd never been so pertinently conscious of it before, but when I said it I immediately recognised it, so it must have been there all along, like the inside of a jacket you wear every day:

"You know what really frightens me, Prof?" He quietly stared at me through the smoke of his pipe, waiting for me to explain. "Here we're going on gathering our bits of information. Sometimes it seems to come to a standstill, yet all the time we're making progress, step by step. But suppose one day the picture is complete and we know everything that happened to him down to the smallest detail – then I'll still not know anything about his life."

"Aren't you asking too much?" he said. "What can one man really know about another? Even two people who live together and love one another. I've often thought about it, you know—" The fart sounded almost reassuring when it came. "My wife. Our marriage. All right, I was years older than she, and I suppose if you really think about it the marriage was doomed right from the beginning. But I still thought, at the time, that we knew each other. I was absolutely convinced of it. Until she took her things and walked out on me. Then, for the first time, I realised I'd been living beside another person for practically twenty-four hours a day without knowing a thing about her. Same with the chaps who were in that German camp with me: shared everything, got really close. Then something would happen, the most paltry little thing, and you would discover that you really were total strangers, each one desperately alone in the world. You're on your own, Ben. All the time."

"Perhaps it is because one tends to take things for granted," I said, unconvinced by his words. "But as far as Gordon is concerned, here I'm actually working on him day and night. It's not a passive relationship, I'm actively involved with him every moment of my life. But when all is said and done, what have I really got? Facts, facts, details. What does it tell me about *him*, this man, this Gordon Ngubene who must exist somewhere behind all the facts? And what about all the people flocking to me for help? What do I know about them? We talk to each other, we touch each other, yet we're strangers from different worlds.

220

It's like people on two trains passing each other. You hear a shout, you shout back, but it's just sound, you have no idea of what the other man has said."

"At least you heard him shout."

"That's not much comfort."

"Who knows?" He moved one of his bishops. "Most people have got so used to their passing trains that they don't even look up any more when they hear the shout."

"Sometimes I think I envy them."

His eyes shone with malicious glee. "Matter of choice," he said. "You can also stop asking questions if you want to, can't you? All you need to do is accept that 'such things happen'."

"Is one really free to choose – or are you chosen?"

"You think there's much difference? Did Adam and Eve choose to eat the apple? Or did the Devil choose for them? Or had God willed it like that from the beginning? I mean, He may have figured it out this way: If that tree looked just like all the others they might never notice it; but by placing His ban on it He made damned sure they would have a go at it. Perhaps that was why God could sleep so peacefully and contentedly on the seventh day."

"At least, I assume, they knew what they were doing."

"Don't *you*?"

"I once thought I knew. I was convinced I was going into it with my eyes wide open. But I don't think I expected it to be quite so dark around me."

Without answering directly, as if suddenly struck by a new idea, Bruwer pushed back his chair and climbed a small step-ladder in search of a book on a top shelf. From there he said over his shoulder: "You'll know more about it than I do, it's your subject. But don't you agree that the meaning, the true meaning, of eras like those of Pericles or the Medici lay in the fact that a whole society, in fact a whole civilisation, seemed to be moving in the same gear and in the same direction?" It was accompanied by the familiar and reassuring crackle. "In such an era there is almost no need to make your own decisions: your society does it for you and you find yourself in complete harmony with it. On the other hand there are times like ours, when history hasn't settled on a firm new course yet. Then every man is on his own. Each has to find his own definitions, and each man's freedom threatens that of all the others. What is the result? Terrorism. And I'm not referring only to the actions of the trained terrorist but also to those of an organised state whose institutions endanger one's essential humanity." He resumed his search. "Ah, here it is." When he came down he handed me the book he'd found. Merleau-Ponty. Unfortunately in French, which I cannot read. He seemed disappointed but I promised him I would try to find an English copy.

And all the time, day by day, there was the awareness of being surveyed. Going shopping in a supermarket of a Saturday morning there would be the sudden recognition of a checkered sports jacket in the crowd: Lieutenant Venter with the friendly, boyish face and curly hair; or Vosloo, the squarely built man with the dark complexion; or Koch, the tall athletic one with the large hands. Usually it was no more than a glimpse, often too brief to feel really sure that it had in fact been one of them. Perhaps it was his imagination. One reached a stage where one was expecting them everywhere, even in church.

The letters in his mailbox, the envelopes slit open as if whoever had opened them had been too contemptuous even to bother about sealing them again – unless, of course, that, too, was done deliberately so he would *know* his mail was read by others. There never was anything of real importance: who would possibly send him letters endangering the security of the State? What annoyed him was the feeling, like the day in his study when they had searched his box of chess-pieces and the bowl of polished stones, that nothing belonging to him was treated with respect; nothing was sacred or private to them. "It's like living in an aquarium," he once noted on a page torn from an exercise book, "your every move scrutinised by eyes watching you through glass and water, surveying even the motion of your gills as you breathe."

Or elsewhere (dated 14 September): "It's only when you realise that you're being watched like this that you learn to look at yourself with new eyes. You learn to judge differently, to discover what is really essential about your needs and what may be discarded. Perhaps one should be grateful! – It teaches you to purify yourself, to rid yourself of whatever is redundant, to rely less on your own strength or judgement and more on grace. Everything permitted you is pure grace. For any moment of the day or night they may decide to pounce. Even in your sleep you are exposed. And the mere fact that, from day to day, from one hour to the next, you can say: *This day, this hour is still granted me* — becomes an experience so intensely marvellous that you learn to praise the Lord in a new way. Is this the way a leper feels as he takes leave of his limbs one by one? Or a man suffering from a terminal cancer? Oh it is a dry season. But infinitely precious in its own way."

He didn't always react so positively. Most of the notes from those months talk about depression, worry, doubt, uncertainty. Tension at home, with Susan. Quarrels on the telephone, with Suzette. Tiffs with colleagues.

It was possible to get used to those episodes of petty intimidation which recurred regularly, to learn to live with them, even to get bored by them. But there were others too. Finding a hammer-and-sickle painted on his door one morning. On another day, as he got into his car to drive home after school, the discovery of all four tyres cut to shreds. The anonymous telephone calls, often at two or three o'clock at night. Susan's nerves were giving in, leading to hysterical outbursts or bouts of crying that left both of them dismayed.

What Ben found most unsettling was to be confronted, in his class-room, by large printed slogans on the blackboard, inanities which sent sniggers through the class. Somehow his colleagues also knew about it; and once, in the presence of all the other staff members, Koos Cloete asked scathingly: "How can a teacher expect his pupils to look up to him unless his own conduct is beyond reproach?"

18 September. Noticed Johan looking dishevelled after school. Shirt torn, one black eye, lips swollen. At first he refused to say anything. In the end I managed to wheedle it from him. Couple of Standard Nines, he said. Been taunting him for weeks, calling his father a nigger lover. This morning he couldn't take it any more. Did a good demolition job but there were too many of them. Worst of all: while it was happening one of the teachers came past and pretended not to see.

He still wasn't intimidated. "Dad, if they start again tomorrow I'm going to beat the shit out of them."

"What's the use, Johan?"

"I won't have them insulting you."

"It doesn't hurt *me*."

Johan spoke with difficulty because of his swollen mouth, but he was too angry to be quiet: "I tried to reason with them, but they wouldn't listen. They don't even know what you're trying to do."

"You sure *you* know?" I had to ask him, however hard it was.

He turned his head so that his only good eye could look squarely at me. "Yes, I know," he said impetuously. "And only if you stop doing it I'll have reason to be ashamed of you."

He appeared very embarrassed by what he'd blurted out. Perhaps I shouldn't have asked. And I didn't want to add to his discomfort by thanking him. We sat staring straight ahead while I drove us home. But in that one startling, wonderful moment I knew it was worthwhile after all: if only for the sake of hearing those words from my son.

As we stopped beside the house he looked at me again, winking with his good eye: "Better not tell Mum what it was all about. I don't think she'll like it."

Of a completely different order was the shock Ben received when he returned to Dan Levinson's office for a consultation about one of the people who had come to him for help. Levinson was as brusque and as busy as always, but what upset Ben was the visitors he had with him – the two advocates who had acted in the inquest on Gordon's death, De Villiers on behalf of the family, Louw for the police.

"You have met, haven't you?" Levinson said.

"Of course." Ben greeted De Villiers heartily, then turned to Louw with a scowl. To his surprise the latter was very cordial. And the three lawyers spent another fifteen minutes chatting and joking before the advocates left.

"I never thought I'd meet Louw in your office," Ben remarked uneasily.

"Why not? We've known each other for years."

"But – after Gordon's inquest—?"

Levinson laughed, patting him on the shoulder in a comradely gesture. "Good heavens, man, we're all pros. You don't expect us to mix our jobs with our lives, do you? Well, what is it today? Incidentally, did you get my last account?"

6

Early in October four or five of Ben's colleagues were called in by the Special Branch and questioned about him. How long they'd known him, what they knew about his politics, his activities and interests, his association with Gordon Ngubene; whether they were aware of his "regular" visits to Soweto; whether they ever visited him and, if so, whether they had ever met blacks in his home, etc.

Young Viviers was the first to come back to Ben to tell him all about his interview. "But I told them straight they were wasting their time, Oom Ben. I said quite a few things, I think, which they should have been told a long time ago."

"I appreciate it, Viviers. But—"

The young man was too agitated to wait for him to finish. "Then they started asking questions about myself too. Whether I was 'co-operating' with you. What I knew about the ANC and so on. In the end they became all fatherly and said to me: 'Mr Viviers, you come from a good Afrikaans family. We can see you have strong feelings about things. Well, it's a free country and every man is entitled to his own views. But there's one thing you've got to realise: it's people like you the Communists are looking for. You don't realise how easy it is to play into their hands. Before you know where you are, they're using you for their own purposes.'"

"I'm sorry, Viviers," Ben said. "I didn't want you to get involved too."

"Why should you be sorry? If they think they can intimidate me they have a surprise coming." Adding, with a smile of satisfaction, "Just as well it was me they called in for questioning. Some of the others might have said some nasty things about you, I know what they're like."

But soon, of course, it became known that Viviers had not been the only one. Ben had become used to hearing from friends that discreet inquiries had been made about him. But the deliberately organised way in which it had taken place this time, and the fact that his colleagues had been drawn into it, was a blow to him; as was the suspicion that the whole move had been arranged in such a way as to make sure that it would reach his ears. He was not worried by the thought that anything of significance might have come to light in the process: what dismayed him was that there was nothing he could do about it, no countermove he could possibly make.

The other teachers involved in the interrogation did not dismiss it as lightly as Viviers had. To the jovial Carelse it had been, like nearly everything else in his carefree life, a huge joke. He openly talked about it in the common-room, finding in the episode ammunition for weeks of unmalicious and inane joking: "How's the terrorist this morning?" – "I say, Oom Ben, can't you lend me one of your bombs? I'd like to blow up the Standard Sevens" – "How's the weather in Moscow today?"

A few of the others began to ignore him more pointedly than before. Without looking at him Ferreira, of English, hinted about "some people who are going to burn their fingers".

Koos Cloete broached it, in his usual aggressive manner, in the common room at tea-time:

"In all the years I've spent teaching it has never yet been necessary for the Security Police to come and discuss one of my teachers with me. I've seen it coming, mind you. But I never thought it would actually come to this."

"I'm quite prepared to sort out the whole matter with you," Ben said, finding it difficult to restrain his anger. "I have nothing to be ashamed of."

"Anything can be twisted to make a good impression, Mr Du

Toit. All I can say to you at this stage is that the Department has very strict regulations about this sort of thing. And you know it as well as I do."

"If you will allow me half an hour in your office, I'll explain everything."

"Is there something you don't want your colleagues to hear then?"

Ben had to draw his breath in deeply to retain his self-control. "I'm prepared to tell you anything you want to know. Anywhere. If you really are worried about me."

"It's more important to make it out with your own conscience," said Cloete. "Before you become an embarrassment to the school."

Not wanting to say anything untoward, Ben went back to his own classroom. Thank God there was a free period ahead. For a long time he sat unmoving, pulling at his pipe, staring across the rows of empty desks. Slowly his anger abated. Clarity returned. And, with it, the knowledge of what to do. It was so obvious that he found it hard to understand why he hadn't thought about it before.

Early in the afternoon he went back to John Vorster Square. In the parking garage in the basement he took the automatic lift. He wrote Colonel Viljoen's name on the form the guard pushed towards him. Ten minutes later he was back in front of the same desk where he had been so many months before. This time Viljoen was alone; but even so, Ben remained conscious of people appearing noiselessly and invisibly in the door behind his back, staring at him, disappearing into the corridors. He had no idea of where in the big blue building Stolz was; perhaps he wasn't even there today. Still he was aware of the man's presence. His dark staring eyes. The thin line of the white scar on his cheekbone. And somewhere behind this awareness, with the sudden violence of a blow in the solar plexus, the memory of Gordon's face and frail body, his hat pressed against his chest with two hands. *If it was me, all right. But he is my child and I must know. God is my witness today: I cannot stop before I know what happened to him and where they buried him. His body belongs to me. It is my son's body.*

The amiable, tanned, middle-aged face opposite him. The

grey crew-cut. Leaning back in his chair balanced on two legs. "What can I do for you, Mr Du Toit? I do feel honoured."

"Colonel, I thought it was high time we had a frank discussion."

"I'm very glad to hear that. What is it you would like to discuss?"

"I think you know very well."

"Please be more specific." The hint of a small muscle flickering in his cheek.

"I'm not sure how you people operate. But you must be aware of the fact that your men have been waging a campaign of intimidation against me for months on end."

"You must be exaggerating, Mr Du Toit."

"You know that they searched my house, don't you?"

"Simple routine. I trust they were polite?"

"Of course they were. That's not the point. What about all the other things? Questioning my colleagues about me."

"Why should that upset you? I'm sure you don't have anything to hide."

"It's not that, Colonel. It's – well, you know what people are like. They start talking. All sorts of rumours are being spread. One's family has to bear the brunt."

A quiet chuckle. "Mr Du Toit, I'm no doctor but it seems to me what you need is a good holiday." Adding, with the smallest hint of an undertone: "Just to get away from it all for a while."

"There are other things too," Ben persisted, refusing to be put off. "My telephone. My mail."

"What about your telephone and your mail?"

"Don't tell me you're not aware of it, Colonel."

"Of what?"

Ben could feel a throbbing in his temple. "When I come into my classroom, I find insults scrawled all over the board. There was a hammer-and-sickle painted on my front door. I've had my car tyres cut to bits. Night after night we're pestered by anonymous phone calls."

The Colonel allowed his chair to tilt forward, back on the floor. He leaned over. "Have you reported all this to the police?"

"What's the use?"

228

"That is what they're there for, isn't it?"

"All I want to know, Colonel, is why don't you leave me in peace?"

"Now wait, wait a minute, Mr Du Toit. You're not trying to blame me for it, are you?"

He had no choice but to persist: "Colonel, why is it so important to you people to stop my inquiries about Gordon Ngubene?"

"Is that what you're doing?"

It seemed as if he would never be allowed an opening. And yet he had persuaded himself that with this man, unlike all the others, he could be frank; and that he would get an equally frank reply. He'd thought that they would speak the same language. For a while he sat staring at the framed photograph of the two blond boys, standing at an angle on the desk between them.

"Colonel," he said, suddenly impetuous, "doesn't it haunt you sometimes? Don't you wake up at night about what happened to Gordon?"

"All the available evidence was placed before a competent magistrate who examined everything in depth and gave his finding."

"What about the evidence that was deliberately kept from the court?"

"Well, now! Mr Du Toit, if you possess any information that may be of use to us I trust you won't hesitate to discuss it with me."

Ben looked at him, rigid on his straight-backed chair.

The Colonel leaned over more closely towards him, his tone darkening: "Because if there are facts you are deliberately hiding from us, Mr Du Toit – if you give us reason to believe that you may be involved in activities that may be dangerous both to yourself and to us – then I can foresee some problems."

"Is that a threat, Colonel?" he asked, his jaws very tight.

Col Viljoen smiled. "Let's call it a warning," he said. "A friendly warning. You know, sometimes one does something with the best of intentions, but because you're so deeply involved you may not realise all the implications."

"You mean I'm being used by the Communists?" He found

229

it difficult to tone down the sarcasm.

"Why do you say that?"

"That's what your men told one of my colleagues."

Viljoen made a brief note on a sheet of ruled paper lying on the desk before him. From where he sat Ben couldn't decipher it; but more than anything else that had happened during the interview it made his heart contract.

"So you really have nothing to tell me, Colonel?"

"I was looking forward to hearing something from *you*, Mr Du Toit."

"Then I won't waste your time any longer."

Ben got up. When he came to the door the Colonel said quietly behind him: "I'm sure we'll see each other again, Mr Du Toit."

That night, when they were all asleep, except for Johan who was still studying in his room, three shots were fired from the street into Ben's living-room. The TV screen was shattered, but fortunately there was no further damage. He reported it to the police, but the culprit was never found. The doctor had to be called to attend to Susan.

7

He was diffident about going to the press, even after discussing it with Melanie.

"I don't think you have any choice left, Ben," she said. "There was a time when you had to keep it as private as possible. You and Stanley and I, all three of us. But there's a point of no return. If you keep it to yourself now they may try to silence you altogether. Your safety lies in making it known. And if you really want to do something for Gordon you'll just have to use the press."

"And how long before they start using *me*?"

"The final choice remains your own."

"I'm sure your paper would love the scoop!" he said in a sudden gust of aggressiveness.

"No, Ben," she said quietly. "I know I'm being a very bad journalist now but I don't want it to break in my paper. Go to an Afrikaans paper. That's the only place where it will really carry any weight. You know what the government thinks of the 'English press'."

Even at that point he still tried to postpone it by first making an appointment to see George Ahlers, the company director his sister Helena had married.

The office, the size of a ballroom, was on the top floor of an ultramodern building overlooking most of the city. Heavy armchairs, low glass table, mahogany desk with a writing surface in calfskin. Long boardroom table surrounded by fake-antique chairs; cut-glass water carafes and blotters in leather frames at every seat. Elephant's-ear and Delicious Monster in large ceramic pots. The whole room dominated by the lordly presence of George Ahlers: large-limbed and athletic, well over six feet tall, in navy suit and pale blue shirt, a tie proclaiming dazzling good taste. He had a balding head with a fringe of longish grey hair over his ears. Ruddy face. Cigar and signet ring.

In his worn brown suit Ben felt like a poor relation coming to ask a favour – a feeling aggravated by George's show of urbanity.

"Well, well, Ben, haven't seen you in years. Have a seat. Cigar?"

"No thank you, George."

"And how's Susan?"

"She's fine. I've come on business."

"Really? Did you inherit a fortune or what?"

After he had explained the matter George's joviality was visibly dampened. "Ben, you know I'd just love to help you. Frightful story. But what can I possibly do?"

"I thought big businessmen like you might have access to the government. So I wondered—"

"Your father-in-law is an M.P., isn't he?"

"He's already given me the cold shoulder. And I need someone with contacts right at the top."

"It's hopeless, Ben. You're making a sad mistake if you seriously think big business in this country has an open door to the government. In an industrial country like the U.S. maybe. But not here. There's a one-way street running from politics to business. Not the other way." He blew out a small cloud of cigar smoke, relishing it. "Even supposing I can approach a Cabinet Minister — just for argument's sake — what do you think will happen? In my position I'm dependent on permits, concessions, goodwill." With perfect timing he tapped the ash from his cigar into a crystal ashtray. "Once I get involved in this sort of thing it's tickets." He changed into a more comfortable reclining position. "But tell me, when are you and Susan coming over to see us? We've got so much to talk about."

6 October. Today: Andries Lourens. One of the most pleasant people I've ever had dealings with. I went to him on Melanie's advice, because of his paper's outspoken progressiveness and his own reputation for fairness and clearheadedness. Not always popular with the establishment, but they pay attention to him. Even knowing all this in advance I was still pleasantly surprised by the man. Obviously up to his neck in work, a weekend edition on the point of going to press, but he instantly made time for me. Spent more than an hour together in the topsy-turvy office clearly meant for work, not comfort. Cigarette stubs all over the place. Bundles of cuttings and small typed or handwritten sheets hanging from metal clamps or washing-pegs on a board behind him.

When I told him what I was working on, handing him the summary I'd compiled last night, he showed deep and immediate interest. Lines between the eyes; much older, seen from close by like that, than one had expected. Sallow complexion. Perspiration on his forehead. Candidate for a coronary?

But just as I was beginning to feel hopeful he suddenly shook his head, moving his hand backwards through his black hair, looking up with his keen but tired eyes:

"Mr Du Toit . . . I can't say it really comes as a shock to me.

Do you know how much similar information we've had these last few months? Sometimes it seems as if the whole country has gone berserk."

"It's in your power to help put an end to it, Mr Lourens. You reach thousands of readers."

"Do you know how many readers we've been losing lately? Our circulation figures—" He reached out towards a crammed wire-basket on the corner of his desk, but allowed his arm to drop back almost hopelessly. "Let me put it this way," he said. "I know exactly how much injustice is happening all around us. But to make a drastic move at the wrong moment will simply have the opposite effect from the one we want. Our readers are already accusing the Afrikaans press of turning against them. We've got to take them with us, Mr Du Toit, not estrange them."

"So – you'd rather not do anything about it?"

"Mr Du Toit." His hand resting on my small pile of papers. "If I publish this story tomorrow I may just as well shut up shop the next day."

"I don't believe it."

"Can't you see what's happening in the country?" he asked wearily. "The beginnings of urban terrorism. Russia and Cuba on our borders. Even the U.S. ready to stab us in the back."

"And so we must learn to live with this disgrace in our midst, just because it's ours?"

"Not living with it by condoning it. But by learning to have more understanding. By awaiting a more opportune moment. And then to start putting it right from the inside, step by step."

"And in the meantime the Gordon Ngubenes must go on dying one after the other?"

"Don't get me wrong, Mr Du Toit. But you must realise" – how many times have I heard those words before? – "you must realise it's fatal to plunge in right now. I mean, try to think about it objectively. What other party in this country is in a position to lead us peacefully into the future? I'm not suggesting for a moment that everything is as it should be inside the National Party. But it's the only vehicle we have for achieving something. We cannot afford to put any more ammunition into the hands of our enemies."

233

And much more in the same vein. All of it, I believe, with the sincerest of intentions. More and more I realise that my real problem is benevolence, Christianity, understanding, decency. Not open hostility: one can work out a strategy to counter that. But this thick, heavy porridge of good intentions on the part of people obstructing you 'for your own good', trying to 'protect you against yourself'.

"Please, Mr Du Toit," he said in the end. "Do me one favour: don't take that file to the English press. That will be a sure way to thwart your own cause and destroy yourself. It's a kiss of death. I promise you, it's for your own good. And I give you my word: as soon as the climate improves I shall personally come back to you."

He didn't go to Melanie's paper. She herself was against it – in case anyone had seen Ben with her in the past. It would be too easy to put two and two together; and she desperately wanted to protect him.

The Sunday paper was not only willing but eager to publish the story. Front page. And most obliging, promising not to give any hint of their source. It would be signed by one of their senior reporters, as the result of "the paper's own private investigation".

The report certainly caused a stir that Sunday. But not all the repercussions were predictable. Within days the Department of Justice instituted a claim for libel against the newspaper. An interdict was requested by the Commissioner of Police for the source of the information to be divulged; the reporter, Richard Harrison, received a summons, and when he refused to name his informant in court he was sentenced to a year's imprisonment.

Ben, too, did not escape the immediate consequences. It was obvious that no one close to him had much doubt about his hand in the story. Already on the Monday morning a cutting of the report was stuck to his blackboard. Suzette telephoned. Two of his co-elders in church visited him to drop a hint that the time had come for him to resign from the church council. And the Rev Bester did not offer much more than token resistance when, later in the week, he did just that.

By the Wednesday his principal went so far as to summon him to his office: for once, it seemed, the matter was too serious to be dealt with in the common room. On his desk lay the front page of the previous Sunday's paper. And without any preliminaries Cloete asked:

"I assume you are familiar with this?"

"Yes, I read it."

"I didn't ask whether you'd read it, Mr Du Toit. I want to know whether you had anything to do with it."

"What makes you think so?"

Mr Cloete was in no mood for evasiveness. "According to my information it was you who spilled the story in the English press."

"May I ask where you got your information?"

"How much did they pay you, I wonder?" Cloete panted in his asthmatic way. "Thirty silver pieces, Mr Du Toit?"

"That's a disgusting thing to say!"

"To think that an Afrikaner should sell his soul like this!" Cloete went on, unable to restrain himself. "For a bit of money and some cheap publicity."

"Mr Cloete, I don't know what publicity you're talking about. My name isn't mentioned anywhere in the report. And as far as money is concerned, you're being libellous."

"You accuse me of being libellous?" For a moment Ben feared the principal would have an apoplexy. For several minutes Cloete sat wiping his perspiring face with a large white handkerchief. At last, in a smothered voice, he said: "I want you to regard this as a final warning, Mr Du Toit. The school cannot afford to keep political agitators on its staff."

The same afternoon he found the parcel in his mailbox. Intrigued, he looked at it from all sides, for he hadn't ordered anything and there was no birthday in the family in the near future. The postmark was too indistinct for him to decipher. The stamp was from Lesotho. Fortunately, just as he started opening it, he noticed a small length of wire protruding from the paper. And immediately he knew. He took the parcel to the police station. The next day they confirmed that it had been a bomb. No one was ever arrested in connection with it.

26 October. Stanley, late this afternoon, for the first time in weeks. Don't know how he manages to come and go unseen. Probably approaches through the yard of the back neighbours, scaling the fence. Not, I suppose, that it really matters.

Stanley's news: the old cleaner who'd told him about Gordon's clothes had disappeared. Just disappeared. A week ago already, and still no sign of him.

I was forced to draw up a balance sheet in my mind. On the one side, all the bits and pieces we'd assembled so far. Not an unimpressive list by any means – at first glance. But then the debit side. Isn't the price becoming too high? I'm not thinking of what I have to go through, worried and harassed and hounded day by day. But the *others*. Especially the others. Because, at least partly, it is through my involvement that they have to suffer.

The cleaner: "disappeared".

Dr Hassiem: banished to Pietersburg.

Julius Nqakula: in jail.

The nurse: detained.

Richard Harrison: sentenced to jail – even though he's going to appeal.

And who else? Who is next? Are all our names written on some secret list, ready to be ticked off as our time comes?

I wanted to "clean up" Gordon's name, as Emily had put it. But all I've done so far is to plunge other people into the abyss. Including Gordon? It's like a nightmare, when I wake up at night, wondering in a sweat: Suppose I'd never tried to intercede for him after they'd detained him – would he have survived then? Am I the leper spreading disease to whoever comes close enough?

And if I examine closely what we've gathered so laboriously over so many months: what does all our evidence *really* amount to? Much circumstantial evidence, oh certainly. Corroborating what we'd presumed or suspected in the beginning. But is there really anything quite indisputable? Let's assume for a moment it all points towards a crime that was committed. Even more specifically: a crime committed by Captain Stolz. Even then there is nothing, nothing final, nothing incontrovertible, nothing "beyond all reasonable doubt". There is only one person in the whole world who can tell the truth about Gordon's death, and that is Stolz himself. And he is untouchable, protected by the entire bulwark of his formidable system.

There was a time when I thought: *All right, Stolz, now it's you and me. Now I know my enemy. Now we can fight hand to hand, man to man.*

How naïve, how foolish of me.

Today I realise that this is the worst of all: that I can no longer single out my enemy and give him a name. I can't challenge him to a duel. What is set up against me is not a man, not even a group of people, but a thing, a something, a vague amorphous something, an invisible ubiquitous power that inspects my mail and taps my telephone and indoctrinates my colleagues and incites the pupils against me and cuts up the tyres of my car and paints signs on my door and fires shots into my home and send me bombs in the mail, a power that follows me wherever I go, day and night, day and night, frustrating me, intimidating me, playing with me according to rules devised and whimsically changed by itself.

So there is nothing I can really do, no effective countermove to execute, since I do not even know where my dark, invisible enemy is lurking or from where he will pounce next time. And at any moment, if it pleases him, he can destroy me. It all depends solely on his fancy. He may decide that he wanted only to scare me and that he is now tired of playing with me and that in future he'll leave me alone; or he may decide that this is only the beginning, and that he is going to push me until he can have his way with me. And where and when is that?

"I can't go on," I said to Stanley. "There's nothing I can do any more. I'm tired. I'm numb. All I want is some peace to regain my perspective and to find time for my family and myself again."

"Jeez, man, if you opt out now, it's exactly what they wanted all along, don't you see? Then you playing squarely into their hands."

"How do I know what they want? I know nothing any more. I don't *want* to know."

237

"Shit, I thought you had more guts than this." The shattering contempt in his deep voice. "Lanie, what you suffering now is what chaps like me suffer all our fucking lives, from the day we give our first shout to the day they dig us into the ground. Now you come and tell me you can't go on? Come again."

"What can I do then? Tell me."

"How d'you mean what can you do? Just keep on, don't quit. That's enough. If you survive – you want to bet on it? – there's a hell of a lot of others who going to survive with you. But if you sink now, it's a plain mess. You *got* to, man. You got to prove it."

"Prove what to whom?"

"Does it matter? To them. To yourself. To me. To every goddamn bloke who's going to die of natural causes in their hands unless you carry on." He was holding my two shoulders in his great hands, more furious than I'd ever seen him before, shaking me until my teeth were chattering. "You hear me? Lanie? You hear me? You got to, you bloody fucking bastard. You trying to tell me I been wasting all my time on you? I got a lot of money on you, lanie. And we sticking together, you and I. Okay? We gonna survive, man. I tell you."

8

31 October. A weekend decisive in its own mysterious manner – even though it had nothing to do with Gordon or with whatever I have been involved in these months. Was that the reason? All I know is that I jumped at it when Melanie so unexpectedly suggested it in the midst of last week's deep depression.

In the past I often went off for a weekend like this; even a full week if it was holiday-time. On my own, or with a group of schoolboys, or some good friends, occasionally with Johan. Susan never went with us. Doesn't like the veld. Even openly contemptuous about such "backveld" urges.

In the last few years I've never done so any more. Don't know why. So perhaps understandably Susan was annoyed when I broached it. ("I've arranged to go to the Magaliesberg this weekend," I said, as casually as possible. "With a friend, Professor Phil Bruwer. Hope you don't mind.")

"I thought you'd outgrown this childish urge of yours at last."

"It'll do me a world of good to get away for a while."

"Don't you think I'd like to get away too?"

"But you never cared for climbing or hiking or camping."

"I'm not talking about that either. We can go somewhere together."

"Why don't you spend the weekend with Suzette?"

She looked at me in silence. It shocked me to see how old her eyes had grown. And there was something slovenly about her appearance after all these years of fastidious grooming.

We didn't discuss it again. And two days ago, Saturday morning, when Susan was in town, they came round to pick me up. Prof Bruwer and Melanie and I squeezed into the front of the old Land Rover that had seen better days – a replica of its owner; and equally indestructible, it seemed. Melanie let the top down. Sun and wind. The cobweb pattern of a crack in the windscreen. Stuffing protruding from the seats.

A white warm day, once we'd left the city behind. Not much rain so far this year and the grass hadn't sprouted yet since winter. Brittle as straw. Scorched red earth. Here and there, in irrigation areas, patches of varying green. Then bare veld again. At last the rocky ridges of the foothills. A landscape older than men, burnt bare by the sun, blown empty by the wind, all secrets exposed to the sky. The more fertile narrow valleys among rows of hills made an almost anachronistic impression with their trees and fields and red-roofed houses. Man hasn't really taken root here yet; it is still unclaimed territory. His existence is temporary and, if the earth should decide to shrug him off, which would happen quite effortlessly, he would leave no sign behind. The only permanence is that of rocks, the petrified bones of a vast skeleton. Ancient Africa.

From time to time we passed someone or something. A broken windmill. A dam of rusty corrugated iron. The wreck of an old car. A cowherd in a tattered hat, a fluttering red rag tied to a stick in his hand, following his small herd of cattle. A man on a bicycle.

Reminiscences of my childhood. Driving with Pa, in the spider or the little green Ford, Helena and I played the immemorial game of claiming for ourselves whatever was seen first. "My house." "My sheep." "My dam." And, whenever we passed a black man or woman or child: "My servant." How natural it had all seemed then. How imperceptibly had our patterns fossilised around us, inside us. Was that where it had all started, in such innocence? – You are black, and so you are my servant. I am white, which makes me your master. *Cursed be Canaan; a servant of servants shall he be unto his brethren.*

The old Land Rover shook and shuddered on its way, especially after Bruwer had turned off the tarred road to follow a maze of small dusty tracks deeper into the hills. Conversation was impossible in that din. Not that it was necessary, or even desirable. Almost fatalistically one resigned oneself to that process of stripping away whatever was redundant in order to be exposed to the essential. Even thoughts were luxuries to be shaken and blown out of one's mind. And what returned to me from my childhood was not thoughts but immediate and elemental images, things, realities.

Deep in the tumbled rocky mountains we stopped on a farm owned by friends of Bruwer's. A deep and fertile valley, a poplar grove, a paved furrow in which water came rushing down from a dam on the slope behind the house of solid stone. A stoep fenced in with wire-mesh. A large cage filled with canaries and parakeets. Flower-beds. Chickens scratching and squealing and squawking in the yard. A single calf in a pen, lowing wretchedly at regular intervals. Two charming old people, Mr and Mrs Greyling. The old man's hands covered with grease and soil; broken nails; a white segment on his forehead above the tanned leather of his face, where the hat had kept the sun away. The old woman large and shapeless, like a mattress stuffed with down; a broad-brimmed straw hat on her wispy hair, a large mole with a tuft of coarse black hair on her chin; badly fitting dentures pushed forward by her tongue whenever she wasn't talking. As soon as we had stopped she came waddling towards us from the labourers' houses several hundred yards away. One of the children had a fever, she said, and she'd been spending all night nursing it.

We sat on the wide cool stoep, drinking tea and chatting effortlessly. Nothing of importance. The drought and the prospects of rain; the labourers becoming less dependable and more "cheeky"; the strawberry harvest; last night's radio news. There was something wholesome about getting involved in trivialities again.

They wouldn't let us go without dinner. Roast leg of lamb, rice and roast potatoes, peas and beans and carrots from the garden, homeground coffee. It was past three before we could shoulder our rucksacks and set out on the footpath up the steep slope behind the stone house, into Phil Bruwer's mountain wilderness.

He led the way in his heavy climbing boots and grey stockings and wide khaki shorts flapping round his bony knees. Brown sinewy calves. Leaning forward under the weight of the rucksack stained and faded with age. The beret with its jaunty guinea-fowl feather. Well-worn beech stick. Perspiration on his weatherbeaten face, his beard stained by tobacco juice. Melanie on his heels, in an old shirt of her father's, the tails tied in a knot on her bare belly; cut-off jeans with frayed edges; lithe brown legs; tennis shoes. And I beside her, sometimes falling behind.

The mountains aren't particularly high in those parts, but steeper than one might suspect from below. A curious sensation: it isn't you who go higher but the world that recedes from you, slipping away to leave you more desolate in that thin and translucent air. A mere hint of a breeze, just sufficient to suddenly sting your face with coolness when you stop in a sweat. The dry rustling of the grass. Occasionally a small bird or a lizard.

We stopped repeatedly to rest or look about. The old man tired more easily than I'd expected. It didn't escape Melanie either; and it must have worried her for once I heard her asking him whether he was all right. It annoyed him. But I noticed that after that she would more frequently find some pretext for interrupting the climb, stopping to point out a rock-formation or a succulent or the shape of a tree-stump, or something in the valley far below us.

On a particularly rocky slope we passed a cluster of huts, a small flock of goats, naked black children playing among the brittle shrubs, a lonely old man squatting in the sun in front of his doorway smoking a long-stemmed pipe and raising a thin arm to salute us.

"Why don't we build us a little hut up here too?" I said lightly, nostalgically "A vegetable garden, a few goats, a fire, a roof overhead, a clay wall to keep out wind and rain. Then we can all sit here peacefully watching the clouds drift by."

"I can just see the two of you sitting there smoking your pipes while I have to do all the work," said Melanie.

"Nothing wrong with a patriarchal system," I replied, laughing.

"Don't worry, I'll give you more than enough to keep you busy," she promised. "You can teach the children."

I'm sure she meant it quite innocently. Still, when she said it – *the children* – there suddenly was a different kind of silence between us, a different awareness. In the candid light of the sun she was looking at me, and I looked back. The fineness of her features, the large dark eyes wide apart, the gentle swelling of her lips, her hair moving in the breeze, her narrow shoulders straining against the weight of the rucksack, the faded khaki shirt with its knotted tails, baring her belly, the navel an intricate little knot fitting tightly into its cavity. For a moment all that mattered was simply being there, relinquishing the world, isolated in that immense space.

Inevitably her father nipped our silly and extravagant romanticising in the bud.

"Impossible to turn your back to the world," he said. "We're living in the wrong age. We've tasted a different forbidden fruit, so we have no choice but to go back." A neatly timed punctuation mark; and then he was off on one of his tangential anecdotes. "Old friend of mine, Helmut Krueger, German from South-West Africa, was interned during the War. But old Helmut had always been a clever bastard, so one day he

242

escaped, clinging to the chassis of a truck that used to deliver vegetables to the camp." Out of breath, he sat down on a rock. "So far so good. But when he got back to South-West, he found that all his friends and neighbours had either gone away or been interned; and he himself couldn't show his face for fear of being recaptured. So life became pretty dreary." He started fiddling with his pipe.

"What happened then?" I prodded him.

Bruwer smiled impishly. "What could he do? One fine day he just went back to the camp, in the same vegetable truck he'd used to escape. You can imagine the commandant's face at the next roll-call when they found they had one prisoner too many." A resounding crackle. "See what I mean? In the end you always have to go back to your camp. It's our condition. Rousseau was wrong about being free and acquiring fetters later. It's the other way round. We're born in bondage. And from there, if you receive enough grace or if you're mad enough or brave enough, you break free. Until you see the light and return to your camp. We still haven't learned to handle too much freedom, you see, poor miserable creatures that we are." He got up. "Come on. We can't sit around on our backsides all day."

"You're very pale," said Melanie.

"You're imagining things." As he wiped the beads of sweat from his face I could also see the pallor through his deep tan. But without paying attention to us he jerked the rucksack back into position, took his heavy stick and strode on.

However, Melanie saw to it that we settled into a camping spot well before sunset. A small sheltered opening surrounded by large boulders. We gathered wood. Then I stayed behind with him while Melanie went off in search of grass and shrubs she could use for bedding under her sleeping bag. I sat looking at her until she disappeared behind a ridge as knobbly as the vertebrae of some prehistoric animal: how I would have loved to go with her, but the "proper behaviour" of a lifetime forced me to keep the old man company.

"What are you looking so depressed for?" he asked, and I realised that he'd been watching me closely for some time. "You're in the mountains now, Ben. Forget about the world outside."

"How can I?" I started telling him about the disappointments and dead-ends of the recent weeks, the disappearance of the old cleaner, my visit to John Vorster Square. "If only they would allow me to talk things over with them," I said. "But I just seem to blunder on blindly. They simply won't give me a chance to ask, or to explain, or to discuss."

"What else did you expect?" The familiar crackling sound. "Don't you realise? – discussion, dialogue, call it what you will, is the one thing they dare not allow. For once they start allowing you to ask questions they're forced to admit the very possibility of doubt. And their raison d'être derives from the exclusion of that possibility."

"Why *must* it be so?" I asked.

"Because it's a matter of power. Naked power. That's what brought them there and keeps them there. And power has a way of becoming an end in itself." He began to carry the wood to the spot he'd chosen for the fire. "Once you have your bank account in Switzerland, and your farm in Paraguay, and your villa in France, and your contacts in Hamburg and Bonn and Tokyo – once a flick of your wrist can decide the fate of others – you need a very active conscience to start acting against your own interests. And a conscience doesn't stand up to much heat or cold, it's a delicate sort of plant."

"Then it would be madness to hope for even the most paltry form of change."

He was standing on hands and knees like a Bushman, tending his fire. The sun had gone down and the twilight was darkening. His face red with blowing, gasping for breath, he sat up after a while, wiping his forehead.

"There are only two kinds of madness one should guard against, Ben," he said calmly. "One is the belief that we can do everything. The other is the belief that we can do nothing."

In the deep dusk I saw her coming towards us, and my heart gave a jump. Through what unfathomable ways does a thing like this announce itself to one? – it's like a seed you put in the earth; and one day, miraculously, a plant breaks through the soil, and suddenly nothing can deny its existence any more. In just that way I knew, the instant I saw her approaching from afar, minute in that infinite dusk, that I loved her. And at the

244

same time I knew it was an impossible thing, going against the grain of everything that had shaped me, everything I believed in.

Almost deliberately I started avoiding her. Not because I was wary of her, but of myself. It was, of course, impossible to keep out of her way altogether. I could manage it while all three of us were preparing supper; but not afterwards. Because the old man left us quite early to bed down in his sleeping bag.

Worried, she went over to sit beside him. "Dad, you sure you're all right?"

He shook his head, annoyed. "A bit tired, that's all. I'm not as young as I used to be, remember."

"I've never known you to get tired so easily."

"Oh stop it. I'm feeling a bit nauseous, something I've eaten. Now leave me alone, I want to sleep."

And so the two of us were left beside the fire. From time to time she would turn her head to look in his direction; once or twice she got up to investigate, but he was sleeping. Whenever the flames began to subside I added more logs to the coals, sending up a spray of red sparks into the dark. Occasionally there was a dry breath of wind. Smoke swirling, temporarily obscuring the stars.

"Why are you so worried about him?" I asked her once.

She was staring into the coals, a cardigan draped loosely over her shoulders to ward off the chilly night air creeping up from behind. "Oh I'm sure he'll be all right in the morning." A long pause. Then she turned to look at me: "What upsets me is the way one gets attached to someone. Then you begin to panic when you suddenly realise—" A fierce shake of her head, sending her dark hair swinging over her shoulders. "Now I'm being silly. I suppose the night does it to one. One's defences are down in the dark."

"You do love him very much, don't you?"

"Of course I do. He's always been with me. That time I was breaking up with Brian he was the only one really to understand – even when I was just battling on blindly, not really knowing what was happening. But that wasn't why I went back to live with him again: I couldn't simply exchange one bond for another. Once one has taken the sort of decision I took then,

245

you've got to be able to go it alone. It's a precondition. Otherwise——" Once again she looked round to where he was sleeping, a dark bundle in the dark; then her eyes returned to the
fire.

"Can one really survive entirely on one's own?" I asked. "Is
it possible to be so totally self-sufficient? Is it wise?"

"I don't want to detach myself from anything. In that sense
you're right, of course. But – to be *dependent* on another person,
to derive your whole sense and substance from another——"

"Isn't that what love is really about?"

"When I left Brian," she said, "he loved me and I loved him.
Inasmuch as we knew anything about love at all." A silence.
Her unavoiding eyes. "If you want to be a journalist, if you're
really serious about it, you've got to give up security, stability,
predictability. Here today, off again tomorrow. Up and down
the face of Africa. Now and then you meet someone who makes
you realise you're also human, you've got human needs, you're
hungry. But you daren't yield. Not quite. Something is always
held back. You may share a few days with him, perhaps a
night." This time she was quiet for a very long time and I was
conscious of nausea lying inside me like a dumb animal. "Then
it's off again."

"What are you trying to achieve?" I asked. "Is it really necessary to punish yourself like that?"

Impulsively she laid her hand on mine. "Ben, don't you think
I would love to be a simple little housewife with a husband I can
meet at the door when he comes home from work at night?
Especially when you are thirty, and you're a woman, and you
know time is running out if you want to have children?" She
shook her head angrily. "But I told you before. This country
doesn't allow me to indulge myself like that. It isn't possible to
lead a private life if you want to live with your conscience. It
tears open everything that's intimate and personal. So it's less
messy to have as little as possible that can be destroyed."

I didn't look at her but deep into the coals, as if trying to
probe beyond them, into the heart of the black earth; and I said
what I could not keep secret any more: "Melanie, I love you."

The slow intake of her breath. I still didn't look at her at all.
But I was aware of her beside me, knowing her more intensely

246

than I had ever known another person: her face and hair and the slight body enclosing her, shoulders and arms and hands with sensitive fingers, small breasts under the loose shirt, and the tense curve of her belly, everything that was hers; and even more exquisitely than her body I knew her presence, and ached for her as the earth aches for rain.

After some time she leaned her head against my shoulder. It was the only caress we exchanged. It would have been possible, I suppose, to express our need and our discovery more intimately. On the hard soil we might have made love that night, body and body together in the dark. But I was afraid, and she too, I think. Afraid of everything that would be defined and circumscribed by such an act; everything which, until that moment, had existed only as possibilities. We owed one another that compassion not to involve each other in more than we could handle or more than was allowed us.

It must have been quite late when we got up. The coals were burning very low, their light a dull red glow on her face. She turned to me and, standing on her toes, briefly pressed her lips against mine. Then turned away quickly and went to her sleeping bag beside the old man who was breathing deeply and unevenly.

I stacked more wood on the fire, made a brief excursion into the night, and returned to my own bag. Slept restlessly for a few hours before I woke up again and remained lying, my head on my arms, staring up at the stars. Jackals cavorting eerily in the distance. Pushing myself up on an elbow I looked at the two dark shapes beside me in the flickering light of the coals. The old man nearer to me. Then she, Melanie. From very far back came her playful, theatrical words: *When one person unexpectedly finds himself on the edge of another — don't you think that's the most dangerous thing that can happen to anyone?*

I could lie down no longer. The jackals had stopped howling. But her nearness and her almost inaudible breathing disturbed me. I pulled a few heavy logs to the smouldering fire and with the help of some brushwood coaxed the flames back into life. Then sat down beside it, wrapped in my sleeping bag, and lit my pipe. Once or twice I heard the old man moaning in his sleep. There was no sound from Melanie. It felt like keeping

247

watch by the bedside of a sleeping child.

This was what it had come to. But what was "this"? Peace, grace, a moment of insight, or a still greater wilderness? Night around us, as dark as faith.

My thoughts wandered back, all the way. Childhood. University. Lydenburg. Krugersdorp. Then Johannesburg. Susan. Our children. Responsibilities. The empty predictable rhythms of my existence. And then the change of direction, so slowly that I'd barely noticed it. Jonathan. Gordon. Emily. Stanley. Melanie. Behind every name an immensity like that of the night. I felt myself groping on the edge of a strange abyss. Utterly alone.

I thought: There you lie sleeping, two yards away from me, yet I dare not touch you. And yet: because you're there, because we are both alone in this same night, it is possible for me to go on, to go on believing in the possibility of something whole and necessary.

The bitter cold of the predawn. A breeze stirring. Stars fading and turning grey. The early, murky light pushing up from the horizon. A landscape slowly revealed. The simple secrets of the night exposed, intricate and indecent in the light.

At sunrise I started making coffee and before I'd finished the old man joined me beside the fire, looking very pale and shivering.

"What's the matter, Prof?"

"Don't know. Still this nauseous feeling. Can't breathe properly." He rubbed his chest and stretched his arms to expand his lungs; then looked round uneasily. "Don't mention it to Melanie. It will just upset her and I know it's nothing, really."

It wasn't necessary to mention it to her. She saw it at the first glance when she joined us a few minutes later. And after breakfast, which none of us enjoyed, she insisted on turning back in spite of his indignant protests. Neither of us made any reference to the previous night. In this daylight it appeared preposterous and absurd. For the last kilometre or so we had to support him between us. Melanie drove back from the Greylings' farm. I wanted to go home with them to give a hand, but she insisted on taking me back first.

All day I waited anxiously. In the evening she telephoned. He was in the intensive care unit in hospital. Heart attack.

Late this afternoon I went to their house but it was deserted. Tonight she phoned again. He is no longer critical, but still very weak. Will probably have to spend several weeks in hospital.

"Shall I come over?" I asked.

"No, rather not." A momentary return to the peaceful warmth we'd shared so briefly in the mountains: "Really, it's better this way."

I'm left with the disquieting, ridiculous thought: Is Phil Bruwer the latest victim of my leprosy?

But I dare not give way to a new depression. Whatever happens from now on I must remember that one night we were together on the mountain. It is the truth, however unreal it seems in retrospect. And for the sake of that memory, even though I can give no logical explanation for it, I must go on. Stanley was right, after all. We must endure. We must survive.

9

In late November Phil Bruwer was discharged from hospital. Ben drove him home, Melanie sitting in the back. The old man was shockingly frail and white, but nothing could quell his exuberant spirit.

"I decided not to die just now," he said. "Realised I'm not quite ready for Heaven yet. Too many sordid habits I still have to conquer." With some effort, and none of the carefree virtuosity of earlier days, he forced out a fart to illustrate his point. "I mean, suppose I blew out my last breath at the wrong end. St Peter may not approve if a jet-propelled angel came whizzing through his gates like that."

Even with the anxiety about Bruwer's health alleviated Ben

249

still had his hands full. There was no decline in the stream of people coming to him for help. The work permits. The reference books. The trouble with police or urban authorities: married men refusing to live in single quarters among tsotsis and wanting to bring their families to town; children accused of arson and sabotage; women in despair when their townships were cleaned up systematically after the discovery of an ammunition dump. Once a pathetic old couple in well-worn Sunday clothes: a month ago their son of fifteen had been sent to Robben Island and now they had been informed of his death – a heart attack, according to the prison authorities; but how was it possible, they said, he'd always been a healthy boy. And they had been instructed to collect the body in Cape Town before next Wednesday, otherwise it would be buried by the government. But they had no money: the old man was ill and out of work; and the woman's wages as a domestic servant, twenty rand per month, were not enough.

Most of the callers were referred to Stanley or to Dan Levinson; some of the trickier cases to Melanie. The old couple in search of their son's body Ben also mentioned in a phone-call to his father-in-law. The latter immediately set to work and arranged for the body to be sent to Johannesburg by train at State expense. That, however, was the end of the matter: the "heart attack" was never cleared up, and apart from Melanie's newspaper the press gave it no publicity.

Depressing as it was, his constant involvement in new problems helped to keep Ben going. While people still came to him for help at least there was something to keep him occupied – even though all this remained peripheral to what really mattered to him: the dogged search for new light on the deaths of Gordon and Jonathan. The information gathered in those months was less dramatic than some of the earlier discoveries. Still, he continued to add new bits to his store. And provided one didn't expect too much, provided one didn't try to think in terms of a destination yet, there was some sense in the slow progress. Ben kept hoping that Emily's policeman, Johnson Seroke, would return, convinced as he was that the man held the key to the final important breakthrough. In the meantime he had to content himself by registering the sluggish motion which carried them forward step by step. Looking ahead, one tended to lose courage. But looking back it was impossible to deny the length of road already travelled.

Then, in the first week of December, came an unexpected reverse when it was reported that Dan Levinson had fled the country, crossing the border to Botswana (risking his life against well-nigh impossible odds, the newspapers claimed), and proceeding to London where he had been granted political asylum. There he embarked on a series of press interviews to explain how his position in South Africa had become intolerable and how his life had been threatened. He announced that he had brought a stack of files with him, from which he would compile a book to finally expose the iniquities of the Security Police. Photographs of him were plastered all over the newspapers, taken in night clubs or at sumptuous receptions, mostly in the company of starlets and the wives of publishers. He vehemently denied reports from South Africa that he had smuggled out thousands of rands of trust money, including the deposits of black clients. But several of the people referred to Levinson by Ben came back to him when the news broke, with complaints about exorbitant fees the lawyer had charged them – while Ben had already paid for their consultations himself, either out of his own pocket or with money supplied by Melanie's newspaper fund.

The loss of so many original statements and documents shook Ben. Fortunately he had kept signed copies of almost everything in the secret compartment of his tools cupboard, which softened the blow. Even so he was shattered when he was first told about it by Stanley.

"My God," he said. "How could he do that to us? I *trusted* him!"

Stanley, perhaps predictably, shook with laughter. "Come on, lanie, you got to admit it: he caught us for suckers. I thought he was a bloody shark right from the word go. But I never thought he was such a good actor too." With relish he spread open the newspaper again to read aloud the full report of how, in a violent storm in the middle of the night, Levinson had crawled for miles on all fours through the minefields of a closely patrolled area before crossing the border to Botswana. "He's a

251

made man, I tell you. He'll get enough mileage out of this to last him for years. And look at the two of us with our pants round our ankles. You know, I think it's time we caught some shine too. Why don't we follow him? Then we find ourselves two fancy blondes over there" – his hands described the appropriate curves – "and we live happily ever after. How about it, hey?"

"It's not funny, Stanley."

Stanley stared hard at him for a while. Then he said: "You slipping, lanie. What you need is a proper *stokvel*."

"What's that?" Ben asked warily.

"You see? You don't even know what it is. Why don't you come with me this Friday, then we have a solid *stokvel* right through to Sunday night." Noticing Ben's uncomprehending look, Stanley explained, exploding again with mirth: "It's a party, lanie. Not every which way's party, but the sort where you dance non-stop till you pass out. And then we bring you round with *popla* and we push some meat down your throat and there you go again. Lanie, I promise you, by the time you get to Sunday night – if you survive so long – we just hang you out with the washing for a week, and then you're a new man. Born again. That's what you need."

Grimacing stiffly, Ben asked: "And is that the only remedy you can offer?"

"Better than castor oil, lanie. You not laughing enough. That's what you need, man. If a man can't laugh to clean out his stomach, if you can't tell the world to get fucked, then it's tickets." A resounding blow on Ben's shoulders. "And I don't want to see your balls crushed, man. We got a long way to go still."

Ben managed a wry smile. "All right, Stanley," he said. "I'll stay with you." A brief pause, then he said: "What else is there for me to do?"

His son-in-law, Suzette's husband Chris, was not prepared to get involved himself, but through his influence in "inner circles" he arranged an interview with a Cabinet Minister for Ben. And on an afternoon early in December he drove to Pretoria.

A functional, panelled office in the Union Buildings. Cluttered desk. In one corner, below a colourful map of the country, a small table with a water carafe and an open Family Bible. The Minister was a jocular man with a bull-neck and large round shoulders, large hands, smooth hair, wearing steel-framed glasses with double lenses. For a few minutes they indulged in small-talk. The Minister enquired about his work and his family, commented on the vocation of a teacher, the promise of the younger generation, the sound character of the boys on the border, protecting the nation against the evils of Communism. Then, without any change of inflexion, he said:

"I believe there is something you would like to discuss with me, Mr Du Toit?"

Once again – how often had he done so already? how many more times to go? – Ben gave a resumé of Gordon's story up to the day of his death.

"Every man has the democratic right to die," said the Minister, smiling.

Ben looked at him in silence. "Do you really believe he committed suicide?" he asked tersely.

"It is standard practice among Communists to escape interrogation."

"Mr Minister, Gordon Ngubene was murdered." As briefly as he could he summarised the results of his enquiries.

There was no sign of the big man's earlier jocularity as his eyes surveyed Ben in a cold stare. "Mr Du Toit, I hope you realise the seriousness of the allegations you're making against people who have been performing a thankless but indispensable task under very difficult circumstances?"

"I knew Gordon," he said, strained. "An ordinary, decent man who would never think of harming anyone. And when they killed his son—"

"The son, as far as I know, was shot with several other agitators in a violent demonstration."

"Jonathan died in a cell after two months in detention. I have evidence that he had been seen in hospital in a serious condition shortly before his death."

"Are you absolutely sure you're not being manipulated by people with very dubious intentions, Mr Du Toit?"

253

Ben placed his hands on the arm-rests of his chair, preparing to get up. "Does that mean you are not willing to have the matter investigated?"

"Tell me," said the Minister, "it was you who leaked the story to the English press some time ago, wasn't it?"

He felt his face grow hot. "Yes," he said, tight-lipped. "I had no option after our own newspapers turned me away."

"With very good reason, I should imagine. They probably realised the harm it would do to the Party if something like that was shouted from the rooftops. Especially by people who hardly know what they're talking about."

"I was thinking of the country's interests, not those of the Party," said Ben.

"Do you really think you can separate the two, Mr Du Toit?"

Ben pushed himself up, but sank back again. "Mr Minister." He was doing his utmost to control himself, but his voice was trembling. "Do you realise that if you send me away with empty hands today there will be no hope left of having the matter investigated officially?"

"Oh, I won't send you away with empty hands," said the Minister, with a smile that bared his teeth. "I shall ask the Security Police to go into the matter and to report back to me."

10

26 December. Miserable Christmas yesterday. Desolate ever since Melanie and her father left for the Cape a week ago. Cornered in a house filled with relatives. And even Linda was sulky, red-eyed because we'd kept her away from her Pieter over the festive days: it was her last Christmas at home, next year she'll be married, so we selfishly wanted her for ourselves. Susan's

parents moved in several days ago. Suzette and Chris came over from Pretoria in the morning, followed by Helena and George just before dinner. For the first time in God knows how many years the whole family was assembled.

But I couldn't shake off my glumness. Had been looking forward to taking my old moth-eaten Father Christmas outfit from the cupboard to entertain my grandson, but Suzette would have none of it:

"Good heavens, Dad, we're not so old-fashioned any more. Hennie knows this Father Christmas stuff is all nonsense. We don't believe in bringing up our children on lies."

For the sake of Christmas I swallowed my annoyance. As it was, I had my hands full trying to control all the hidden tensions in the family. Helena, corsetted and bluntly streamlined, hair tinted and dress designed for a much younger figure by some Frenchman with an unpronounceable name – ever ready to make Susan cringe by hinting how much a poor teacher's wife had to miss in life. Suzette bitching Linda for sulking about such a nondescript little man whom she insisted on calling His Holiness. George, a cigar stuck permanently to his mouth, irritating Chris by pretending to know better about everything. Susan, tense and nervous, nagging because Johan refused to give a hand with fetching and carrying. Father-in-law begrudging younger men like George and Chris their easy success, and stung by the lack of adequate reward for the years he'd fought and suffered for the Party. And all of them antagonistic towards me for "betraying" the family in some mysterious manner, turning me into the scapegoat for all their own resentments.

However, at last we were all squeezed in round the table (enlarged by adding a much lower tea-table from the stoep to one end), leaving preciously little elbow-space for eating. And one really needed space to do justice to Susan's turkey and leg of lamb and topside, yellow rice with raisins, peas, sweet-potatoes with cinnamon, stewed fruit, sugarbeans, and the salads contributed by Louisa and Suzette (avocado, carrot, asparagus, cucumber, moulded in gelatine, like plastic wreaths at a funeral). In addition, there were two flower arrangements with "Japanese" lines threatening the territorial integrity of some plates; a cluster of candles sending small brass angels

255

spinning in a tinkling merry-go-round; and a rather odd assortment of wine glasses. (Susan: "Ben keeps on promising he'll buy us a proper set, but you know what he's like"; Helena, sweetly: "When George came back from his last overseas trip he brought us a whole crate of crystal glasses from Stockholm: he has the right contacts, of course.")

"Will you say grace for us, Father?"

The heads bowed in meek acquiescence to Father-in-law's interminable prayer: having failed to reach the top in politics his only compensation lies in pouring it all into the patient ear of the Almighty.

There was an unfortunate interruption when, halfway through the prayer, little Hennie escaped from the clutches of his black nanny in the backyard and came running in to express at the top of his voice his need to respond to an urgent call of nature. After a momentary stumble, Father-in-law made an admirable comeback, resuming his prayer over the food which was cooling off in direct proportion to Susan's rising blood pressure. At last the formalities were over, the crackers cracked and the paper hats donned, the plates filled to capacity and George's eloquent toast drunk.

A feeling of constrained magnanimity began to spread as, in that sweltering summer heat, stuffed into our Sunday best, we sat sweating and masticating, grimly scooping vast quantities of food into our tortured insides. Susan and I were the only ones not tempted by the cornucopia, she because of the state of her nerves, I because I simply had no appetite.

The plates had just been removed to be replaced by bowls filled with the enormous old-fashioned Christmas pudding Mother-in-law had baked months ago, when there was a loud knock on the front door.

Johan opened.

And suddenly Stanley erupted into the room like a great black bull in white suit and white shoes, brown shirt and scarlet tie, with matching handkerchief protruding from his breast pocket. For a moment he stood swaying in the middle of the floor; it was obvious at a glance that he'd had more than enough to drink.

Then he bellowed: "Lanie!" Followed by a wide gesture that

sent a flower arrangement toppling from a tall table, and a greeting in a broad, mock-American accent: "Hi folks!"

It was deadly quiet round the dining table; not even the sound of a spoon clinking against china.

Like a sleepwalker I got up and approached him on the thick, tousled pile of Susan's new carpet. All those eyes following me.

"Stanley! What are you doing here?"

"It's Christmas, isn't it? I've come to celebrate. Compliments of the season to everybody." He made another gesture as if to embrace the whole family.

"Is there something you wanted to see me about, Stanley?" I tried to keep my voice down so only he could hear. "Shall we go through to my study?"

"Fuck your study, man!" It reverberated through the room.

I looked round, and turned back to him. "Well, if you prefer to sit down here—?"

"Sure." He staggered to the nearest arm-chair and lowered his massive body into it, jumping up again with staggering ease to put an arm round my shoulders: "Join the happy family, eh? Who's this lot?"

"You've had too much to drink, Stanley."

"Of course. Why not? It's the season of goodwill, isn't it? Peace on earth and all that crap."

A sombre black figure rose from the dining table. "Who is this kaffir?" asked Father-in-law.

A moment of total silence. Then Stanley doubled up with laughter. His face purple, Father-in-law came towards us and I had to step in between them.

"Why don't you tell the *boer* who this kaffir is?" asked Stanley, wiping the tears of hilarity from his face.

"Ben?" said Father-in-law.

"Tell him we're old pals, lanie." Once again Stanley put his arm across my shoulders, causing me to stagger under his weight. "Or aren't we? Hey?"

"Of course we are, Stanley," I said soothingly. "Father, we can discuss this later. I'll explain everything."

In deathly silence Father-in-law looked round. "Mother," he said, "let's go. We don't seem to be welcome here any more."

All of a sudden there was pandemonium. Susan trying to

stop her father and being bitched by Helena. George gently restraining his wife, only to be shouted at by Suzette. Johan turning on his sister. Linda bursting into tears and running into the passage sobbing. A rush for the front door.

Without warning the room was empty around us. Only the angels were still tinkling merrily above their almost burnt-out candles. On the plates lay the remains of Mother-in-law's Christmas pudding. And in the middle of the floor Stanley was stumbling this way and that, helpless with cascading, bellowing laughter.

"Jeez, lanie!" He was practically sobbing. "Ever in your fucking life seen such a stampede?"

"Maybe you think it's funny, Stanley. But I don't. Do you realise what you've done?"

"Me? I only came to celebrate, I tell you." Another fit of laughter.

From the spare room next door came the sounds of Mother-in-law's sobbing and her husband's voice, soothing at first, then growing in volume as his annoyance increased.

"Well?" said Stanley, recovered temporarily. "Happy Christmas anyway." He put out his hand.

I had no wish to take his hand and did so only to humour him.

"Who was that old cunt with the potbelly and black suit, looks like an undertaker?"

"My father-in-law." Adding deliberately: "M.P."

"You joking?" I shook my head. He started laughing again. "Jeez, you got all the right connections. And here I fucked it all up for you. Sorry, man." He didn't look repentant at all

"Would you like something to eat?"

"You kept the scraps for me?"

That really made me angry. "Now pull yourself together, Stanley! Say what you've come to say. Otherwise go to hell."

His laughter changed into a broad grin. "Right," he said. "Dead right. Put the kaffir in his place."

"What's the matter with you today? I just don't understand you."

"Don't kid yourself, lanie. What the hell do you understand anyway?"

"Did you come here to tell me something or to shout at me?"

"What makes you think there's anything I'd like to tell you?"

Although I knew how ludicrous it was – Stanley must be twice my size – I grabbed him by the shoulders and started shaking him.

"Are you going to talk?" I said. "What's wrong with you?"

"Let me go." Stanley shoved me off, sending me staggering as he stood reeling on his own legs, planted far apart on the shaggy carpet.

"You're disgraceful," I said. "Instead of keeping Emily company on a day like this you just make trouble for other people. Don't you think she needs you?"

Abruptly he stopped swaying, glaring at me with bloodshot eyes, breathing heavily.

"What do you know about Emily?" he sneered.

"Stanley. Please." I was pleading with him now. "All I'm trying to say—"

"Emily is dead," said Stanley.

The angels went on spinning, tinkling. But that was the only sound I was aware of, and the only movement, in the house.

"What did you say?"

"You deaf then?"

"What is it? For God's sake, Stanley, tell me!"

"No. You want to celebrate." He started singing: "Oh come, all ye faithful—" But he stopped in the middle of a line, staring at me as if he'd forgotten where he was. "Haven't you heard about Robert?" he asked.

"What Robert?"

"Her son. The one who ran away after Gordon died."

"What about him?"

"He got shot with two of his friends when they crossed the border from Mozambique yesterday. Carrying guns and stuff. Walked slap-bang into an army patrol."

"And then?" I felt alone in a great ringing void.

"Heard the news this morning, so I had to go and tell Emily. She was very quiet. No fuss, no tears, no nothing. Then she told me to go. How was I to know? She looked all right to me. And then she—" Suddenly his voice broke.

"What happened, Stanley? Don't cry. Oh, my God, Stanley, please!"

"She went to the station. Orlando station. All the way on foot. They say she must have sat there for over an hour, because it's Christmas, there's only a few trains. And then she jumped in front of it on the tracks. Zap, one time."

For a moment it seemed as if he was going to burst out laughing again; but this time it was crying. I had to dig my feet into the thick carpet to support that dead weight leaning against me and shaking with sobs.

And I was still standing like that, my arms around him, when the two old people came from the spare room carrying their bags and followed by Susan, going through the front door to their car parked beside the house.

Last night she said: "I asked you once before whether you knew what you were doing, what you're letting yourself in for?"

I said: "All I know is that it is impossible to stop now. If I can't go on believing in what I'm doing I'll go mad."

"It doesn't seem to matter to you how many other people you drive mad in the process."

"Please try." It was difficult to find words. "I know you're upset, Susan. But try not to exaggerate."

"Exaggerate? After what happened today?"

"Stanley didn't know what he was doing. Emily is dead. Can't you understand that?"

She inhaled deeply, slowly, and spent a long time rubbing stuff into her cheeks. "Don't you think enough people have died by now?" she said at last. "Won't you ever learn?"

I sat staring helplessly at her image in the mirror: "Are you blaming me for their deaths now?"

"I didn't mean that. But nothing you have done has made any difference. There's nothing you can hope to do. When are you going to accept it?"

"Never."

"What about the price you pay for it?"

For a moment I closed my eyes painfully, wearily. "I've *got* to, Susan."

"I don't think you're all there any more," she said in cold

staccato words. "You've lost all balance and perspective. You're blind to everything else in the world."

I shook my head.

"Shall I tell you why?" she went on.

I made no attempt to answer.

"Because all that matters to you is Ben Du Toit. For a long time now it's had nothing to do with Gordon or with Jonathan or anybody else. You don't want to give up, that's all. You started fighting and now you refuse to admit defeat even though you no longer know who you're fighting, or why."

"You don't understand, Susan."

"I know very well I don't understand. I damned well don't even want to try to understand any longer. All I'm concerned with now is to make sure I won't be dragged down with you."

"What do you mean?"

"There's nothing I can do for you any more, Ben. There's nothing I can do for our marriage. And God knows it did matter to me once. But now it's time I looked after myself. To make sure I don't lose the few scraps that remain after you've broken down my last bit of dignity today."

"Are you going away then?"

"It's immaterial whether I go or stay," she said. "If I have to go I'll go. For the moment I suppose I may just as well stay. But something is over between us, and I want you to know it."

That stark white face in the mirror. There must have been a time, years ago, when we loved one another. But I can no longer even yearn back for it, because I've forgotten what it used to be like.

11

The reopening of the schools seemed to provide a new impetus to events. A new wave of anonymous telephone calls, another vandalistic attack on his car, the entire front wall of his home sprayed with slogans, coarse insults on his blackboard, at night the sound of footsteps going round the house. Until he, too, accepted the need for a watchdog; but within a fortnight of acquiring one it was poisoned. Susan's state reached a new and disturbing low; her doctor called Ben for a serious discussion of her condition. And even when nothing specific was happening there was the gnawing awareness of that invisible and shapeless power pursuing him. For the first time in his life he was having trouble getting to sleep at night, lying awake for hours, staring into the dark, wondering, wondering. When would they strike next, and what form would it take this time?

He rose exhausted in the mornings, and came home from school exhausted, went to bed exhausted, only to lie awake again. School imposed a measure of wholesome discipline on his life, but at the same time it was becoming more difficult to cope with, more unmanageable, an anxiety and an irritation, on some days almost anguish. The disapproval of his colleagues. Cloete's silent antagonism. Carelse's feeble jokes. And the enthusiastic loyalty of young Viviers sometimes proved even more aggravating than the disdain of the others.

Then there was Stanley, coming and going as before. How on earth he managed to do so unseen and unfollowed was beyond Ben's comprehension. In terms of any logic he should have been picked up or silenced months before. But Stanley, Ben had to conclude, was an artist of survival; seated behind the wheel of his taxi, the big Dodge, his *etembalami*, closer to him than wife or kin, he went his mysterious way without turning a hair. Christmas day was the only occasion Ben had ever seen him lose control. Never again. And surrounding the highly charged moments he burst into Ben's life, emerging from the night and dissolving into it again, the complex riddle of his life remained his own.

From time to time he went off on one of his "trips", to Botswana, or Lesotho, or Swaziland. Smuggling, most likely. (But what? Hash, money, guns, or men—?)

In the last week of January Phil Bruwer had to go back to hospital. He hadn't had another attack, but his condition had deteriorated so much that the doctors felt he should be kept under constant surveillance. Melanie had to fly back from the Cape, abandoning the project she'd been working on. A few times she and Ben visited the old man together, but it was depressing as, for once, it seemed as if his indomitable spirit had given up.

"I've never been afraid to die," she told Ben. "I can accept whatever happens to myself and I've been close enough to death to realise it doesn't make so much difference." Her large black eyes turned to him: "But I'm scared for him. Scared of losing him."

"You've never been afraid of loneliness before."

She shook her head pensively. "It's not that. It's the bond as such. The idea of continuity. A sort of reassuring stability. I mean, anything outside one may change, one may change oneself, but as long as you know there's something that goes on unchanged, like a river running down to the sea, you have a sense of security, or faith, or whatever you want to call it. Sometimes I think that is why I have such an overwhelming urge to have a child." A deliberate, mocking laugh. "You see, one keeps clinging to one's own little hope for eternity. Even if you've given up Father Christmas."

12 February. And now Susan. Have noticed something in her these last few days. Thought it was just a new phase in her nervous state, in spite of the sedatives she takes in ever growing doses. But this time it turned out to be different, and worse. Her contract with the SABC revoked finally. Convincing arguments about "new blood" and "tight budget" etc. But the producer she usually worked with told her the truth over a cup of tea. The fact that she was my wife was becoming an embarrassment to them. One never knew when my name might be linked to some scandal. He didn't know where it came from. His superiors had simply told him that they had "information".

It all came out last night. When I came into the bedroom she sat waiting for me. The day after Christmas she'd moved into the bedroom that used to be the girls', so I was wary of this unexpected new overture. She in her nightie without a gown, seated on the foot of my bed. A nervous, twitching smile.

"You not asleep yet?" I asked.

She shook her head. "I was waiting for you."

"I still had some work to do."

"Doesn't matter."

The trivialities, the inanities one can indulge in!

"I thought you were going to the theatre tonight?" I said.

"No, I cancelled it. Didn't feel like it."

"It would have done you good to go out."

"I'm too tired."

"You're always tired nowadays."

"Does it surprise you?"

"It's my fault. Is that what you're trying to say?"

Suddenly a hint of panic in her: "I'm sorry, Ben. Please, I didn't come here to reproach you for anything. It's just – it *can't* go on like this."

"It won't. I'm sure something will happen soon. One has just got to see it through."

"Every time you believe 'something will happen'. Can't you see it's only getting worse? Just worse and worse all the time."

"No."

Then she told me about the SABC.

"It's the only thing I had left to keep me going, Ben." She began to cry, even though I could see she was trying to fight it. For a while I stood looking at her hopelessly. If a thing like this goes on so slowly, day by day, you tend not to notice the difference. But last night, I don't know why, I suddenly looked at our wedding portrait on the wall above the dressing table. And it shook me to think it was the same woman. That beaming, self-assured, strong, healthy, blond girl and this weary old woman in the nightie made for someone much younger, the pathetic white lace leaving her arms bare, the loose folds of skin on her upper arms, the wrinkly neck, the streaks of grey no longer camouflaged in her hair, the face distorted with crying. The same woman. My wife. And my fault?

After a while I sat down beside her, holding her so she could cry properly. Her sagging breasts. She didn't even try to hide them: she who'd always been so ashamed of her body when it was young and beautiful. Now that she'd grown old she didn't mind my seeing. Was it carelessness or despair?

How is it possible that even in agony, even in revulsion, one

264

can be roused to desire? Or was it something I tried to avenge on her? All those years of inhibitions; the passion I had discovered in her on a few rare and unforgettable nights of our life together, only to be almost aggressively repressed afterwards. Sin, wrong, evil. Always occupied, always busy, running, achieving things, grasping at success, frantic efforts to deny the body and its real demands. And now, all of a sudden, pressed against me, exposed, exhibited, made available. Blindly I took her, and in our agonising struggle she left the imprint of her nails on my shoulders as she cried and blubbered against me; and for once it was I who turned away in shame afterwards, remaining with my back to her.

A very long time.

When she spoke again at last her voice was completely controlled.

"It didn't work, did it?"

"I'm sorry. I don't know what got into me."

"I'm not talking about tonight. All these years."

I didn't answer, reluctant to argue.

"Perhaps we never tried hard enough. Perhaps I never understood you properly. Neither of us really understood, did we?"

"Susan, we've brought up three children. We've always got along fine."

"Perhaps that's the worst. That one can get along so well in hell."

"You're exhausted, you're not seeing it the way you should."

"I think for the first time in my life I'm seeing it as I should."

"What are you going to do?"

I looked round. She was sitting upright, the bedspread drawn defensively round her shoulders in spite of the warm night.

"I want to go to my parents for a while. Just to regain my balance. To give you a chance. So that we can think it over calmly and clearly. It's no use if we're both so involved that we can't breathe properly."

What could I do? I nodded. "I suppose you do need a holiday."

"So you agree?" She got up.

265

"It was your idea."

"But you think I should go?"

"Yes, to breathe some fresh air. To give us a chance, as you said."

She went as far as the door. I was still sitting on the bed.

She looked round: "You're not even trying to hold me back," she said, the passion in her voice more naked than her misused body had been a little while ago.

The worst was that there was nothing I could say. Realising for the first time what a total stranger she was. And if she was a stranger to me, the woman I had lived with for so many years, how could I presume ever to understand anything else?

25 February. I'm making fewer and fewer notes. Less and less to say. But it's a year today. It feels like yesterday, that evening I stood in the kitchen eating my sardines from the tin. *A detainee in terms of the Terrorism Act, one Gordon Ngubene, has been found dead in his cell this morning. According to a spokesman of the Security Police,* etcetera.

And what have I achieved in this year? Adding everything together it still, God knows, amounts to nothing. I'm trying to persevere. I'm trying to persuade myself that we're making progress. But how much of it is illusion? Is there anything I really know, anything I can be absolutely certain of? In weaker moments I fear that Susan might have been right: am I losing my mind?

Am I mad – or is it the world? Where does the madness of the world begin? And if it is madness, why is it permitted? Who allows it?

Stanley, two days ago already: Johnson Seroke shot dead by unknown persons. Emily's Special Branch man, my one remaining hope. Now he too. Late at night, according to Stanley. Knock on the door. When he opened they fired five shots at point-blank range. Face, chest, stomach. Leading articles in several papers yesterday. Interviews with police officers: "All those voices that usually cry out against deaths in detention are strangely silent now that a member of the Security Police has died in the service of his country. This black man's life, sacrificed on the altar of our national survival in the face of senseless terrorism, should be pondered by all those who never have a good word for the police and their ceaseless efforts to keep this country stable and prosperous—"

But I know why Johnson Seroke died. It doesn't take much imagination.

How much longer must the list grow of those who pay the price of my efforts to clear Gordon's name?

Or is this yet another symptom of my madness? That I am no longer able to think anything but the worst of my adversaries? That in a monstrous way I'm simplifying the whole complicated situation by turning all those from the "other side" into criminals of whom I can believe only evil? That I turn mere suspicions into facts, in order to place them in the most horrible light? If this is true I have become their equal in every respect. A worthy opponent!

But if I can no longer believe that right is on my side, if I can no longer believe in the imperative to go on: what will become of me?

7 *March.* Beginning, end, point of no return: what was it? Decisive, undoubtedly. Separate from everything else that has happened so far – or rooted in it? Have been going round for days now, unable to write about it, yet desperate to do so. Frightened by its finality? Afraid of myself? I can no longer avoid it. Otherwise I shall never be able to get past it.

Saturday 4 March.

The rock-bottom of loneliness. No sign of Stanley since the news about Johnson Seroke. I know he has to be more careful than ever, but still. No word from Susan. Johan off to a farm with friends. This is no life for a young boy. (But how touching when he said: "You sure you'll be okay, Dad? I'll stay here if you need me.") More than a week since I last visited Phil Bruwer in hospital. Melanie working full-time. You reach a danger point if you're forced to keep your own company for too long. The temptation of masochism.

But where to go, and who to turn to? Who has not rejected me yet? Young Viviers? The jovial Carelse? Until they, too, have to pay the price. I suppose the Rev Buster may have welcomed me. But I couldn't face the prospect of discussing the state of my soul with him. I don't think my soul is really so important any more.

Tried to work. Forced myself to go through all my notes again, turning the sorting process into some game of solitaire. Then stacked away everything again in the tools cupboard and drove off.

But the old house with the curved verandah was dark and empty. Walked round it. Cats' saucers on the back stoep. No curtains drawn but everything dark inside. What room hers? As if it mattered! Simply to know, to draw some solace from it. Adolescent. That's why older men should steer clear of love. Makes them ridiculous.

Sat on the front steps for a long time, smoking. Nothing happened. Almost relieved when I got up to go to the front gate. Felt "saved". Dear God, from what? Fate worse than death? Ben Du Toit, you should have your head read.

Still, much more at peace. Resigned to going home again and facing my solitude.

But before I'd reached the gate – I really have to fix it for them one day, the slats are falling out – her small car turned into the back yard. I actually felt almost regretful. It might have been avoided so easily. (How can I talk about "avoiding"? At that moment, surely, I had no anticipation, no hope, no conception of what was to happen. And yet it seems to me there must be such subtle subterranean ways of knowing in advance.)

"Ben?!" When she saw me coming round the corner of the house. "Is that you? You gave me a fright."

"I've been here for a while. Was on the point of leaving."

"I went to see Dad in hospital."

"How is he?"

"No change."

She unlocked the kitchen door and unhesitatingly led the way down the dark passage – I stumbled over a cat – to the living room. The murky yellow light seemed to illuminate more than just the room. She was wearing a dress with a prim high collar.

"I'll make us some coffee."

"Shall I give you a hand?"

"No. Make yourself at home."

The room became meaningless without her. From the kitchen came sounds of cups tinkling, the hiss of a kettle. Then she came back. I took the tray from her. We sat drinking in silence. Was she embarrassed too? But why? I felt like a stranger on a formal visit.

When her cup was empty she put on a record, turning the volume down very low.

"More coffee?"

"No thanks."

The cats were purring again. The music made the room more habitable, more hospitable, the book-filled shelves a protection against the world.

"Any idea when your father will come home again?"

"No. The doctors seem reasonably satisfied, but they don't want to take any chances. And he's growing impatient."

It was a relief to talk about him. By discussing him it was possible to say what we had to suppress about ourselves. The first evening in this room. The night in the mountains.

Another silence.

"I hope I'm not keeping you from your work?"

"No," she said. "There's nothing important at the moment. And next Friday I'm off again."

"Where to this time?"

"Kenya." She smiled. "I'll have to rely on my British passport again."

"Aren't you scared of being caught one day?"

"Oh I'll manage all right."

"Isn't it exhausting to go on like this, immersing yourself in one thing after another, never really settling down?"

269

"Sometimes. But it keeps one on one's toes."

I couldn't help saying: "At least you have more to show for your efforts than I've achieved these last few months."

"How do you measure results?" Her eyes were warm and sympathetic. "I think we're really very similar in many ways. We both seem to have a greater capacity for experiencing things than for understanding them."

"Perhaps it's just as well. Sometimes it seems to me that to really understand would drive one mad."

It had grown late. A warm night with the balminess of early autumn. We spoke less as the evening wore on, but it was easier to communicate. The old intimacy had returned, in that cosy room still bearing vaguely the smell of her father's tobacco, through the mustiness of books and cats and well-worn carpets.

It must have been past midnight when I got up reluctantly. "I suppose it's time to go."

"Do you have 'obligations'?" With light, ironical emphasis.

"No, there's nobody else at home."

Why hadn't I told her about Susan before? To protect myself? I'm not sure. Anyway, there was no reason to keep it secret any longer. I told her. She made no comment, but there was a change in her dark eyes. Pensive, almost grave, she got out of her chair, facing me.

She'd kicked off her shoes earlier, making her even smaller, almost teenage in appearance, a slip of a girl; and yet mature and sobered, illusions shed, and with that deeper compassion either unknown to youth or underestimated by it.

"Why don't you stay here then?" she said.

I hesitated, trying to fathom her real meaning. As if she were guessing my thoughts, she added calmly: "I'll make you a bed in the spare room. Then you needn't drive home at this ungodly hour."

"I'd love to stay. I can't really face the prospect of an empty house."

"Both of us will have to get used to empty houses."

She went out ahead of me, soundless on her narrow feet. We didn't speak again. I helped her make the bed in the spare room; a beautifully carved old wooden bedstead. All thoughts suspended.

When we'd finished we looked at each other across the bed. I was aware of the tightness of my smile.

"I'm also going to turn in," she said, moving away.

"Melanie."

Without a word she looked round.

"Stay here with me."

For a moment I thought she was going to say yes. My throat was dry. I wanted to put out my hand to touch her but the broad bed was between us.

Then she said: "No. I don't think I should."

I knew she was right. We were so close. Anything might happen. But suppose it did: what then? What would become of us? How could we possibly cope with it in our demented world?

It was better, if more desolate, this way. She didn't come round the bed to kiss me goodnight. With a small, agonised smile she went to the door. Did she hesitate there? Was she waiting for me to call her back? I desperately wanted to. But merely by inviting her I had already gone far enough. I couldn't risk any more.

I couldn't hear which way she went, her feet made no sound. Here and there, from time to time, a floorboard creaked in the big dark house, but it might have been of old age, no indication of her whereabouts. For a very long time I remained there beside the bed with the covers drawn back from the pillows. Taking stock of everything, as if an inventory were of vital importance. The pattern of the old-fashioned wallpaper. The bedside table stacked with books. A small bookshelf against the wall. A dressing table with a large oval mirror. A large Victorian wardrobe with a pile of suitcases on top.

After several minutes I went over to the window. The curtains were not drawn; one of the side-windows stood open. Looking out across the back garden. Grass and trees. Darkness. The day's fragrant warmth still lingering in the stillness. Crickets and frogs.

It amazed me that desolation could be so peaceful. For her refusal and her turning away had sealed something very finally. Something hopeful, however extravagant or presumptuous, which had now been closed gently and serenely before me, like a door clicking shut before I could enter.

And then she came back. When I turned my head she was standing there beside me, close enough to touch. She was naked. I stared at her in utter silence. She was clearly timid; fearful, I think, that I might find her provocative. But she made no attempt to turn away. She must have known that it was as necessary for me to gaze as it was for her to be gazed at. I had become the mirror she'd spoken of before. *You look at yourself naked. A face, a body you've seen in the mirror every day of your life. Except you've never really seen it. You've never really looked. And now, all of a sudden—*

All our previous moments seemed to converge in this one. Chronology and consequence became irrelevant. Time was stripped from us the way one removes one's clothes to make love.

The candour of her body. Her presence was total, and overwhelming. I feel quite ridiculous trying to grasp it now with nothing but words. How paltry it sounds, almost offensive, reduced to description. But what else can I do? Silence would be denial.

Her hair undone, loose and heavy on her shoulders. Her breasts so incredibly small, mere swellings, with dark, elongated, erect nipples. The smooth belly with the exquisite little knot in its hollow. Below, the trim triangular thicket of black hair between her legs.

But it is not that. Nothing I can enumerate or adequately name. What mattered was that in her nakedness she was making herself available to me. The incomprehensible gift of herself. What else do we have to offer?

Those words of months ago, on the eve of everything: *Once in one's life, just once, one should have enough faith in something to risk everything for it.*

We didn't pull the sheets up over us. She didn't even want me to put off the light. Like two children playing the game for the first time we wanted to see everything, touch everything, discover everything. A newness, as of birth. The smooth movements of her limbs. The scent of her hair. My whole face covered with it, my mouth filled with it. The slightness of her breasts against my cheek. Her nipples tautening between my lips. Her deft hands. Her sex distending, opening deeply to

272

my touch, in wet and secret warmth. Our two bodies mingling on the edge of our precipice. The marvel and mystery of the flesh. Her voice in my ear. Her urgent breathing. Her teeth biting into my shoulder. The hairy bulge of her mound, a fleshy fist yielding under my pressure and sucking me inside.

But it was not that. It wasn't that at all. What I was conscious of, what I can recapture now, was what I could feel and see and touch and hear and taste. But it wasn't that. Not those limbs I can catalogue one by one, trying desperately to grope back to what really happened. Something else, something wholly different. Bodies purified through ecstasy, in light and darkness. Until at last and out of breath we became still again. Exhausted, I lay against her listening to the deep rhythm of her breathing, her mouth still half-open, and behind her moist lips the dull glistening of her teeth, her small breasts bruised, the puckered nipples slack, on her belly the snail-trails of our love; one knee bent outwards, the leg relaxed, and in the dark mat of her love-hair the exposed and mangled furrow, the moist inner lips still swollen with invisible blood. The full frank miracle of her body alive even in that sleep of exhaustion and fulfilment. I couldn't get enough of looking at her, trying to quench the thirst of years and years in a single night. I had to cram myself with her so that, all five senses replete with her, there would be nothing left of myself at all. The final consummation would be to break right through the senses and plunge into the darkness beyond, into that love of which our passion had been but the celebration and the token. *Behold, thou art fair, my love.*

The urgency of my desire slaked, I felt a new serenity. Propped up on one elbow I lay looking at her in peace and awe, touching her, caressing her very gently, still unable to believe my eyes, or my hands, or my tongue. I wasn't sleepy. It was presumptuous even to think of sleep while I had her there beside me to look at, to touch, to reaffirm the unbelievable reality of her body. I had to keep awake and keep watch, probing every possibility of this brief tenderness while it was so precariously and incredibly ours.

Happiness? It was one of the saddest nights of my life, an ageless sadness that insinuated itself into the very heart of this new world and deepened slowly into anguish and agony. There she was sleeping, closer to me than anyone had ever been to me, exposed and available, utterly trusting, at my disposal to love, to look at, to touch, to explore, to enter: and yet, in that peaceful deep sleep more remote than any star, ungraspable, forever apart. I knew her eyes and the inside of her mouth, her nipples in rest and arousal, every limb of her slight smooth body, every individual finger and toe; I could examine if I wished each separate secret hair. And yet it amounted to nothing, nothing at all. Our bodies had joined and turned and clasped, and shared the spasms of pleasure and of pain. But having touched, we were again separate; and in her sleep, as she smiled, or whimpered, or lay breathing quietly, she was as far from me as if we'd never met. I wanted to cry. But the ache was too deep to be relieved by tears.

It must have been near sunrise when I fell asleep beside her. When I woke up it was broad daylight and the birds were singing in the trees outside. On the bedside table the lamp was still burning, a dull and futile yellow stain on the brilliant morning. What had awakened me was the movement of her hands over me, the way I had caressed her in the night while she'd been sleeping so remotely. There was no haste: it was Sunday, and nothing and no-one required us or made demands on us; and very slowly she allowed me to return from sleep, and once more to cover her body with mine, breaking back into the hidden warmth of her body – a sensation like diving into lukewarm water, as if not only my penis but all of me, all I'd ever been or could hope to be, were drawn into her, immersed in her; until, after the implosion, consciousness ebbed back, throbbing dully and painfully, as I knew once more what it meant to feel and to be alive, to be exposed, and to fear.

Because I know only too well – and I knew it then, too, in that incongruous light where the lamp was trying so bravely to hold its own against the unmerciful glare of the day – that we love one another, but that neither of us can redeem the other. And that through the love of our bodies we have been drawn into history. We are no longer outside it, but involved in all that is definable, calculable in terms of months or years, manoeuvrable, shockable, destructible. And in that sadness more profound than I had ever known, I went away at last.

274

Three weeks later Susan returned from Cape Town. Not quite her old self yet, but more relaxed, more prepared, more determined to try again. Two days after her return, on Thursday 30 March, Ben found, when he came home from school (Johan had stayed behind for cadets), a large brown envelope in the mailbox, addressed to her. He took it inside with his own post.

There was no letter in the envelope, only a photograph. An ordinary eight-by-ten on glossy paper. Not a very clear shot, as if the light had been bad. A background of fuzzy, out-of-focus wallpaper, a bedside table, a crumpled bed; a man and a girl naked in a position of intimate caressing, apparently preparing for intercourse.

Susan was on the point of tearing it up in disgust when something prompted her to take a closer look. The girl, the dark-haired girl, was a stranger to her. The man with her was middle-aged, and immediately recognisable in spite of the heavy grain. The man was Ben.

FOUR

When he opened the door Captain Stolz was waiting on the stoep. For months on end he'd been waiting for them to come back, assuming that it was only a matter of time. Especially after the photograph had arrived in the mail. Still, his notes leave one in no doubt about the shock he received when it actually happened that afternoon: it was the third of April, a day before Melanie was due to return from Kenya. The officer was alone. That in itself must have meant something.

"Can we talk?"

Ben would have preferred to refuse him entry, but he was much too shaken to react. Mechanically he stood aside, allowing the lean man in the eternal sports jacket to enter. Perhaps it was also, in an irrational way, a relief at last to have an adversary of flesh and blood opposite him again, someone he could recognise and pin down, someone to talk to, even in blind hate.

Stolz was, at least to begin with, much more congenial than before, enquiring about Ben's health, his wife, his work at school.

In the end, pulling him up short, Ben said tartly: "I'm sure you didn't come here to ask about my family, Captain."

A glint of amusement in Stolz's dark eyes. "Why not?"

"I've never had the impression that you were very interested in my private affairs."

"Mr Du Toit, I've come here today" – he crossed his long legs comfortably – "because I feel sure we can come to an understanding."

"Really?"

"Don't you think this business has gone on long enough?"

279

"That's for you people to decide, isn't it?"

"Now be honest: has all the evidence you've been collecting in connection with Gordon Ngubene brought you one step closer to the sort of truth you were looking for?"

"Yes, I think so."

A brief pause. "I really hoped we could talk man to man."

"I don't think it's still possible, Captain. If it ever was. Not between you and me."

"Pity." Stolz shifted on his chair. "It really is a great pity. Mind if I smoke?"

Ben made a gesture.

"Things don't quite seem to be going your way, do they?" said Stolz after he'd lit his cigarette.

"That's your opinion, not mine."

"Let's put it this way: certain things have happened that might cause you considerable embarrassment if they were to leak out."

Ben felt tense, the skin tightening on his jaws. But without taking his eyes from Stolz he asked: "What makes you think so?"

"Now look," said Stolz, "just between the two of us: we're all made of flesh and blood, we've all got our little flaws. And if a man should get it into his head to – shall we say, sample the grass on the other side of the fence, well, that's his own business. Provided it's kept quiet, of course. Because it would be rather unpleasant if people found out about it, not so? I mean, especially if he is in the public eye. A teacher, for instance."

In the seemingly interminable silence that followed they sat weighing each other.

"Why don't you come out with it?" Ben asked at last. Although he hadn't meant to, he took out his pipe to keep his hands occupied.

"Mr Du Toit, what I'm going to say to you now is in strict confidence—" He seemed to be waiting for reaction, but Ben only shrugged. "I suppose you know there are photographs in circulation which may cause you some discomfort," said Stolz. "It so happened that I came across one of them myself."

"It doesn't surprise me, Captain. After all, they were taken on your instructions, weren't they?"

Stolz laughed, not very pleasantly. "You're not serious are you, Mr Du Toit? Really, as if we haven't got enough to do as it is."

"It surprised me too. To think of all the manpower, all the money, all the time you're spending on someone like me. There must be many bigger and more serious problems to occupy you?"

"I'm glad you're seeing it that way. That's why I'm here today. On this friendly visit." He emphasised the words slightly as he sat watching the thin line of smoke blown from his mouth. "You see, that stuff was brought to my attention, so I thought it was my duty to tell you about it."

"Why?"

"Because I don't like to see an ordinary decent man like you being victimised in such a sordid way."

In spite of himself, Ben smiled stiffly. "What you really mean, I presume, is: if I'm willing to co-operate, if I stop being an embarrassment or a threat to you, the photographs will remain harmlessly filed away somewhere?"

"I wouldn't exactly put it in those words. Let's just say I may be able to use my influence to make sure that a private indiscretion isn't used against you."

"And in exchange I must keep my mouth shut?"

"Well, don't you think it's high time we allowed the dead to rest in peace? What possible sense could there be in continuing to waste time and energy the way you've been doing this past year?"

"Suppose I refuse?"

The smoke was blown out very slowly. "I'm not trying to influence you, Mr Du Toit. But think it over."

Ben got up. "I won't be blackmailed, Captain. Not even by you."

Stolz didn't move in his chair. "Now don't rush things. I'm offering you a chance."

"You mean my very last chance?"

"One never knows."

"I still haven't uncovered the full truth I'm looking for, Captain," Ben said quietly. "But I have a pretty good idea of what it's going to look like. And I won't allow anyone or anything to come between me and that truth."

Slowly and deliberately Stolz stubbed out his cigarette in the ashtray. "Is that your final answer?"

"You didn't really expect anything else, did you?"

"Perhaps I did." Stolz looked him in the eyes. "Are you sure you realise what you're exposing yourself to? Those people — whoever they may be — can make things very difficult for you indeed."

"Then those people will have to live with their own conscience. I trust you will give them the message, Captain."

A very slight hint of a blush moved across the officer's face, causing the thin line of the scar to show up more sharply on his cheekbone.

"Well, that's that then. Good-bye."

Ignoring Stolz's hand Ben went past him and opened the door of his study. Neither said another word.

What amazed Ben was the discovery that there was no anger against the man left in him. He almost, momentarily, felt sorry for him. *You're a prisoner just like me. The only difference is that you don't know it.*

There was no sign of Melanie at the airport when Ben went there the next afternoon to meet her. The stewardess he approached for help pressed the buttons of a computer and confirmed that Melanie's name was on the passengers' list all right; but after she'd gone off to make further enquiries an official in uniform approached Ben to tell him that the stewardess had been mistaken. There had been no person by that name on the flight from Nairobi.

Prof Bruwer received the news with surprising equanimity when Ben visited him in hospital the same evening. Nothing to worry about, he said. Melanie often changed her mind at the last moment. Perhaps she'd found something new to investigate. Another day or two and she would be back. He found Ben's anxiety amusing; nothing more.

The next day there was a cable from London: *Safely here. Please don't worry. Will phone. Love, Melanie.*

It was nearly midnight when the call came through. A very bad line, her voice distant and almost unrecognisable.

Ben glanced over his shoulder to make sure Susan's door was shut.

"What's happened? Where are you, Melanie?"

"In London."

"But how did you get there?"

"Were you waiting for me at the airport?"

"Of course. What happened to you?"

"They didn't want to let me through."

For a moment he was too shocked to speak. Then he asked: "You mean—you were there too?"

A distant laugh, smothered and unsettling. "Of course I was."

It hit him forcibly. "The passport?"

"Yes. Undesirable immigrant. Promptly deported."

"But you're not an immigrant. You're as South African as I am."

"No longer. One forfeits one's citizenship, didn't you know?"

"I don't believe it." All his thoughts seemed to get stuck, idiotically, in the violent simplicity of the discovery that she would never come back.

"Will you please tell Dad? But break it gently. I don't want to upset him in his condition."

"Melanie, is there anything I—"

"Not for the moment." A strange, weary matter-of-factness in her voice. As if she had already withdrawn herself. Perhaps she was scared to show emotion. Especially on the telephone. "Just look after Dad, Ben. Please."

"Don't worry."

"We can make other arrangements later. Perhaps. I haven't had time to think yet."

"Where can I get in touch with you?"

"Through the newspaper. I'll let you know. Perhaps we can think of something. At the moment it's all messed up."

"But, my God, Melanie—!"

"Please don't talk now, Ben." The immensity of the distance between us. Seas, continents. "It'll be all right." For a while the line became inaudible.

"Melanie, are you still there?"

"Yes, I'm here. Listen——"

"Tell me, for God's sake——"

"I'm tired, Ben. I haven't slept for thirty-six hours. I can't think of anything right now."

"Can I phone you somewhere tomorrow?"

"I'll write."

"Please!"

"Just look after yourself. And tell Dad." Tersely, tensely, almost irritably. Or was it just the line?

"Melanie, are you quite sure——"

The telephone died in his hand.

Ten minutes later it rang again. This time there was silence on the other side. And then a man's voice chuckling, before the receiver was put down again.

2

It felt as if her letter would never come. And the tension of waiting, the daily disappointment at the mailbox, sapped his nervous energy as much as anything else that had happened to him. Had the letter been intercepted? That possibility in itself brought home the futility of his anger to him in a more nauseating way than even the discovery of the photograph had done. However vicious the pressures he had been submitted to, they had all been related to his efforts in connection with Gordon. But now Melanie had been drawn into it, involving what was most private in his existence.

Interminable nights of lying awake. Groping back to that unbelievable night, so farfetched in his memories that he sometimes wondered whether it had been a hallucination. All he had to sustain him was the vividness of those memories. The achingly vulnerable, barely noticeable swelling of her breasts. The long dark nipples and their golden aureoles. The taste of her hair in his mouth. Her quicksilver tongue. Her rising voice. The slickness of her sex opening under the soft mat of hair. But the acute physicality of those very memories was disturbing. It had been so much more than that, hadn't it? Unless their love in itself had been an illusion, a fever-dream in a desert?

And on the other hand, the painful fantasies: that she'd deliberately decided not to write because she wanted to withdraw from him; that she'd grasped at the opportunity to escape from him because he'd become an embarrassment to her. Worst of all: that she herself had been planted by them, instructed from the very beginning to play cat-and-mouse with him in order to find out what he knew and who his collaborators were. Surely that was madness! And yet it had become such an effort merely to drag oneself from one day to the next that nothing really appeared more outrageous than anything else.

Perhaps everything had become part of one vast mirage. Perhaps he'd imagined the whole persecution. Perhaps there was an illness in his brain, a tumour, a cancerous growth, a malignant accumulation of cells causing him to lose touch with what was really happening. What was 'real', what was pure paranoia? But if that were so, was it possible for a madman to be aware of his own madness?

If only it had been a real desert and he a real fugitive running from a real enemy in helicopters or jeeps or on foot. If only it had been a real desert in which one could die of thirst or exposure, where one could go blind of the intolerable white glare, where one could shrivel up and bleach out like a dried bone in the sun: for then, at least, one would know what was happening; it would be possible to foresee the end, to make your peace with God and with the world, to prepare yourself for what lay in store. But now – now there was nothing. Only this blind uncontrollable motion carrying him with it, not even sure whether it was actually moving; as imperceptible as the motion of the earth under his feet.

The events and minor afflictions of every day hardly served as landmarks any more, having become part of that general blind motion. The telephone calls. The car following him into town.

Even the more serious incidents: the crude bomb hurled through his study window one evening while he was with Phil Bruwer in hospital (thank God Susan had gone to spend a few days with Suzette; and Johan was able to put out the fire before much damage could be done). The shots fired through the windscreen of his car while he was returning from an aimless zigzagging trip through the streets on another night. Was it just his luck that he hadn't been hit: or had they missed him deliberately?

In the beginning he was relieved by the Easter holidays, not having to worry about the tedious duties imposed by his school routine. But soon he came to regret it, missing the security of that very routine, infinitely preferable to this dizzy, unpredictable course from day to day. The pale autumn days growing ever more wintry. The leaves falling, the trees barer, drier. All sap invisible, unbelievable. All softness, all tenderness, all femininity, all gentle humanity, compassion, burnt away. Dry, dry, and colourless. An inhospitable autumn.

And all the time, in a steady, ceaseless flow, the people coming to him for help. Enough to drive him out of his mind. What was there he could really and effectively do? The widely divergent requests: heart-rending, serious, mendacious, banal. – The young black man from the Free State, illegally in search of work because his family was starving on the farm: four rand in cash and half a bag of mealie-meal a month. Twice before he'd tried to run away, only to be brought back and beaten to within an inch of his life by his master; but the third time he'd escaped and now the Baas must help him. – The woman whose wages were stolen in a supermarket. – The man who'd just spent eight months in jail and received six cuts with the cane because he had been impudent enough to tell his white master's teenage daughter, "You're a pretty girl."

It was getting boring. He couldn't go on with it. But he was overrun by their collective agony. *The Baas must help me. There is no one else.* Sometimes he lost his temper. "For God's sake stop pestering me! Dan Levinson has fled the country. Melanie has gone. I hardly ever see Stanley any more. There's no one I can send you to. Leave me alone. I can't do it any longer."

Stanley did come round again, late one night when Ben was

in his study, unable to face another sleepless night in bed.

"I say, lanie! Why you looking like a bloody fish on dry ground?"

"Stanley! What brought you here?"

"Just blew in." Large and bristling with life his virile presence flooded the little room. Like so many times in the past he seemed to act like a generator, charging all the inanimate objects around him – carpet, desk, lamp, books, everything – with secret uncontrollable energy.

"Got you another bit for your jigsaw. Not much, but so what?"

"What is it?"

"The driver of the police van that took Jonathan to hospital that time."

Ben sighed. "You think it will be of any use?"

"I thought you wanted everything."

"I know. But I'm tired."

"What you need is a fling. Why don't you find yourself a girl? Fuck the shit out of her. Trust me."

"This is no time for joking, Stanley!"

"Sorry, man. Just thought it would help."

They sat looking at one another, each waiting for the other to say something. At last Ben sighed. "All right, give me the driver's name."

After he had taken down the particulars he listlessly pushed away the paper, looking up.

"You think we may still win in the end, Stanley?" he asked wearily.

"Of course not." Stanley seemed surprised at the very idea. "But that's not the point, man."

"*Is* there any point?"

"We can't win, lanie. But we needn't lose either. What matters is to stick around."

"I wish I could be as sure of it as you seem to be."

"I got children, lanie. I told you long ago. What happens to me don't matter. But if I quit now it's tickets with them too." His bulky torso supported on his arms, he leaned over the desk. "Got to do *something*, man. Even if my own people will spit on me if they knew I was here with you tonight."

287

"Why?" Ben asked, startled.

"Because I'm old-fashioned enough to sit here scheming with a white man. Make no mistake, lanie, my people are in a black mood. My children too. They speak a different language from you and me." He got up. "It won't be easy to come back here again. There's informers all over the bloody place. It's a hell of a time, lanie."

"Are you also abandoning me now?"

"I won't drop you lanie. But we got to be careful." He put out his hand. "See you."

"Where are you off to this time?"

"Just a trip."

"Then you'll be back sometime."

"Sure." He laughed, taking Ben's hand in both of his. "We'll be together again, sure's tomorrow. You know something? The day will come when I won't have to dodge your neighbours' fucking dogs at night no more. We'll walk out here in broad daylight together, man. Down the streets, left-right, all the way. Arm in arm, I tell you. Right through the world, lanie. No one to stop us. Just think of it." He bent over, limp with glee. "You and me, man. And no bastard to stop us saying: 'Hey, where's that *domboek*?'"

He was still laughing, a great sad booming sound. And suddenly he was gone and it was very quiet in the room. It was the last time they saw each other.

Beside him, Susan went her own way, distant and aloof. They spoke very little, exchanging a few indispensable words at table, but no more. When he did make an attempt to start a conversation, asking a question or offering an explanation, she sat looking down, studying her nails in that absorbed way a woman has when she wants to convey to you that she finds you boring.

Actually, Linda was the only one he still spoke to, telephoning her from time to time; but it often happened that in the middle of a conversation he would become absent-minded, forgetting what he'd wanted to tell her.

And Phil Bruwer, of course, even though Melanie was an unspoken obstacle between them. The old man constantly spoke about her, but Ben found it difficult to respond. Although the old man was her father – perhaps because of it? – she was too painfully private to discuss.

Her newspaper had carried a prominent report about the confiscation of her South African passport, intimating that it might have some connection "with a private investigation she had been conducting in connection with the death in detention of Gordon Ngubene a year ago". Curiously enough, though, they never followed it up. The Sunday paper continued to refer to Gordon's story at irregular intervals, owing mainly to the perseverence of one or two young reporters who kept in touch with Ben about it; but even that was losing momentum. A few readers' letters specifically requested the newspaper to drop the 'tedious affair'.

"You can't blame them, really," said Prof Bruwer. "People's memories are short, you know. They mean well. But in a world that has seen Hitler and Biafra and Viet Nam and Bangladesh the life of a single man doesn't mean much. People are moved only on the quantitative level. Bigger and better."

It was the day Ben brought the old man home. The doctors still were not very happy with his progress but neither was he ill enough to be kept in hospital. And since Melanie's departure he had become more short-tempered and restless. He would not be at ease again before he was back in his own home and pottering in his own garden. Ben had arranged for a full-time nurse to attend to him – much against the old man's wishes – and with that care taken from his shoulders he stayed away until, a few days before the reopening of the schools, Bruwer telephoned him and asked him to come over.

There was a letter for him from Melanie. It came so unexpectedly that he could only stare at the unstamped envelope in disbelief.

"Came inside my own letter," explained the old man, chuckling contentedly. "She sent it to an old friend of mine and he brought it round this morning. Take your time, I won't interrupt."

It was not a long letter, and strangely sober in tone. Almost feverishly he scanned it in search of some deeper meaning, some subtle intimate reference in the prosaic account of how she had been stopped by Customs at Jan Smuts airport, escorted to a private office and put on a British Airways flight returning to London later the same evening. A brief, unemotional statement about her concern for him and her father. The assurance that there was nothing for them to worry about; she would be all right and had, in fact, already been officially transferred to her newspaper's Fleet Street bureau. And then, at last:

What follows is for your eyes only. Please don't let Dad find out. I started writing an article about Gordon, thinking it might be a good idea to spill all the beans over here. But before I could finish it I received an unexpected visit. Distinguished gentleman, very British in appearance, but betrayed by his accent. (Unless I'm imagining things: one starts doubting one's own judgement.) He said very suavely that he felt sure I wouldn't be so rash as to publish anything about Gordon in Britain. "What can stop me?" I asked. "Common decency," he said. "You wouldn't like to cause your old father any trouble, would you?"

So here I am, stumped. But we must not lose heart, Ben. Please don't let what has happened to me interfere with what you have to do. Despair is a waste of time. Dad will need your help. You must go on. You must endure. You've got to, for Gordon and Jonathan. But also for your own sake. For mine. For ours. Please. As far as I am concerned, I want you to know that I do not regret for one moment a single thing that has happened between us.

For a long time he sat looking at the letter on his lap before he folded it very meticulously and put it back in the envelope.

"Satisfied?" asked the old man, his eyes twinkling with amusement.

He made up his mind very quickly. It was hardly a conscious decision: simply the acceptance of what had become inevitable.

"Prof, there's something I've got to tell you."

"That you and Melanie are in love?"

"How do you know?"

"I'm not blind, Ben."

"It's more than being in love. I want you to know. One night, just before she left for Kenya—"

"Why do you tell it to me?"

"Because that is the reason they took away her citizenship. Not to punish her for anything. But to get at *me*. They took photographs of us and tried to blackmail me. And when I refused, they took it out on her. Because they knew how it would hit me."

Very calm, his head bowed, the old man sat opposite him.

"I don't want you to go on receiving me in your house after I've been responsible for what has happened."

"They've been eyeing her for a long time, Ben."

"But I was the last straw."

"Does it really matter what pretext they used?"

"How can I look you in the eyes again?"

"Blaming oneself can be a bloody sterile pastime."

"How can I not blame myself?"

"We owe it to ourselves to look beyond this thing, Ben. I think we owe it to Melanie too." He took the pipe the doctors had expressly forbidden him and started scratching out the dry ash. "You know, what amazes me is to wonder what sort of world this is, what sort of society, in which it is possible for the state to persecute and try to break a man with a thing like this. How does such a system come into being? Where does it start? And who allows it to have its way?"

"Isn't it enough to know that it happens?"

"What will become of us if we ever stop asking questions?"

"But where do these questions lead to?"

"No matter where the hell they lead to. The important thing is to bloody well go on asking." Breathing deeply, more upset than I had seen him in a long time, he struck match after match to light his pipe. "And we'd better keep asking until we've cleared up our own responsibility in the matter too."

"How can we be responsible for what happened?" said Ben. "We're rebelling against it!"

"There may not have been any specific thing we did." He inhaled the smoke, savouring it, relaxing slowly. "Perhaps it's something we *didn't* do. Something we neglected when there was still time to stop the rot. When we turned a blind eye just because it was 'our people' who committed the crimes."

For a long time they sat in silence.

"You don't blame me for what happened to Melanie then?"

"You're not children any more." With an angry gesture he moved his hand across his face. In the twilight Ben hadn't noticed the tears before. "Can you beat it?" the old man said.

"After all these years this tobacco is getting too strong for me."

Monday 24 April. Brief phone-call from Cloete this morning. Wanted to see me urgently. I was surprised by his haste. Why couldn't he wait until school started again tomorrow? Still, when it came I was very calm. Unless I'm simply getting punch-drunk. But really, there was relief in knowing that one more thing was being taken from me, another burden removed. One marvels at how humble one's real needs can be. Acceptance of one's own insignificance. A wholesome and sobering experience.

Brown envelope on his desk. He didn't open it in my presence. No need. I'd seen Susan's.

"Mr Du Toit, I don't think it is necessary to tell you how shocked I was. All these months I've been confident – I mean, I've always been prepared to stand by you. But in the present circumstances—" He was panting heavily, like the bellows in Pa's primitive smithy on the farm so many years ago; the winter mornings white with frost; the sheep outside; the dog lying in front of the fire; the spray of sparks. His voice went on relentlessly: " – one's first responsibility, don't you agree? The school, the pupils entrusted to our care. I think you'll appreciate that you leave me no choice in the matter. I have been in touch with the Department. There will have to be a formal enquiry, of course. But until such time—"

"It won't be necessary, Mr Cloete. If you wish I can write out my resignation while I'm here."

"I had hoped you would offer to do so. It will make things so much easier for all concerned."

Was it really necessary for him to have discussed it with the rest of the staff? Or is there no sense in hoping to be spared even the most blatant humiliation? There were four or five of them in the common room as I came from Cloete's study.

Carelse in great form: "Now really, I take my hat off to you. You should start a stud farm."

Viviers unexpectedly sullen, avoiding me until the last moment. Then, following me outside, as if he'd suddenly made up his mind: "Mr Du Toit" – no longer *Oom Ben* – "I hope you don't mind my saying so, but I do feel you've let me

292

down terribly. I've always taken your side, from the very first day. I really thought you were concerned with an important cause, and with basic principles. But to do what you have done now—"

I didn't want to discuss it with Susan. Not so soon, not today. But tonight at supper – thank God there were only the two of us – when she said something about my clothes for tomorow I could no longer put it off.

"I'm not going to school tomorrow."

She stared at me in amazement.

"I offered them my resignation this morning."

"Are you out of your mind then?"

"Cloete was prepared to offer me the honourable alternative."

"Are you trying to tell me—"

"He also received a photograph in the mail."

I couldn't take my eyes off her: the way one feels compelled to stare at an accident happening in front of you. It makes you feel nauseous, yet you're fascinated by it, mesmerised, you can't look the other way.

"Then they all know about it now." It was a flat statement, not a question. "All this time I've been forcing myself to think it was something for you and me to come to terms with. God knows it was bad enough as it was. But at least it was kept between us."

That was all she said. After supper she went to her room without clearing the table. I came to the study. It is past midnight now. Half an hour ago she came to me. Very calm. Her formidable self-control.

"I've made up my mind, Ben. If it's all right with you I'll still stay here tonight. But I shall clear out in the morning."

"Don't."

Why did I say that? Was there any alternative? Why was it suddenly so important for me to restrain her, to hold on to her? It was unworthy of me. Because it wasn't for herself I was trying to hold her back, only for my own sake. This terrible anguish. Not this too. Not total solitude.

She smiled painfully. "Really, Ben, you can be so childish."

I wanted to get up and go to her, but I was afraid my legs

might fail me. I remained where I was. And without looking round again she went away.

3

Understandably, the waves rippled through the whole family, in one shock after another.

After a fierce argument with Susan Johan stayed on in the house with Ben. Whether she had told him the whole truth is difficult to determine; in any case, the boy lost his temper completely:

"You've all been against Dad from the beginning. But he's my father and I'm staying right here. The whole world can go to hell for all I care!"

Linda's reaction, on the other hand, upset Ben deeply. She was so thoughtless as to bring her Pieter with her for the uncomfortable, passionate, final discussion. That Ben had been making life so difficult for all of them, she said, she could still accept because she had kept faith in his integrity and his good intentions. She might not have been in agreement with his methods or the particular direction he'd chosen, but she had never doubted his motives. He was her father and she'd loved him and respected him; she'd been willing to defend him against all comers. But what had happened now was too much. This – this sordid, disgusting thing. And to think it was common knowledge by now. How could he expect her ever to raise her head in public again to face anyone squarely? What had become of the values he'd preached to them? The temple of God. Now this. How could he hope ever to demand respect from her again? All right, it was her Christian duty to forgive. But she would never be able to forget. Never. She was lying awake at night, or crying herself to sleep. The horror of it. The only way in which to keep her own self-respect was to take her final leave of him, there and then.

Pieter assured Ben that he would continue to pray for him. Afterwards they drove back to Pretoria in the young man's secondhand Volkswagen.

In a totally different way it was Suzette's reaction Ben found by far the most unexpected. Only a day after Susan had left she arrived at the house in her sleek new sports car. In a near-panic Ben's first thought was to get away as soon as possible. Her antagonism was the last thing he could face at that moment. But immediately he saw her he discovered in her something different from the hostility he'd grown accustomed to. Tall and blond and beautifully groomed, she came towards him, but without that aggressive self-assurance which had so often rattled him. Biting her lip she glanced up nervously, pressed an impulsive, awkward kiss on his cheek and started fumbling with her snake-skin handbag. As if she was the culprit expecting recrimination. Tense, agitated, evasive.

"Are you here all on your own?"

He looked at her guardedly. "I thought you knew?"

"What I meant was—" Once again the furtive glance in his direction, her whole manner apologetic. "Isn't there anything you need?"

"I can manage all right."

She stood up nervously. "Shall I make us some tea?"

"Don't bother."

"I'm thirsty. I'm sure it will do you good too."

"Suzette." He couldn't play this game any longer. "If you've come to talk to me about what happened—"

"Yes, I have." Her cool blue eyes looked at him, but with an expresssion of concern, not accusation.

"Don't you think I've heard enough about it lately? From all sides."

"I didn't come to reproach you, Dad."

"What else?" He looked straight at her.

"I wanted you to know that I understand."

He couldn't help thinking bitterly: *Oh I understand your understanding. You've never had much respect for the sanctity of marriage.* But

295

he said nothing, waiting for her to continue.

She found it difficult; he could see her struggling with herself. "Dad, what I mean is – Well, I'm not blaming Mum for going away. I know she's had a bad time. But these last few weeks I've been battling with it day and night. And I know now" – once again the hesitant glance as if she expected him to condemn her – "for the first time I think I know what you also had to go through. This past year. And even before that. And so I thought – I can't agree with all of it, and I'm not sure I always understood you well, but I respect you for what you are. And all I can hope for is that I haven't waited too long to tell you."

He bowed his head. Dully, dazedly, he said: "Let's go and make the tea."

They didn't mention it again that morning, preferring to restrict their conversation to harmless small-talk about his grandchild, and her work for the magazine, and Johan's studies, gossip, even the weather. But when she returned on other days it became easier to talk about what was of more concern to him, including Gordon and what had happened and what was still happening. And much against his will – though there was an almost childlike eagerness in him as well – she even referred to Melanie. Gradually her visits became part of his routine. Every other day or so she would drive over in the morning to tidy up, and make tea, and have a chat. A new Suzette he still found hard to believe, even though he accepted the change with almost sentimental gratitude.

There were days when her presence irritated him – he'd become possessive about his solitude, his hours in the empty house, his silence – but once she'd left he would discover that he actually missed her. Perhaps not so much for herself as for the opportunity of talking to someone, of being in someone's company. It was different from the blind loyalty of his son. – Contact with Johan was limited to non-commital remarks at table, going out to a café or a restaurant; attending a rugby match. Mainly, they played chess, which offered the opportunity to communicate without a need to talk. But Ben was becoming absent-minded, relying on unimaginative standard openings, neglecting to follow up properly so that he usually had to pay a heavy toll in the middle games; more often than not losing the endgames through lack of concentration. — What Suzette offered him was the understanding and sympathy of an eloquent, mature woman, sustaining his confidence just when it had begun to crumble. Young Dominee Bester also came to see him, but only once. He offered to read from the Bible and say a prayer, but Ben declined.

"Oom Ben, don't you see it's useless to kick against the pricks? Why don't we rather try to do away with this thing?"

"It can never be done away with while Gordon and Jonathan lie unavenged in their graves."

"Vengeance belongs to God, not to us." The young man was pleading with great seriousness. "There is a bitterness in you which makes me very unhappy. I find something hard in you which I never knew before."

"How well did you really know me, Dominee?" he asked, staring through the smoke with smarting eyes. They were both smoking; and he hadn't slept the previous night.

"Hasn't it gone far enough, Oom Ben?" asked the minister. "There has been so much destruction and devastation in your lives already."

He seemed to gaze inward at the battlefield of his own life. "There would be no sense in it unless I'm prepared to pay the full price, Dominee."

"But don't you see the arrogance, the terrible presumption in this urge you have to go on regardless and to suffer more and more in the process? Don't you see it's something like the perversion of those medieval Catholics who went into ecstasies flogging themselves? There is no humility in that, Oom Ben. It's naked pride."

"Who is doing the flogging now, Dominee?"

"But don't you understand? 'I'm trying to help you. It's not too late."

"How do you want to help me? What do you want to do?" His thoughts were wandering; he found it hard to concentrate.

"We can stop this divorce for a start."

He shook his head.

"After all the years you two have lived together? I refuse to believe a relationship can be ended just like that."

"Susan and I have nothing to say to one another any more, Dominee. It's all over. She is exhausted. I'm not blaming her for anything."

"One can always try to search one's own heart."

He sat listening tensely, suspiciously, waiting for it to come.

"This other woman, Oom Ben."

"I won't have her dragged into this!" he exploded, losing all control instantly. "You know nothing about her."

"But if we want to achieve something with this discussion—" His voice trembled with loving kindness.

"You want to achieve something that no longer interests me," he said, choking. "My life is my own."

"We all belong to God."

"If that is so He certainly made a sorry mess of my life!" he said. After a while he calmed down. "And I prefer not to blame Him for it. I'd rather take the responsibility myself."

"Do you remember the night you came to me, just after the court inquest? If only you'd listened to me then."

"If I'd listened to you then I wouldn't have had a conscience left tonight. God knows I may have lost everything else. But I still have my conscience."

"There are so many things that go by the name of 'conscience'," said the Rev Bester quietly. "That, too, may be a matter of pride. It may be a way of taking God's work from His hands and trying to do it ourselves."

"Perhaps the very reason it's misused so often makes it such a precious thing, Dominee. No outsider can ever understand. I know nothing about your conscience, and you don't know about mine. I've often wondered whether that isn't the true meaning of faith. To know, to know in the face of God, that you have no choice but to do what you are doing. And to take the responsibility for it." Through the smoke, more dense than before, he peered at the young man in silence; at last he said, the pipe trembling in his hand: "I'm prepared. Whether I'm right or wrong I don't know. But I'm prepared."

5 May. Would I have had the nerve to do it if Phil Bruwer hadn't been rushed back to hospital? But what's the use of wondering?

The matron phoned yesterday. Apparently he'd heard from the Department of the Interior that his passport would not be renewed for him to visit Melanie in London. And just after lunch he'd had another attack. Not a very bad one, but he was kept in intensive care and they wouldn't allow me to see him. "Relatives only."

Talked to Johan. But his eagerness to "help" is an embarrassment. What does he really understand? What can I really discuss with him? How can I explain to him this oppressive feeling in me, threatening to overwhelm me? I can no longer eat or sleep. Cornered. Claustrophobic. A bumblebee in a bottle.

Tried to contact Stanley, although I knew it was unwise. Not from home, of course, not even from the public booth a few streets away, but from a different suburb altogether. Paranoic! No reply. Tried three more times in the course of the evening. At last came through to a woman who said he was out "on business". She promised to tell him the lanie had phoned. Still nothing by this morning. By eleven o'clock I couldn't bear it any more. Just to hear a human voice. Even the Dominee's! But only his wife was at the vicarage. Child-woman, blond and dazed – from having too many children too soon? – but with a certain anaemic charm. Offered me tea. I accepted in pure desperation. Trampled by toddlers. Then fled again.

Considered driving to Pretoria to Suzette. But reluctant. Her sympathy and filial concern is my only consolation at the moment; yet I feel uncomfortable in her presence. Unable to cope with the change in her, however much I welcome it. Have given up trying to fathom her, or anyone else. Weary.

And so I went to Soweto.

The ultimate madness? I couldn't care a damn. I just had to. Hoping I'd find Stanley there. Anyone I knew. Ridiculous, I suppose, but it seemed to me more likely to find someone there than here in my own neighbourhood.

Drove in circles first, stopping from time to time to make sure I wasn't followed. There is a certain satisfaction in these cops-and-robbers games. Tests one's ingenuity, keeps you awake, helps you concentrate, helps you survive. To endure. Not to go mad.

Slowed down when I reached the power-station. I'd only been there twice before with Stanley, once in the dark. And it's a veritable maze of paths and tracks. Managed to stay roughly on course. Across the railway-line and in among the houses. But then I lost my way. Drove this way and that, losing all sense of direction in the dense cloud of smoke that obscured the sun. Stopped twice to ask the way. The first time a group of playing children froze in their tracks when they saw me, staring dumbly past me, refusing to reply. Then found a barber in front of an open door, his client seated on a bentwood chair in the dusty street, a soiled sheet draped over his shoulders. He explained to me how I should set about it.

There were a few youngsters on the street corner when I stopped in front of Stanley's house. They pretended not to hear when I asked them whether he was at home. Perhaps that should have warned me, but I could think of nothing but getting to him.

Knocked. All was silent. Knocked again. At last a woman opened. Young, attractive, Afro hairstyle. Stared at me suspiciously for a moment and tried to close the door, but I held it open.

"I've come to see Stanley."

"He is not here."

"I'm Ben Du Toit. He often came to my place."

She stared hard at me, still resentful, but as if the name had rung a bell.

"I phoned several times yesterday. Left a message for him to get in touch with me."

"He is not here," she repeated sullenly.

I looked round helplessly. The youngsters were still standing on the corner, hands thrust into their pockets, staring.

"You must go now," she said. "There will be trouble."

"What sort of trouble?"

"For you. For Stanley. For all of us."

300

"Are you his wife?"

Ignoring the question she said: "They are looking for him."

"Who?"

"They."

"Does he know it?" I asked anxiously. Not Stanley too. He is the only one that remains. He has got to survive.

"He has gone away," she said bluntly. "I think to Swaziland. He will not come back soon. He knows they are waiting for him."

"What about you?" I asked. "And his children? Do you need anything?"

She seemed to find the question amusing, smiling broadly. "We need nothing. He has made provision for us." Then, serious once more: "You must go now. You cannot come in. They will find out."

I turned away, hesitated, and looked back: "But – if he comes back – will you tell him?"

A brief motion of her head, but whether it was a nod or a refusal I couldn't make out. She closed the door.

Lost and dejected, I remained outside. What now? Where could I go? Back home, as if nothing had happened? And what then?

I was so deeply lost in my own perplexing thoughts that I never saw them coming closer. By the time I looked up they were standing in a tight group between me and the car. In the background I could see others approaching casually. The very slowness of their movement made me suspicious. As if there were no need for them to hurry: as if they were very sure about the outcome.

I gave a few steps towards the car, then stopped, uncertain. They were still staring at me in stony silence, their young dark faces expressionless.

"Stanley isn't home," I said, feeling foolish, trying to establish some sort of random contact. My throat was dry.

They didn't move. From behind, the others were drawing closer. How on earth had they learned about my presence?

"I'm Stanley's friend," I said again.

No answer.

Trying not to reveal my apprehension I gave another step, taking out my car keys.

Everything started happening very quickly, in a great confusion of movement and sound. Someone slammed the bunch of keys from my hand. As I stooped to pick them up I was knocked down from behind, sprawling in the dust, but holding on to the keys. A wave of bodies tumbling over me. I tried to scuttle away on all fours, but as I was pushing myself up against the car I was grabbed again. A kick in the stomach. I doubled forward. Knee in the kidneys. For a moment I was dizzy with pain. But I knew if I stayed there it would be the end. I still can't explain how I did it, but in the confusion of the fight I managed to make my way round the car to open the driver's door. Thank God the others were locked. As I sank into my seat the door was wrenched open again. I kicked blindly. Caught someone's hand in the door. Noticing a big dark crowd approaching in the distance, I turned the key with shaking hands.

Thought of Melanie who, in just such a throng, had given the Black Power salute to be let through scot-free. But I had none of her presence of mind.

All I did was to turn the window down an inch or so to shout at them: "Don't you understand? I'm on your side!" My voice breaking with hysteria.

Then the first stone hit the body of the car. Numerous hands grabbed hold of the back, rocking it, trying to lift the wheels off the ground. More stones clanging against the sides. Only one remedy: I reversed full-speed, catching them off balance, sending them sprawling. Then forward, tyres whizzing and kicking up a cloud of dust and pebbles.

At the first corner a few of them stood waiting for me. The window on my side was shattered by a brick that barely missed my head, landing on the empty seat beside me. For a moment I lost control of the car, zigzagging down the road, scattering children and chickens, miraculously missing them all.

It couldn't have been more than a minute or two but it felt never-ending. Then I was in another township. Children playing with worn-out tyres or the rims of bicycles. Women shouting at the top of their voices from one streetcorner to the next. Broken cars littering bare stretches of veld. Rubbish dumps with clusters of people scratching and digging. Only this time there was nothing commonplace or peaceful about it. Everything was hostile, alien, ominous. I had no idea of where to turn to; at the same time I was still too scared to stop. I simply went on driving and driving, reckless and without direction, nearly breaking the axles in potholes and ditches in the road, often missing pedestrians by inches, leaving them behind in a cloud of dust, swearing and jumping and shaking their fists at me. Up and down the streets, from one township to the other.

After a long time I forced myself to stop in a burnt-down patch of open veld. Just sat there to try and calm down again, breathing deeply. My limbs bruised. My head aching. My clothes torn and covered with dust. My hands grazed. My whole body shivering with cold fever. I waited until I felt more or less in control of myself before I finally started the car again and drove on to a shopping centre where I could ask my way. By that time, it turned out, I was at the very opposite end of Soweto, near the cemetery. Where Gordon lay buried.

Only then did it really strike me: the strange way in which one tended to live in circles, passing again and again the same decaying landmarks from earlier times. One circle had now been completed. In this place, Stanley's Sofasonke City, in a demonstration similar to the one I'd just been involved in, Jonathan had been arrested. For me, that had been the beginning of everything. And suddenly there was something very orderly about it all: it seemed predestined that I had to return to that place on that day.

Back home I took a bath and changed my clothes. Swallowed a few tablets. Lay down. But I couldn't sleep. Every now and then I started shivering again, quite uncontrollably.

I had never been so close to death before.

For a long time, as I lay there trying to clear my mind, I couldn't think coherently at all, conscious only of a terrible, blind bitterness. Why had they singled me out? Didn't they understand? Had everything I'd gone through on their behalf been utterly in vain? Did it really count for nothing? What had happened to logic, meaning, sense?

But I feel much calmer now. It helps to discipline oneself like this, writing it down to see it set out on paper, to try and weigh it

303

and find some significance in it.

Prof Bruwer: *There are only two kinds of madness one should guard against, Ben. One is the belief that we can do everything. The other is the belief that we can do nothing.*

I wanted to help. Right. I meant it very sincerely. But I wanted to do it on my terms. And I am white, they are black. I thought it was still possible to reach beyond our whiteness and blackness. I thought that to reach out and touch hands across the gulf would be sufficient in itself. But I grasped so little, really: as if good intentions from my side could solve it all. It was presumptuous of me. In an ordinary world, in a natural one, I might have succeeded. But not in this deranged, divided age. I can do all I can for Gordon or the scores of others who have come to me; I can imagine myself in their shoes, I can project myself into their suffering. But I cannot, ever, live their lives for them. So what else could come of it but failure?

Whether I like it or not, whether I feel like cursing my own condition or not – and that would only serve to confirm my impotence – *I am white.* This is the small, final, terrifying truth of my broken world. I am white. And because I'm white I am born into a state of privilege. Even if I fight the system that has reduced us to this I remain white, and favoured by the very circumstances I abhor. Even if I'm hated, and ostracised, and persecuted, and in the end destroyed, nothing can make me black. And so those who are cannot but remain suspicious of me. In their eyes my very efforts to identify myself with Gordon, with all the Gordons, would be obscene. Every gesture I make, every act I commit in my efforts to help them makes it more difficult for them to define their real needs and discover for themselves their integrity and affirm their own dignity. How else could we hope to arrive beyond predator and prey, helper and helped, white and black, and find redemption?

On the other hand: what can I do but what I have done? I cannot choose not to intervene: that would be a denial and a mockery not only of everything I believe in, but of the hope that compassion may survive among men. By not acting as I did I would deny the very possibility of that gulf to be bridged.

If I act, I cannot but lose. But if I do not act, it is a different kind of defeat, equally decisive and maybe worse. Because then

I will not even have a conscience left.

The end seems ineluctable: failure, defeat, loss. The only choice I have left is whether I am prepared to salvage a little honour, a little decency, a little humanity – or nothing. It seems as if a sacrifice is impossible to avoid, whatever way one looks at it. But at least one has the choice between a wholly futile sacrifice and one that might, in the long run, open up a possibility, however negligible or dubious, of something better, less sordid and more noble, for our children. My own, and Gordon's, and Stanley's.

They live on. We, the fathers, have lost.

How dare I presume to say: *He is my friend*, or even, more cautiously, *I think I know him*? At the very most we are like two strangers meeting in the white wintry veld and sitting down together for a while to smoke a pipe before proceeding on their separate ways. No more.

Alone. Alone to the very end. I. Stanley. Melanie. Every one of us. But to have been granted the grace of meeting and touching so fleetingly: is that not the most awesome and wonderful thing one can hope for in this world?

How strange, this rare stillness. Even this winter landscape, bared of humanity and with the vultures circling over it, is beautiful in its own way. We still have much to learn about the subtleties of God's infinite grace.

In the beginning there is turmoil. Then it subsides, leaving a silence: but it is a silence of confusion and incomprehension, not true stillness but an inability to hear properly, a turbulent silence. And it is only when one ventures much more deeply into suffering, it seems to me, that one may learn to accept it as indispensable for the attainment of a truly serene silence. I have not reached it yet. But I think I am very close now. And that hope sustains me.

Surely, if Ben had not been quite so exhausted, so close to the limits of his endurance, he would have suspected something. And if he'd known in time he might have taken some precautionary measures. But there is no point in speculation. After all, she was his own child, and how could one expect him to look for ulterior motives in the disarming sympathy she so unexpectedly offered him?

On the Sunday he and Johan drove to Pretoria to have dinner with Suzette and her family. Not that he was at all eager to embark on the journey, but she had insisted so strongly on the telephone that he couldn't refuse. Moreover, he felt an overwhelming need to be with someone he could talk to.

The car windows had not been replaced yet and he was worried about being stopped by traffic police, but fortunately nothing happened.

"What on earth has happened to the car?" Suzette asked, shocked, the moment she saw him. "It looks as if you've been to war."

"It was something of the sort." He smiled wearily. "Fortunately I came out of it unscathed."

"What happened?"

"Just a mob beside the road, few days ago." He was reluctant to go into particulars.

After the sumptuous dinner, prepared by Suzette's full-time cook, Ben felt more relaxed. The good food, the wine, the tasteful interior decoration straight from the pages of her own glossy magazine, the chance of playing with his grandchild before the boy was taken away by his nanny, everything added to a new and cherished feeling of ease and warmth. Suzette led him outside to recline on deck-chairs in the gentle late-autumn warmth beside the pool, where their coffee was served. Chris, in the meantime, had taken Johan to the study to show him something. Only afterwards did it occur to Ben that it might have been deliberately arranged.

She referred to the state of the car again. "Please, Dad, you really must be careful. Think of what might have happened!

One never knows these days."

"It'll take more than a few stones to get rid of me," he said lightly, unwilling to be drawn into an argument.

"Why didn't you have it repaired? You can't drive around like that."

"Nothing wrong with the engine. Anyway, I'll have it fixed this week. Just haven't had the time yet."

"What keeps you so busy?"

"All sorts of odds and ends."

She probably guessed that he was hedging for suddenly, her voice warm with sympathy, she asked: "Or is it a matter of money?"

"Oh no, not at all."

"You must promise me you'll tell me if there's anything Chris and I could do to help."

"I will." He looked at her, smiling slowly: "You know, I still think it's incredible, the way the two of us used to be in each other's hair all the time – and now, these last few weeks—"

"Sometimes it takes a jolt to open one's eyes. There's so much I'd like to make up for, Dad."

She had the sun behind her. A slender, elegant, blond young woman; every hair in its place, no sign of a crease in her expensive, severely simple dress, undoubtedly from Paris or New York. The firm lines of her high cheekbones, the stubbornness of her chin. The very image of Susan, years ago.

"Don't you find it unbearably lonely at home, Dad? When Johan is away to school—"

"Not really." He changed his legs, avoiding her eyes. "One gets used to it. Gives me time to think. And there's all my papers and stuff to sort and bring up to date."

"About Gordon?"

"Yes, that too."

"You amaze me." There was nothing bitchy in her voice; it sounded more like admiration. "The way you manage to keep at it, no matter what happens."

He said uneasily: "I suppose one just does what one can."

"Most other people would have given up long ago." A calculated pause: "But is it really worth your while, Dad?"

307

"It's all I have."

"But I'm concerned about you, Dad. That bomb the other day. What if Johan hadn't been there to put out the fire? The whole house could have burned down."

"Not necessarily. The study is well apart from the rest."

"But suppose all your papers had been destroyed? Everything you've been collecting about Gordon?"

He smiled, putting his cup on the low table beside his deckchair; he was feeling quite relaxed now, in that lazy May sunshine. "Don't worry," he said, "they'll never lay hands on that."

"Where on earth do you keep the stuff?" she asked casually.

"I made a false bottom for my tools cupboard, you see. A long time ago already. Nobody will ever think of looking there."

"More coffee?"

"No, thank you."

She poured some for herself, all of a sudden curiously energetic. He looked at her fondly, enjoying the luxury of her attentiveness, indulging himself, abandoning himself to her sympathy, and to the caressing of the autumn sun, the dull afterglow of the red wine.

It was only on the way back, late that afternoon, that he thought in sudden panic: What if Suzette had had something very specific in mind when she'd questioned him so carefully, with so much studied nonchalance?

Angrily he rejected the thought. How could one think that of one's own child? What sense would remain in the world if one no longer had the right to trust one's own family?

He wondered whether he should discuss it with Johan. But the wind made such a noise through the broken windows that conversation was almost ruled out. Without realising it he was driving faster and faster.

"Watch out for speedcops!" Johan shouted.

"I'm driving my normal speed," he grumbled, easing his foot off the accelerator. But he was impatient now, brooding, deeply perturbed.

Even though he despised himself for his own suspicions, for harbouring the mere thought, he knew he would have no peace of mind before he'd done something to allay his fears. And while Johan was away to church that evening he unscrewed the small trap-door in the wooden casement of the bath and transported all his documents to the new hiding-place, meticulously screwing the lid back after he'd finished.

One night later that week the garage was burgled so cautiously and professionally that neither Ben nor Johan was disturbed by the slightest noise. It was only when he came to his car the next morning that Ben discovered what had happened. The entire tools cupboard had been methodically ripped apart and the contents lay strewn all over the garage floor.

EPILOGUE

Very little remains before I arrive back where I started with Ben's story. A senseless circle – or a spiral moving slowly inward after all? Almost lightly I clutched at another man's life to avoid or exorcise the problem of my own. I discovered very soon that no half-measures were possible. Either evasion or total immersion. And yet, with almost everything written down, what have I resolved of the enigma that tantalised me so? Ben: my friend the stranger. The disturbing truth is that even as I prepare to finish it off I know that he will not let go of me again. I cannot grasp him: neither can I rid myself of him. There is no absolution from the guilt of having tried.

I am left with a sense of hopelessness. In my efforts to do justice to him, I may have achieved the opposite. We belong to different dimensions: one man lived, another wrote; one looked forward, the other back; he was there, and I am here.

No wonder he remains beyond my reach. It is like walking in the dark with a lamp and seeing blunt objects appearing and disappearing in the narrow beam of light, but remaining incapable of forming an image of the territory as such. It is still a wilderness. But it was either this – or nothing at all.

Immediately after discovering the burglary in his garage Ben drove in to town and telephoned me from a booth at the station. An hour later I met him in front of Bakker's bookshop. The strange, thin, fugitive creature so different from the man I thought I'd known.

The rest is mostly guesswork or deduction, in which I may be influenced by the same paranoia he had written about; but it must be told.

313

He posted his papers and notebooks from Pretoria. And I like to imagine that, for once, he allowed himself a touch of irony by first telephoning Suzette to say:

"Please do me a favour, my dear. Remember those notes we spoke about – all that stuff in connection with Gordon, you know: well, it's just occurred to me it may not be so safe with me after all. Do you think I could bring it over so you could store it for me?"

One can imagine how she would try to suppress her excitement, saying eagerly: "Of course, Dad. But why take the trouble of bringing it here? I'll come over to collect it."

"No, don't worry. I'll bring it myself."

In that way, of course, he would eliminate the risk of being followed: knowing that everything was to be deposited with Suzette they wouldn't bother to tail him to Pretoria. And an hour or so later, quiet, pale, content, he would hand in his package at the parcel counter of the post office in Pretoria and then drive out to Suzette's home on Waterkloof Ridge.

She would come out to meet him. Her eyes would eagerly search the car. Slowly her face would drop as he explained casually: "You know, I thought about it again. I've landed so many people in trouble that I'd rather not compromise you in any way. So I decided I'd rather burn the whole lot. I must admit it's a load off my mind."

Of course she wouldn't dare to give away her feelings; her lovely make-up acting as a mask to her shock and anger.

A few days later the parcel was delivered at my house. And then he was killed.

That, I thought, was the end of it.

But fully one week after his funeral his last letter reached me. Dated 23 May, the night of his death:

I really didn't mean to bother you again, but now I have to. Hopefully for the last time. I have just had another anonymous call. A man's voice. Saying they would be coming for me tonight, something to that effect. I've had so many of these calls before that I've learned to shrug them off. But I have the feeling that this time it's serious. It may just be the state of my nerves, but I don't think so. Please forgive me if I'm troubling you unnecessarily. But just in case it really is serious I want to warn you in time. Johan isn't here tonight. And anyway I wouldn't like to upset him unduly.

The caller spoke English, but with an Afrikaans accent. Something very familiar about it, even though he was trying to smother it, probably by holding a handkerchief over the receiver. It was he. I'm quite convinced of it.

There have been two more burglaries at my house this past week. I know what they're looking for. They are not prepared to wait any longer.

If I am right in my suspicion it is imperative that you know about it.

One feels a strange calm at a moment like this. I have always liked end-games best. If it hadn't happened in this way, they would have found another. I know I couldn't possibly have gone on like this for much longer. The only satisfaction I can still hope for is that everything will not end here with me. Then I shall truly be able to say, with Melanie: "I do not regret for one moment a single thing that has happened."

At about eleven o'clock that night he was run over by a car. According to the newspaper report the accident occurred when he was on his way to post a letter. But how could the reporter have known it, unless Ben still had the letter with him when it happened? And if he had, then who posted it afterwards? And why?

Would that explain the week's delay before it was delivered? Of course, it may quite simply be due to Johannesburg's notorious postal services. On the other hand it is possible that having found it on his body and perused it they decided I should receive it. In which case they could have had only one motive: to keep me under surveillance; to follow the trail from here.

They cannot be so obtuse as not to realise I would be suspicious about the delayed delivery. If that is so, they deliberately intended it as a warning or a threat, by making sure that I would be conscious of being watched.

Then why did I go ahead by writing it all down here? Purely from sentimental loyalty to a friend I had neglected for years? Or to pay some form of conscience money to Susan? It is better not to pry too deeply into one's own motives.

Is everything really beginning anew with me? And if so: how far to go? Will one ever succeed in breaking the vicious circle? Or isn't that so important? Is it really just a matter of going on, purely and simply? Prodded, possibly, by some dull, guilty feeling of responsibility towards something Ben might have believed in: something man is capable of being but which he isn't very often allowed to be?

I don't know.

Perhaps all one can really hope for, all I am entitled to, is no more than this: to write it down. To report what I know. So that it will not be possible for any man ever to say again: *I knew nothing about it.*

1976. 1978–1979.